THE SOUND OF MURDER

A Veronica Shade Thriller

Book 3

Patrick Logan

This book is a work of fiction. Names, characters, places, and incidents in this book are either entirely imaginary or are used fictitiously. Any resemblance to actual people, living or dead, or of places, events, or locales is entirely coincidental.

Copyright © Patrick Logan 2023
Interior design: © Patrick Logan 2023
All rights reserved.

This book, or parts thereof, cannot be reproduced, scanned, or disseminated in any print or electronic form.

First Edition: February 2023

For my three girls.
May your inspiring curiosity be rewarded with lives full of incredible stories.

Prologue

"MORE BILLS, RONNIE. MORE BILLS."

Ronald Milligan raised his eyes from his coffee and stared at his wife. Sporting a long white nightshirt, she stood with her back to him, her shoulders hunched.

He sighed.

I thought we agreed not to talk about money in front of Laura?

Ronald glanced to his left and offered his daughter a wan smile.

"Bill? I'm sorry, honey, you've mistaken me for someone else. My name's Ronnie."

Laura giggled and slurped Cheerios off her spoon.

"You think this is funny?"

Both of their smiles vanished.

"You really think this is funny, Ronnie?" Zinnia Milligan had since turned and was flapping a handful of envelopes in her right hand. "How long do you think this is gonna last before they cut off the TV?"

"They're gonna cut off the TV?" Laura asked, her eyes going wide.

Ronnie patted her head.

"No, they're not." Then, to Zinnia, he said, "I'm doing the best I can here. I've already worked three overtime shifts this week."

Zinnia's face dropped and Ronnie stood with the intention of comforting his wife. But the woman was having none of it. At thirty-six, Zinnia was still as attractive as the day they'd met. Smooth dark skin, full lips, and the most intense eyes that he'd ever come across.

But at this moment, as a sneer crept onto her face, she looked absolutely hideous.

2 LOGAN

"Well, clearly whatever you're doing is not good enough."

If his daughter wasn't there, if Laura wasn't sitting beside him and staring at them both, Ronnie would've been tempted to say what had been on his mind for the last three months. *I'm working overtime and you're not even trying to get a job. It might not be your fault that you were let go—the hotel industry, like everything else, is constantly downsizing. But you could* try. *You could change out of that fucking nightgown that you wear day in and day out and* try. *Hell, if you don't want to work, that's fine— you could just stay home with Laura. That would save us a bundle on daycare costs.*

"Nothing? You've got nothing to say for yourself?"

Ronnie had to bite his tongue to avoid speaking. After an intense stare that lasted several seconds, Zinnia raspberried her lips and shook her head. Then she turned her attention to that damn cell phone that never left her sight.

Ronnie took a final sip of his coffee.

"I love you, sweetheart," he said.

"I love you too, Daddy."

Ronnie bent, kissed his daughter on the forehead, and then smoothed her curly black hair.

"I'll be home late tonight."

Zinnia didn't even look up from her phone.

With a sigh, Ronnie grabbed his Bear County Deputy hat off the counter, put it on, and then dipped the brim toward his daughter.

"I'll be back, pilgrim."

***

People have this idea about law enforcement—about cops, State Troopers, County Deputies. They think that they get their jollies pulling people over for exceeding the speed limit by as little as a single mile per hour.

This couldn't be further from the truth.

Pulling people over meant paperwork. And Ronnie Milligan would much rather just sit in his car and listen to a podcast or audiobook all day, take his mind off his failing marriage than fill out forms.

But there was a difference between speeding and *speeding*. Even on rural roads, Ronnie would only allow a twenty, maybe twenty-five percent over the limit buffer. But if anything looked reckless or dangerous?

He wouldn't hesitate to flick on his siren and lights.

And when Ronnie clocked the white Mazda sedan going eighty in a fifty zone? That was exactly what he did.

There was always a moment when you put on your lights that your adrenaline spiked. No matter how benign the traffic stop, this surge always got Ronnie's heart pumping.

The driver of the Mazda pulled over immediately, the car's bald tires sending so much dust and dirt into the air that he couldn't read the license plate.

Radio coverage was spotty out here, but he called in the traffic stop anyway after parking about twelve feet behind the white car. The dust settled enough for him to see a single person in the vehicle. A man, most likely, wearing a ball cap.

Ronnie adjusted his belt, made sure his holster hadn't shifted while sitting and got out of his car. As he approached, his initial observation was confirmed: one occupant, male, medium to small build. Ronnie pressed the index finger of his right hand against the rear taillight, leaving a distinct print behind.

Then he continued to the driver's side window, which had been rolled down.

"License and registration please."

The man in the driver seat had a burgundy cap pulled low over his dark eyes. It was some sort of workout hat, with a kettle bell in the center and some cliched quote in a circle around it. He was pale, with black hair that covered his ears.

"Both are in here. They're wedged in pretty good. Can't get them out."

The man handed over a small black wallet. Inside were both his registration and license.

He could work with this.

"Was I speeding?"

"You were speeding all right. Please stay in your vehicle, sir. I'll be right back."

Ronnie retreated to his car. He was trying to remove the man's license when the top of the wallet opened. Inside, he spotted five crisp one-hundred-dollar bills.

Ronnie lowered the wallet to his lap as he looked through the windshield at the white Mazda.

The outline of the driver was completely still, hands on the wheel, head straight.

Fuck.

This was no accident—this was a bribe.

Fuck.

Ronnie's eyes dropped to the money.

He'd never taken a bribe before. *Never.* He knew that others did, on occasion—they called it 'letting you go with a warning'. Not giving a warning, but letting you go with one. A simple, yet important distinction.

Five hundred dollars.

Enough to pay off two or maybe three bills. TV, cell phone, electrical. Five hundred bucks wasn't like winning the lottery, but it would help. It would help a great deal.

In the back of his mind, an alarm started to ring.

Five hundred bucks? That was a large bribe for a speeding ticket that wouldn't come to even half that much.

When Ronnie started justifying the size of the bribe—unpaid parking tickets or too many demerit points, maybe even expired insurance—he knew that he'd already committed to taking the money.

There was no one around. Nobody would ever know about it.

And it *would* help.

Ronnie chewed his lip as he thought about what his daughter had said earlier that morning.

"They're gonna cut off the TV?"

Fuck it.

Ronnie removed the money from the wallet and jammed it into his pocket. Then he got out of the car and walked back to the Mazda. Now that the dust had settled, he saw several cans of paint in the backseat.

"I'm letting you go with a warning," Ronnie said as he passed the man back his wallet. The words made his tongue feel dirty.

"Thank you so much, officer. You don't know what this means to me."

"Hmm."

Ronnie's gaze fell on the backseat.

"You doin' some painting?"

"Oh, yes, officer. Lots of painting today. Lots of painting."

"All right, you have a good day. And slow down."

"Of course. Thanks again."

Ronnie stepped back and the Mazda slowly pulled onto the road. As he watched it recede into the horizon, the deputy couldn't help but think that he'd just made the biggest mistake of his entire life.

***

He couldn't believe his luck.

He shouldn't have been speeding in the first place, which was idiotic, but his bribe—five hundred bucks—had actually worked. That had been an extremely high-risk decision. If the deputy had been one of those by-the-book type of guys, he'd be screwed. He would have been arrested and his car impounded.

And a closer inspection would have revealed a lot more than some cans of paint. Yet, even though he'd gotten away, his dark eyes continued to flick to the rearview mirror, expecting to see red and blue flashing lights appear at any moment.

But as time passed—a minute, three, ten—he began to relax. And exactly thirteen minutes after the deputy had pulled him over, he heard the first bang.

Just a dull thud from the trunk, but a moment later, this was followed by muffled screams.

Then words... words that he could just make out, shrill as they were.

"Let me out of here! Let me the fuck out of here!"

And that's when the man started to smile.

"Hey, you want me to sing you a song?" he said loudly, not sure if the woman he had bound and gagged before throwing her in the trunk of his car could hear him. "Yeah? Good. Because I have the perfect song for you. It's one that we used to sing as kids—I think you're going to like it. Ready? Here goes... One, two, I'm coming for you..."

PART ONE: THE INTERVIEW

Chapter 1

"No, no—I-I don't want to do this," Detective Veronica Shade said, shaking her head back and forth. "This is a bad idea, Steve."

She felt a comforting hand on the small of her back and looked up at Sheriff Steve Burns. Even though he had encouraged her to accept the offer to go on TV and talk about the dollmaker, she knew that he wouldn't push her if she didn't want to do it.

Sometimes, Veronica wished the man wasn't so sweet. Sometimes, giving her a nudge was exactly what she needed.

And this PR interview was what the City of Greenham PD needed, not her. At least, that was what Internal Affairs thought when they'd reached out to talk shows in and around Portland. An about-face from trying to stay out of the news after the disaster that was Ken Cameron and then the forced retirement of her father, Peter Shade, as Police Captain.

But when Veronica looked up at Steve's soft blue eyes, she knew he would never push her.

He didn't even have to say anything—it was written all over his face.

If you don't want to go ahead with this, Veronica, we can just go home. We can just get back in the car and drive the forty minutes home. Or, if you want, we can stay in Portland, catch a movie instead.

"Shit. Can't you just be mean for once?"

Steve smirked. When he wasn't in uniform, Bear County Sheriff Steve Burns looked younger than his thirty-eight years. In uniform, he was going on fifty. But then when he grinned like this? He looked like a child.

"You almost ready? Detective Shade, are you almost ready to go on?"

The handler appeared out of nowhere. A diminutive woman with short brown hair and big eyes made bigger by oversized glasses that were as likely to be stylish as they were ironic. Without waiting for an answer, she used a powder brush to dab Veronica's forehead. That sealed it.

She was going to do this.

She had to.

Veronica let the woman work for several seconds before casually brushing her aside.

It wasn't just Steve and IA who had encouraged her to go on the talk show, it had been her psychiatrist, Dr. Jane Bernard, as well. This was most surprising. After the dollmaker, she'd expected Jane to tell her to lay low. Veronica had taken three months off following her brother's death, but only three weeks after shooting and killing the dollmaker. She'd been cleared for duty after the mandatory week of psych evals, followed by two weeks of rest and relaxation.

Veronica had been so certain that Jane would be against the idea, that she'd almost forgotten to even broach the subject. When she had, Jane had instantly been in favor of it, citing that it would be good for her recovery.

Recovery from what, Veronica wasn't sure.

That left only Veronica.

If it hadn't been for her father, for Peter Shade being forced to retire, Veronica would've said no. Even though it was silly to think that her garnering positive press for the department would in any way help him be reinstated, deep down, that was her hope.

If nothing else, it would help rebuild his reputation. The mayor and the police department had gone through with their promise to keep the real reason for Peter's retirement a secret, but people in law enforcement were good at reading between the lines.

They knew that Captain Shade's retirement had been anything but voluntary. Not for a man like him, a man who only knew one thing: being a cop.

"Right, so if you would just follow me…" The handler held an arm out in front of her.

Veronica took one step before realizing that Steve was still holding her back.

"Just stay calm, have fun. I'll be right here if you need me." He leaned down and kissed her on the lips.

They'd been together for almost a year now, living together for most of that time. And while they both had hectic schedules, what with her moving quickly up the City of Greenham detective ranks, and him as the sheriff of the largest county in Oregon, they still spent every night in each other's arms.

And no matter how many times he kissed her, Veronica felt a flutter in her stomach. She pushed him away before becoming lost in the sensation.

Steve grinned and then mouthed the words "go get 'em".

The woman led her up two steps and across a dark stage. The lights were blinding here, artificial and deliberate. Veronica shielded her face with her hand, but the woman gently pulled her arm back down.

"You'll get used to it, don't ruin your makeup."

There were two large blue armchairs on the stage, with a circular table made of glass between them. Sitting on top of the table was an artificial plant.

Veronica was guided to the chair on the right and as soon as she'd sat, another woman appeared.

The eponymous *Marlowe,* which was written in cursive neon tubing on a fake brick wall behind them, took up residence in the other chair.

She was pretty: blonde with red lips and sporting a stylish dark suit. Undoubtedly intimidating to most people, but not to Veronica Shade.

Not to the detective who had seen her brother burn in front of her and who had put a bullet in the dollmaker's forehead.

"Detective Shade, are you ready?"

Veronica smiled, took a deep breath, and then readied herself for the live TV interview.

Chapter 2

VERONICA OBSERVED THE CAMERAMAN HOLD up three fingers, then two. On one, he pointed at the stage and a red light above the camera that read 'LIVE' came on.

Marlowe's body was angled toward Veronica, but her face was aimed directly at the camera straight ahead.

"Welcome back," the host said, with her characteristic TV beam. "I am so proud—*so* proud to have a very special guest with us today. Ladies, we all know how difficult it is for a woman to succeed in certain industries, even today. Even in 2023."

With every word the woman muttered, Veronica felt her teeth clench a little tighter. They'd gone over the format: a series of soft-ball questions about the dollmaker, her work as a detective, followed by fielding questions from women who aspired to enter law enforcement. Not once had this cringe-worthy introduction been mentioned.

"Law enforcement is particularly difficult for women and people who identify as non-binary. Which is why I am excited to speak to someone who has not only succeeded as a female in the City of Greenham Police Department but *excelled*. A woman who has been through her share of tribulations, from being sexually assaulted by a fellow officer to being kidnapped by a husband and wife team who murdered women and left their bodies in the Hilltona Forest, but who never gave up. Please, put your hands together and help me welcome Detective Veronica Shade."

The crowd erupted into applause, augmented by Foley sounds pumped through the speakers, but Veronica felt sick to her stomach. She hadn't even considered the idea that Ken Cameron would be mentioned.

This was supposed to be about bringing down the dollmaker. That was what they'd discussed and what they'd agreed on. Details would be scant, nothing more than what the sheriff had revealed in his multiple press conference, with an emphasis on Veronica's involvement.

Marlowe, still beaming, looked over at her.

"Welcome, Detective Shade."

"Please, just Veronica."

This response was automatic and rehearsed, something that Marlowe had called setting the scene and leveling the playing field.

"And thank you for having me," Veronica continued, working on autopilot now.

"No, thank you. Thank you for what you do. Thank you for keeping us all safe."

More applause.

"Right? *Right?*" Marlowe clapped twice. "Now, please, tell us what it's like being a woman in a predominantly male industry? One that is historically full of toxic masculinity?"

Veronica felt her brow crease and forced it straight.

In preparation for her interview, she had watched and suffered through two episodes of *Marlowe*. It was clear that the host had a tendency to go off script, but this felt more like a hard right and not a subtle deviation. Veronica had been instructed to 'go with the flow', but she had other ideas.

Redirect the stream where she wanted to go.

"The Greenham Police Department has only been good to me. Yes, there was an issue in the past, but that has been dealt with in a more than satisfactory way. What I can say is that I have one of the greatest partners that I could ever ask for. Detective Freddie Furlow is a fantastic detective and an even better man."

She expected further applause, but whoever's finger was on the button to illuminate the sign had fallen asleep. And while Veronica thought she had done a good job of hiding the annoyance from her face, Marlowe was an absolute ventriloquist dummy.

"Right." Marlowe licked her lips. "Well, I'm just glad to see a woman moving up the ranks as you have. Is it correct that you are the youngest detective in all of Greenham?"

"I am." Veronica felt a tinge of pride.

"Congratulations. Now," the woman leaned forward dramatically, placing her elbows on her thighs, "tell us about the night you were kidnapped."

Veronica began massaging the back of her hand with her opposite thumb where she'd been burned, but then stopped herself.

"Well, Bear County had already arrested Gordon Trammel for multiple homicides—the man the media called the dollmaker. But there were some inconsistencies, and the idea of an accomplice was bantered around. See, the real issue was that the cars that—"

"Sounds terrifying. But what must've been more frightening is when you were actually abducted. What was going through your head? Did you think about the possibility of becoming a doll?"

A dramatic, collective intake of breath.

"I wouldn't say I was abducted, not really. But I'd rather focus on the evidence that—"

"Veronica, I know this can be difficult. But as a victim of abuse and trauma myself, I know first-hand that talking, opening up about our experiences is the only way to move on. The only way that we can grow."

For the first time since the interview began, Veronica broke eye contact and scanned the audience. She saw Steve off to one side, angrily gesturing at a cameraman.

This was absolute dog shit.

Veronica hadn't come here to be paraded around as a champion of women's rights. She'd come here to talk about what happened and how effective police work and evidence collection had led to the capture and death of those behind the dollmaker murders.

She'd come here to pump Greenham PD's tires.

"I don't mind talking about it," Veronica said flatly. "But I'd rather talk about how we took a woman murderer off the streets. I'd rather talk about how the hard work myself, but also others, including my detective partner Detective Furlow, and the Bear County Sheriff, made sure to stop these people before anyone else was hurt."

"But it was a woman, right? It was Gloria Trammel and not her husband who actually killed those young girls?"

"Yes… but both her and her husband are responsible."

Veronica tried not to picture little Bev Trammel, her pigtails, tongue in her cheek as she attempted to perform a new yo-yo trick.

Bev was off-limits. Veronica had made that crystal clear. If Marlowe so much as hinted at the girl's involvement, she would stand up and walk off the set.

"Hmm. But everyone believed that it was Gordon all along—working alone. Isn't that right?"

Even though Marlowe exercised restraint, her implication was clear: the male cops thought these violent crimes could have only been committed by a man.

A bizarre and twisted way of calling out inequality.

Yes, women are capable of depraved and horrific acts, too. We're just as sick as you are. How dare you think differently?

"I wouldn't say everyone thought Gordon was working alone. In a case, we look at the evidence and sometimes—"

Marlowe stopped her by holding up a hand. Then she turned to the audience.

"Hold that thought, Veronica—I would love to continue this discussion with you, but first, we need to take a break."

More clapping, camera panning, then the *LIVE* light switched off.

"What are you doing?" the woman said with such venom that Veronica actually pulled back. Even more surprising was that Veronica saw a hint of a yellow aura encircling the woman's face and head. "This is my show. That's my name over there." She pointed at the neon lettering on the wall. "*My* show. So, if I lead you in a direction—"

"This is not what we agreed to," Veronica said, finding her voice. "I have no problem speaking about the dollmaker, but I won't lie to fit an agenda."

"You were told that we might go a little off topic."

Marlowe's yellow aura had become burnt.

Was the woman really that pissed that she would resort to violence?

Veronica considered, very briefly, that she was just projecting. Her synesthesia was never perfect but ever since the fire that had taken her brother's life, it had become less reliable.

"A little off topic? That was more than a little—"

"Dahlia! *Dahlia!*" Marlowe hollered.

The mousy handler appeared out of nowhere.

"Yes?"

"You told me *she* was prepped. You told me *she* was going to go along with things."

Dahlia clutched a clipboard to her chest and said nothing.
What the hell? What happened to women empowerment? This wasn't right.

"Leave her alone," Veronica said.

Marlowe shot lasers at Veronica with her eyes and the glowing aura extended more than three inches from her head now.

"Don't tell me what to do. Did you forget that this is my—"

"Did you forget that I'm a detective," Veronica shot back feeling the heat rise in her cheeks. "Remember that before you do or say something that you might regret."

Marlowe sneered and she glared at Dahlia.

"Let's just skip to the call-in part of the show."

Steve came on stage, pushing by a burly cameraman. Veronica stood as he approached.

"This is bullshit," he said into her ear. "Let's just go."

Marlowe overheard but rather than exacerbate her anger, this seemed to amuse the woman.

If Veronica left with Steve now, she knew how the rest of the show would go. And it wouldn't be good. Comments would be made, disparaging ones, ones related to setting women's rights back.

Further damage to Greenham PD's reputation would be done.

Veronica was trapped and the sinister grin spreading on Marlowe's lips was an indication that the woman knew it.

"I'll stay," Veronica said. "But I agree, let's take some calls."

Dahlia nodded so vigorously that her thick glasses threatened to fall off her face.

"Fine."

"Ten seconds to air," a man bellowed.

Dahlia started to guide Marlowe to her seat, but the host pushed her away. Veronica waited for the other woman to sit first before she lowered herself into the plush blue armchair.

Marlowe scowled at Veronica, and Veronica smiled back. They stayed locked like this, two twelve-point bucks intertwined, neither giving an inch. Then the red 'LIVE' light came on and the woman's face transformed.

"Welcome back. I'm here with survivor and feminist Greenham PD's youngest detective Veronica Shade."

Oh, fuck you, Veronica thought. But she had to respect the woman for sticking to her guns.

"I know that you guys have many questions for our esteemed guest, so we are opening our phone lines right now. The number's on the screen—feel free to ask Detective Shade anything you want."

This wasn't true, of course. Veronica had been assured that all calls would be vetted and only softballs would come through.

But that was before.

"Who do we have on the line now?"

Marlowe put a finger to her ear.

"Stacy from Portland. Stacy from Portland, what question do you have for Veronica?"

The sound came from a speaker overhead, giving it an otherworldly quality.

"Hi—Hi, Veronica. First of all, I just wanted to say that you're an inspiration to me. After seeing you on the news, I enrolled in a criminal justice degree at the local college."

A smattering of applause.

"Thank you."

"What's your question, Stacy?"

"My question is... were you scared? Were you scared when you were in the dollmaker's home?"

Veronica briefly considered that this could be a plant, someone from Marlowe's staff, but she decided to answer anyway.

"Yes. Yes, I was frightened." She pictured Gloria Trammel's shaking hand pointing a gun at her chest. She cleared her throat. "To be honest, I was terrified. This job can be scary at times, rewarding, sure, but also frightening. If anybody tells you differently, they're lying."

Marlowe's face gave nothing away.

"Thank you, Stacy, for your call. Next up, we have Pearl from Montréal? Is that right?"

"Yes," Pearl said with a hint of a French accent. "I'm a big fan of yours, Veronica."

These calls went on for the better part of five minutes and true to Marlowe's word, they were softballs. And Veronica actually enjoyed answering them. Unlike her esteemed host, she had no delusions that her presence on this shitty daytime talk show was driving feminism forward, but, as the old adage goes, if she could inspire just one person...

"We have time for one more call. Is this..." Marlowe pushed her finger against her ear again and nodded. "...ah yes, Gina? Gina, are you there?"

There was a pause, one that lasted the better part of three seconds.

Marlowe looked at Dahlia who just shrugged.

Then there was a click, and someone spoke.

Only, it wasn't Gina.

"Hello, Veronica," a man said. "Or should I call you Lucy?"

Chapter 3

Veronica froze completely.

Lucy.

The man on the phone had called her Lucy… her birth name. How was that possible?

When Veronica had been six, two men had broken into her home while everyone was asleep. They'd tied her up, along with her dad, brother, and mother. Then the sadistic fucks had played a game of *EENIE, MEENIE, MINEY, MO*.

Veronica was *MO*. Then they'd made her choose: only one person was coming out of that house alive, and it was up to her to pick.

She'd chosen herself.

The will to survive is ingrained at birth, Lucy.

The men had set the house on fire with the Davis family still inside. Police Officer Peter Shade arrived first on the scene and found Veronica sitting on the grass, alone, frightened, and confused. Unwilling to put her in the system, he'd broken all the rules and adopted her. He changed her name from Lucy Davis to Veronica Shade and they'd moved around constantly, Peter doing everything in his power to keep Veronica's past a secret.

And it had worked. Until someone came looking for her.

Benny Davis hadn't died in the fire, but nobody had adopted him.

He'd festered and stewed, spending most of his time in an orphanage called Renaissance Home, which had a less-than-stellar reputation.

Eventually, he found his sister—he found Veronica.

And he'd tried to get her to commit suicide. To right what he perceived as a wrong committed nearly two decades ago.

In the end, Benjamin 'Benny' Davis, now going by the name Holland Toler, had started a fire of his own. Veronica and Steve had escaped, her brother had not.

There were only three people who knew the story of Veronica's past life, of Lucy Davis: her father, Peter Shade; her psychiatrist, Dr. Jane Bernard; and herself.

And the voice on the phone now was none of these people.

As her shock settled, Veronica became aware of the colors. Unlike when Marlowe had become furious and her aura had pulsed, the colors weren't originating from one distinct location, like the host's face and head.

Instead, they were everywhere. Perhaps it was the fact that the booming voice came from above, or maybe because this reveal had the potential to ruin her—whatever the reason, her vision was nearly completely obscured.

It was as if someone had taken a moist napkin and dotted it with yellow, orange, and red watercolors. The wet paper made these drops bloom and she was staring through this filter, coloring her world with a fire that only existed inside her mind.

Rarely had her synesthesia been this extreme, this visceral.

Veronica expected the call to be cut, to move on, for the colors to fade. But Marlowe—that *bitch*—waved her hand, signaling to whoever was behind the scenes to keep the call rolling.

"Lucy?" Marlowe asked. "I think you're mistaken. I'm here with Detective Veronica Shade."

"You're mistaken. The woman seated across from you is Lucy Davis." The stranger's gruff baritone voice through the speakers was enough to make the plumes in front of her eyes dance. "Ah, you're seeing them now, aren't you? The colors. Lucy, you're seeing the colors in front of your face. The ones from the fire."

It was a dream. It *had to be a dream*

Her heart started to race, and now, adding to the disorienting kaleidoscope of colors, blue entered the fray. A light, blossoming blue inspired by the slick, cold sweat that had formed on her skin.

"I'm sorry, sir, I think you're confused, I think you're referring to someone else." Marlowe shrugged as if she had no control over the situation.

"Veronica Shade was born Lucy Davis." The man almost sounded seductive. "That's her real name. I know about her family, about what happened to them. I know about her synesthesia, too."

Veronica swallowed hard. Marlowe was listening intently to her earpiece, probably getting a quick lesson on what the hell synesthesia was.

"Who are you?" she asked softly.

"Who am I?" the voice boomed. "Who are *you*? Are you Lucy Davis, daughter of Trevor and Roberta Davis, sister to Benjamin, also known as Holland Toler? Or are you Veronica Shade, a detective who got promoted because your adopted daddy was the police captain?"

Out of the corner of her eye, Veronica spotted movement. Sheriff Burns was trying to come onto the stage again, but security was blocking the way.

"Or are you the detective who uses her *disease*, her synesthesia, to solve cases? Sees flames when there is only violence, sees blue when people are nervous and sweating?" Simply mentioning these manifestations made everything in front of Veronica throb and shake. "Is a human lie detector? Smells gas when somebody isn't telling the truth. Let me ask you something, do you smell gas right now, Lucy? Am *I* lying to you? Am I making this all up?"

Veronica started to tremble. Steve had told her to remain calm and Dahlia had instructed her to act normally no matter what happened. No sudden movements, limited hand gestures. No profanity.

But Veronica felt like jumping to her feet, throttling the air with her hands, while uttering every curse word she'd ever known.

Everything her father had done, everything he'd sacrificed to keep her secret safe was ruined.

"Excuse me, are you saying that —"

"Are you the same girl who used to hate her brother singing to you? Taunting you with a song? *Lu, lu, lu, la, laaaaa, laaa.*" Truth be told, since her brother's death, Veronica hadn't heard that song inside her head. But now, even though the voice was different and the cadence slightly off, it made tears well in her eyes. "Well, I have a new song for you, Veronica Shade."

Marlowe finally made a gesture to hang up and move on. This had gone from interesting to too bizarre to be of much interest.

But, once again, whoever was on the switchboard was napping.

"You ready? Here goes: *one, two, I'm coming for you. Three four, lock your door. Five, six, I crossed the river Styx. Seven, eight, I've sealed your fate.* Veronica, your first—"

Two things happened at nearly exactly the same time: the audio cut out and Steve came to her side.

Somewhere in the back of her mind, she realized that Marlowe was apologizing to the audience for the strange interruption and that after another short break, they'd be back with Veronica Shade.

This was a lie.

Veronica didn't need her synesthesia to know this.

It was a lie because she wasn't going to be back.

This whole thing had been a mistake, and now some psychopath had aired all of her secrets on live TV.

That song...

Veronica closed her eyes.

La, la, la, la, laaaaa, laaa.

Her brother used to tease her with that song. And when the two men had broken into their home, Veronica's mother had instructed Benny to cover his ears and sing. She promised him that everything would be okay.

That was also a lie.

But after Benny had committed suicide, the song had strangely disappeared from inside Veronica's head.

And now it was back. Only Veronica had a feeling that this new tune was even more ominous.

One, two, I'm coming for you. Three, four, lock your door. Five, six, I crossed the river Styx. Seven, eight, I've sealed your fate.

Chapter 4

"YOU PLANNED THIS. YOU PLANNED this from the very beginning," Sheriff Steve Burns said, pointing a finger directly at Marlowe's chest.

The woman raised her hands, feigning innocence.

"All the calls were screened. I don't know how—"

"Bullshit," Steve snapped. Veronica had seen her boyfriend angry before, but never this angry. His face had turned red, and his eyes were thin slits. "Bullshit!"

The quarrel had gathered a crowd and the burly security guards who had stopped the sheriff from storming the stage earlier were now working their way between them.

"Sheriff, I'm sorry that this didn't work out the way you wanted it to," Marlowe said in a condescending tone. "But this is live TV—this stuff happens. Some wacko tricked our screeners and ran his mouth. This isn't—"

"Don't give me that shit. You could have ended the call the second you realized it wasn't Gina. Instead, you kept it going on purpose. You don't give a shit about Veronica or the feminist movement. All you care about is ratings."

Steve was coming dangerously close to Marlowe now, and one of her security reached for his arm. Never in a million years would Sheriff Steve Burns strike a woman, but everyone had their breaking point. And nowadays, words have the potential to get you in nearly as much trouble as your firsts.

As much as Veronica appreciated the man coming to her aid, it wasn't worth him losing his job or worse.

Veronica replaced the security guard's hand on Steve's shoulder with her own.

"Steve, come on."

Thinking that it was still the security guard, the sheriff shook free of her hold.

"Steve, let's go."

Drawn by her tone, the man finally turned his head to look at her. For a moment, Veronica didn't even recognize him. His eyes were wild, untethered, his pupils dilated. White paste clung to the corners of his lips.

Steve snarled, shot one final scathing look at Marlowe, and then stormed out, not even looking back to make sure that she was following.

Neither of them said anything until they were back in his car. Even then, Veronica just sat in silence, thinking about what had just happened.

A psychopath had found her out.

Veronica and her father had hidden her past as best they could, but if you knew where to look, you could find out anything about anyone.

"I'm sorry, Veronica. I should have gotten to you earlier and made them end the call. It's just—I thought it was a prank at first."

Veronica was rubbing the backs of her hands furiously. No longer being in the studio meant that she no longer saw the colors, but the echoes of her visions remained, like the spots on your retinas after staring at the sun for a little too long.

I thought it was a prank at first.

Meaning, now he thought differently. And of course, he would. Veronica might be able to convince others that she had no idea what the man on the phone was talking about, but pleading ignorance would not fly with Steve.

He'd seen her.

He'd seen her reaction.

This would make for a very interesting dinner conversation.

Veronica's hands were burning—she was rubbing so hard that her skin was on the verge of blistering. Steve reached out and put a stop to her frantic massaging.

"It's not your fault," she said softly. "I could've gotten up and left." But she couldn't have—not really. Veronica had been too blind and disoriented to move. "Did he say... did he say his name?"

Steve was staring straight ahead, his jaw clenched. Since the dollmaker, he'd grown his beard even longer. It wasn't quite scraggly but was well on its way. Veronica preferred it shorter but didn't mind the rugged look, either.

"I don't think so. They said that the caller was Gina, but that's obviously not the case."

"Yeah."

More silence as Steve pulled away from the studio and headed back to Bear County. Veronica knew that her focus should be on denial or damage control, but instead all she could think about was who called and how they'd obtained their information.

Her father was retired, but busier than ever. He took cooking classes every day. But even if the man sat on his ass drinking Bud and watching old college football games, Peter Shade wouldn't tell anyone about her. That made zero sense.

Then there was Dr. Jane Bernard... she knew everything—*absolutely* everything. But not only did Veronica consider the woman a friend, but the psychiatrist also had a legal obligation to keep their discussions private. Besides, Jane had kept her secret for nearly twenty years... why reveal Veronica's true identity to the world now?

But who else?

Her partner, Detective Freddie Furlow? No, he didn't know everything the man on the phone had disclosed. He knew some of it—he was the one who had saved Veronica and Steve from the fire that her brother had set. But he didn't know about the song or her synesthesia.

Steve?

Veronica looked over at the sheriff again.

Ludicrous.

The only other person that she could think of was Dylan Hall, the reformed drug dealer and addict turned confidential informant. Dylan had known her brother from their time in the Renaissance Home orphanage. Did Benny tell him about the fire? The twisted game that Trent Alberts and Herb Thornton made Veronica play? Maybe. But Benny didn't know about her synesthesia. Her condition had been forged by that horrific night but hadn't been actualized until much later when the girl in her elementary school committed suicide.

Dylan could be irrational, but Veronica had always been kind to him. She'd kept him out of prison and was the only one who supported him when Ken Cameron—

"Ken," she said the name almost breathlessly.

The sheriff, who had been lost in thought, glanced at her.

"What's that?"

"Ken Cameron. Is he still in prison? It could have been him."

It didn't sound like Ken—Ken was a cocky frat boy, whereas the man on the phone sounded rough. But a voice changer wasn't out of the question.

"I have no idea," Steve admitted. "You want me to take you home? I have a few things I need to clear up, but I should be able to break away early and join you."

Veronica had been granted the day off to do the fucking interview, so she had no need to get back to work. But the idea of being alone with her thoughts was almost unbearable.

She checked her phone. It was only two-fifteen.

And then Veronica saw the messages.

Two dozen, maybe more. There were so many that she had to scroll for nearly five seconds before reaching the end.

"Shit," she muttered, closing her phone.

She looked skyward.

"Veronica? What that guy was saying, the stuff about... sniffing lies? I've seen you—"

"Not now. Later—I promise I'll explain later." She looked out the window and bit her lip. "I don't want to go home, Steve. Take me back to the precinct. Please."

Steve made a face.

"You sure? There's gonna be a lot of ques—"

Veronica straightened.

One, two, I'm coming for you.

"Yeah, I know it's gonna be a shit show. But, hey, you know what they say: it's better to peel a Band-Aid off fast than slow."

Chapter 5

VERONICA HAD HOPED THAT HER partner, Detective Freddie Furlow, would be waiting outside the precinct for her as he did most days. But not only was he not there, but he was also one of the few people she knew who *hadn't* tried to reach her after the interview.

When her father had 'voluntarily retired' as police captain, Freddie had been there to calm her down, to make sure she didn't say or do something in front of either the union rep, the mayor, or anyone else present who could make her life extremely uncomfortable.

Without Freddie, Veronica was second-guessing her decision to go back to the office. But to her surprise, there was nobody waiting for her out front, no media, no crowd, no colleagues, and when she exited the elevator on the second floor, no one approached her there either.

There were people in the office—the floor was shared by a half dozen detectives and three times as many beat cops—but they were all buried in their work, seemingly not taking notice of her.

Did the episode not air? Was the LIVE sign, like everything else about Marlowe, a lie?

That wouldn't explain the messages, but—

A man seated at a desk next to the captain's office rose to his feet.

Veronica sneered and balled her hands into firsts.

"What the hell are you doing here?"

"I came to see you, actually," the man replied.

Veronica looked him up and down. He was still wearing those damn double-monk strap shoes and pants that didn't quite reach his ankles. His white dress shirt looked straight from the packaging.

"Don't come near me," Veronica warned, now pointing at the man's chest. "After what you did to my dad—"

The door to the captain's office, what had once been her father's, opened. The man who stared out couldn't have been more different than Peter Shade. Whereas her dad was a big man, larger-than-life, the new captain, Pierre Bottel, was thin and lean, maybe five foot ten, hundred and sixty pounds. He had a rust-colored mustache, and even though he was only in his early fifties, he was nearly completely bald.

Pierre wore gold wire rim glasses more befitting an accountant than a police captain.

When it was announced that Pierre would replace her father, a man not from Greenham but all the way from Washington, D.C., Veronica had secretly been pleased. This feeling persisted after looking him up. It was like breaking up with someone. You never wanted your ex to date someone who looked like you, or God forbid, just a little *better* than you—bigger tits, flatter stomach, rounder ass. You wanted them to date someone completely different so that you could convince yourself that it wasn't you, it was just that they had a different type.

And then she'd met Captain Pierre Bottel. Veronica very much wanted to hate the man, but, to his credit, Pierre had been more than fair to her.

But Internal Affairs Officer Cole Batherson? He was different. He was scum. Initially called in to investigate how a man like Ken Cameron had managed to stay undetected for as long as he had, and to determine if sociopathy, narcissism, and antisocial personality disorder were a systemic trait, Cole had hung around like a bad smell. In the end, he was the one who had submitted the report that had lost her father his job.

"Detective Shade." For such a thin man, Captain Bottel had an unexpectedly commanding voice. "Can you please join me inside my office?"

Try as she might, Veronica couldn't completely wipe the sneer off her face.

"Officer Batherson, you too."

Veronica shot the man a look, one that said, don't walk beside me if you want to walk at all, then entered the captain's office.

"Take a seat, please," Pierre said as he took up residence behind his desk.

"I'd prefer to stand."

The captain looked up at her through his gold glasses.

"Sit, please."

Veronica nodded and sat. Cole had no choice but to take a seat in the chair beside her because it was the only other one in the room.

"I caught your interview, Veronica. I'm sorry." Pierre didn't believe in preamble. He usually didn't believe in apologies, either. One of the few similarities between her father and the new captain was that for them, it was about the job and only the job.

"I-I didn't want to do it." Veronica loathed sounding defensive, but like rubbing her hands the way she was now, it was instinctual. It was also a mistake—her first response should have been to deny the caller's claims. "It-it was just some weird fanboy spouting nonsense. Waste of time. No big deal."

Pierre stared at her so intently that Veronica wondered if the captain could smell the gasoline scent generated by her lie.

"I just wanted to let you know that we're planning to issue a brief media release refuting the claims made by the caller. Nothing specific, just a short note."

"Is that why he's here?" Veronica spat, not granting Cole the dignity of looking in his direction.

"No. Cole Batherson is here because another media outlet has asked to do a profile on you."

Veronica craned her neck forward.

"You can't be serious." Pierre's response came in the form of a glare. This was another similarity between her father and the captain, Veronica realized at that moment. Neither liked to be questioned. But this... this was too much. "After this morning's disaster? I won't. No way."

"Detective Shade, this request came from the New York Times."

Veronica was unimpressed.

"So? I don't care if the Pope wants an interview, I'm done. Today was—" *a fucking absolute disaster* "—a mess. I'm fine with what you said before, a small press release. But that's it."

Another stare.

"Detective Shade, this will be different. This will—"

"How? How will it be different?"

"For one, we control the narrative. Cole will be writing the article."

Veronica crossed her arms and leaned back in her chair.

"That's what I was told about *Marlowe*, that everything was in our control. Softball questions, a couple of callers. Nothing too deep, nothing personal."

Captain Bottel sighed.

"Detective Shade, this is non-negotiable."

"What? Why? Why can't we just do a small release, like you said?"

"We can, and we will. But the reason why we need to do this article, why it's not up for debate, is because someone will look into what that caller said on the talk show if they aren't already."

"So? Who cares?"

Veronica's throat felt tight.

She already knew the answer before the captain opened his mouth.

"I care. And so should you. We need to control the narrative, Detective Shade, because even if you deny what was said a million times, someone will eventually dig up irrefutable proof that everything mentioned on *Marlowe* was true."

Chapter 6

VERONICA WAS FUMING AS SHE stormed out of the captain's office.

...everything mentioned on Marlowe *was true? Really? What does Pierre Bottel know about my life? Nothing. He isn't even from around here.*

The man was just grasping at straws. Probably thought that her pain and suffering was an opportunity presented: use the freak to boost Greenham PD's rep, maybe gain a few new recruits, and get some great numbers for the mayor to use in his next campaign.

Well, fuck him.

And fuck Freddie, too. Where the hell is he? He's supposed to have my back.

Instead, he'd left her alone to be railroaded by two men.

Veronica scooped up her laptop and was headed toward the stairway when Cole spoke up.

"Veronica?"

The hurt in Cole Batherson's eyes threatened to crack through her anger. But then she remembered that this was the man who had gotten her father fired for missing a meeting with the mayor.

Because they were attending a funeral... a funeral of a fellow cop, no less.

Veronica flipped him the middle finger and left.

She kept her head down until she got behind the wheel of her car but before opening her laptop, her eyes fell on a book on the passenger seat—Daddy's Little Girls by Dan Padavona. Nervous about the interview, Veronica hadn't slept well last night. She'd gotten up early and decided to drive around, trying to clear her head. She was in Matheson when she remembered that the Public Library had called on Friday. Steve had mentioned that he'd been waiting for this book, but they'd spent so much of the weekend preparing for the interview that he hadn't had time to go pick it up. Veronica thought it would be a nice surprise for the man who'd offered her so much support over the past few months.

And yet, she'd been so wrapped up in her own head that she'd completely forgotten about it.

The familiar tightness that was guilt manifested, began to attack her stomach. She should have been honest with Steve. She should have told him about her synesthesia.

About her brother.

While Steve's primary concern during and in the moments following the interview with Marlowe had been her safety, she saw hurt in his eyes—the type of hurt that only came with the realization that your partner didn't fully trust you.

I'll tell you everything, Steve. Once I figure out who's behind this, I'll tell you everything you want to know.

Veronica deliberately held her breath for fear of what she might smell. When she was confident that if her synesthesia had acted up, that any gasoline odor would have since dissipated, she finally inhaled and addressed her laptop. She was still convinced that, somehow, Ken Cameron was behind all of this, his vendetta against her so deep-rooted that even prison couldn't temper it. The man had been passed over for detective in favor of Veronica, and then she'd shot down his advances. Ultimately, he'd arranged the kidnapping of a city councilor's daughter. This had signaled the beginning of the end for Captain Peter Shade, a career police officer who had managed, despite having to move constantly to protect Veronica's true identity, to make it to as high and prestigious a post as captain. And Peter had *loved* his job.

Ken had taken that away from him. In return, the bastard had received eight years in prison for his crimes, and...

Veronica's frown deepened as she stared at the database on her laptop.

... he was still behind bars.

"Shit."

Veronica raised her eyes.

It could still be him, she rationalized. *Ken still had contacts outside prison. He had access to a phone, the Internet. The man was determined and—*

Seeing Freddie stopped her train of thought. Her morbidly obese partner was standing by the corner of the City of Greenham Police Department. Veronica's first instinct was to roll down the window and shout to him, to ask him where the hell he'd been, but the expression on his face made her hesitate.

A mixture of shock and fear.

Partially obscured by Freddie's girth was another man. A juxtaposition of her partner, FBI Agent Jake Keller was in excellent shape. He had short blond hair brushed to one side and dark blue eyes. But he shared something in common with Freddie: a dour look.

What the hell is he doing here? Veronica wondered.

She'd met the man only once—Agent Keller had granted them access to then incarcerated serial killer, Trent Alberts, the same man who had broken into the Davises' home and made them play his sadistic, murderous game.

Blue hues came off Freddie in waves, but this was pretty much a constant—his immense size meant that he was perpetually sweating. But the two men's collective posture was undeniable.

They weren't discussing dinner plans.

Keller finished what he was saying, and Freddie gave him a reluctant nod. Then the detective jammed his hands into his pockets and hunched forward. Keller grabbed the back of his arm and gave it a reassuring squeeze.

There was something wrong with Freddie. His face was downcast, eyes sunken. Veronica couldn't remember a time he'd looked this bad, which was saying something about a man whose diet consisted solely of saturated fats and mass quantities of sodium.

And yet, she still held her tongue.

Agent Keller said something else and then left, leaving Freddie alone. Veronica continued to watch him for a few seconds longer but then, when her partner started to make his way in his characteristic saunter around the corner of the building, she finally called out.

It was too late, Freddie was out of earshot.

Veronica quickly dialed his number. She saw him pull out his phone, look at it, then slip it back into his pocket without answering.

Then he was gone.

"What the hell?"

Veronica moved to start the car, intending on going after him, when she nudged the forgotten laptop resting on her lap.

Ken Cameron's mug shot stared back at her. It was almost more sinister now that it was tilted at an odd angle.

Freddie could wait.

This could not.

Fuck Pierre Bottel and Cole Batherson and their New York Times Pulitzer prize-winning bullshit.

This wasn't about them.

This was about her.

It was Ken—it had to be. After he'd been arrested, Ken had used his contacts in the department to dig into her past. Many people disliked Veronica for what she'd done to the disgruntled officer. Marlowe was right about one thing: there was a residual element of bro-culture that still existed in the police department. Even though Ken's guilt was irrefutable, there were those who believed that he was family, a fellow blue blood, and that his discretions should have been dealt with in-house.

That's how things were done in the past.

But as Peter Shade always liked to say, the past is boring—it's already happened. The future is far more interesting.

And Veronica's future was no different.

Especially because it involved meeting a man who despised her. A man whom she'd put behind bars for eight years.

One, two, I'm coming for you.

Veronica shuddered and started her car.

Yeah, I'm coming for you, too, asshole.

Chapter 7

BEAR COUNTY CORRECTIONAL WAS LOCATED about forty miles south of the City of Greenham. After conviction and sentencing, the judge had ordered Ken Cameron into the custody of the City of Greenham Jail. At the last minute, however, his lawyer made a desperate plea to move Ken somewhere where he was less likely to encounter the criminals that he'd put behind bars.

Where it would be safer for him.

Veronica couldn't care less for the man's safety, but the judge had been sympathetic. Ken's attorney had asked for placement out-of-state, but the best the judge was willing to do was send him to Bear County. This was met with backlash, with the attorney of the convicted claiming that everyone in Bear County would know that his client had been a cop. The judge quickly countered that they had asked to keep Ken away from people he might have arrested, not conceal his identity. And as all major offenders in Greenham are sent to Portland and not Bear County, the judge had effectively granted the request.

Hearing this had brought a rare smile to Veronica's lips.

This twist of fate would also prove helpful for her current situation. Bear County Correctional was staffed by Bear County Deputies. And if you wanted to see a prisoner without approval or an appointment, dating and living with the Bear County Sheriff would come in handy.

The first deputy she encountered asked for her ID. She flashed it, and he appeared to recognize her name.

"Detective Shade, what can I do for you?" The man asked. He was older than Steve, with gray hair at his temples and oddly wide-set eyes.

"I would like to speak to an inmate," she said flatly.

The man didn't so much as raise an eyebrow at this. It wasn't uncommon for detectives to visit inmates without prior approval. Often times, cases required expediency, which is the antithesis of bureaucracy. And while crossing jurisdictions and law enforcement departments was unusual, she had Sheriff Burns' name in her back pocket as a last resort.

"Name?"

"Ken Cameron."

Was that a tiny twitch of the man's gray eyebrows? Veronica thought it was, but the deputy kept a straight face.

"Let me see if I can arrange that for you."

The man began typing on the keyboard in front of him.

"I would also like his call logs."

"Of course. How far back?"

Veronica took a second before saying, "About two weeks."

The man nodded, typed some more, and then Veronica heard the whirring of an ancient printer start up from somewhere beneath the deputy's desk. As they waited for the printout to complete, the deputy got on the phone and said a few words.

He hung up and then handed over the single-page printout.

Veronica was immediately disappointed. There were but four numbers on the list, three of which were repeated several times: Pierce and Brown, the law firm that had represented Ken Cameron at his trial.

The other number belonged to Blair Cameron, probably Ken's sister or mother.

And none of the calls had been made earlier today.

But while discouraged, to Veronica, this didn't mean that Ken hadn't been behind the call. He could have just as easily used a burner phone or paid another inmate and given him a script to read.

"This is it?"

"Yep. Want me to go back a little further?"

"Yeah, give me the last month... no, make that the last two months of calls."

"Sure."

The deputy returned to his keyboard a third time when the phone rang. He answered, staring at Veronica as he did.

"All right, I'll send her in. Thanks."

"You came at a good time, Detective Shade. Mr. Cameron just finished his lunch and was on his way back to his cell. A guard will detour him to a meeting room. And I'll have those call logs ready for you on your way out."

"Thank you."

The man smiled and then the large metal door buzzed and unlocked.

Bear County Correctional was a medium-security prison, catering mostly to inmates convicted of non-violent offenses—drugs, theft, and the occasional stalker.

As a result, prisoners here had more freedoms than at a higher security facility. During the day, they could generally come and go as they pleased. There was a library, a TV room, and even a basketball court, but time on the latter was regulated. Inmates had daily access to the Internet, but what they could see and visit while online was highly regulated and controlled.

The deputy that greeted her on the other side was of medium build with large hands and a heavy brow characteristic of a much larger person. The way he moved, ambled was the word that came to mind, was reminiscent of someone who once carried a lot more weight on their body but had gone to great lengths to get back into shape.

Veronica's mind turned to Freddie, of how her partner was in desperate need of weight loss. He might hate running, but he had to do *something*. The man was a ticking time bomb.

Freddie...

She pictured her partner's sallow cheeks, the fear in his eyes. *What's going on with you, Freddie?*

He had taken Peter Shade's dismissal hard—the two men went way back—but this was something else.

What the hell did Agent Keller say to him?

"He's not very talkative," the deputy remarked. "Usually just keeps to himself."

For a second, Veronica thought that the deputy was speaking about Freddie.

"I didn't tell him who's come to visit, by the way. So, he might be... well, he might be surprised to see you."

Surprised in this context meant furious. And if this random deputy knew exactly who Veronica was, not in relation to the sheriff, but to Ken Cameron?

Talkative or not, she suspected that Ken had uttered his fair share of choice words relating to a Detective Veronica Shade.

Criminals aren't generally known to be a particularly introspective bunch. In her experience, they would rather blame their own mothers than accept responsibility for their actions.

"Appreciate the heads-up."

"He's just in here." The man indicated a thick dark-blue door with the number one plastered on it. "Now, Ken is cuffed, but not to the table. If you would prefer—"

"That's fine."

The man slipped a key into the lock and turned it.

"If you need anything at all, Detective Shade, just holler."

With that, the deputy opened the door, and Veronica stepped into the interrogation room.

Chapter 8

THE SECOND SHERIFF STEVE BURNS dropped Veronica off at her precinct, he pulled a loose, innocuous pill from his pocket. Not quite the size of one of those colorful ROCKETS candies, the white disk had 40 engraved into it.

Forty milligrams of Oxycontin.

When his back had been torn to ribbons by a black bear, the doctor had prescribed him a dosage regiment of 10mg twice a day of the powerful long-term opioid. That had been more than a month ago.

His injuries had since healed and his prescription run out, but something other than a series of nasty scars remained.

A yearning for the numbness that the drug provided.

Steve rolled the pill between thumb and forefinger.

You stole this. You broke into the evidence locker and stole it.

This self-shaming was intended to make him toss the pill out the window. The reality was it didn't even work as a stall tactic.

Steve dry-swallowed the Oxy.

The first time he'd stolen these pills from the evidence locker, he'd done it because he was still in pain. He'd been smart about it then, turned off the cameras, and taken only a few. The second time, the pain was gone, and he'd been dumb. Not only had he taken all the remaining pills, but he'd also left the cameras recording.

What's worse, was that the next time he had legitimate business in the evidence locker, Steve reviewed the footage.

It was gone. Not because it hadn't been recorded—it had—but because someone else had deleted it.

And this stranger was no guardian angel. If he had to guess, Chief Deputy Marcus McVeigh was the person responsible.

And when it suited the man best, the video would miraculously resurface.

Steve would bet his life on it.

Perhaps more frightening than his blatant disregard for the law was the fact that he'd gone from 10mg twice a day to three times forty in record time.

Shit, he'd popped one right before Veronica's interview had started, and by the end of it, he was so desperate for another that he'd nearly strangled the woman with the red lips and fake everything.

I need help.

But so did Veronica.

And right now, she was more important.

Until today, Sheriff Steve Burns had never heard of synesthesia. He knew of Veronica's past, though—he knew what happened to her family, and the sick game that Trent and Herb had made her play.

Veronica's brother had told him. He'd told him everything while Steve was bound and gagged inside that burnt shell of a home.

Steve had also seen firsthand Veronica's almost supernatural ability to tell if someone was lying, most recently when Gordon Trammel had claimed to have killed those girls and had tried to convince them that he was the dollmaker. Steve himself could tell that something was off about the confession, but it was Veronica's confidence, her sheer insistence that he was lying that was the difference between their inclinations.

What did the creep on the phone say?

She smelled gasoline when someone lied?

It was fantastical, and perhaps he was just imagining it, but Steve thought he remembered Veronica's nose twitching ever so slightly anytime she asked a question.

What else had he said?

She saw colors when there was violence?

Two hours of researching synesthesia on his work computer offered little with regards to insight into this condition.

As he understood it, synesthesia was a mixing of senses—seeing or hearing or tasting or feeling or smelling things that weren't there? Tasting honey, for instance, when you hear Beethoven's fifth. Seeing purple everywhere when you read the number six. An insatiable forearm itch stimulated by the sweet scent of roses.

What the hell did it all mean?

And if what the caller said was true... a big if... why the *fuck* hadn't Veronica mentioned it?

The apparent lack of trust stung. Stung hard. Stung hard enough for him to want to reach into his pocket and take another Oxy.

The only thing that stopped him was the realization that he only had a finite number of pills left.

The irony was, Steve had secrets of his own. Secrets that rivaled hers in both magnitude and severity.

And as disturbing as their mutual mistrust was, it didn't change the fact that he loved her. There was no doubt in Steve's mind that he loved Veronica Shade. Whether she loved him back was still up in the air.

Steve sighed and massaged the bridge of his nose and the inner corners of his eyes.

He had shit to do, of course. Even though he never overtly flaunted his relationship with Veronica, people knew that they were together. As such, anything that happened to her reflected on him. If he had still been a State Trooper, this would never have happened. But he wasn't—he was an elected official. And he needed to do damage control.

Steve had already received three phone calls—from the Kleinmans' as well as two other substantial donors to his campaign, and he'd let them all go to voicemail.

Instead of working, he was researching.

His cell phone buzzed, and Steve realized that he'd zoned out—his computer was beeping because his finger was holding down the 'O' key.

Steve cleared his throat and looked at his phone, expecting it to be another donor checking in.

It wasn't, and he answered on the second ring.

"Yeah?" He cleared his throat again.

"Sheriff, I've been trying to reach you on the radio, but I haven't been able to get through."

Steve glanced at his radio, which he'd taken off his lapel and laid on the corner of the desk. He'd turned it off.

"Sorry, batteries are dead," he lied. "What can I do for you, McVeigh?"

Hand over my badge and gun? Hold out my wrists for you to cuff them?

"We found a body... female."

The sheriff straightened.

"Body? Cause of death?"

"That's the thing, I'm not really sure."

"OD? Do you see any track marks? Where are you, McVeigh? Where's the body?"

"I can't—" McVeigh was clearly struggling to keep up with the rapid-fire questions. "I'm in Matheson, but I can't tell cause or manner of death."

"What do you mean?"

"I think you gotta come look at this, Sheriff... everything... everything is covered in paint, believe it or not. Yellow, orange, and red paint."

Chapter 9

ALMOST A YEAR AGO TO the day, Veronica had participated in another jailhouse interview. Then, she'd sat across from one of the two men who had broken into her house when she'd been a child: Trent Alberts, one of the cruelest men to ever live.

How else could you describe a man who made a six-year-old choose a single family member to survive and then was forced to watch the others be burned alive?

Now, the man before her was despicable, but not nearly as sadistic or frightening.

"Oh no," Ken Cameron said, baring his teeth. "Not *you*."

Veronica observed the man whom she used to work beside.

Prison had not been kind to ex-City of Greenham police officer Ken Cameron. Before being convicted, he'd been muscular, if a bit fluffy, and had a young, round face. Now, he was drawn, thin, bordering on malnourished, and his eyes were heavily hooded. There was a fresh scar on his chin in the shape of an apostrophe.

Even his voice seemed different. Older, perhaps. The voice of a man who'd started smoking at an early age and when he'd decided to quit, permanent damage had already been done to his vocal cords.

"Yes, *me*," Veronica replied, electing to stand rather than sit across from the man in the orange jumper.

"You ruined my fucking life, you know that?" Ken spat, his eyes disappearing almost completely beneath the swollen lids. "You took everything away from me. You know what it's like being a cop in prison, Veronica?"

Despite his words, Veronica detected no threat of violence here. Most likely, that had been beaten out of him early on during his sentence. And while she knew better than to entertain the man, she couldn't help herself.

"No, I don't. And I won't ever know."

Ken sneered.

"Fuck you."

"You did this to yourself, you egotistical bastard," Veronica shot back. A simple curse normally wouldn't make her this hostile, but there was nothing usual or typical about today. "The sad thing is," she continued, unable to stop now that she'd started down this track, "you were actually a decent cop. You know what I think? If you kept your head on straight, you probably would have made detective in a couple of years. Maybe even sooner."

Ken glared at her.

"I would've made detective before you if my daddy was captain."

"Well, he's not the captain anymore."

Veronica wasn't sure why she said this but instantly regretted it.

"Oh, yeah?" Ken became smug. "What happened? Did he finally get canned for helping you out?"

Not far from the truth.

Veronica felt a pang of guilt and immediately changed the subject.

"I didn't come here to talk about my father."

"Then why the fuck did you come here, Veronica? To rub it in? After nearly a year, you'd think—"

"How did you find out about my past, Ken?"

The question startled the convict.

"What?"

"My past," Veronica repeated. "Who told you? Did you hack Dr. Bernard's files? Is that how you found out about me?"

Ken leaned back in his chair. He tried to cross his arms over his chest, but the cuffs wouldn't allow for it. His hands rested in his lap, instead.

"Are you high?"

This was not how Veronica envisioned things going down. She'd expected Ken to initially deny the allegations, but then his narcissistic nature would take over. He'd laugh and mock her, tell her he was going to call every news station in Oregon to talk about her past. Try to ruin her.

Maybe he'd even attempt to antagonize her to the point of violence.

But, so far, this wasn't the case. Ken looked legitimately confused by her questions. Still, Veronica decided to push a little harder. Prison changed people and while Ken hadn't been even a half-decent liar back when he'd been a cop, he might be one now.

"Did you call the TV station during my interview?"

Ken stared blankly at her for a full second before replying.

"I'm not telling you shit."

This sort of reply was typically a surrogate for no, but Veronica wanted to hear him say it.

"Just tell me. Tell me that it was you and I'll leave you alone."

Veronica knew that she was coming off as desperate, but that was because she was.

"Why would I tell you anything?" Ken said, licking his lips. "You're the one who put me in this place. I owe you nothing."

Veronica was tempted to remind Ken Cameron a second time that it had been his actions that had landed him behind bars, but that felt like going backward.

"What do you want? You want me to admit that you calling in pissed me off? That it got to me?" she shrugged. "Okay, it did—it got to me. I mean, I'm here, right? So, why not just admit it?"

Ken observed her.

"You know what, I'll tell you—I'll tell you, but first, you have to tell *me* something."

Veronica didn't like the idea of playing games with the manipulative bastard, but her badgering the man was getting nowhere.

"What? What do you want to know?"

"You said your daddy is no longer captain. I want to know why?"

Veronica was torn. She didn't know how this information could be useful or even interesting to a man who would never be a cop again, which made the request curious.

She also didn't see any immediate harm in telling him at least part of the truth.

"Internal affairs were pissed off, thought that somehow, for some reason, my dad should have identified *you* as a narcissist, a sociopath. They blamed him for not knowing that there was a rat in his department."

Ken ignored the insults.

"And it took them a year to let him go? I don't think so, Veronica. Tell me what really happened or I'm going to sit here with my mouth closed until the guard comes and tells me it's time for bed."

Ken was telling the truth. And had she been in her right state of mind, Veronica would have just come up with a convincing lie to appease the man.

But she was too tired, too desperate to get away from the stench of self-pity.

Veronica sighed and offered Ken some facsimile of the truth.

"Sorry to break it to you, but it wasn't anything salacious. After what you did, IA came in to babysit everyone. They were just looking for a scapegoat, someone to take some of the blame for your actions. Someone not yet disgraced. Captain Shade missed a meeting with the mayor because of a funeral and they canned him for it. That's it."

"No way."

"Yes, way," Veronica countered.

"I don't think so—it was something *you* did. It had to be. I know it."

Veronica raised one shoulder.

"Sorry to disappoint. I told you what you wanted to know, now it's your turn."

Ken continued to observe for several moments. Then his grin became lecherous.

"Yeah, I called into the show. Told them *aaaall* about you, Veronica—wait, where are you going?"

Even before he opened his mouth, she knew that what was going to come out was a lie. She saw it in those hooded eyes.

Then she smelled it in the form of gasoline.

Veronica banged on the door.

"We're done here," she announced to the guard.

"No, wait—I called the show. It was me."

Veronica looked over her shoulder at the pathetic man in the orange jumpsuit.

"Yeah? What was the name of the show then, smart guy?"

Ken's lips quivered as the door opened.

"Hey! Come back! It was me, I called. Hey! *Hey!*"

The guard slammed the door on Ken and then to Veronica, he said, "You get what you come for?"

"Yeah."

Unfortunately, while she had her answer, it wasn't the one she'd wanted. And when Detective Veronica Shade left Bear County Correctional, she did so with more questions than when she'd arrived.

Chapter 10

"Shit," Sheriff Steve Burns grumbled. He put his hands on his hips and stared at the scene before him.

"Shit is right. Got a strange call this morning, gave this address," Deputy McVeigh said. "I sent a deputy to perform a wellness check, but nobody answered the door. He said he peered through the frosted glass and saw what he thought was a fire at first. Made the executive decision to kick down the door." McVeigh waved a hand over the front hallway and adjacent family room. "As you can see, no fire."

It definitely wasn't a fire, but the sheriff wasn't sure what he was looking at. It was as if someone had taken buckets of paint and splashed them in streaks over pretty much everything: the floor, walls, furniture. In some places, the stains even reached the ceiling. Steve noticed three distinct colors—orange, red, and yellow—but they were mixed together in most places due to the haphazard method used to empty the cans.

Seeing this, Steve couldn't help but recall the gravelly voice emanating from the speakers above Veronica's and Marlowe's heads.

..sees flames when there is only violence?

This couldn't possibly be related, could it?

"Where's the body?"

"On the couch," McVeigh replied. "You might want to put these on."

The deputy offered him fabric shoe covers. Steve took them, slipped them on, and then made his way into the house.

"I'm not much of a painter, but this seems like a hell of a lot of paint," he said.

"Yep. I'm thinking like maybe six of those five gallon jugs? We can get an expert in later to figure out exactly how much. But it is a lot."

The sheriff pushed the brim of his hat back.

"Which means whoever was in here had to make multiple trips to bring the paint cans in from the car."

"Unless there was more than one of them," McVeigh remarked.

Sheriff Steve Burns nodded but said nothing. He looked to the driveway, then the curb, noting that other than his deputy's vehicles, there were no other cars in the immediate vicinity.

"Either way, I have some men canvassing the area, asking neighbors if they saw anything."

"Good. Now, where is the body?"

"In here."

McVeigh directed the sheriff to the left and into the family room. There was even more paint here than in the front hallway, with puddles so thick in some places that they rippled with every step the two men took. The closed blinds that covered the front bay window were coated in streaks of red, orange, and yellow, but the main focus was the couch.

"I don't—" *see it,* was what Steve was about to say when he finally spotted the victim. Or at least, part of them.

A foot covered in yellow paint and thus blending into the couch cushions jutted up from the far end. The way it was oriented suggested that the body lay on the floor on the other side. Steve carefully walked around the couch, nearly slipping several times on the thick, syrupy liquid.

And there she was.

The scene was already disorienting from all the paint, but the way the body was positioned added to the confusion.

Based on the angle of the leg, she should have been face down, with one foot on the arm of the couch, and the other on the ground. And, at first, Steve thought this was the case. But then, through the paint that, like everything else in the room, covered the corpse, he saw her nose and eyes.

Her head had been turned almost completely backward.

"And you couldn't tell cause of death?" Steve asked as he moved even closer to the body. "What did you think happened? Contortionist gone wrong?"

"No, I—"

"Then what? The painters decided to do the job with her just lying there? Figured, what the hell, she won't care if we pretty much do the worst job ever?"

"You asked about an OD, and I—"

"She was killed, McVeigh. Broken neck." Steve clucked his tongue. His mouth was dry, and his cheeks felt warm. "Any idea who the victim is?"

"The home belongs to Gina Braden. Apparently, she works at the Matheson Public Library."

Steve went from flushed to burning hot in a fraction of a second. An uncomfortable tingling rose in his cheeks and the tops of his ears.

"Sheriff?"

It took Steve several seconds to collect himself.

"I know her." This sounded strange. "I mean, I *knew* her. Goddamn it, I knew her well."

Chapter 11

THE FIRST THING THAT VERONICA did after driving away from Bear County Correctional was open her phone. She needed someone to talk to, and the first person who came to mind was Freddie. But the sheer number of texts and missed calls were intimidating, and Veronica couldn't handle them right now.

She placed the phone on the passenger seat.

The caller to the show wasn't Ken Cameron. Ken Cameron was a despicable piece of shit and a liar, but he wasn't resourceful enough to obtain the information that the caller had spewed while inside prison. And all she'd accomplished by visiting the prison was providing him with more ammunition should they ever cross paths again. Unlikely, but Veronica thought that sitting in the courtroom and listening to Ken's sentence being read was the final time she'd have to see his face.

Not only that, but Veronica had also wasted about two hours, and she was no closer to finding out who the mysterious man on the phone had been or who might've leaked her secrets.

Her intention had been to head back to the precinct, but she quickly changed her mind. Cole Batherson was there. And while this time he claimed to be on her side, the idea of sitting down and eating crumpets and talking about what it was like to be a chick cop in a dude precinct was nauseating.

How the man could flip sides like that, going from following them around and snitching on every little procedural error or misstep, to writing a puff piece about Veronica was a mystery not even Robert Langdon could solve.

No way would she trust him with any personal details. Although, thanks to Ghostface—*hello, Lucy*—there was enough information in the ether now that he might be able to comprise a George R.R. Martin length book out of it.

She could only hope it took as long to write.

Thoughts of Cole inevitably led to her father, of Peter Shade sitting on the couch, eyes glazed from watching daytime TV.

Veronica shook her head. That wasn't her father—thankfully, he wouldn't have caught her *Marlowe* interview just yet. But he was alone and that made her feel guilty. It wasn't completely her fault that her father had never married or met someone, but Veronica felt partly to blame. It was hard to hold down a relationship while moving around constantly with an adopted child while attempting to keep her true identity a secret.

After a quick stop to pick up a six-pack of craft IPAs, Veronica drove to the house that most qualified as her childhood home. It was the middle of the afternoon, but Peter was retired, and she needed a drink… or three.

Nobody answered on the first knock. Nor the second.

Veronica knocked a third time, harder now. The lack of a response was curious because her father's Buick was in the driveway and Peter's abhorrence for walking anywhere rivaled Freddie's distaste for running.

When there was still no movement from within, she backed away and looked up at the window above the garage, which was her father's bedroom.

The curtain swayed.

"Dad?" she hollered. "Dad, you in there?"

An eye. Veronica spotted a bespectacled eye between the curtain and the window frame.

Peter Shade didn't wear glasses.

Veronica returned to the front door and pounded with the base of her palm.

"Dad? What's going on? You in there?"

She tried the doorknob and found it locked.

Peter never locked the door.

"Dad?"

Horrible thoughts entered her brain. Thoughts about petty criminals exacting their revenge on a retired police captain.

"Fuck it."

Veronica knocked one final time, and then reared back and delivered a kick next to the door handle.

If the deadbolt had been engaged, she probably would've ended up with a sore ankle and not much else. But it wasn't, and the frame shattered inward. Veronica stepped into the house, gun drawn.

"Dad!"

A muffled cry came from the second floor, and Veronica mounted the stairs two at a time. She grabbed the bedroom door handle, expecting it to be locked as well, but it wasn't. She opened it, leading with the gun.

And then somebody screamed.

Chapter 12

"I JUST—I JUST NEED a minute."

Sheriff Steve Burns stumbled out of the house, nearly slipping on a thick puddle of red paint. He almost forgot to take his shoe covers off before hurrying across the lawn. Deputies, who had just arrived on the scene, were looking at him strangely, but he didn't care.

What he cared about was popping another pill. Under the guise of retrieving something from the front seat of his car, he leaned out of sight and gnashed an Oxy tab between his molars. Then he called the Matheson Public Library, which he had on speed dial.

Please, pick up. Gina, please, pick up.

The call was forwarded to an answering machine.

Fuck.

Steve knew Gina Braden well. Even though he didn't read as much now as he used to, what with being so busy, he still made time for it.

In the evenings, when Veronica elected to watch TV, Steve crawled into bed and read a book. In fact, Gina had just called him last week, telling him that a new release that he had reserved was available.

He'd been intending to go in and pick it up sometime in the next few days.

And now Gina was dead.

Both librarians were dead.

The first, Maggie Cernak, had hung herself in Steve's barn. He still couldn't sell his place because of it, although this seemed trivial by comparison.

And now this… a broken neck and gallons of paint.

What the hell did it all mean?

The front door of Gina's house hung open, and he could clearly see the vibrant spilled paint.

His first thought was that this had something to do with Veronica, with her interview, and the caller.

But that couldn't be. Veronica wasn't a reader—he doubted she'd been to a library in years. And even if she had, it would make more sense for her to visit Greenham's public library. Not only was it closer, but it was much larger and better stocked.

Steve preferred Matheson's only because it was near where he used to live, and after Maggie's death, he made a point of staying loyal, offering support to any patrons who knew and missed Maggie.

Then what was with the paint? Had the killer used it to cover his tracks?

It was perhaps the most nonsensical and elaborate method of concealing evidence Steve had ever heard of.

And it made no sense.

As he stared off into space, lost in thought, a car pulled up and the Bear County Coroner got out: 63-year-old Kristin Newberry. A lawyer by trade, Kristin was a no-nonsense professional woman whom Sheriff Burns had come to know and appreciate over the past year. She did good work, but more importantly than that, she knew her limitations. And Kristin wasn't afraid to call in help.

Today, however, her gray hair was messy, half in a bun and half out, and she had darker than usual eye bags.

The sheriff wiped his lips in case there was any white residue on them and then waved his arm as he walked over to the coroner.

"Kristin, thanks for coming as fast as you did." This close up, Kristin didn't just look tired, she looked exhausted. "Everything okay?"

Kristin moved her head in a circular motion, not committing to a nod or shake.

"It's this case I'm working. I can't seem to..." As if just realizing who she was speaking to, Kristin suddenly stopped herself. "I'm sorry. But I'm here, and I'm ready to see the body."

A black CSU van pulled up behind Kristin's car and a tech whom Steve only knew as CSU Paulie got out. He was still young looking, but like any job that was even tangentially related to law enforcement, you aged more rapidly than the rest of the population.

No longer did Paulie appear thirteen. Now, he was a mid- to late-teenager, acne scars and all.

"What happened here?" the man asked, joining the two of them on the front stoop. No introduction, no offer to shake hands.

CSU Paulie was a strange one, but Steve suspected that anyone in his business was bound to be a little odd.

"No fucking idea," the sheriff said under his breath. He cleared his throat for what felt like the thousandth time. "One body inside, it looks like a broken neck after an altercation. I know the victim, she was a librarian at the Matheson Public Library. Paint is everywhere. I'm not sure—"

"Don't tell me it's Gina?" Kristin said in a tone that suggested she was familiar with the victim.

"Unfortunately, yeah. Did you know her?"

Kristin frowned.

"Not well. I saw her at the library once, and I even tried one of her CrossFit classes. She was... insane."

That was one way of describing the woman, who was built like a brick shithouse. Intense was another. CrossFitters often got a bad rap, with outsiders calling the sport cliquey and culty.

But Gina had only ever been kind to Steve and everyone else he witnessed her interacting with.

"Shit."

Normally, Steve tried to stay objective about the crimes he investigated and to keep his emotions out of it. Lately, that had proven next to impossible.

"Everything okay, Sheriff?"

It was CSU Paulie who asked the question, but Kristin was also interested in the answer.

His hand was shaking, and he made a fist to force it to stop. Not exactly the type of leadership they were expecting from the Sheriff of Bear County.

"To be perfectly honest? I'm not okay. It's been one of those days. I'm guessing you guys don't watch too much daytime TV? Talk shows?"

"I wish I had time. Last thing I saw was *How to Catch a Predator*," Kristin said.

"Hey, you know how the show ended, right?" CSU Paulie chimed in. "Why it went off the air?"

"Something about a district attorney?" Kristin rolled her bottom lip. "I don't remember."

"Yeah, in Texas, there was this—"

"Let's focus, guys," the sheriff said, finally taking charge. "As I was saying, one victim inside with a broken neck. Paint is pretty much everywhere in the entrance and family room, where the body is located."

"It's going to be next to impossible to collect evidence with all this paint," Paulie remarked. "Is it still wet?"

"Yeah, it's soaked. Make sure you put shoe covers on before you go in."

"You're not coming?" Kristin inquired.

The sheriff glanced through the door at all the paint.

"No, I'm not. Let me know if you find anything." He caught another queer expression on Kristin's face before he turned and grabbed the closest deputy. "McVeigh said that someone called in, and that led to the wellness check?"

"Yeah," the deputy, whose name Steve couldn't recall, replied. When no further information was forthcoming, the sheriff made a face.

"What was the message, Deputy?"

"Ah, I didn't hear it. I don't even know—"

The sheriff let go of the deputy.

"Great help you are." Steve looked around, searching for someone he recognized. He spotted a tall thin deputy walking down the driveway. "Lancaster!"

The man turned.

"Good afternoon, Sheriff," he said in his Southern drawl.

Steve waved him over.

"Deputy, did you hear the call that led to the wellness check?"

"*Ah-yup*, but I can do you one better. Got the recordin' right here."

Deputy Lancaster scrolled through his messages then pressed play and held his phone at arm's reach.

All Sheriff Burns needed to hear was the first two words and everything suddenly fell into place.

"One, two, I'm coming for you."

Chapter 13

IT WAS A FEMALE SCREAM, which was probably the only reason Veronica didn't shoot. That, and the lack of any striking oranges or reds. She didn't completely lower the gun, though, as she was still trying to wrap her head around what she was seeing.

Peter Shade was on the bed, sitting up. His lower half was covered in a sheet, but his chest was bare, revealing a rather substantial thatch of gray chest hair. The woman who had screamed had medium-length brown hair and was wearing only a pair of white panties. She was covering her breasts with one arm and twisting her body protectively. There was so much blue sweat coming off her, that Veronica couldn't clearly make out her face.

Half-naked man in bed, half-naked sweaty woman standing over him.

Had her mind been wired differently, Veronica wouldn't have taken so long to figure out what was going on. But if her mind had been wired differently, her father would still have his job and she'd likely be a clerk at Walmart.

"Oh, shit," she cursed. "I'm sorry."

"Veronica," her father said sharply. "What the hell are you doing here?"

Veronica felt her face redden and she began to back out of the bedroom.

"I'm sorry," she repeated.

What a fucking nightmare. Just when I thought this day couldn't get any worse, I walk in on my father screwing a woman in the middle of the afternoon. Veronica winced. *Walk in? You kicked down the front door and barged in with your gun drawn.*

"I'm sorry, Dad!" she shouted over her shoulder as she descended the stairs nearly as quickly as she'd mounted.

This was so stupid, she thought. *So* fucking *stupid.*

"I'll fix the door, promise!"

"Veronica, wait!"

Her father was on the upper landing now, but she didn't slow.

"No, it's okay, I'll be back tomorrow!"

"Veronica!"

Peter's tone finally made her look up. He was still shirtless, but thankfully he was now sporting a pair of gray sweatpants. He was gripping the railing in meaty hands. There was blue coming off the top of his head, thin wisps almost like cigarette smoke, but nothing compared to the woman's.

"Veronica, you're not a kid, don't run. Don't be silly."

Veronica scratched the back of her head.

"This is so dumb," she said, mostly to herself.

Embarrassing and dumb and… goddamnit.

Veronica kicked a piece of splintered wood that had once been part of the door frame.

"I'll fix the door. I just—I called and knocked and saw someone upstairs. I didn't—my bad, Dad."

"I don't give a shit about the door, Veronica."

Peter Shade's face was a mask of seriousness as he started down the stairs. The man knew her well, knew that something was wrong even in the absence of her gross overreaction.

To say that the caller had her on edge would be a massive understatement. And if his goal was to get her to behave as irrationally as possible, then he'd already succeeded in spades.

Why hadn't she tried calling her dad? Or going around back to see if the door to the porch where he sneaked away to smoke cigarettes was unlocked?

Even when she'd raced after the man who was lurking outside Shooter's, the man she thought was the dollmaker, she hadn't behaved this illogically.

Her father appeared in front of Veronica. Had he not been bare-chested, she was certain he would have hugged her. Or at least considered it.

"What's wrong, V?" Peter half-smiled. "And are those for me?"

It took a while for Veronica to realize that despite everything, she still inexplicably held the six-pack of IPAs in one hand. Maybe she hadn't lost her mind entirely. Maybe her priorities were still intact.

"For both of us, I think."

Embarrassment lingered, but like the intensity of her synesthesia, it had waned somewhat. Veronica doubted that the awkwardness of walking in on your parent having sex would ever go away entirely—irrespective of the age of either party—but it was manageable for now.

Veronica finally put the case of beer down. Both she and Peter grabbed one and opened them, the characteristic sound of pressure being released from each of the cans oddly in sync.

"What's so important that you felt the need to break down my door to tell me?"

Peter sipped his beer. He was unusually cavalier about the episode, which would have disarmed her had he been fully dressed.

"I'm guessing you didn't catch *Marlowe* this morning?" Veronica stared at the beer as she spoke.

"*Marlowe?*"

Veronica huffed.

"Trashy talk show. I didn't tell you about it because—"

"Here, put this on, Pete," a female voice suggested.

Veronica had forgotten all about the mysterious woman. But that voice... it sounded familiar.

The woman had since dressed in a white blouse and gray slacks. She tossed a sweatshirt to Peter who caught it and slipped it over his head.

Veronica caught this in her periphery because she couldn't take her focus off the woman.

"Veronica, we both think—" her dad began.

"You have to be shitting me."

"Veronica—"

"No, you have to be *shitting* me, Dad. This isn't happening. This isn't *fucking* happening!"

Chapter 14

ONE, TWO, I'M COMING FOR you.

It was haunting, chilling, and it sounded exactly the same as this morning.

"Can you trace the call?" Sheriff Burns asked, his eyes boring into Deputy Lancaster's.

"I already tried." The deputy's speech was even slower than usual and did not reflect the gravity of the situation. "No dice, Sheriff. Caller used some sort of scrambler."

The sheriff sighed and rubbed his face with both palms.

"Okay, okay, play it one more time, please."

This time, the sheriff kept his eyes closed and he listened as closely as he could.

The words were clear and distinct, except for the last one—*you*—which was almost whispered. And then, when the caller stated Gina's address, his cadence was quick and almost excited. There was no background noise to speak of, nor any distinguishing or remarkable sounds.

Just a creepy nursery rhyme and an address.

Steve was almost positive it was the same voice as the man who had called into *Marlowe*, but that was the only thing he'd established.

The sheriff's eyes snapped open.

"Alright, send that to me."

"Sure thing, Sheriff."

Steve spotted Deputy McVeigh removing his shoe covers at the entrance of Gina's home and waved him over.

"McVeigh, I want this shit locked down. No media presence—absolutely none. Tarps, covers, whatever you have to do, I don't want anyone seeing inside the home. Got it?"

McVeigh nodded, but the sheriff, not satisfied with the lackluster response, reached out and grabbed the man's shoulder.

"I mean it, Marcus. Nobody is to see inside. Let the other deputies know that if I find out they leaked anything to the press, they'll be looking for a new job come Monday."

"Yes, sir."

To emphasize his point, Steve gave the man's shoulder a squeeze.

"*Nobody.*"

Steve stared directly into Deputy McVeigh's eyes, silently conveying how important it was to keep the crime scene a secret.

Finally convinced he'd gotten his point across, he left. Steve got into his car and ripped across the city, going back to the place where this nightmare had begun.

Back to that bitch Marlowe and her goddamn TV show.

The security guards made a lame attempt to prevent Steve from entering the building, but a quick tap of the gold shield on his right breast was enough to make them stand down.

Even though he'd only been gone for a few hours—four, at most—*Marlowe's* had been transformed. In fact, it was so unrecognizable to the sheriff that he thought that either he was in the wrong location or that this had all been an elaborate gag, the kind where people changed the scenery when you turned around to make you think you were going crazy.

And it almost worked.

Instead of pink cursive writing of the eponymous host's name on a faux brick wall, block letters on a futuristic background read: TRUMP THE DEALER.

"What the hell?"

"Sheriff?"

Steve turned and saw the diminutive handler with her thick glasses and short brown hair staring at him as if he was an apparition. The woman, clearly not used to being remembered, stated her name out of habit.

"I'm Dahlia."

Steve gave her a curt nod.

"What happened to Marlowe? What happened to the set?" He waved his hands about like a man trying to tell if there was fog in the air or if it was lightly raining.

"Marlowe leaves almost immediately after taping—always does. Then the crew comes in and tears the set down, rebuilds it for the next show. I was actually just heading out." Dahlia tilted her head downward. Peering over the thick frames of her glasses, Steve realized that the woman had pretty eyes. "I didn't get a chance to say how sorry I am about what happened. I'm guessing you're here because of tomorrow's show?"

"Tomorrow's show?"

"Yeah, apparently, the ratings were so good today that Marlowe decided to skip the scheduled guest and do a special feature on synesthesia instead." The word synesthesia came out with a lot of Zs.

Steve was incredulous.

"You're kidding me."

"Nooo." Dahlia cowered a little. "I'm sorry—I thought you knew. And I don't have control over what Marlowe talks about."

"Fuck."

What a disaster.

Steve made a mental note to do whatever he could to shut this down. Which, realistically, was absolutely nothing.

"I'm not here for that. I need to hear the phone call—the entire phone call."

Dahlia's eyes snapped up and now, distorted by the thick lenses, her eyes just looked beady.

"Marlowe doesn't like people looking at raw footage. She says that it's her IP and nobody else's. She even fights with studio execs when they try to pull unaired footage for promos or outtakes."

"I don't care about the footage," Steve said flatly. "I just want to hear the audiotape, I want to hear the call from when they spoke to the producer or whoever answers the phone here until they hung up."

Dahlia was still shaking her head.

"I know, I know, but Marlowe... it's not just video. It's audio and still pictures, too. She doesn't let anyone but her have access to them. If you want, I have a copy of this morning's episode I can give you? I might even be able to get her to sign it tomorrow morning."

"What? No—I'm not interested in the video. I want the *audio*. I know you're just doing your job, and to be honest with you, I don't have jurisdiction here in Portland—I'm the Bear County Sheriff and Portland falls within Multnomah County boundaries. But I know Sheriff Theo Flowers quite well. If I call in one of my many favors, I can guarantee he drives out here within the hour. Now I know, we'll need a subpoena for those tapes, and that would take some time—a day, maybe two. The problem with that is, he's gonna have to station his men here at all times, and in plain view, to make sure that the tapes do not leave the premises. That will make tomorrow morning's recording of *Marlowe* quite difficult. Not just logistically, but aesthetically."

Dahlia shifted her weight from foot to foot. Steve got the impression that she wanted to help but was scared to do so. He didn't blame her—Marlowe treated her like a slave.

"I'm really sorry, Sheriff. Do whatever you have to do, call in your sheriff buddy, get the deputies here, but I can't get you the tapes. I'd lose my job, and Marlowe will make sure that nobody hires me, like, ever again."

Steve tried to think of another way to obtain the audiotape, but only one thing came to mind.

And after explicitly instructing McVeigh to make sure that no media so much as got a sniff of what happened at Gina Braden's house, was he really going to share everything with a woman who worked for the biggest mouthpiece in Portland?

He sighed.

There was no other way.

"Dahlia, I'm not here because of what happened to Detective Veronica Shade. I'm not here because of any of that. I'm here investigating a murder."

Dahlia's mouth became a perfect lowercase 'o'.

"What? Is it… is it Veronica?"

Steve was taken aback by this.

"No—God, no, not Veronica, someone else. And I think..." The sheriff paused, mentally selecting his words with caution. "I think that the person responsible might have called into the show this morning."

Chapter 15

"My previous appointment was canceled, so I decided to stop by," Dr. Jane Bernard explained. Half of her blouse was untucked, and she was having significant difficulty shoving it into her slacks.

Veronica squinted at her psychiatrist.

"You decided to stop by and… what? Accidentally fell on my dad's dick?"

"Veronica," Peter admonished. "Don't be a child."

Veronica's eyes bounced from Jane to her father. For some reason, she started thinking about their Sunday dinners, a ritual they'd shared for years now. A time and place to enjoy excellent food, to decompress, and chat about everything *except* for work. It had been just the two of them for so long, but now Steve joined them every once in a while. What's next? Was their Sunday family time destined to become a recurring couples date? Would Jane sit across from her, holding her dad's hand, laughing just a little too hard at Veronica's jokes?

There was something odd about the way she was feeling, a sort of reversal of roles—her being overprotective of her dad and not vice-versa—but this realization didn't make Veronica feel any more comfortable with the situation.

Maybe it wasn't that she was opposed to sharing her father, maybe it was the person he chose that was unsettling.

Did it have to be Dr. Jane Bernard? Did it have to be the only person who knows more about me than you, Dad?

"How long has this been going on for?"

"Your father and I—" Jane began, but Veronica immediately shut her down. It was the woman's tone—it was exactly the same as during their sessions. In Jane's office, this made her feel comfortable. In her father's home, it came off as patronizing.

"Save it," she snapped. "Dad, what's going on here?"

Her father held her stare. There were many people who would crumble beneath Veronica's authoritative voice and look, which was befitting of someone much larger than her five-foot-five frame. It was also her strange gold-flecked eyes that made others back down.

But not Peter Shade.

Not even now, after she'd barged in on him when he was half naked.

Not now, not ever.

"I don't need to explain anything to you, V. And I won't." It was Veronica who looked away first. "But you came here in the middle of the day wanting to ask me something?" Peter held his hands out, one with a beer, one without. "I'm here for you."

Veronica cast a surreptitious glance in Jane's direction and the woman caught the hint.

"I'm gonna see myself out."

Veronica expected her father to say, *no, stay, you have every right to be here.* After all, you're my lover and Veronica's stepmother.

She cringed.

But Peter didn't say anything at all. He just nodded in Jane's general direction.

Veronica was suddenly reminded of why she'd come here in the first place: the mysterious caller. The man who had revealed her secrets to the daytime talk show community.

She huffed and massaged her forehead.

Was it serendipity that they were both here?

Maybe.

More likely just luck. Good and bad, as it turned out.

"No." Veronica's voice was little more than a whisper. "Stay."

Jane, who was halfway to the front door, and still somehow struggling to tuck in her damn shirt, stopped.

"Yeah, stay," she repeated even though neither Jane nor her father had said anything. "There's something… there's something I need to talk to you both about."

***

It took the better part of fifteen minutes to tell the story about what happened earlier that morning, starting with the reasons why she'd decided to do the interview in the first place. Her voice caught when she spoke of the caller, of what he'd revealed before singing that creepy song.

With every word, her father's eyes narrowed a little more and his posture became increasingly protective. She could tell that he had dozens of questions for her. She could also tell that he was confused by most of what she'd said.

This came as a relief; whatever Jane's and Peter's relationship was, it didn't appear to include sharing patient/doctor-privileged information.

Not yet, anyway.

Despite her father's eagerness, it was actually Jane who spoke first.

"I'm so sorry, Veronica," she said with genuine sympathy. "That must have been terrible for you. And you said the show was live?"

Veronica nodded.

"I'm sorry," Jane repeated.

"I've never… I've never heard of synesthesia before." Peter took a large haul of his beer. "That's real? I mean, what he said, that's… you?"

Over the years, there had been many an occasion where Veronica had considered revealing her condition to her father. But at the last minute, for reasons she didn't fully understand, she'd always pulled the plug.

Perhaps it was that she didn't want to burden the already overworked man. Raising her by himself hadn't been easy. It wasn't that Veronica was a bad kid, if there was such a thing, but Peter had limited experience when it came to parenting. His own father and mother had both worked hard jobs and long hours—money had been tight, time together as a family even more so.

Or maybe it was because Peter, as a career cop, lacked something in the compassion and empathy department and that's what Veronica thought she needed. As with most children, their parents' personalities rubbed off on them, helping mold who they became as adults. Peter's difficulty in displaying affection and the fact that her synesthesia made hanging out in crowds next to impossible, contributed to why, at twenty-four, Steve was Veronica's first serious boyfriend.

"Yes."

Veronica felt more heat rise in her cheeks.

Or maybe she was just embarrassed to be different.

"I don't... I don't really understand."

Veronica huffed.

"Me neither."

"Did you always have this... this..." Peter's face contorted as he struggled to find the right word.

"Condition," Jane finished for him.

"Right, *condition*," Veronica agreed. Synesthesia wasn't a disease or a mental illness. It was a neurological condition. Nothing to be embarrassed or ashamed about. "I don't think I've always had it. I—" she glanced at Jane, "*we* think that it might have something to do with the trauma I suffered as a child. I'm not really sure because I don't remember anything before that time."

This wasn't exactly true, and Veronica tried her best not to sniff the subtle hint of gas she knew was all around her.

She remembered bits and pieces of before. She remembered her brother as a young boy with blond hair, playing with his yo-yo.

But now wasn't the time to reminisce or explain the finer details of her synesthesia.

"The real question is, how did this man know these things?" Veronica's eyes remained locked on Jane as she spoke. "Things that I only ever told *you*?"

Chapter 16

TRUE TO HER WORD, LESS than ten minutes later, a skittish-looking Dahlia strode up to the sheriff's window less than half a block from the Portland studio.

Her eyes were downcast, and her shoulders rolled forward. Steve suspected she did this to avoid being noticed, but all it did was make her look more suspicious.

He didn't care either way.

Strumming his fingers anxiously on his thigh, Steve had passed the time thinking about Veronica and her synesthesia. From the phone call to the research, it all seemed like a strange dream to him. There was an unbelievable quality to not just Veronica's claims, but to others' stories that he'd read online. But then his fingers had tapped the Oxy tabs buried deep in his pocket and Steve began to feel something that wasn't really there. There was no swirl of colors or the scent of diesel fuel.

But there were feelings of expectation. Of impending euphoria.

Of no longer feeling any pain.

The wounds that he'd suffered from the black bear and the burns from the fire that Holland Toler had set had mostly healed.

But the pain… the pain wasn't gone. The pain was more indelible than the scars.

And then there was Lieutenant Philip Crouch. A verifiable asshole who just happened to remind him of a past he'd done everything to put behind him.

Well, my real problem is what happened to your wife. She was my friend, you know? A good friend. And when I find out you guys get into a fight and the next thing I know she's gone and there's about a gallon of blood on your kitchen floor? That's my fucking problem.

The urge to take another pill was nearly impossible to resist. If Dahlia hadn't appeared just then, he might have indulged. And then Steve would have probably been lost in a stupor for the next five hours or so.

"I couldn't get the actual tapes," the woman said, eyes still locked on her shoes.

Steve's scowl deepened.

"I'm going to have to call—" *Sheriff Flowers*, he started to say. But then Dahlia looked up and offered him a coquettish grin.

"But... but I managed to record the call with my cell phone."

Dahlia thrust her hand into the open window, indicating for the sheriff to press play on her phone.

Steve was confused by her strange attitude, but then he recalled how the woman cowered in Marlowe's presence. He chalked it up to Dahlia being proud of doing something on her own, even if it was clandestine in nature.

He pressed play, and the recording began with a female voice.

"This isn't it." Steve shook his head and tried to hand the phone back. "It was a man on the—"

"Just listen."

The sheriff reluctantly pulled the phone back into the car.

"Hi, thank you for calling *Marlowe*. Can you please tell me your name?"

"Gina. My name's Gina."

Adrenaline surged.

Steve had completely forgotten that Marlowe had announced that someone named Gina had called in to the show.

Gina... was it her? Was it Gina Braden?

The sheriff concentrated hard on the voice.

"Okay, Gina, what is your question for Detective Shade?"

There was a lengthy pause.

"I want to know what it's like being such a strong woman in a male-dominated environment."

Even though her words were constricted, it was her—Steve was sure of it. It was the smiling woman who always kept the stack of books Sheriff Burns reserved in a special pile for him. It was the woman who recommended new releases, tried to convince him to join CrossFit, and teased him about his ever-lengthening beard.

"Thank you. If we choose to have you on, please remember to keep your question short and brief."

The recording ended.

"That's it?"

Dahlia shook her head and took the phone back.

"There's more."

The sheriff felt his chest tighten as he was transported back to this morning.

"Hello, Veronica." A husky male voice said. "I've been waiting a long time to talk to you. Or should I call you Lucy?"

The recording included Veronica's increasingly frantic replies, as well as Marlowe's not-so-subtle encouragement of this must-see TV.

Eventually, he heard his own voice, muted, barely audible, instructing them to hang up.

I should've been stronger. I should've been louder. I should've made them cut it off.

And then came the song.

One, two, I'm coming for you. Three four, lock your door. Five, six, I crossed the river Styx. Seven, eight, I've sealed your fate. Veronica, your first victim awaits.

Steve leaned toward the phone.

He didn't remember the mysterious man concluding with, *Veronica, your first victim awaits.*

"It kept recording even after the producer turned off the speakers above the stage," Dahlia said, picking up on his confusion. "Sheriff, do you think that the victim that he's talking about is the one that you found?"

The sheriff just looked at her.

This was exactly what he thought. He believed that the caller had kidnapped Gina and forced her to speak on the phone. Then, after her usefulness had expired, the man had broken her neck and covered her in paint.

Steve's upper lip pulled back, revealing his teeth.

"I'm going to send this to my phone." Without asking, he texted himself both audio files. Then he gave Dahlia her cell and thanked her.

Before she could offer so much as 'you're welcome' he left the woman with the oversized glasses in the dust.

Back at Gina's house, Steve had had an inkling that the librarian's death was related to the talk show phone call. Now, he was absolutely sure of it.

And that meant that Veronica Shade was in danger.

Chapter 17

"VERONICA, I WOULD NEVER TALK about your sessions or anyone else's. *Never.*"

Veronica leaned in close, aware that her father was staring at her, probably thinking that she was smelling for a lie. Which she was.

Truth is, Veronica hadn't meant for her words to sound so accusatory, but now that she was thinking more clearly, she realized that the only person who knew about everything was Jane.

But to her dismay, she smelled nothing. Jane and her father were sweating now, but less so than when she'd burst into the bedroom.

It had to be her. It *had* to be.

Who else knew about her brother and her synesthesia? About the fire?

Veronica was tempted to ask further questions, but she was sure her dad would shut her down. Dr. Jane Bernard felt no compulsion to defend herself, either, which would have been a characteristic of someone who was being dishonest.

Despite these facts, Veronica was unable to let go of this stubborn idea. A more sinister possibility was that Jane was using her knowledge of Veronica's synesthesia against her. If anyone knew how to lie without being detected, it was her. And if this was all just some elaborate set-up, then Jane could have practiced *ad nauseum*. Hell, the whole, *your synesthesia isn't infallible* bit could have just been a way for her to place doubt in case Veronica detected anything unusual.

The problem was, if Jane truly was the person behind the phone call, what in the world was her motivation?

Money?

Money was the ultimate motivator.

Only, Dr. Jane Bernard had never been a flashy woman and so far as Veronica knew, she made decent coin working with patients. And her contract with the City of Greenham PD must bring in some—not a lot, but some—income. The woman drove a nice car and her office, while not to Veronica's taste, was furnished with upscale pieces.

Jealousy?

She didn't think so. Any psychiatrist worth their salt would quickly come to the conclusion that there was nothing any woman could say or do to keep Peter away from his daughter for long.

Blackmail?

Possibly... but for what?

"Veronica?" Peter asked, and she finally peeled her piercing stare away from Jane. Several awkward seconds had gone by without anyone saying a word. Her poor father was probably giving her time to activate her superpowers.

It dawned on Veronica that her life had changed this morning. Life as she knew it had been irrevocably altered.

People would never look at her the same way. Colleagues, friends, Steve...

How could she explain this to Steve?

Perhaps flat denial, as boorish a concept as it was, was the way to go.

"Veronica?"

"Somebody told him," she said, her voice weak. "Somebody told him about me."

At that moment, Veronica wanted nothing more than for her father to come and hold her and tell her everything was going to be okay.

But Peter couldn't do that. Because that wasn't who he was.

Peter Shade was objective and calculated. And his intractable personality was reflected in the next thing he said.

"Do you take notes of your sessions with my daughter?"

Jane nodded.

"Of course."

"Digital or paper?"

Veronica immediately understood what her father was getting at, as did Jane.

"Paper. I haven't had a break in and nothing's been stolen, at least not as far as I know." She cocked her head in Veronica's direction. "We can go check though. Yeah, I think that's a good idea. I'm going to head to my office right now."

This had to be it. Someone broke into Jane's office, found my files, and stole them. Now, they're getting their jollies by harassing a Greenham Detective.

There were holes in this theory, but it made more sense than Ken Cameron or Dr. Jane Bernard being behind it.

"And I'm coming with you," Veronica said in a tone that ensured nobody would confuse her demand as a request.

***

Dr. Bernard strongly suggested they take the same car, but Veronica declined the offer. She didn't feel in the mood to be probed and questioned by Jane, for the woman to fall into psychiatrist mode.

Her focus was singular.

She wanted to find out who this man was who had so publicly shamed her, and why.

Everything else was just a distraction.

As she followed closely behind Dr. Bernard, Veronica found herself thinking of Captain Bottel and Cole Batherson. They were clearly giving her space, but they would have to meet again soon. Veronica wondered if it was too late to do an about-face. The captain had leaned into this whole thing, the whole *Marlowe* debacle, but Cole hadn't written anything yet.

Deny, deny, deny.

While searching for Sarah Sawyer's true identity, Steve had contacted someone who had the clearance to view originals of heavily redacted documents.

Maybe this source could do the opposite, hide Veronica's birth name so deeply that no one would ever be able to find it.

As for the New York Times? Cole Batherson could write an article about the mole on her ass for all she cared. Veronica was done with PR. If the City of Greenham PD wanted to boost its reputation, it could take out a series of bus ads.

Unlike Sheriff Burns, Veronica wasn't an elected official.

She was an employee, someone hired to do a job.

And she was fucking good at it. Veronica had figured out what happened to Trent and Herb's survivors, and she'd killed the dollmaker. The *real* dollmaker: Gloria Trammel.

She had put a bullet in the bitch's head before she could kill anybody else, Veronica included.

Her cell phone rang and grateful for the distraction, Veronica answered.

"Hi, Steve," she said, unsure of how to act. Embarrassed? They had been through a lot together, and Steve knew some of her secrets. Ashamed? That made no sense.

Veronica was only ashamed of one thing, and now that her brother was dead, she was confident that it had died with him.

Trent Alberts' terrible voice echoed in her mind.

You get to pick which member of your family survives, little one. Eenie, meenie, miney, mo, you get to pick the only person besides me and Herb who gets to leave this house alive.

"Veronica?" Steve sounded distraught. "Can we meet?"

She stared at Dr. Bernard's license plate, two car lengths in front of her.

"Can it wait? I'm trying to figure out who called into the show."

"And? Do you know who it is?" Now he sounded desperate.

"Not yet. I think maybe someone broke into Dr. Bernard's office and stole my files. What do you need? Is it important?"

"It's about the case."

"What case?"

He couldn't be referring to the *Marlowe* phone call. Turning it into a 'case' would make it official and much more difficult to just pass off as the ramblings of a madman.

Deny, deny, deny.

"Veronica, there's been a murder. And… and I think you're gonna want to see this one for yourself."

Chapter 18

"Who is it? Who's the victim?" Veronica barked the second she got out of her car. The front of the modest home was almost completely covered by a series of dark gray tarps. One obscured the bay window, and a tunnel had been created to shroud the front door.

Sheriff Burns refused to say much over the phone, other than the fact they were investigating the death of a single victim.

Nothing he'd said supported such a level of secrecy as this.

"It was Gina."

Veronica, who had been trying to see inside the house, craned her neck to look at Steve. He had dark circles under his eyes and there was a sheen to his face, even though it was cool out. Veronica had seen him a few hours ago, and he'd looked fairly normal. Now, he looked like shit.

Maybe he's coming down with something, she thought.

"Who?"

The name didn't immediately ring a bell.

"Gina Braden, the librarian from Matheson?"

A series of goosebumps rippled across her flesh.

"Gina Braden? I—I saw her—I saw her this morning."

Her voice was soft, barely audible, but Steve picked up every word.

"You're kidding."

"No."

Veronica reached through the open window of her car and grabbed the book from beneath her laptop.

She held it out to Steve, but he just stared at it, confusion plastered across his features.

"Daddy's Little Girls," Veronica said in way of explanation. "I knew you had it reserved, so this morning when I couldn't sleep, I drove into Matheson and picked it up. I forgot about it until..." until right before I went to visit Ken Cameron in your prison. "I forgot about it until now."

Steve took the book and turned it over repeatedly in his hands as if it was the first book he'd ever held.

"Is it really Gina? She... she looked fine this morning."

A stupid comment, but Veronica was still processing this information. In her mind, she pictured the woman's smiling face, her banal commentary—*Sheriff Burns is going to looove this one*—and her cheery disposition.

Veronica's eyes went back to the oddly covered home.

Less than half an hour ago, she'd been racing across the city toward Dr. Jane Bernard's office, her singular desire to figure out who had fucked with her on *Marlowe*.

That seemed irrelevant now.

"What happened to her, Steve?"

"Don't know yet. Someone broke her neck."

"Jesus."

"But—but, Veronica, there's more," the sheriff said, his voice cracking.

He really is coming down with something.

"It's about the guy who called into the show."

Part of Veronica still didn't believe the sheriff that Gina was dead, and the second he'd said, 'broken neck' she'd started across the street.

"Veronica?"

"I don't care about the show," she said, waving her hand over her shoulder.

Not now, anyway.

"Wait, Veronica!" Steve struggled to keep up. "God dammit."

Veronica tried not to think of Maggie Cernak, the woman who had hung herself in the sheriff's barn. She'd also been a Matheson librarian. Veronica had crossed paths with Gina while investigating her colleague's death. The woman was in incredible shape, a dedicated CrossFitter, but her kind and friendly demeanor quickly debunked any stereotypes. The woman had been shocked and frightened. She'd also handed over a spare key to Maggie's place, where Veronica had discovered the deceased woman's cat.

The cat that oddly shared her birth name.

This morning, Gina had handed her the book with heavily calloused hands and Veronica had signed for it.

And now she was dead.

It seemed impossible.

An odd thought occurred to her then.

Here today, gone tomorrow.

She shook her head.

Here this morning, gone this afternoon.

"Veronica!"

Steve's shout was loud enough to gain the attention of several deputies hanging out in front of Gina's home. One, in particular, met Veronica's gaze. He had a round face, freckles on the bridge of his nose, and was wearing a deputy shirt that was just a little too tight—a medium when he was better suited for a large.

It was Chief Deputy Marcus McVeigh.

"Detective Shade," the man said with a nod.

Veronica didn't acknowledge the deputy. While she was still trying to wrap her head around the political aspects of her boyfriend's job, she knew that Deputy McVeigh was vying for his position.

Steve was tight-lipped about most of the inner workings of the Bear County Sheriff's Department, not wanting to burden her with the drama, but Veronica could read between the lines. Some of the things that Deputy McVeigh did were in the County's best interests, but others, like trying to throw Steve under the bus during the dollmaker investigation, benefited nobody but himself.

Veronica frowned and continued toward the crime scene tunnel. McVeigh didn't initially move, but when she was within three feet of him, he reluctantly stepped aside.

"Veronica! *Veronica!*"

Veronica ignored the sheriff and swiped the tarp aside with the back of her hand. But she didn't enter Gina Braden's home.

Instead, Veronica Shade entered a burning inferno where everything and everyone was on fire.

PART TWO: FIRE, GAS, AND SWEAT

Chapter 19

VERONICA TRIED HER BEST TO control her breathing. She did this before she entered Gina Braden's home and she did this after she entered Gina Braden's home.

It didn't work.

This place was one of intense violence.

It was a place of murder.

Veronica had been to the scenes of more than a dozen murders but never had her synesthesia been this potent. She was used to flashes of color, vibrant yet semi-transparent swatches of yellow, orange, red, and the entire spectrum in between. Occasionally, these colors exploded like fireworks that burned her retinas and melted into the fabric of the world itself.

But this was different.

And it was overwhelming.

It was as if the colors were actively accosting her senses. Some of them were solid stripes, others nearly pellucid blooms. It made for a disorienting illusion, one that messed with her depth perception and sent her center of balance out of kilter.

Veronica had never experienced anything like it.

She gagged, swooned, and was about to go down when someone grabbed her around the waist. Her first thought was that it was Deputy McVeigh, and she tried to push him off.

"It's okay, it's me."

Comforted by Sheriff Burns' whisper, Veronica allowed herself to be half-carried out of Gina's house.

As she sat on the front lawn, she heard the tarp behind her folding back into place, hiding the ephemeral crime scene from view.

What the fuck just happened?

Veronica shut her eyes and tried for a good thirty seconds to slow her heart rate and regulate her breathing.

"Steve? What happened in there?" Veronica wasn't sure her voice was loud enough for the sheriff to hear.

He put a hand on her upper back and rubbed gently. If Steve had heard her, he didn't let on.

"Breathe," he said. "Take a deep breath."

Even behind closed lids, the heat map was nearly as visible as it had been inside Gina's home.

"I've never—I've never seen anything like that."

Steve continued to massage her back.

"Anybody have any water? Can someone please get the detective a bottle of water?" Then in her ear, he said, "Just relax—breathe."

Veronica finally opened her eyes and looked up at the sheriff. The way he was grinding his teeth and his eyes darted about, she thought that he needed to heed his own advice.

She also was annoyed that he was babying her but knew that he meant well.

Veronica cleared her throat and tried to speak forcefully. She settled on a weak tremor.

"Steve, I-I know you heard what the man said on the phone, but this was different. What-what-what happened in there?"

Over the years, Veronica had developed mechanisms to cope with her synesthesia, and she lived with the condition as best she could. It was never easy—crowds were a nightmare—but she'd gotten used to it. The first time she'd seen these colors, in the bathroom of her elementary school, it had been terrifying. Seeing something that wasn't actually there blurs the distinction between reality and fantasy, confusing the mind and body. In some ways, what she experienced was similar to the effects of a mild dose of a hallucinogenic drug—psilocybin, for instance—but the main difference was that consumption was the cause.

Seemingly *de novo* hallucinations were often indicative of a pathology—a migraine aura, for instance, foretelling intense and crippling pain. Or a brain tumor spreading its pseudopod-like extensions deeper and deeper into one's brain matter. Early on, Dr. Bernard had explored these options as a possible cause for what Veronica saw, smelled, and heard, but they were all eventually ruled out.

Another main difference is that the effects of a drug typically wear off, even though the paranoia of remaining in this altered state is often the driving factor behind bad trips.

Not so with Veronica's synesthesia—it had been with her for nearly twenty years, and there was no sobering up from this nightmare.

Looking around now did nothing to assuage the fear of being a prisoner to this new, unpalatable version of her condition.

The tarp was closed, and she could no longer see into the house, but the colors had followed her outside. Smears of warm colors marred the concrete steps, on the walkway, the grass, her...

"Shoes," Veronica whispered.

There was yellow and orange paint on the soles of her shoes. This too was new.

Steve handed her a bottle, and she drank from it. Water dribbled down her chin, which she wiped away with the back of her hand.

"It's just paint," Steve said. "Someone spilled paint everywhere. All over the floor, walls, even the body."

"Paint?" Veronica was still trying to come to grips with what she'd seen.

Steve nodded. His lips looked incredibly dry, so after another sip, Veronica offered him the water bottle.

He declined.

"I tried to warn you before you went in. I think—I think you should listen to this."

The sheriff pulled his cell phone out and played an audio clip.

Veronica's heart rate had finally calmed down, but upon hearing the voice, the song, it began thumping away again.

One, two, I'm coming for you.

"It's him. It's the man from the show," she said.

"That's what I thought, too. But listen again."

This time Veronica drowned out everything except for the recording. She was no longer one hundred percent certain that it was the same man. In the studio, she'd heard him speak over loudspeakers. Now, the song emanated from a small iPhone speaker.

Both times, Veronica had been emotionally charged.

"I-I don't know. It *could* be him."

"I'm not sure either," Steve admitted.

They stared at each other for some time, neither wanting to say what was on their minds. Others were staring, too. A handful of deputies and a crime scene tech Veronica didn't recognize.

"What are you looking at?" she demanded.

Eyes dropped. Feet shuffled.

This time, when Steve went to comfort her by rubbing her shoulders and back, she moved out of his reach.

The reality was, it didn't matter who was on the phone, or whether it was the same man from *Marlowe*.

Veronica pictured Gina lying on the ground, her neck viciously broken, her body coated in thick globs of warm-colored paint.

What mattered was that whoever was behind this had done it for her.

And that meant that Veronica was to blame for another death.

Chapter 20

EVENTUALLY, VERONICA CAME TO HER senses. She finished the bottle of water and then retreated to her car.

With so many deputies and CSU techs milling about, it was only a matter of time before the media caught wind of the crime and showed up.

Veronica wasn't ready for that just yet.

They would ask questions. Questions about why a beloved librarian who spent her free time tossing kettle bells in the air was brutally murdered in her own home.

Even though Steve hadn't said as much, Veronica knew that nothing was taken. This wasn't a robbery gone wrong.

This wasn't even about Gina Braden. It was about *her*—about Veronica Shade.

And Gina wasn't the first person to die because of Veronica.

There was Gloria Trammel, the dollmaker, whom she had shot and killed no more than a month ago.

Veronica had passed her psych eval with flying colors, but she had a wealth of experience with the profession. And passing didn't mean that what happened didn't affect her, that she didn't think about that day.

Killing Gloria wasn't the issue, but that was all the psychiatrist wanted to talk about. Perhaps if it had been Dr. Bernard who had been on her case, and not Dr. Cookie-Cutter, things would be different.

Jane would have known what to ask.

For Veronica, it wasn't about Gloria.

It was about the woman's daughter, about little Beverly 'Bev' Trammel, who was so proud of her yo-yo tricks that she couldn't wait to show them off.

Veronica had put the six-year-old in harm's way to save herself.

The will to survive is ingrained at birth, Lucy.

Just thinking of Bev brought about other memories. Memories of a time when another child was put in danger because of—

EENIE.

—her. A child who—

MEENIE.

—watched his parents burn to death. Heard them scream—

MINEY.

—as their skin bubbled and peeled and their hair caught fire. Benny Davis may have spoken that line about survival, but clearly, it didn't apply to him. After all, he'd taken his own life, setting himself alight and bringing everything full circle.

MO.

Veronica shut her eyes, trying to keep her thoughts from going back to that time. It served no purpose. It was of no benefit to her. She had to focus on the present, on figuring out who the caller was and what the fuck he wanted.

The past is boring—it's already happened. The future is far more interesting.

That was her father's favorite saying, and while it may be true, Veronica knew that the past and future were on the same continuum and that the former heavily influenced the latter.

What we do today shapes who we are tomorrow.

Today, the man on the phone had killed Gina Braden.

Tomorrow, Veronica would take his life.

One, two, I'm coming for you.

"Then come for me, bitch," she hissed. "Come for me, not—"

"Veronica? There's more I think you should hear."

She startled, not realizing that Steve had approached. But while startled, Veronica wasn't surprised.

There was always more.

Gloria Trammel could've stopped after she'd murdered Felize Hoffman after she caught the woman in the jester makeup fornicating with her husband.

But no, she had to make more dolls.

Trent Alberts and Herb Thornton didn't stop after the first home they broke into and played their sick game.

They kept going, and going, and going...

There was something incredibly virulent about violence, something pathogenic, parasitic, but unlike normal diseases, there was no vaccine or antibiotics for the treatment of murder.

There was only proliferation and metastasis.

That was why, over time, serial killers became more sadistic, creative, *unhinged*.

Murder had a tendency to spread.

"What is it?" Veronica asked dryly.

"Back at *Marlowe's*, we didn't hear everything—there was more. Listen."

The first thing Veronica heard on the recording was Gina Braden's voice. She sounded terrified, and Veronica clenched her jaw so tightly that her molars started to ache.

Then it was *him*.

The man with the song. But it was different this time.

"Veronica, your first victim awaits? I don't—I don't remember that."

"They cut the audio right before he said it live."

Veronica stretched her chin forward, easing some of the pressure in her lower jaw.

"He had her. This guy, whoever the hell he is, grabbed Gina and made her call into the show. Then he brought her here and killed her." Veronica squinted. "I-I saw her earlier. Like, maybe seven-thirty, at the library."

"And you went on *Marlowe* just after nine. Did you notice anybody suspicious at the library?"

Veronica thought back to earlier that morning, which felt like a hundred years ago.

It had been early, and the library was nearly empty. She remembered a white car, or maybe it was silver, in the parking lot. There had also been a black Subaru there as well, not quite a truck, but larger than a car.

Veronica had parked behind the black vehicle and remembered smirking at the bumper sticker which included clipart of a kettle bell and the quote *Be Stronger than Your Excuses* around the image.

Veronica glanced at Gina's driveway. It was empty.

"Her car," she said, "I'm pretty sure Gina's car was there. There was another one, too. A white, older car. I dunno."

"What about people? Anyone in the library that early in the morning?"

Veronica wracked her brain. She thought she remembered a man with dark hair browsing one of the shelves but couldn't be sure.

"I don't know."

Steve nodded.

"That's okay, I sent someone over there to check it out."

"What about the call? Where did it come from?"

"Took some work, but we eventually traced it back to Gina's own cell."

"Shit."

Veronica watched as Deputy McVeigh stepped through the tarp and onto the pain-streaked stoop.

"Any evidence inside?" she asked, already knowing the answer.

"Doubt there's anything useful. So much fucking paint." Veronica grimaced.

"Anybody see how the paint got into Gina's house?"

"I have my men going door-to-door."

Veronica turned her gaze to the street. Gina lived in a middle-class neighborhood, which didn't work in their favor. The driveways of almost every single family home, Gina's included, were empty.

People were at work.

"Someone had to see," she whispered. And then she noticed it: halfway up the block parked at the side of the road was a weathered white sedan. "That-that looks like the car from the library."

"Where?"

"There."

Veronica smeared the soles of her shoes on the grass and started to walk toward the vehicle.

"I'll send one of my deputies to—Veronica?"

Veronica was already off on a brisk walk, which became a jog when she heard the car start and saw exhaust pump from the muffler.

"Hey! Stop! Greenham PD! Put your car in park and exit the vehicle!"

Chapter 21

THE DRIVER DIDN'T PUT HIS car in park, nor did they get out. Instead, the car peeled away from the curb, spraying dust in Veronica's direction. She was still a quarter block away and couldn't make out the tag number. And even though she knew it was a lost cause, Veronica started to sprint after the car anyway.

She gave up when it made a left and disappeared from sight less than a minute later.

Sweat dripped from her forehead as she returned to Steve. She was angered to see that the man had barely moved.

"What the hell, Steve?"

"What happened?" The fact that he still held his phone in his hand indicated that not only did he not run after her but had no intention of doing so.

"What happened? I think that was the same car as at the library!"

Steve screwed up his face.

"I'll have one of my deputies—"

"What's with you?" Veronica snapped.

Everything was lazy, slow—everything was, *I'll get my deputies to check it out.*

"I'm just trying to figure this out, Veronica."

"Well, try harder."

Steve's behavior wasn't just out of character, but it was odd and didn't reflect the gravity of the situation.

"What happened?" Unlike Steve, Deputy McVeigh appeared as serious as ever. He glanced at her forehead, and Veronica wiped the sweat away with her hand. Blue tendrils trailed her fingers like afterglow.

"White sedan, peeled away from the curb when I told them to get out. I think it might be the same one from the library this morning."

McVeigh lowered his head ever so slightly.

"You were at the library this morning."

For some reason, Veronica was tempted to lie.

"Yeah, she was there picking up a book for me," the sheriff replied for her.

Deputy McVeigh nodded and then returned his attention to Veronica.

"Did you get a tag number? Make? Model?"

Veronica shook her head.

"Maybe a Mazda? Not sure. They were Oregon plates, but that's all I got." She glanced quickly at Steve. "Maybe it was just someone who noticed all the commotion and wanted to get a quick video."

"I'll get somebody to check if there are any red-light cameras around here."

"How's it going in there?" the sheriff asked.

McVeigh held his hands out, which were covered in dark orange, nearly brown paint.

"We're not going to get anything. Coroner is about to remove the body and maybe back in the morgue she can tell us more, but I wouldn't get your hopes up."

Veronica couldn't help but notice McVeigh was taking the lead on this case. She knew the issues that Steve had with his chief deputy, knew of the latter's aspirations, as well, but the sheriff seemed... disinterested, at best.

What the hell is going on with you, Steve?

It wasn't just today, either. Over the past few weeks, ever since the bear attack, really, Steve had become less engaged in everything. Even the sex, which used to be passionate, frenzied, had become routine.

Veronica knew that Steve had bad dreams. Often, he would cry out in his sleep and wake her up. During these episodes, which had gone from once or twice weekly to nearly every night, there was so much blue from his intense sweating that he looked like Dr. Manhattan. The first time, Veronica had said nothing.

But when these nightmares happened again and again, she eventually brought it up.

Steve said he couldn't remember his dreams, but Veronica knew he was lying.

Deputy McVeigh's lapel radio squelched, and he answered it.

"McVeigh, over."

"Deputy, it's Archie. I'm about half a block away on the east side of the street. Number—" there was a short pause—"512. Woman says she saw something earlier today. Over."

McVeigh raised his eyes.

"Stay there, I'll be there shortly, over."

It took a physical nudging to get Steve to move with McVeigh, let alone take the lead. The tension mounted when Veronica saw the deputy standing with a woman on the front porch of a house with a massive American Flag hanging limply above the door. She was in a worn blue bathrobe and was incessantly flicking a cigarette.

Veronica suddenly got a bad feeling in the pit of her stomach. If she'd been asked to describe the type of woman who might enjoy daytime talk shows, this was her.

Perhaps Steve recognized this as well because while he quickly introduced himself to the woman, who said her name was Linda, he didn't bother introducing Veronica. But when he also neglected to introduce Chief Deputy McVeigh, Veronica figured that this might have just been an oversight.

"Linda was saying that she saw Gina earlier today—two, maybe three hours ago," Deputy Archie informed them.

Linda took an obnoxiously long pull on her cigarette before speaking.

"Yeah, I saw Gina—at least I think it was her. She was wearing that hat she likes, the one she wears to the gym or aerobics or whatever? Anyways, I saw her carrying paint buckets inside. A lot of 'em. I thought she was starting a remodel, or something. Either that or it was just one of those weird workouts them types do. Always lifting things." The woman shuddered and took another drag. "Don't know why any woman would like to look like that, all them veins and muscles."

"Was she alone?" Veronica asked. For the first time since approaching, Linda's heavy eyes landed on her.

"I think so. It's not like I was staring, you know? I saw her bring some of them paint cans in and then I went back inside. She lives alone, though." The woman lowered her voice. "I think she's a lesbian."

"Right—and did you see what kind of car she was driving?"

"Yeah, her—" Linda paused to smoke. "You know what? I was gonna say it was her car, but it *wasn't* her car. It was like an old, white beater. She drives a black Subaru."

"Did you know the model? Did you get a license plate number?" the sheriff asked.

"No, sorry."

Veronica resisted the urge to glare at Steve.

We could have caught him. He was right there... watching.

McVeigh quickly got on his radio and put an APB out for a white, older model car, possibly a Mazda, with Oregon plates.

"What happened to her, anyway?" Linda asked. She was trying to overhear what McVeigh was saying. "Did someone break into her home? Because I've heard—"

"Linda," Sheriff Burns said forcefully. "What time did you see Gina carrying paint into her house?"

Linda shrugged.

"I dunno. Nine-thirty? It was just—" Once again, the woman looked at Veronica and she knew, in a single heartbeat what was coming next. It was impossible to stop. "I was watching my show!" Excitement crept into her voice. "*Marlowe!* You—you were on it! You were on the show!"

Veronica scowled.

"Wrong person. Sorry."

"No, it was you! The detective with the superpowers! Detective, *uhh*, Shade, right? What—"

Veronica's face reddened. McVeigh had since finished putting out the APB and was staring at her with a queer expression on his face.

"Wrong person."

Veronica walked backward off the porch.

"What's her name?" Linda asked Steve. "Detective Shade, right? It is her—I know it's her."

"Thank you for your help, if you remember anything—"

"You see them colors now?" Linda hollered. "Hey, Detective, you going to be on the show again tomorrow? Marlowe's doing a special on you. Barely anybody gets to do *Marlowe* twice. Unheard of. You're like *famous.*"

Famous.

Now that was a scary thought. Famous peoples' pasts were aired like dirty laundry.

And Veronica's laundry wasn't just dirty.

It was downright filthy.

Chapter 22

VERONICA WAS FUMING WHEN SHE got back to Gina Braden's house.

Deep down, she knew that Steve wasn't to blame for this—for any of this—but at the moment, she was pissed at him.

If only he'd been faster, if only he hadn't been so dopey from lack of sleep or whatever it was, they might have been able to catch the guy in the car.

Why didn't he trust her? Hadn't her instincts—her synesthesia—proven reliable enough in the past?

She was right about the suicide girls. She was right about the dollmaker.

She was right about the fucking car.

"I didn't tell McVeigh about the show." Veronica whipped around. Steve had a vacant expression on his face. "I didn't know what to tell—"

"Fuck the show."

Steve licked his lips.

"Are you—are you okay?"

"What?" Veronica snapped. "Am *I* okay? *Me*? You're the one moping around. I don't know what's gotten into you, but you need to knock it off. We already have one murder on our hands, and I don't know about you, but I don't think this is the end."

On our *hands...*

The words echoed in her mind. Veronica had been in this situation before, on the outside, looking in.

Not this time, she decided.

"I want on this case, Steve."

The sheriff looked shocked at her outburst, and Veronica wasn't sure why. He knew her, knew her strong personality, and while her venomous tongue was typically reserved for others, this wasn't their first spat.

"I want on this case, Sheriff Burns," she repeated, this time using his title.

Veronica was preparing for pushback, expecting a similar response to the one she'd received when trying to get involved in the hunt for the dollmaker.

You're not ready. You need to ease back into things.

But Steve surprised her by shrugging.

"Alright. I'll reach out to Captain Bottel."

And just like that, he got on the phone.

Veronica listened halfheartedly for a few moments before pulling out her cell. She ignored the missed calls and unread texts and wrote to her partner, whom she hadn't seen since this morning.

Freddie, where are you? Enjoying a little afternoon snack?

Veronica sent the message with a read receipt, which didn't come.

"Yes," she overheard Steve say, "Special Consultant. Correct, like in the Trammel case. I am aware."

She looked down at her phone again.

Her message remained unread.

Veronica had been so wrapped up in her own disaster of a day that she had forgotten all about seeing Freddie with FBI Special Agent Jake Keller.

If her partner had been smiling and laughing, she probably wouldn't have thought anything of it.

But Freddie had looked downright dour.

Veronica chewed the inside of her cheek as she fired off another text.

Being pulled onto a Bear County case. Matheson librarian, deceased. Call me.

Veronica wanted to add more, but including additional information in a text was unadvisable.

"He wants to speak to you."

Veronica accepted the phone from Steve and put it to her ear.

"Detective Shade."

"Detective, it's Captain Bottel. Bear County Sheriff Steve Burns has requested your assistance on a recent crime as a Special Consultant."

The formality was jarring. If the captain knew so much about her that he was certain what the caller on *Marlowe* said was true, then he was definitely aware of Veronica's relationship with the sheriff.

"Yes," Veronica said without hesitation. "Yes, I want on the case."

"Okay, but you still need to check in every few days."

Veronica glanced down at her phone. Neither of her messages had been read.

"What about Freddie—sorry, Detective Furlow?"

There was a second of dead air before the captain said, "Detective Furlow has taken a few days of personal leave."

Still formal, but there was a hint of something else in the man's voice—condescension, perhaps, as if she should already know this, being Freddie's partner and all.

"Is everything okay?"

"You're going to have to ask him that."

"Yes, sir. Thank you for—"

"Is Cole with you?"

"I—wh—who?"

The about-face was more than jolting. It was as if she was speaking with a different person now.

"Internal Affairs Officer Cole Batherson. I was wondering if he was with you."

She was about to ask why he would be with *her*, but then she remembered the Times article.

Forget the article, Veronica nearly said. *I'm investigating a fucking murder.*

She settled on, "I haven't seen him since leaving your office this morning."

"All right. Detective Shade, please remember to check in."

Just like that, the man hung up.

Even after the line went dead, Veronica stared at the phone.

Freddie on personal leave, Cole Batherson following her around, Steve acting as if nothing mattered.

A killer on the loose leaving a trail of bodies while revealing all her secrets.

What a fucking Monday.

Steve had his hands in his pockets and didn't make the effort to take his phone back.

Fine, Veronica thought. *If he doesn't want to take charge, then I will.*

"Come with me," she ordered, opening the passenger door to her car for him.

"Where we going? McVeigh already has two dozen deputies driving around Matheson looking for any and all white cars."

Veronica shook her head.

"The white car's gone. This case is about me, Sheriff. And no one knows me better than Dr. Jane Bernard."

Chapter 23

"I JUST FOUND OUT," FBI Agent Jake Keller said. "When I saw you earlier, the only thing listed was his name."

They were in Jake's car, his dark-gray Town & Country, driving from the City of Greenham toward Portland. Freddie, who hadn't eaten yet today even though it was well past noon, felt his blood sugar bottom out. He was starting to shake, and he was also starting to sweat.

"I don't get it—part of a DEA sting? How could he be involved in a sting?"

Jake ran his hand through his short blond hair.

"I don't know, Freddie. As I said, I just heard about it."

Freddie looked at his longtime friend for a moment. The fact that the man wouldn't meet his eyes was telling.

"You're holding back." Jake sucked his bottom lip into his mouth. "Jake, please."

Freddie was desperate for more information, but he knew better than to push. After all, the man was doing him a favor. A *second* favor, in fact. The first had been getting him and Veronica in to see convicted serial killer Trent Alberts before the man was executed.

"Troy Allison brought him in," Jake said flatly.

Freddie groaned and he understood his friend's apprehension in revealing this to him.

Despite having been a cop for the better part of three decades in one capacity or another, Freddie had only collaborated with the DEA a handful of times. Each occasion had been the result of an overdose. These being as common as they were, however, the DEA was only called in when there was what the captain determined to be an inordinate amount of product present—which, in Freddie's experience, was about a kilo or more.

He'd met DEA Agent Troy Allison on one such call. And once had been enough for Freddie to get a read on the man.

And it wasn't good.

Any hopes that Freddie had in asking for some leniency, some professional courtesy, was dashed, even with FBI Agent Keller in tow.

Troy Allison was notorious for being a stickler for the rules. Under no circumstances would he succumb to pressure or allow for any sort of favoritism.

Everybody knew this from the man serving slop in the County Jail to the captain of the City of Greenham Police Department.

In an industry seemingly governed by nepotism, Troy Allison wouldn't even grant the mayor's kin an extra bottle of water if it wasn't mandated in the Constitution.

"Fuck." Freddie uttered the word like a breath.

"Yeah," Keller said as confirmation. "Yeah."

They drove in silence the rest of the way, Freddie's mind racing with ideas on how to leverage Troy.

The only possible thing he could come up with was getting Cole Batherson involved. The man might be internal affairs on the PD side, but he could have connections in a parallel department of the DEA.

It wasn't just a stretch, but a goddamn taffy pull.

Still...

Cole Batherson was good at his job. As much as Veronica detested him, the man *was* good. And if it were up to Freddie, he'd tell the truth; he wouldn't let his partner go on thinking that the reason her father had been forced into retirement was that he'd missed a meeting with the mayor.

What really happened spoke to Cole's character.

He'd done them all a favor.

Especially Veronica.

Could he be counted on to do another?

Freddie sighed as Agent Keller pulled up to a nondescript gray building on the outskirts of Matheson.

Unlike the Greenham police department and the FBI, the DEA liked to keep a low profile. The building was in such rough shape that it was a broken window from being condemned.

It fit Troy Allison's personality perfectly. No frills, no surprises.

The idea of pressuring the agent on his home turf was almost laughable.

And what Agent Keller said next eradicated what little confidence Freddie may have had left.

"I have to warn you, Freddie, Agent Allison and I butt heads."

Not 'butted heads', as in past tense, but as in, we butt heads often.

There goes the idea of storming in with the FBI. Two departments versus one.

"I get it. You going to wait in the car?"

"I can walk you to the door, but I don't think it's in either of our best interests for me to actually see the man or vice versa."

Freddie nodded.

They got out of the car, and Agent Keller, clearly more familiar with this landscape, led the way to the front doors. He pulled one wide and Freddie leaned over and said, "Thanks for the head's up, Jake. Appreciate it."

"Good luck, Freddie."

"Thanks."

Freddie patted his friend on the shoulder and entered the DEA stronghold.

Unlike the modern interior of the City of Greenham PD, there was no front desk, no receptionist, not so much as a computer. If you didn't know you were entering a DEA building, nothing inside would tip you off.

But somebody was watching the door. It had barely closed behind Freddie's massive waist when another door, a side door, this one with a heavy lock and a window reinforced by metal screening, opened.

DEA Agent Troy Allison was a cross between Michael Chiklis from The Shield and Tom Selleck: he was big, bald, and had a thick brown mustache. He was wearing a black vest with the letters DEA on the chest, a green T-shirt, and light-blue jeans.

"You lost, buddy?" Troy asked. He didn't have a toothpick in his mouth, but Freddie imagined that if he did, this was the point where he would pull it out and point it at him.

"I'm here to see Randall."

While Troy's eyebrows weren't as impressive as his mustache, they were full, and they both rose up his forehead.

Freddie pulled out his detective shield, noting that Troy's hand instinctively went to the butt of the gun on his hip as he did.

"I'm here to see my son."

Chapter 24

IT WAS INEVITABLE THAT ALONE in the car with Steve, he would again confront her about her synesthesia.

Her reply came much easier than Veronica would have thought, considering that this was only the second person she'd ever told about her condition.

"I've been working with Dr. Bernard for years, trying to understand it. What we know is that when someone's lying, my brain, my subconscious brain, picks up on subtle cues, the way a poker player can detect an opponent's tells. Only I'm not even aware of what these are. But my fucked-up brain informs me by making me smell gasoline."

In her head, it made sense. Spoken out loud, less so. But Veronica lacked both the insight and vocabulary to explain her condition better.

"What about the sweating? He mentioned sweating... and violence?"

"When someone sweats, even if they're trying to hide it, I can tell. You know when it's cool out, but someone is sweating from a long run? And there's steam coming off them? I see that all the time, only for me, it's blue. And the more someone sweats, the more opaque and concentrated these... watercolors become. As for violence? Well, if I enter a scene where violence has occurred, then I see what to me looks like a fire dancing before my eyes: yellow, red, orange, everything in between. Just like the way I can tell a lie, my brain can also pick up on cues of impending violence, too. That's how I knew that Gloria Trammel was going to shoot me. I had to act."

A justification for something unchallenged. A classic guilt-coping mechanism.

Bev could have been killed. Gloria could have shot and killed both of you.

If Steve noticed, he didn't say anything—he didn't say anything at all. He just stared straight ahead. Twice, Veronica saw him open his mouth to speak, only to give up and just lick his lips instead.

Finally, he said, "And this is because of what happened to you when you were a young girl?"

Now it was Veronica's turn to search for words.

"I think." She shrugged. "Probably, but it didn't really start until much later when I was a bit older. Dr. Bernard said that's not uncommon."

"What was the trigger?"

"What do you mean? I told you. We think it started after Trent and Herb broke in. They lied about letting us go—they lied while splashing gasoline everywhere. And Trent was wearing this blue T-shirt—when he fought with my dad, sweat stains started to spread. The sweat I see now coming off people's bodies is kinda like that. And the fire… well…" Veronica let her sentence trail off.

She didn't want to talk about this anymore. It was too painful. Too raw.

Veronica took her hands off the steering wheel for a moment to aggressively rub the back of her hands.

"Is that it?"

It wasn't just the question, but the tone that surprised her.

"What? What are you getting at, Steve?"

There was something else on his mind, and Veronica wished he would just spit it out.

"Nothing." He scratched his neck absently. "Except… why didn't you tell me?"

Veronica laughed. It was a terrible sound, one that captured the emotion of the day, and she let it out in a single, obnoxious bleat.

"Tell you that I see things? That I can smell a lie and see sweat and predict violence? Yeah, I guess I should have told you that on our first date. Would have gone over really well." While Veronica had explained her condition as best she could, her eyes had been locked on the road. Now, she glanced over at the sheriff. The look of contempt on his face inspired a flash of anger. "What? Like you tell me everything? Okay, Steve, what are these dreams you've been having? *Hmm?*"

A lie was on the tip of his tongue—*I don't remember my dreams*—but given the context of their discussion, he decided better of it.

"That's what I thought."

They arrived at the building that hosted Dr. Bernard's office, a two-story structure in an upscale zip code of Greenham. In addition to her psychiatric practice, it also housed a tax consultant, a florist, and other mundane businesses on the ground floor, and apartments on the second.

Veronica spotted Dr. Bernard's vehicle in the parking lot as well as several others.

Unfortunately, none of them were the white Mazda she'd seen outside Gina's home.

"That's her car," Veronica remarked. "I was following Jane here when you called. We think maybe someone broke in. Stole her notes on me. Come—it's this way."

Unlike the florist, who had a door from the main parking lot directly into his shop, both the tax consultant and Dr. Bernard's office could only be reached by using the tenant's entrance and walking down a hallway.

"It's—"

Veronica stopped. Dr. Jane Bernard's door was slightly ajar.

"Jane?" Veronica unclipped her gun holster. "Jane? You in there?"

Steve was beside her as she placed one hand on the partially open door while leaning away from the opening. A simple nod at Steve and they acted in perfect coordination: Veronica pushed the door wide, and Steve, gun drawn, cleared the room.

A second later, he came back out.

"She's not here."

Veronica already had her phone out and was dialing Jane's number when she looked into the familiar office.

The office itself was separated into two halves of roughly equal size: a front waiting area, and the back where Jane did her sessions.

The fire that danced in front of her eyes was everywhere, but most of the deep reds were concentrated near Jane's desk and the row of cabinets behind it. The hallucination wasn't nearly as visceral as it had been back at Gina's. Veronica felt no nausea, no overwhelming urge to empty her stomach's contents on the grass, but it was uncomfortable, like the beginning of a cramp.

"Something happened here." Veronica shook her head. "Something bad."

"What is—"

Veronica held up a finger.

"Do you hear that?"

The buzzing was coming from beneath Jane's desk. Veronica hurried over and bent to pick it up.

"She was here," Veronica said, her voice tight. "This is Jane's cell phone."

Chapter 25

"DAD, IS JANE WITH YOU?" Veronica asked.

"No, I thought you guys were together. Is everything okay?"

Veronica looked about Dr. Bernard's office. The lingering colors were still there, an indication of violence. And her cell phone... nobody forgot their cell phone under a desk these days. It was your watch, your daily planner, your link to the world.

"I don't know, Dad," she said honestly. "I think something bad might've happened to her."

"What do you mean? Weren't you together? You know what—tell me where you are. I'm coming to you."

"No—it's probably nothing." Veronica shut her eyes. "Stay home. Stay safe. I'll call you when I find her."

Even though Peter Shade was no longer a cop, this was Oregon, and he had a small, but impressive cadre of guns at his disposal.

Stay safe was a metaphor for be prepared.

Veronica wasn't yet convinced that her father was in danger, but first Gina and now Jane...

Jane's fine. She just dropped her phone.

"Veronica?"

And left her office door open when they suspected that someone had already broken in and stolen her files. Sure. Makes sense.

"Just stay home and stay safe. I'll call you as soon as I know anything."

Veronica hung up before her dad could continue the argument. She figured there was a fifty-fifty chance that he would listen to her because, like Veronica, Peter Shade was as stubborn as they came.

"I called CSU Paulie, he's on his way. Just wrapping up at Gina's home," Steve informed her.

"Good."

Veronica walked over to the wall of filing cabinets behind Jane's desk. The dark blue cubes were stacked three high and four long. They reminded Veronica of old high school lockers, complete with horizontal slits in the front to allow for air flow. She had asked about them once, as they seemed out of place in the office's otherwise neutral decor. Jane had said that while she'd initially purchased them because of their aesthetic—Dr. Bernard was a lot of things, an interior designer not being one of them—she admitted that their familiarity served to comfort some of her younger patients.

Veronica grabbed one of the combination locks on a locker door and pulled. It was rock solid.

"I need to get inside these." Steve grimaced and shifted his weight onto one foot. "What's wrong? The killer knows me, Steve. He knows me the way only Jane knows me. She didn't tell him, so that means he got into here."

Veronica tapped the metal.

"How?" he asked.

Veronica opened the desk drawers, hoping, but not expecting, to find a list of combinations for the four locks.

There was none, of course.

"I don't know but I bet CSU Paulie has something that can break these open."

Another grimace from the sheriff.

"What? What's the problem?"

"It's just—they're sensitive files, patient files. Even with a warrant I don't know if it would cover these. And getting a warrant will be tough. All we have is Jane's cell phone and your… intuition."

"All we *have*?" Veronica said, feeling venom on her tongue. "Are you forgetting about the dead body? Gina was murdered and—"

Her phone rang and she glanced at the caller ID.

It was Cole Batherson.

Veronica declined the call.

"Let's say we open the cabinets," Steve said, continuing his thought. "What do you expect to find?"

"For one, my files. If they're not in there, we know that he has them."

Steve cocked his head.

"I'll give you that, but it doesn't really help us."

"What do you mean? Then we'll know that it's me he's after."

Steve, always the rationalist, immediately spotted a problem with her logic.

"Which is the assumption that you and I are working on already. Look—"

"No," Veronica shook her head. "No, don't do that—don't patronize me."

"Sorry. But if the pages are in there, we won't know whether the killer took a photo of them or copied them and put them back."

"What if there are fingerprints on them?"

Even Veronica knew how unlikely this was.

"If this is the same guy, he put paint all over—"

"Okay, fine. Let me think for a moment."

Steve was making sense and Veronica knew that even if they managed to break into the cabinets, in the rare event that they found anything, it would be inadmissible in court. Not typically her main concern but it was a valid consideration. Yet, knowing these facts did nothing to assuage the intense desire to open the damn cabinets and look inside. Perhaps an infinitesimal part of this urge was curiosity, of wanting to know what Jane had written about her over all these years.

But it was more than that.

This had nothing to do with her synesthesia, either; this was something else. The nagging notion that there was something in these cabinets, something that would help them find the killer.

"How long until the tech gets here?"

Her phone rang again, and Veronica, annoyed at the second interruption, answered it this time.

"Cole, if this is about—"

"I'm far away, but I'm safe," Cole interrupted.

"What? What are you talking about?"

There was a muffled cry and then Cole returned to the line.

He took a shuddering breath, then said, "Three, four, lock your door."

Chapter 26

"Cole? Cole! Where are you?"

The line was dead.

"What'd he say?" Steve demanded.

Veronica was having a hard time swallowing the lump that had formed in her throat.

"He said—" she shook her head. "Fuck, he said, *three, four, lock your door.*"

Steve immediately sprang to action. He squeezed his lapel radio three times.

"I'm going to trace the call."

"It was from him—it was from Cole Batherson's cell."

"Doesn't matter. I can trace where the call came from."

Sheriff Burns got on his radio, speaking to dispatch, while Veronica just stared at her phone. This was a nightmare.

First Gina, then Jane, now Cole?

What the hell was going on?

A myriad of questions raced through Veronica's mind at lightning speed.

Why are they doing this? What did I do to them?

"Tracy, hold on a second," Steve said into his shoulder. "Veronica, you smell that?"

All Veronica heard was Cole's voice.

I'm far away, but I'm safe.

"Hmm?"

"I said, it smells like gas in here."

Veronica sniffed the air but noticed no difference from moments ago... because Cole had lied to her, and she'd smelled gas over the phone.

Most of the time, her subconscious required line of sight to put together visual cues indicative of a lie: shifting eye movement, feet positioning, even microscopic drops of sweat. Not so in this case. Cole's voice was sufficient to initiate the smell of gasoline somewhere deep within her confused parietal lobe.

"Oh, shit," Veronica said suddenly, her eyes darting about the room. "Cole said he was safe, that he was far away. Both were lies." She inhaled deeply, but it was impossible for her to discern between the phantom smell and the actual odor. "He's-he's here somewhere. Close."

But they'd already searched both halves of Dr. Bernard's office and there was no one else there. In the area where Jane had her sessions, there was nowhere to hide. But in the front room…

Veronica pushed by Steve and hurried to the front closet. She whipped it open preparing to leap backward or forward or do something.

A lone umbrella and a light spring jacket inspired no such action.

"Damn."

"It's getting stronger," Steve remarked from near Jane's desk.

"The lockers?"

Steve immediately tapped one of them, saying the man's name as he did. Then he tilted it before moving onto the next. Veronica could tell that the lockers were heavy from the way the vein in Steve's left arm bulged, but he wasn't straining enough to suggest that there was a body inside one of them.

It didn't make sense, anyway. Veronica had been standing right next to them when her phone had rung.

She inhaled deeply, trying to use her nose like a Bloodhound's to lead her to the source. A useless task, until she began to detect something more than gas.

"Fire. I smell fire."

Steve inhaled deeply.

"Yeah, I smell it, too. Where's it coming from?"

There was no fireplace in Dr. Bernhard's office, of course, but Veronica's mind was still desperately trying to come up with a benign explanation for everything.

She followed the growing smell of fire toward the lockers as Steve got back on his radio, this time requesting a fire truck.

The blue metal was cool to the touch, but the smell was more intense, and now Veronica thought she *heard* fire.

What the fuck is going on?

"I think it's coming from here?"

Steve touched the cabinets as she'd just done, but then reached above them and pressed his palm against the wall.

"It's hot. It's fucking hot."

Veronica craned to see behind the cabinets but didn't notice a secret door or anything like that.

It has to be coming from the other side, she thought. *It has to be.*

Veronica left Dr. Bernard's office and stood in the hallway. No sign of fire.

She leaned back into the office where Steve was still touching the wall like a confused mime.

"You check upstairs," she yelled. "Could be coming from one of the apartments. I'm going around back."

Veronica left before Steve could ask questions. She ran outside, looped behind the building and then stopped.

It was probably just her eyes playing tricks on her, but she thought she saw a white car in her periphery, slowly moving away from the building. When she looked, it was gone.

Either way, she wasn't chasing cars now.

Cole had said he was safe and that he was far away.

Both had been lies.

There were several doors behind the building, but one, in particular, caught her eye. While the others were labeled with the business they were associated with, one was not. It was also located beside a half-full dumpster.

Veronica couldn't be certain, but it appeared to be located near where she thought Dr. Bernard's office was on the other side. It also oddly looked like one of Jane's locker cabinets—it was metal and the same dark blue color—but this had to be a coincidence.

She tried the handle, only to cry out and pull her hand back immediately. It wasn't just hot, it was scalding.

"Cole?"

Veronica kicked the door.

"Cole, you in there?"

Veronica listened.

She could hear fire behind the door and what might have been someone stirring. Veronica covered her hand with her sleeve and grabbed the handle again. This time, the heat was bearable, and she pulled.

It was locked.

"Cole!"

Veronica delivered another hard kick to the door.

"Cole!"

This time there was a reply: a muffled cry.

"Hang in there!"

Veronica ran back to the front of the building, and into the hallway.

"Steve?"

He wasn't in Jane's office—he was probably upstairs knocking on apartment doors.

Veronica spotted the location of the fire immediately. The drywall above the lockers was turning a dark gray and was bowing a little.

"Steve!"

She grabbed the corner of the closest cabinet and pulled. It wobbled but didn't topple. Grunting, Veronica slid her fingers between the wall and the cabinet, ignored the heat, and yanked with all her might.

She barely managed to get out of the way as the first cabinet came crashing down. The row of four lockers was somehow connected from behind, and the second groaned, and then fell as well. The last two followed with a squeal of twisted metal.

The wall behind the lockers was completely black.

Knowing that if Cole was in the janitor's locker, or whatever the hell the room was on the other side, he didn't have much time, Veronica drove her foot into the center of the black stain.

Weakened by the fire, her shoe went right through the drywall with ease. The hole she made was the size of a dinner plate, and as the air from Dr. Bernard's office was sucked into the hungry fire, flames erupted from the opening.

Veronica jumped backward to avoid being burned only to bump into someone. Thinking it was the man from the phone, the one who sang the song, she whipped around.

It was Steve.

"You okay? The fire—"

She shook him off.

"The wall! I think Cole is in there! You have to save him!"

Chapter 27

"I DIDN'T KNOW HE WAS your son," DEA Agent Troy Allison said. There was no hint of apology in the man's voice, he was simply stating a fact. With big, broad shoulders, and a bald head that was shaved daily, Troy was an intimidating figure. It wasn't just his size that conveyed this, but also his eyes. They were dark and hard, and almost always partially squinted. This had given rise to thick creases at the corners that rivaled those on his forehead with respect to their depth.

"I appreciate you letting me see him," Freddie said as he followed the man down a dingy hallway. The lighting was cirrhotic, giving everything from the walls to the linoleum floor a burnt yellow hue.

Troy shrugged.

"He's not under arrest... yet."

Freddie wasn't sure how to interpret this comment. Were they wrong about Troy? Was he giving him an out?

Not under arrest... yet.

Did he expect a bribe? A favor exchange?

What?

"Look," the man said. "I ain't gonna lie to you—as a courtesy to a fellow officer, I'll tell you straight."

"Please."

"Your son was arrested with a kilo of pure heroin."

Freddie's eyes bulged.

"No—can't be. Not Randall."

The man's eyes went from half-squinted to two-thirds closed.

"When's the last time you spoke to your son, Detective Furlow? Because he didn't mention you. And I know how you guys work. I got a son myself. I tell him the same thing you probably told Randall. If you ever get in trouble with the law, real trouble, drop my name, tell 'em to give me a call. Randall didn't do that."

Freddie wasn't sure how to answer.

He went with ambiguous.

"Haven't spoken to him in a while," he admitted. "But a kilogram? That's absurd."

In truth, it had been close to three years since Freddie had spoken to either of his sons. And while his eldest, Tom, had always been more on the experimental side when it came to recreational drugs, Randall was the responsible one.

What the hell happened?

"*Uh-huh.* Absurd, but true. A kilo. Now, I'm not sure if you're versed on—"

"Five years minimum," Freddie said.

Troy looked at him curiously for a second before nodding. "That's right. But this case is a little trickier than others."

Freddie felt a headache coming on.

I should have eaten something... why the hell didn't I eat?

"What do you mean?"

"Well, the heroin that your son was found with wasn't just your run-of-the-mill powder. A couple of years back there was this massive scandal in New York City. The mayor, Ken Smith, was involved in a drug trafficking ring?"

"What does this have to do with Randall?"

"Well, here's the thing, the heroin that this mayor was importing was straight from Colombia. Because he was getting it from the source, it was cheaper and purer than the other garbage on the street. Pretty much forced all competition out of business."

Freddie wasn't sure why he was getting this lecture on the New York City heroin trade, but he knew better than to rush the man.

"Anyway, everything came crashing down, and dear mayor Ken Smith is presumed dead. This here—" Troy took out a massive cell phone in a protective case that looked capable of withstanding a nuclear blast. "—is the logo on Ken's product."

He showed Freddie a picture of brown paper upon which was an image, mostly just an outline, of a snake with an eyeball in its mouth.

"You ever seen that before?"

"No."

"Well, me neither. Until I arrested your son, that is. You see, Detective Furlow, his kilo of smack was wrapped in this paper. Now, I'll be the first to admit it, I didn't even know what it meant—who keeps up with what they do o'er there in New York? But I reached out to some of my contacts out east, and they were none too happy about this. They thought it was gone for good. They got all worried, you see, thinkin' that Ken was back or some shit. And then they started calling my boss, telling him that they need a source."

And there it was. The irony of the situation was that while Agent Allison was opposed to making any sort of deals with a fellow cop, he had no such qualms when it came to negotiating with a criminal. DEA Agents were addicted to moving up the ladder, the allure of catching Tony Montana at the very top so captivating, that not even a man as scrupulous as Troy Allison could resist.

"You want him to flip."

Troy shrugged.

"I mean, we don't want this—" he shook his phone, "—on the streets."

Freddie sucked his teeth.

"Look, Detective, I can't tell you what to do. All's I know is that your son ain't even on the first level of the pyramid. I would hate for him to spend the next five years in a cell for this."

Freddie was incensed. He was angry enough that if maybe he'd had a full stomach he might have even done something about it. As it stood, all he could do was nod like an idiot.

"Anyways, he's in here."

They'd come to a stop in front of a door and Freddie made the mistake of looking through the grime-smeared window.

He wasn't prepared to see Randall—not like this.

"You got five minutes, Detective Furlow. Five minutes, then I'm going to formally arrest and charge your son."

Chapter 28

STEVE HAD MUCH LARGER BOOTS than Veronica. Several well-placed kicks combined with the surge of the fire dying down allowed Veronica a clear view of what she'd correctly assumed was a janitorial closet.

"Oh my God," she gasped. "He's in there! Cole's in there!"

Somewhere far away, she heard the sound of a firetruck.

Steve heard it, too, and realized that it wasn't going to get here in time. Saying nothing, he brought the crook of his elbow to his face, turned sideways to make himself as narrow as possible, and dove into what remained of the wall. His right shoulder clipped a dangling piece of charred drywall, as did his right knee.

If the situation had been different, Veronica might've laughed. Whoever had built this room clearly hadn't made it to code and not only did Steve somehow manage to avoid striking any studs, but he left behind a near-perfect, cartoon-like outline of his body.

Veronica had every intention of following the sheriff through and would have easily fit through his contour.

But she couldn't do it. The fire was hot and the smoke thick, but that wasn't the problem.

It was that this fire looked so much like the one in her house all those years ago, the one that had taken her parents' lives.

"No," Veronica whimpered. She was already on her knees, but now she sat on her rear and scooted away from the hole in the wall. "Please."

She could make out dark shapes in the glowing fire. They were indistinguishable, mere shadows, but she knew they were her mom and dad, was absolutely certain that they were Trevor and Roberta Davis.

"Please."

There was a grunt, and a shape filled the opening.

"Veronica, give me a hand!"

Steve's voice brought her back to the present. He was dragging something—Cole—and he was no longer the same shape and couldn't fit through the opening.

"Veronica!"

She kicked some drywall free, and then guided him between the studs. The sheriff barely made it through and when he did, he immediately tripped on the corner of the fallen locker. Steve went down hard and the form collapsed on top of him.

"Cole!"

The man's eyes were closed, his hands bound behind his back, and there was a piece of duct tape covering his mouth. His face was gray with soot.

Veronica rushed to him as Steve wriggled out from beneath his body. She pulled the tape off. It stretched Cole's lips painfully away from his face and Veronica, like a mother just having given birth and not hearing her baby cry, knew that something was wrong when he didn't so much as groan.

"Shit."

Desperate now, she placed her ear on his chest and listened. Nothing.

"He's not breathing, Steve. He's not breathing!"

Steve tried to push her out of the way, but Veronica had already commenced CPR. Thirty chest compressions, then two breaths, just as she was taught.

Or was it fifteen and two?

She kept going, even as she heard Steve yelling at somebody to hurry up, that they had an officer in need of immediate medical attention.

Thirty compressions, two breaths. Thirty compressions, two breaths.

"It's not working!"

As Veronica continued to administer CPR, she couldn't help but think of all those cheesy movies in which the doctor pronounces their patient dead, but the wife, mother, daughter, whoever, screams that it can't be, and they jump in to take over.

It always works in the movies.

But Cole still wasn't breathing...

"No." Veronica pumped even harder. "No, I'm not going to—"

Cole's eyes opened wide, and he sucked in a massive breath, which became a violent cough when his lungs were only half inflated.

With Steve's help, she managed to roll Cole onto his side. He sputtered and vomited a thin liquid, and that's when Veronica heard it.

A wet fizzle.

Her first thought was that Cole was making the sound.

He wasn't.

It was coming from the janitor's closet.

And it sounded familiar.

It sounded like something from her past. Something long buried.

Veronica's vision suddenly went red—completely red, as if someone had taken acrylic paint and coated her corneas with it.

"Down!" she screamed. "Steve, get down!"

Veronica didn't know if he heard in time. All she could do was react.

Veronica turned her face away from the hole in the wall and shielded Cole's body as the gasoline canister exploded into a ball of fire.

Chapter 29

"DAD?"

It wasn't a surprised *'Dad'*. It wasn't a shocked *'Dad'*. It wasn't even a thankful *'Dad'*.

The word *'Dad'* came out of Randall's mouth like *'fuck you, Dad'*, or *'what the hell do you think you're doing here, dad'*?

And this was what Detective Freddie Furlow deserved. But they didn't have time to dissect old wounds.

"Randall, we only have five minutes. We need to talk fast."

The boy, for that's what he still was to Freddie even though he was twenty-one now, was thinner than he remembered. In stark contrast to Freddie's morbid obesity, Randall Furlow, now Randall Byers, was five feet eleven, one hundred and seventy-five pounds. He had dark hair like his father's, but he got his angled features from his mother.

Hazel eyes, ears that were slightly too small for his head, and while Freddie's complexion leaned toward pink, Randall's skin was olive. To Freddie's surprise, his son wasn't handcuffed or restrained in any way. So, when he rocketed to his feet, his metal chair scraped angrily across the floor. And when he tried to back away, Randall didn't realize how small a room they were in, and he bumped up against the cold concrete wall.

"What the hell are you doing here?"

No *'Dad'*, now. No *'Dad'* at all.

Freddie held his hands out to his sides, trying to calm his son.

"Randall, please, we don't have much time."

"I don't want you in here," Randall nearly whispered.

"Randy—"

"No, I don't want you here!" he repeated, his voice bordering on a shout, now. "Guards! *Guards!*"

Nothing happened. The door behind Freddie remained closed.

"No one's coming, Randy. We don't have much time, and if we don't figure something out, you are going to be charged. And then you'll probably spend five years in prison. Do you understand me?"

Randall wasn't fazed by this, which to Freddie, meant one of two things: either the gravity of the situation hadn't sunk in yet, or he didn't care.

It had to be the former.

"I know you changed your name, Randall, but that won't help you. Once you're on the inside, they'll know who you are—they'll find out that you're a cop's son. And if that happens..." Freddie let his sentence trail off. Sometimes, not saying something was more powerful than trying to paint a vivid picture. And judging by the way that Randall screwed up his mouth, he got the point. "You need to tell me who gave you that heroin."

The transition that Freddie saw in his son's eyes was nearly instantaneous. Randall went from undaunted to terrified.

"I-I can't. I can't."

Hands still out, Freddie took a step forward. Randall remained rooted in place.

"You can, and you *have* to."

"No, I can't," Randall reiterated.

"Randy, you *have* to," Freddie implored, his hands becoming fists. "If you don't, there's nothing I—"

"They have Kevin, Dad."

Freddie's jaw fell open.

"What?"

"Yeah." Randall started to shake all over. "They told me that if I didn't sell the heroin, they'd kill him. Dad, they're going to fucking kill Kevin."

Freddie clenched his jaw. He didn't need to ask any questions—he knew what had happened because he'd seen it before.

His eldest son, Kevin, had gotten in deep. Not just hanging out with the wrong crowd, but becoming the wrong crowd: using, and selling a little on the side to make enough cash for his next fix. But the thing about the wrong crowd is that there's always one worse. And while you were new to the game, they weren't. They tempted you, fronted you a little coke or smack, told you to sell it. Told you that if you did a good job, they'd let you keep some of the profits and give you more.

But it was a scam.

The second you accepted that package, you became a target. And not by rival dealers, but to those who were so generous, by your own crew. It was staged to look like a random robbery, but it was all planned from the start. They'd jump you, rough you up a little, and steal their drugs back.

Having no choice but to return with your tail between your legs, you tell them what happened. They act like it's no big deal, that if you work hard, you can pay off your debt. That, too, is a scam. They bleed you dry, exploit you for everything you have. And when you have nothing left to give, they use you to draw someone else in.

Someone close to you.

Like your brother.

Freddie had seen it dozens of times before.

"Fuck," he cursed.

"I didn't know what was going on, Dad, I didn't—"

"Quiet," Freddie hissed.

Dad. Now, this is the I need help, *Dad.*

But Freddie didn't know how to give it.

"I need to think."

Only he couldn't do that because there was a loud knock on the door behind him. He turned and saw Agent Allison's large bald head, warped by the filthy glass.

Time's up.

"Dad, what do we do?"

Pleading *Dad.* I'm still a kid, *Dad,* and no matter what happened, you were supposed to protect me, *Dad.*

And you failed.

Freddie closed his eyes and took a deep breath as he heard the door being opened behind him. It sounded like the jaw of a giant metallic dragon becoming unhinged, preparing to spew fire.

"Randall, keep your mouth shut. Don't say a single word, okay? I'm going to fix this. Just don't speak."

"Detective Furlow?" Agent Allison said.

"Do you understand, Randall?"

Randall nodded and this caused the tears that had been welling in his eyes to spill down his cheeks. He was a boy again.

"I need you to say it, Randall."

"I'm going to keep my mouth shut, Dad."

"Good."

Freddie wanted so much to go to his son and hold him, squeeze him, tell him that everything was going to be okay.

But that was a lie.

And if there's one thing that Detective Freddie Furlow hated more than kale, it was lying.

And he hated kale a hell of a lot.

"Good," Freddie repeated, giving his son a professional nod.

Then he turned and stepped into the dingy hallway with the bald DEA Agent. He waited for the door to be closed behind him—no dragon fire this time—before fixing Troy with a hard stare.

"Forty-eight hours," Freddie said. "Don't charge him for forty-eight hours, and I promise you I'll find out who is behind this."

Agent Allison sighed.

"Detective Furlow, when I said—"

Freddie reached out, came within inches of grabbing Troy by the front of his vest, before stopping his hands in midair.

"You want to move up the food chain, then give me forty-eight hours. That's it. Give me forty-eight fucking hours."

Chapter 30

VERONICA COUGHED AND STUMBLED. SHE was waving her hand frantically in front of her face, but the thick smoke and her watering eyes made it near impossible to see.

"Steve," she tried to say, but the word degenerated into a coughing fit halfway through.

She bumped into something hard and, thinking that it was the door, she shoved.

It didn't budge.

Veronica wasn't sure where she was. She thought she'd made it out of Dr. Bernard's office and was now in the hall, but nothing made sense to her. The smoke, fire, heat, alarms, all of it, combined with her erratic synesthesia, made orienting herself nearly impossible.

She shuffled a little to her left, again trying to find the door, but her palms touched only drywall.

"Come on, come on," she managed without a cough. Veronica hunched lower, knowing that eventually, she would have to press her belly to the floor to avoid inhaling any more smoke.

Her head was spinning from oxygen deprivation and her movements had become languid.

Instead of relying on touch, Veronica resorted to using her ears to try to find her way out. Cutting through the hiss and crackle of the fire—behind her, the fire was behind her—was the whine of a firetruck. Her first step was to her right, but the sound dampened ever so slightly. She went left, running her fingers along the wall as she moved.

Drywall, drywall, drywall… *glass!*

Veronica pushed again and this time she felt something give. And then she heard the whoosh of air being sucked into the building.

Strong hands gripped her shoulders. Still blind, her first instinct was that this was the man on the phone.

One, two, I've got you!

Veronica resisted, but the only way to break free was to go backward into the fire.

"No!"

The fingers dug into her flesh.

"Help!" She started to cough again. "Hel—"

"It's me," Steve said, breaking into a sputtering cough of his own. "It's me, Veronica."

Relief.

Veronica stopped resisting and allowed herself to be pulled forward. They moved quickly, but she somehow managed to stay on her feet. In seconds, her airways cleared. In a minute, she could see—her vision was still watery, but clear enough that she was no longer at risk of tripping.

Someone else came into view, a man in a reflective vest. Steve passed her off, and a mask was immediately placed over Veronica's nose and mouth.

"Steve?"

Her mask fogged and Veronica gave up and just let go.

Many hands were on her, guiding her, and then she was in the air.

Behind her lids, Veronica saw another fire. The fire from her childhood.

The fire that had taken her parents' lives and had forever changed both her and her brother.

The tears from the smoke became tears of emotion.

"We've got you, Detective Shade," a stranger said.

A hand slipped into hers and even before Steve spoke, she knew it was his. She'd traced the burn pattern on his skin for many hours while he slept fitfully beside her.

"I'm right here, I won't leave you."

As Veronica was hoisted and placed onto a gurney, she saw Steve. His hat was gone, and the left collar of his shirt was singed. His eyes were red, and his face was gray with ash and soot.

Veronica went to take the mask off, wanting to ask about Cole, but Steve stayed her hand.

"Keep it on, please."

Veronica shook her head, and she extended the mask away from her face.

"Cole?" She barely recognized her voice. "Where—" she coughed once, "—is Cole?"

"He's dead."

That's what Veronica heard in her head, but Steve's voice was drowned out by the warbling whine of a firetruck entering the parking lot.

Fire destroys everything, which meant that Cole had to be dead.

Lucy Davis had died in a fire.

Steve squeezed her hand.

"I think he's going to be okay, Veronica. I think we got to him in time."

Veronica felt a massive weight being lifted off her shoulders. Her neck and shoulder muscles relaxed, and she allowed herself to sink into the gurney.

The man in the white car may have murdered Gina Braden, but Cole had escaped.

They'd saved him.

Veronica replaced the mask on her face.

They'd come here looking for—

Her sense of joy evaporated.

They'd saved Cole, but the man still had Dr. Jane Bernard.

This time when Veronica tried to remove the mask, one of the EMTs stopped her.

"Ma'am, keep the—"

Veronica wrenched free and pulled the mask back, her eyes daring the EMT to try to stop her again.

"The files," she said, her voice somehow more hoarse than moments ago.

"What?" Steve asked. He turned and spat something dark and thick onto the ground. "What files?"

"The files," Veronica repeated. "Steve, you have to save the files. You have to put out the fire… if you don't save those files, we're never going to find Jane."

Chapter 31

THINKING THAT IT WAS VERONICA, Detective Freddie Furlow didn't pick up his phone when it first rang. But on the third ring, it became clear that whoever was calling wasn't going to stop. And while he'd been correct on the caller's surname, he'd been wrong about the given name.

It was Peter Shade, ex-Greenham PD captain, and longtime friend.

Freddie took a shallow breath, tried to lift his mood by putting on a fake smile, and then answered.

"Pete, how's retirement treating you?"

"Where are you now?"

Freddie had known Peter Shade for the better part of two decades. They'd first met when Peter had been a beat cop in Matheson. Compared to the city of Greenham, Matheson had a small police force that was only a quarter of the size.

Being several years his younger, Freddie had been in the Academy then. He'd also been much skinnier. Come to think of it, he'd been in a relationship and on his way to being happily married.

Most of the time, police officers weren't keen on associating with recruits in the Academy. Even after graduation, 'boots' weren't treated with the greatest respect. They were either ignored or hazed, which typically involved shining boots and performing other such menial tasks.

But for some reason, after a chance encounter, Peter and Freddie had hit it off and had gone for a beer. That was the start of a lifelong friendship. They weren't 'best friends' by any means but kept in touch, even after Peter had adopted Veronica and was forced to move around all the time. As luck would have it, they had reunited in the Greenham PD. At one time, both had had aspirations of moving up the ranks, but that was before the divorce.

That was before Freddie found contentment in the bottom of a take-out bag.

Still, he liked being a detective, and when Peter had come to him and told him that his daughter was being promoted from foot soldier to detective, the writing was on the wall.

Freddie had a new role, a reprised father-like role of looking after Veronica Shade. And for the most part, he'd done an adequate job. Some minor blips, fewer major ones, but he'd taught Detective Shade the ropes, and kept her from making some of the mistakes that he had.

"Fred, where are you?" Peter asked again.

Freddie stared out the window. He wasn't sure exactly where he was. He'd left the nondescript DEA office in Matheson five minutes ago and was driving aimlessly, hoping that a way to keep his son out of prison would come to him in the form of divine intervention.

"About twenty-five minutes from the station," he said at last, which was true of pretty much anywhere in Matheson relative to Greenham.

"You're not with her?"

"With…"

"With Veronica," Peter snapped. His tone was always sharp, but this level of emotion rarely crept into his friend's voice.

"No," Freddie began hesitantly. "I had something else to take—"

"There's been an accident, Fred. A fire."

"What?"

A fire? *Another* fire?

Freddie pressed on the gas.

"Where is she? Is she okay?"

"Veronica's at the hospital. Doctor says she gonna be all right, but Freddie?"

"Yeah?"

"There's someone hunting her."

Freddie flicked on the red and blue LED light bar embedded in his front grill and pushed the gas even harder.

"What do you mean? What the hell is going on?"

"You didn't see the interview this morning?"

"The *what*?"

Freddie scratched the back of his neck.

Interview... interview...

It clicked.

"That was today?"

Jake Keller's visit had pretty much wiped any other thoughts from Freddie's brain. But once prompted, he remembered everything.

When IA had first come to Veronica with the idea, she'd asked Freddie his opinion. Being naturally protective of her, his instinct had been to say no. But it wasn't his decision to make and as the pressure mounted and Veronica wavered, Freddie changed his 'no' to asking her what she wanted to do.

Veronica's eventual agreement was answer enough. Freddie knew that this had something to do with her father—not that Peter would have ever wanted her to go on TV, not after the lengths the man had gone to keep her life a secret. Rather, it was because Veronica felt it was her responsibility to raise the profile of the Shade name, rebuild it after her father's forced retirement.

Twice, Freddie had nearly told her the whole story behind what happened that day outside of the precinct with the mayor and Cole Batherson.

But he hadn't, because he'd made a promise to Peter to keep his mouth shut.

Now, it seemed like both—the interview and the secret—were horrible ideas.

"The fucking talk show—*Marlowe*."

"Yeah, I remember now, but I didn't see it. What happened?"

"It was a fucking disaster, that's what happened. Some fucking creep called, sang her a song, threatened her on the air."

"What?"

Freddie passed an Amazon delivery truck on the soft shoulder, spraying it with a shower of gravel.

"I haven't seen it yet. But apparently whoever called in wasn't playing around. Said some other stuff, too, stuff that… well, secret stuff about Veronica's life."

Freddie felt his chest tighten. This was the reason why he hadn't wanted Veronica to go on the show in the first place.

"Then what happened?"

"Just spoke to Captain Bottel—you know him, didn't say much. All I can tell you is that someone grabbed Cole Batherson and tied him up at Dr. Jane Bernard's office. When Veronica arrived, he started a fire and ran."

Freddie's head was swimming now. This made less sense *after* his friend's explanation.

"Cole? Like, Internal Affairs, Cole?" Of course, it had to be him, but Freddie needed clarification. "And Dr. Bernard? The head shrink?"

"Yeah."

Nothing further.

"Why would someone try to kill Cole? And what does Dr. Bernard have to do with any of this?"

"It's a long story and I'm not sure I understand it, either. But someone tried to kill Cole and Veronica by lighting a gas can on fire. She barely made it out, and he's in worse shape."

Freddie's mind instantly went to the fire at Veronica Shade's childhood home about a year ago. He remembered running into the flames, remembered the uneasy feeling of the skin and flesh around his waist swinging back and forth.

He remembered dragging Veronica's limp body out and then running back in to rescue the sheriff.

The sheriff…. Steve was supposed to go with Veronica to the interview.

"Where the hell is Sheriff Burns?" Freddie demanded.

"He was with her, and somehow managed to avoid getting burned. I'm on my way to meet up with him at the hospital now. I can debrief you there."

Freddie, who was already flying down residential streets, flicked on his sirens to go with the lights and drove even faster.

"I'll be there in five."

Five minutes was all he had to spare. Freddie had asked Agent Allison for a forty-eight-hour hiatus, but there was no guarantee that the bald man would give him more than one.

Guilt crept in, guilt at rushing to save someone else's kid when his own son was in jeopardy of being thrown in jail. And while, as per Peter's account, Veronica was going to be okay, the same couldn't be said for Randall Furlow.

Chapter 32

THEY WERE TRYING TO GIVE her something. Something to sedate her, to calm her down.

Veronica didn't want it.

She *was* calm—well, relatively so given the circumstances. Admittedly, she wasn't completely in the right frame of mind, but who would be?

The librarian that she visited this morning to grab a book for her sheriff boyfriend had been murdered. The scene had been covered in paint to look like her synesthesia.

To confuse her? To replicate her condition? To send her a message?

Veronica didn't know.

Veronica didn't care.

And then there was Cole Batherson.

Cole Batherson, the internal affairs officer who had been on her ass ever since she'd put Ken Cameron in prison. The man who had been looking over their shoulders, undoubtedly reporting everything they'd done wrong, and who was probably responsible for getting her father kicked out of the PD.

He'd also been tied up, tossed in a broom closet, and set on fire with gasoline.

Gasoline...

Veronica still smelled it now. It was on her clothes, in her nose, clinging to the back of her tongue.

That too was for her—more of her synesthesia exploited.

So, no, she wasn't going to be completely calm in this moment.

Not when they still had no idea where Dr. Jane Bernard was.

"I don't want it," Veronica hissed.

"Ma'am, it's not gonna knock you out, it's just going—"

"My name is Detective Shade." Veronica pushed herself to a seated position on the hospital bed. "And I don't want anything to calm me down. I don't want anything at all."

The nurse looked at the clipboard in her hands as if there were speaking notes on it, a list of responses to say to uncooperative patients.

Veronica always wondered why, in a digital era, nurses were still scribbling things on paper instead of dictating into an iPad or marking a tablet with digital check marks. What happened with all these notes? Were they digitized and stored? Or were they sitting in a filing cabinet somewhere—

Veronica straightened even further until she was at a perfect ninety-degree angle.

"The files."

The nurse glanced up from her paper.

"Excuse me?"

"The files—Dr. Bernard's files. Did they save them from the fire?"

A cock of the head, a blank look.

"The psychiatrist's files," Veronica repeated. "Did they burn?"

The nurse put her pen in her breast pocket and lowered the clipboard to her side.

"I'm sorry, Detective, but I don't know what you're talking about. I'm just here to make sure you're doing okay."

And to sedate me.

Veronica felt her anger rising. Anger and frustration, and even though she knew that the nurse didn't deserve any of her wrath, it took all of her effort not to lash out.

She closed her eyes and turned her head. When she opened them again, she was staring out the open hospital room door. She saw Steve, looking exactly as he did outside Dr. Bernard's office—he hadn't so much as washed his face let alone changed his clothes. He was angry, speaking to a man in a white coat—a doctor, presumably—with shaggy black hair. He was pointing his finger at the man's chest accusingly. The doctor seemed intimidated but continued to shake his head.

"Yes, the doctor will be in shortly," the nurse informed Veronica, following her gaze.

"That him?"

"No, your doctor is Dr. Kinkaid. Are you sure—"

"I don't want anything."

"Hmm."

With that, the nurse left, and Veronica called out to the sheriff.

"Steve?"

Speaking loudly hurt her throat, but Veronica was pleased that the sound of her voice had pretty much returned to normal. After a final aggressive point at the doctor, Steve hurried over.

He slipped his hand into hers.

"How're you feeling?"

"Better. Did I sleep?"

Steve shrugged.

"A little, in the ambulance. Cole is doing okay, too. They knocked him out with something, but he should come around in a few hours."

Veronica nodded and squeezed Steve's hand. The man's rough skin was damp with sweat.

"Did you speak to him before they knocked him out?"

It's not going to knock me out, my ass.

"Yeah, just briefly. He didn't see his attacker—the man was wearing a mask. Said he got hit in the head and woke up in the closet, then the man told him what to say on the phone. He started the fire right before Cole heard us on the other side of the wall."

Veronica considered this. They were so close.

"Why was Cole there in the first place?"

"He doesn't remember. The doctor thinks some of his memory will come back after he sleeps it off, but that's just a guess. Cole has a concussion and the lining of his throat and lungs have been burnt. Thanks to you, his skin is pretty much fine, though."

Veronica gently rubbed her thumb on the scarred flesh on the back of Steve's hand.

"What about Jane?"

Steve looked down and ever so subtly shook his head.

"Fuck."

"I had a deputy go to her home, but she's not there. There's an APB out so, hopefully, she turns up somewhere."

They both knew that this was unlikely. Dr. Jane Bernard wasn't an angry teenager running away from an overprotective parent.

"And the files? Did they manage to save the files?"

The look on Steve's face told her that he didn't hold out much hope that there was anything in there that would help them find whoever was behind this.

But she knew.

The answer was in there.

"Haven't looked inside, of course, but those cabinets are pretty hefty."

"Water damage?"

Steve shook his head.

"No, they used chemicals to put out the fire. None of the structure caught."

Veronica sighed and finally collapsed back down onto the bed.

"Thank God."

Steve pulled his hand out of hers and ran the back of two fingers down her warm cheek. Veronica, soothed by the gesture, closed her eyes, and inhaled deeply.

"Why is this happening?" she whispered. "Why is someone doing this to—"

She'd almost said *to me.*

Veronica was convinced that she was at the heart of this, that it had started with the phone call, or perhaps before, and that she was the ultimate target of this psychopath's twisted game.

But to think about herself at this moment, after what everyone else had been through? That just seemed wrong.

The first person she'd seen this morning had been Gina Braden.

The librarian was strangled hours later.

She'd also spoken to Cole Batherson, had snarled at him before and after meeting with Captain Bottel.

As for Jane Bernard? Veronica had caught her with—

Steve's caresses had nearly lulled her off to sleep, but she was suddenly wide awake.

"My dad! Where's my dad?"

Steve stopped stroking her face.

"I called him while you were in the—"

A commotion in the hallway cut Steve's words short. Two large men were striding loudly toward Veronica's room.

The first was six feet tall, maybe two hundred and twenty pounds. Not all fat, but not all muscle either. He had blond hair and brown eyes. Veronica could smell the reek of cigarettes even before he entered the room.

The second was approximately the same height as the first but had at least seventy pounds on him. Thick jowls stretched the dark skin around his eyes downward.

"V," Peter Shade exclaimed, rushing to her side. Steve took a respectful step back. "Thank God you're alright."

Freddie came next. He looked even worse than when Veronica had seen him speaking to Agent Keller.

"Let's take a little break on these fires, shall we?" her partner said, his voice humorless. "I need some time to train if I'm going to be running in and saving your ass."

Chapter 33

WHILE FREDDIE AND PETER SPOKE to Veronica, Sheriff Steve Burns stepped out of the room.

He walked right by the doctor who had denied him a refill on his Oxy prescription, then made his way to a quiet hallway.

He called McVeigh first.

"Any update on Dr. Bernard?"

"No one has seen her since this morning. We're processing her car from the scene, but nothing so far."

Steve frowned.

"What about the white Mazda?"

"Again, nothing. We're still combing red light cameras throughout the city, and I have some men obtaining ATM footage from the area. Maybe we'll get lucky."

McVeigh's tone suggested that he wasn't hopeful.

Neither was Steve.

He exhaled loudly.

"So, we have this madman running around killing people, kidnapping them, starting fires during the middle of the day and we got nothing? What about Gina Braden?"

"The coroner's not quite done yet, but she says so far there are no surprises. Gina Braden's neck was broken, but she fought hard. Kristin thinks that she might be able to get some material from beneath her nails, but they have to separate it from all the paint first. There is one thing, though."

Steve waited, unsure of the reason behind his chief deputy's hesitation.

"And?"

"We found a pen in her pocket, and we managed to pull several fingerprints off of it. Most belonged to Gina."

"What about the others?" Steve snapped, annoyed at McVeigh's obtuse attitude.

"Just one other person... we matched it to Veronica Shade."

For a second, Steve wasn't sure he'd heard correctly.

"What?"

"The pen in Gina Braden's pocket had a finger and thumbprint on it that matched Detective Veronica Shade's police employment records. Now, I wasn't with her when she went inside, but it's possible that she—"

"No," Steve said flatly. "It's not from that. Veronica told me that she visited the library this morning, signed out a book. Probably used the pen then."

"Right. I'll make a note."

McVeigh seemed oddly skeptical, but Steve let it go.

"What about the fire?"

"Again, no surprises. Started in the broom closet, gasoline used as an accelerant. The jerry can was left behind and that's what exploded. Management didn't recognize the lock on the door. Best guess is that our suspect snipped off the old lock and put his on there after forcing Cole inside. And before you ask, there are no cameras in or outside the building."

Of course, there aren't, Steve thought miserably.

"What about the files?"

Steve wasn't sure if it was desperation or Veronica's insistence that gave him hope that there might be a clue as to the killer's identity in there. Earlier today, he'd thought it extremely unlikely. Now, however, he thought there was a chance that there was at least one clue left behind.

"Pretty much intact. A couple of the cabinet locks broke in the fall, and I glanced at the pages. Even the ones that got some of the fire-retardant chemicals on them seem legible. I'm not sure if you want me to leave them or..."

"Take them to evidence." Steve reconsidered. "Wait, what's the status there? At the building?"

"Still cordoned off. Fire Chief said that while there doesn't appear to be any structural damage, they want to take some time to make sure, given that people live on the second floor. It'll be three, maybe four days before people move back in."

"You know what? Don't do anything with the files just yet. Just make sure that nobody goes near them."

"Got it. There's just one more thing, Sheriff."

There was always *one more thing*. And that one more thing was never a good thing. It was never oh, by the way, we ID'd the murderer, found one of his hairs at the scene, have a video of him abducting Dr. Jane Bernard.

It was always something bad.

And this proved to be no exception.

"What is it?"

"The press. I know you wanted to keep them in the dark, but they're already camping outside Gina's place, desperate to figure out what's going on. There are only a few smaller outlets for now, and the deputies are keeping them at bay, but with the fire happening so close to the murder..." McVeigh's sentence trailed off.

"What about it?"

"I mean, I think it's only a matter of time before they start piecing things together."

Steve's eyes narrowed.

"Piecing what things together?"

"I mean, the fact that... that, uhh, everything is, you know—"

"Just spit it out."

McVeigh cleared his throat.

"That everything is related to Detective Shade. And, given the interview and the high-profile nature of *Marlowe*, there will come a time very soon when we won't have a choice but to address the media."

Steve was surprised that McVeigh had linked things as quickly as he had. But then he remembered the deputy's aspirations. It made sense that he would be all over this. Especially with *Marlowe's* involvement.

...we won't have a choice but to address the media.

We or *I*, McVeigh?

Sheriff Burns felt the urge not just to chastise his Chief Deputy, but to physically throttle him.

Six months ago, Steve had marveled at the man's ability to work the press and relied on him to help navigate Bear County's political landscape. He'd admired the man's ambition, as well.

But that was before Deputy Marcus McVeigh had put lives in danger just to boost his own stock. And that was unacceptable.

But Steve held his tongue.

There was something else that he needed to consider: a video. A video of him stealing out of the evidence locker.

In the end, it was Steve who elected to play politician.

"For now, we have no definitive evidence that this is in any way linked to Detective Shade. As for the media involvement, I will stress that there is a gag order in place. And I mean what I said, deputy: if anyone speaks out, I will make sure they never work in Bear County again. No matter the personal cost."

"I understand." McVeigh was all professional, now. "I'll keep the files at the scene as requested, Sheriff. I'll also reiterate your gag order to the other deputies."

Steve couldn't help but read into the man's words: *your* gag order.

Maybe it was a slip of the tongue, but he didn't think so. McVeigh was too smart for slips of the tongue. Everything the man did and said had a purpose. And his purpose here was clear: if this went south, it was the sheriff's decision; he was the captain, and he would go down with the ship.

"Keep in touch."

Steve hung up the phone and instinctively reached into his pocket.

He was shocked to discover that it was empty. There were no pills left.

I couldn't have possibly taken them all. Did I leave them somewhere?

No, that didn't make sense.

Then where the fuck are they?

Just the idea of not having any left was enough to make him break out into a cold sweat.

Steve walked back to the main hallway and grabbed the first person he saw.

A nurse.

"Excuse me, is Dr. Kinkaid in today?"

Dr. Kinkaid had been the doctor who had stitched and stapled him up after the bear attack. He'd also prescribed him the Oxy.

When Steve had initially run out of pills, he'd asked Dr. Kinkaid for a renewal. It had been granted... once. At the time, he'd said it was the last refill, but if Dr. Kinkaid saw him now, saw the shape he was in, the *pain* he was in?

The doctor would have to renew his 'script. He'd have no choice.

"I'm sorry, but Dr. Kinkaid won't be in this week."

"This week?" Steve licked his tacky lips. "What do you mean?"

The nurse eyed him suspiciously. Steve presumed that if it hadn't been for the gold star on his chest this would be the point where the nurse would consider, at least in the back of her mind, the idea of contacting security.

"I'm sorry, but he's not on rotation this week. If you need to reach him, you should try him at his clinic."

"Thanks," Steve grumbled.

"Not a problem, Sheriff."

He didn't even wait for her to be out of earshot before calling Dr. Kinkaid's number.

"Dr. Kincaid's office, how may I help you?" a cheery woman answered on the second ring.

"This is Sheriff Steve Burns, I'm a—*uhh*—patient of Dr. Kinkaid's. Would I be able to speak to him?"

"Hello, Sheriff. Unfortunately, Dr. Kinkaid isn't in at the moment."

"Really? Where is he?" Again, too sharp, too desperate.

"I'm... I'm sorry, he's unavailable. Would you like me to book you an appointment? Alternatively, if this is an emergency, you can always—"

"Appointment, yeah," he said dryly.

"Alright, just give me a moment, please."

The woman typed enough keys that she could have completed the next George R.R. Martin novel.

"How does Friday sound?"

"Friday?" Steve blurted.

More obnoxious typing.

The sheriff's cold sweat became an icy deluge. It was Monday, and he still had maybe a half-dozen stolen pills left. Popping them like PEZ the way he was, however? There was no possible way his supply would last until Friday.

"Sheriff, I can probably squeeze you in Thursday evening? Dr. Kincaid's schedule is very, very busy this week."

"Are you sure you can't get anything sooner? Like tonight or tomorrow?"

"That would be impossible, unfortunately, as Dr. Kinkaid isn't in the city until Wednesday. I'm afraid that Thursday evening is the earliest available time slot. Would you like me to book it for you?"

"Yes." After a second Steve added, "Please."

The secretary completed the epilogue.

"Okay, Sheriff Burns, you're all set for Thursday at 6:30. I'll see you then."

Steve hung up and then looked around.

Maybe there's someone here I can talk to, someone reasonable who can look at my chart and see that I was attacked by a fucking Black Bear. Someone who—

"Sheriff?"

He whipped around.

Detective Freddie Furlow approached, his wide hips barely clearing an empty gurney pressed against one wall. He looked absolutely terrible, which was saying something because Freddie rarely looked healthy.

"Detective Furlow, thanks for coming."

"Just Fred. Listen, I heard about what happened at the interview. I just wanted to apologize for not being there. And I should have been with her this afternoon, as well."

"It's my fault," Steve said, surprising himself at how easily the admission came. He only really knew Freddie in a professional capacity, and even that was limited, but what he saw, he liked. And Veronica couldn't speak more highly of her partner. "I should have stopped her. I should have told her not to go on the fucking show."

Freddie offered a half-grin.

"Good luck with that—telling Veronica what she can or can't do." The big man sighed, and his smile vanished. "It's not your fault, Sheriff. It's not her fault either."

While Steve might not be politically motivated, he was good at reading between the lines. They both knew that Veronica would blame herself for what happened to Gina and Cole.

And guilt was a dangerous companion, worse than even the Devil whispering in your ear. Guilt made you do things, irrational things, but guilt was a greedy bastard, and its hunger could never be satisfied.

"I know. I know. How is she?"

"Physically?"

Steve nodded.

"She's okay. Already wants to leave."

"Sound like her—sounds like mentally she's all right, too."

Freddie's blank stare suggested he thought differently.

"I think it's best if she stays here for a little bit."

"I agree."

Here, they could station officers outside Veronica's door. There were also cameras everywhere in the hospital and if the psychopath on the phone came in, they'd grab him.

But, deep down, both men knew that they needed something considerably stronger than rational thought to keep Veronica in one place.

Like heavy-duty handcuffs.

And so long as Dr. Jane Bernard was still out there, that the madman still held her captive, and there was a hope, however slim, that she was still alive, even shackles wouldn't be able to keep Veronica from looking for her.

Chapter 34

THERE WERE FOUR OF THEM in the room now: Veronica, Steve, Peter, and Freddie.

They were the most important people in Veronica's life. Sometimes, they were the only people.

And they were all parroting the same party line: rest—stay in bed and rest. If it had only been Steve, she would have just shut this down with a look. With Freddie, she would've bribed him with a double cheeseburger from Daphne's.

Her dad? He was probably the easiest. She would just wait for him to sneak out for "fresh air" before leaving herself.

But the three of them? Veronica couldn't argue with them all at the same time. With no other choice, Veronica reluctantly agreed to stay in bed.

What she was unwilling to negotiate on was being kept apprised of the case. As far as Veronica was concerned, and at the risk of once again sounding self-centered and vain, she *was* the case.

These weren't random acts of violence or a thrill seeker with a type. This was a madman obsessed with her, and hellbent on hurting those around her.

The reason—unknown—was irrelevant.

Steve and Freddie realized this, and perhaps her father did, too. Yet, despite the stakes, they were still treating her with kid gloves. They'd collectively done this once before, and Veronica hadn't liked it then. Now, even after she'd proven capable, after she'd put a bullet in the dollmaker's head, they were doing it again.

Veronica liked it less now.

At least they were willing to share their theories, but Veronica felt an inkling of being placated rather than included.

"This whole thing began with the talk show?" her father asked.

Veronica didn't want to talk about her synesthesia—she'd explained everything as best she could to her dad and Steve and it was clear from her very brief conversation with Freddie that someone—probably Peter—had at least touched on it with him, but it was unavoidable.

"Before—it had to be before," Veronica corrected. "Someone had to know about my… past… and they had to be following me this morning to see me interact with Gina. Then—"

"They found your fingerprints on a pen in her pocket," Steve interrupted.

Veronica was about to say that makes sense, that she used a pen to take out the book for him when she hesitated.

It didn't make sense, not really.

"I—I signed a book out this morning. But the pen I used," Veronica thought hard, making sure that she was certain that what she was going to say next was accurate, "was the kind attached with a beaded chain. You know, the kind they use at banks?"

"Which meant that someone had to see you use it and then pick it up," Freddie offered. "Did you notice anyone there with you?"

Veronica shook her head.

"I told Steve earlier that I think there was a guy there. A guy with dark hair, but I can't be sure. I was… tired and anxious. It was before the interview."

"He's trying to frame you, then," Peter said in his trademarked no bullshit manner.

All eyes were on the ex-police captain, and continuing in typical Peter Shade style, he didn't feel the need to explain something that was self-explanatory.

"Weak," Steve remarked with a shrug. "She was at the show with me. Live on TV when Gina was murdered."

Except...

"With all that paint, I bet it messes with being able to determine the exact time of death," Veronica said. "And, besides, whoever killed her could have waited until the show was over to do it."

The men didn't know about her rushing off to visit Ken Cameron in prison after being called into Chief Bottel's office, which would be more than serviceable as an alibi: Bear County Correction would have a video of her session with the convict.

For reasons Veronica didn't completely understand, however, she was inclined to keep them in the dark about this for the time being.

"It doesn't matter why right now, so long as we can all agree on the link between the victims. The reality is the only way our unsub could have gotten this information was from Dr. Bernard." Out of the corner of her eye, Veronica saw her dad open his mouth, but she continued quickly before he could interrupt. "And there's no way that she would have voluntarily divulged any information. Which means—"

"What if it's *her*?" Freddie suggested.

Veronica couldn't tell if he was being serious or not.

"You can't—"

Freddie interrupted the sheriff.

"No, I don't think so, not really—Dr. Bernard has worked with Greenham PD for years. But allow me to play devil's advocate: she had intimate knowledge of your disease—"

"Condition," Veronica corrected.

"Right, sorry, condition. She also knew about the interview and when it was going to happen. Cole is kidnapped at her office, which was set on fire, and then she suddenly goes missing."

"Without her cell phone or car?" Steve asked.

Freddie had an answer for that, too.

"Could all be staged for it to look like she was taken, like she's one of the victims, and not the one responsible for the taking."

"Cole said it was a man who hit him on the head," Steve countered.

"Right, but he was *hit on the head*. He could be wrong or maybe Dr. Bernard hired someone. We made the mistake before of thinking that it could only have been a man responsible for everything."

A sobering thought.

"Does she have a white car?"

"An old beater? I don't know—I doubt it, but she has the means to acquire one," Freddie answered with a shrug.

"No," Peter said flatly. While his eyes lacked the gold flecks that Veronica's had, they seemed to glow with intensity. "This is impossible—Jane was with me all morning."

Silence.

Then Freddie nodded.

"I was just throwing it out there."

More silence, this time pregnant with a question. For all their machismo, the three alphas in the room were too scared to ask it, so it was on Veronica to pose the question herself.

"Who has it out for me bad enough to kill, right? That's what you guys are wondering?"

None of the men disagreed with her.

"Well, let me see: there's Ken Cameron, but he's behind bars." She got this out of the way first, and fast. "Then there's my brother, but he's dead. Matthew 'Collard' Barnaby and his pal Devon? Maybe. But like Ken, both are in jail. Same for the shady lawyer Peter O'Keefe."

"There's also Alfred Cohen to consider," Freddie said, referring to the young man whose father had commissioned him to knock over his own jewelry store in an elaborate insurance/jewelry heist fraud.

"Also in prison. Doesn't get out for a few weeks."

Everyone looked at Peter.

Veronica was surprised that her father knew this off the top of his head, although she knew she shouldn't be. Retired or not, he was still a cop.

And he was still her dad.

"Wait—what do you mean a few weeks?" Freddie asked, incredulous.

"That's all he's got left. Will be let out in less than a month on good behavior."

"What kind of fucking deal is that?" Freddie snapped. "What about his father, then? The man behind the entire scam?"

"Matthew Cohen is a fat, balding hobbit," Veronica said, not mincing words. "Gina Braden was an active Cross Fitter. No way he overpowers her."

"True."

"What about Gordon Trammel?" Steve asked.

Somehow, Veronica had forgotten about him. The sad, pathetic man who, although he didn't actually kill anyone, helped and was complicit in his wife murdering three innocent women just for looking at him.

Then he'd posed the bodies at her request.

What was even more disgusting, was the fact that they'd used their six-year-old daughter to get the women to stop on the deserted road late at night.

"Last I heard, he is pretty much catatonic. Doesn't say anything. Refuses to eat—need to give him food via gavage." Peter again.

So, that's that.

In the context of finding out who was behind this, it felt like a short list. But there were still more than a handful of people who hated Veronica enough to kill to get her attention.

And that was a handful too many.

"I'll have some of my men look into each one of these potential suspects, see if they can trace their movements earlier in the day," Steve said. "A long shot, but you never know."

"Anyone else you can think of?" Peter asked her directly.

Veronica shook her head.

Feeling the mood shift, Freddie brought the focus back.

"Let's not get too caught up on motive. In my experience, motive can be used as a retrospective justification as much as it can a driving factor. We need to figure *how* this person found out about Veronica's past, then we'll understand the *why*."

Veronica couldn't agree more. She'd tried to steer their conversation in this direction earlier, but she'd lacked her partner's way with words.

"Which brings us back to why we were headed to Dr. Bernard's office in the first place," Steve said. "The doctor's personal files. I just spoke to Deputy McVeigh, and he said that they were all intact. I've told him to keep them there for now."

"They were near the wall where the fire started," Veronica remarked. "It could just be a coincidence, but maybe he meant for them to burn with Cole."

The words were a struggle to get out.

Burn with Cole...

Veronica shuddered and rubbed her palms together.

"Maybe—if they are that important," Steve looked at Veronica, "or if there is something in there that can lead us to this guy, he might come back for them. Bear County and Greenham PD are watching the place now but it would probably be safer to have them in evidence. Problem with that is that press is lurking. More officers, and deputies, more of a risk of something getting out sooner, rather than later."

"What if we moved the files to Matheson instead of Greenham?" Freddie put forth.

"What do you mean?"

"Well, I agree that if we ship them to Greenham, people are going to notice. But if we can ship them to the next county over, to Matheson, they might not pay as much attention. Might slip through the cracks. I'm pretty tight with some of the guys over there, but I'm sure you—" Freddie indicated the sheriff, "—would have no problem getting them to hold on to the evidence for a while, at least."

"Might be a good idea," Steve agreed. "As for actually being able to look at the files, that's a different story. I'll try to get a warrant, but no guarantees even with Dr. Bernard missing."

"I'll go with you," Veronica said.

"No," all three men replied at the same time.

Steve followed this up with a much softer, "You stay and rest. I'll keep you in the loop, promise. I'll also have two deputies stationed outside your door at all times."

The expression on the sheriff's face suggested that he expected her to protest, but Veronica, having already concluded that such a venture was a lost cause, didn't argue.

Instead, she said, "It's you guys who need to be careful. He's out to kill those around me, not hurt me directly."

For now.

But deep down, Veronica knew that this revolved around her. And that meant, eventually, he would come for her.

Seven, eight, I've sealed your fate.

Chapter 35

Even though Veronica had declined any sort of sedative, after being left alone in the room she felt so tired that she considered that someone, probably the nurse with the clipboard, had slipped something into her IV anyway.

But despite her exhaustion, Veronica's sleep was fitful. Every time she felt herself relaxing, flashes of fire, of a yo-yo, pieces of her tumultuous past pulled her back to wakefulness.

After close to three hours of just lying there, repeatedly shutting her eyes and then opening them again to vanquish a swelling nightmare, Veronica gave up all hope of sleep.

She inhaled deeply and rolled onto her back. The smell of acrid smoke and the sweet flavor of gasoline filled her nose and throat. Before the men had left, she'd told them to be careful, that the psychopath was out to hurt them and not her. Despite the fire that had come close to causing her serious damage, Veronica believed that it had been a tactic to mess with her synesthesia, not to kill her—just like the paint at Gina's house. How could she smell a liar if her senses were constantly bombarded with the scent of gasoline?

Whoever was behind this was trying to level the playing field.

But for what?

Driven by frustration, Veronica rose out of the hospital bed. She stretched her legs and back, which were sore from kicking doors and dragging bodies.

Gripping the IV stand in one hand, she slowly walked to the door, every step lubricating her joints.

As per Steve's promise, two deputies sat just outside her room. One appeared to have dozed off, the other impossibly alert as if he were protecting the president from an imminent assassination plot. It was almost comical the way the man's dark eyes roved up and down the hallway.

Veronica recognized neither man, which she suspected had been deliberate. Someone like Deputy McVeigh or Lancaster, someone she'd interacted with in the past, would have been easier to negotiate with.

But regardless of their presence, Veronica wasn't a prisoner here—or, at least, she didn't think she was. She also wasn't naive. If she left the hospital, the first thing that one or both of these deputies would do was call the sheriff. Then he'd drop everything and come to try and convince her to remain in her room.

Sheriff Burns needed to be out there looking for Dr. Bernard, not babysitting Veronica.

It was more than that, though. As much as it pained Veronica to admit it, she was feeling increasingly uncomfortable around Steve. Lately, he'd been agitated, likely from the lack of sleep caused by the nightmares he lied about remembering. When Veronica had first met the man, he'd been rational and calculated, but also a little shy and uncertain. All endearing qualities that had attracted her to him in the first place.

Now, these characteristics were but a shadow cast at dusk: weak, and barely present.

Veronica backed away from the door and found her clothes on a chair beside the bed. The nurse must have put them there because they were neatly folded; she'd seen Steve fold before, which could be best described as a modified roll.

The thought nearly made her smile.

The first thing Veronica did was pull the IV out of the back of her hand. The next, after a glance to make sure that the deputies weren't looking into her room, was to remove her hospital gown.

Veronica had lost weight since the incident at the Trammel house. Her breasts were no longer as full, and her hips were narrower. Her body was still toned, but some of the softer bits that she liked, which contributed to a womanly figure, were gone. Had this been a deliberate effort, she would have no doubt been satisfied with the results. But the fact that Veronica had been less active as of late—she couldn't remember the last time she'd gone for a run or hit the gym—was somewhat alarming.

Something to consider later when this was all over.

Veronica slipped her clothes on, scrunching her nose to avoid breathing in too much of the intense smell of fire that had penetrated deeply into the fabric. She put the hospital gown on top, cinching it tight around the waist.

The door to her room wasn't locked, but the second she opened it, the alert deputy practically leaped to his feet and looked at her, stopping just shy of a salute.

"Detective Shade. Sheriff Burns instructed me to—"

"Relax, I'm not going anywhere." Veronica glanced up the hallway. "Not going far, anyway. I just want to go see Cole Batherson."

The man appeared confused.

"You know, the man who was brought in with me? The one in the fire?"

The deputy made a movement that could have been construed as a nod.

"Right... he's, uhh, he's just down the hall. Room 212, I think?"

And just like that, the man had inadvertently given her the opening she'd sought.

"I just want to see how he's doing."

"I-I don't know." The deputy scratched his chin. "Sheriff Burns—"

"What do you mean, you don't know? Are you arresting me or something?"

He scoffed.

"No, of course not, it's just—"

"Where do you think I'm going to go in this?" she said, tugging on the front of her hospital gown.

The deputy reached for the radio on his shoulder.

"Maybe I should just check—"

"I don't want to worry the sheriff." Veronica's eyes darted to the man's silver name tag. "Deputy Edgerton, I just want to see if he's okay. I don't know what the sheriff told you, but Cole was nearly burned alive because of me." She paused. "All right? Just down the hall. You can watch me." The deputy didn't say yes, but he didn't say no either. "I just want to see if he's okay."

Veronica started to walk, playing up her stiff muscles so as to not alarm the deputy.

234, 233, 230.

She scanned the room numbers as she passed them, her mind still trying to work out who might be behind this.

228, 226, 224, 222.

Could it be a cop?

220, 218, 216.

Was it another Ken Cameron, pissed off because of her promotion?

Veronica didn't think so—maybe six months ago, but now, after nearly a year, her becoming a detective was old news. Someone jealous of the media attention that she'd gotten as a result of killing the dollmaker?

Laughable, considering how things had gone.

Then who?

214, 212, 210.

Veronica found Cole Batherson in room 210. His appearance was startling, and even though she knew that Deputy Edgerton was staring at her, she couldn't help but cover her mouth with her hand and tense her shoulders.

Cole was lying on his back, his eyes closed. Someone had cleaned his face, but there were dark streaks under his square jaw and chin. Some of his hair had been singed on his left temple, giving him a lopsided appearance. Without the fancy shoes and shirt, and with something of a five o'clock shadow, or residual soot, it was impossible to tell which, Cole looked rugged and oddly handsome.

Every time she'd met Cole, it had been at the precinct and there, he'd been more of a thing than a person—an IA Officer instead of Cole. But here, in the hospital, completely disarmed and vulnerable, Veronica saw the man in a different light.

He *was* handsome, she realized. Dark features, good skin. On the thinner side, but that was the trend for people their age.

As if sensing that he was being watched, Cole stirred. Veronica felt a little heat in her cheeks, and she quickly entered the room. In response to the sound of the door closing behind her, Cole's forehead wrinkled, and his eyes opened.

"Bad dream?" she asked as she approached his bed.

"Veronica." He said with a dry cough. "Thank you."

This was unexpected and Veronica couldn't think of what to say. But being speechless didn't explain what she did next. Later, after replaying this event in her mind a dozen times, Veronica would come to the conclusion that her actions weren't about Cole but her brother. That Cole Batherson served as a surrogate for Benny Davis, that Veronica had been overwhelmed by the realization that while she'd saved Cole from a fire, she'd failed to do so with Benny… twice.

But in the moment, it just felt right.

Veronica leaned down and kissed the man on the forehead. His skin was warm on her lips.

Realizing what she'd just done, Veronica pulled back, heat rising in her own face. Cole could have made this incredibly uncomfortable, which it should have been, given the odd circumstances, but he didn't. If anything, he looked appreciative of her affection. Not in a sexual way, but innocently, like a child leaning into a hug from his mother, or, in this case, a kiss.

Absurd, given that they were around the same age, but the idea refused to let go.

During her short hospital stay, four people visited Veronica, and someone cared enough about her to station two more outside her door. She had no idea how many had come to see Cole, but something about his wide-eyed expression, a doughiness to his otherwise hard features, suggested that the number, if not zero, was close to it.

And this made her sad.

Being an internal affairs officer was a lot like being a confidential informant: necessary, but loathed.

Confidential informant... this idea stuck in her head.

"Thank you," Cole said again, although this time it wasn't clear whether he was referring to the kiss or the fact that she'd saved his life.

Veronica got the impression it was both.

She cleared her throat and swallowed the urge to apologize for what happened. The man had effectively bypassed this stage by thanking her preemptively.

"Cole, why were you at Dr. Bernard's office?" Veronica softened her voice, trying to sound more curious than accusatory.

"I was looking—" Cole stopped himself, but it was too late. Veronica knew what he was going to say.

I was looking for you.
She nodded in understanding.
Of course, he was. Because he was trying to do his job, to write a New York Times article about her, of all things. The reason Cole was averse to saying as much was two-fold: he knew how she felt about the article, and he didn't want to make her feel any more guilty about what happened than she already did.

"I never saw the person who hit me. The door was open, and I heard a woman speaking, arguing with someone." The man looked skyward. "Fuck, I'm so stupid."

Veronica had the sudden urge to kiss Cole again, but not on the forehead, this time.

What is wrong with me?

She felt the urge to lean toward the man, so she forced herself to do the opposite.

"Did you… did you see Dr. Bernard?"

"I think so—woman with a bob haircut, small glasses, pointy nose?" Veronica nodded. It was an apt description of her longtime psychiatrist. "Yeah, she was there. I walked into the room, and before I could say anything, a man hit me on the back of the head."

"A man?"

Cole scrunched up his face, and then winced and relaxed.

"Yeah, it was a man's voice."

"And you didn't see him?"

The man lowered his eyes in shame.

"No. I only saw Dr. Bernard and then everything went black. I woke up tied in a broom closet. You know the rest."

When Cole closed his eyes, Veronica felt herself moving forward again. The urge to kiss him was almost unbearable. And she would have, there was no doubt she would have, but then she remembered something, and the spell was broken.

"Why was my dad fired?" she asked, her voice still mellow. "It wasn't because he missed the meeting with the mayor, was it?"

Deep down, she'd always known that this wasn't the case. Veronica had only met the mayor once before, and then only in passing. But by all accounts, the longtime incumbent Tom Dixon wasn't so petty that he would fire the police captain for being late to a meeting, no matter the reason.

"I didn't—" Cole stopped himself. "I was just doing my job."

Because of the pervasive smell of gasoline on her clothes, in her nose, and in the room, Veronica was unable to use her synesthesia to tell if Cole was lying.

But she knew he was.

"Well, your—"

A phone buzzed, thankfully cutting Veronica off before she said something she was bound to regret. Like hers, Cole's clothes were folded neatly on his chair—*See? It was the nurse*—and his phone was sitting on top of it.

It was dark and silent.

Veronica felt as well as heard the second buzz.

It was coming from the pocket of her pants—no one had bothered to remove it after the fire. It was no easy task to remove it from her pocket with the gown over top, but Veronica was successful before the fourth ring.

The number was unlisted.

One, two…

Veronica's breathing became shallow, and she answered with a shaky finger.

"Hello?"

"This is a collect call from Bear County Correctional. Inmate—" the recording paused, and a familiar voice spoke, "Ken Cameron."

The recording came back on, but Veronica was already saying, "Accept."

"Thank you. Your call is now connected."

Recognizing the change in her demeanor, Cole shifted in his bed, preparing to get up. Veronica indicated for him to remain put.

"What the hell do you—"

"Five, six." Ken's voice was timid, wavering. "I crossed the River Styx."

"Ken? *Ken?*"

The line had gone dead.

"*Ken!*"

"Is everything—" Cole coughed. "—is everything all right?"

"No," Veronica said in a gasp, "I have to—I have to go. I have to go, *now*."

"What's going on?"

Veronica didn't answer. She walked to the door, peeling off her hospital gown as she went. In the hallway, she dropped it to the tiled ground and broke into a jog.

"Detective Shade?" Deputy Edgerton shouted. This was followed by a curse. "*Detective Shade!*"

Chapter 36

THREE DOCTORS... ON THE WAY out of the hospital, Sheriff Steve Burns approached three different doctors for an Oxycontin refill. The first two were suddenly too busy to speak to him, even though they'd been sipping coffee and chatting moments before, while the third politely informed him that he should see his regular doctor and that he didn't feel comfortable prescribing anything without a full examination.

Steve returned to the building that housed Dr. Bernard's office empty-handed. He still had a number of pills left, but this was a finite supply, and his main concern was what would happen when they ran out. It wasn't just too risky to steal from the evidence locker again, it was downright suicidal. Someone already had a video of him stealing pills, a video that could not only end his career but put him in jail. For whatever reason, it hadn't surfaced yet, but Steve wasn't so disillusioned that he thought it was gone.

It would surface—it was just a matter of time.

And this realization nagged at him, gnawed at the back of his mind. If it hadn't been for the fact that there was a psycho out there stalking Veronica, most, if not all, of his mental bandwidth would have been exhausted figuring out a solution to this disaster of a problem. What was left of his energy would have been spent figuring out how to get more.

There was a loud bang and one of his deputies cursed.

"Don't damage them," the sheriff shouted.

"Sorry, it slipped," the deputy yelled back. He bent his knees and grabbed the corner of one of the cabinets. With a grunt he lifted and then the two deputies walked it up the ramp and into the back of the cargo van.

To make them easier to move, CSU had separated the locker-style cabinets into their initial units: four, three-and-a-half-foot-tall metal containers. And yet, his deputies still had a hard time huffing them into the van. Based on the way they struggled, Steve suspected that each one, full of files, weighed upwards of a hundred pounds.

"Just be careful!"

They were already dented and banged up from when Veronica had pulled them off the wall, but he didn't want to risk destroying their contents.

He also didn't want to attract any more attention to what they were doing. Unlike at Gina's house, the sheriff couldn't blanket the entire building in tarps. The fire had drawn eyes and the police presence had drawn cameras. But, as of now, those with the cameras were civilians. When people started linking the crimes together, however, this would change. Cell phones would be replaced by much larger devices that would be accompanied by annoying talking heads with microphones.

Like Marlowe...

Steve suddenly remembered what the woman with the thick glasses—Dahlia—had told him when he'd asked for the entire telephone recording.

The ratings were so good today that Marlowe decided to skip the scheduled guest and do a special feature on synesthesia instead.

Marlowe didn't strike the sheriff as a research-heavy production, but all it would take was an overzealous assistant to come looking for a comment from Veronica to find out she was in the hospital.

Then it was just a simple connect the dots.

If there was a way to stop her from going forward with her plan, Sheriff Burns would have. But that, like acquiring another 'script, was out of his control.

A Greenham PD police car, with sirens blaring and lights flashing, pulled into the parking lot. Steve was about to tear a strip off the cop behind the wheel—he'd given explicit instructions, to both his men and Greenham PD, to keep the scene locked down but visible police presence to a minimum—until he saw who got out of the passenger seat.

Bald, mustachioed, and sporting wire-frame glasses, the City of Greenham PD's new captain was like a comical opposite version of the man who had previously held the post. But while they couldn't have looked more different, both men had an air of confidence and a presence that demanded respect.

The man immediately spotted the sheriff and walked over.

"Captain Bottel," he said in a surprisingly baritone voice. He held his hand out.

"Sheriff Steve Burns."

"It's too bad that we had to meet under these circumstances. Even though I'm relatively new here, by all accounts, Dr. Jane Bernard has done great work for the City of Greenham over the years."

The sheriff wasn't sure he liked the way the captain spoke of the woman. It was as if he already considered her dead. And that, in turn, made him question whether or not he should feel the same way. After all, their unsub had already proven that he was capable of murder.

He'd killed Gina and tried to kill Cole... what was stopping him from taking the psychiatrist's life?

A metallic bang ceased this train of thought.

"God dammit, I told you to be careful with those!" he shouted. The sound had come from inside the cube van and no deputy was brave enough to show his face. He turned back to the captain and offered an explanation. "We're trying to keep media involvement to a minimum—I'm shipping the evidence from Dr. Bernard's office to Matheson."

The captain nodded in agreement, but his expression suggested that this was simply a stopgap measure, that the media would be here soon enough.

Yeah, and whose fault is that? The sheriff thought. *Yours, that's who. You were the one who encouraged Veronica to go on that stupid show.*

Normally, Steve wasn't one to become agitated so easily, but today was different. Today, everything annoyed him.

Even Captain Bottel's rust-colored mustache was irritating.

"I just want to make sure that when the media does come calling, we keep yours and Detective Shade's relationship out of the investigation."

The frankness, the sheer bluntness of the comment surprised Steve.

And then it angered him.

"That's my business," he snapped. "All I care about is finding Dr. Bernard. Nothing else matters. Greenham PD politics," Steve replaced the *c* in 'politics' with two *k*s, "are of no interest to me."

The sheriff fell just short of directly saying that this should be the captain's objective, as well. He felt as if he'd gotten his point across already.

And what Bottel said next made it clear that he'd picked up this insinuation.

"That is our primary focus. But for the sake of a potential trial, I think it's best if your involvement in the case is limited. Conflict of interest and all that."

Steve glared at the man. His relationship with Peter Shade meant that he would be, at the bare minimum, reserved when it came to the new captain. But considering that they were destined to work together on Greenham cases moving forward, he'd envisioned a much more amicable greeting and subsequent relationship.

"What are you saying?"

Technically, Sheriff Burns had authority here—he *was* the authority when it came to anything that happened within his county, of which Greenham was a part, but never did he think he would have to use it to suppress a police captain.

But he was coming close to doing that now.

"I'm just saying that we need to be careful, is all."

What happened to your bluntness now, Captain Bottel?

"She's going to be fine, by the way," Steve snapped, annoyed that the man hadn't even asked about how his detective was faring. "Just a little smoke inhalation."

"I know."

Steve clenched his jaw. He couldn't help but feel that the man was deliberately trying to get on his nerves now.

"Captain," a voice said from the darkness.

Even though Steve couldn't make out their features, the outlines of the two big men who approached were unmistakable.

Peter Shade and Detective Freddie Furlow.

Captain Bottel recognized them as well—at least the former.

"Peter? This is a crime scene and—"

"I was with him when I got the call," Freddie lied. "Came straight here."

The captain bristled his mustache, but to preemptively stop any further comment, Steve made sure to stand beside Peter, a silent, and more than a little petty indication of an alliance.

Maybe a reminder, too, that they had one collective goal here: to find Dr. Jane Bernard. They didn't have time for anything else.

Steve waited for Captain Bottel to say something but after a few seconds of silence, it became apparent that the man had swallowed his pride.

"Good. In terms of an update, one of my deputies managed to obtain security footage from a local hardware store," Sheriff Burns said, recounting the information that his deputy had shared with him on the way from the hospital back to the crime scene. "Gina Braden was alone in the store when she purchased the paint."

"Alone?" Freddie asked, eyebrow raised.

"Alone in the store," Steve confirmed, "but not in the parking lot."

"The white car."

"Yep, unfortunately, no images of the driver, but now we have a make: Mazda 3, between 2004 and 2009."

"How did she look in the video?" Freddie asked.

"I haven't seen it, but my deputy says she looks calm."

"Gina must have known him, then. Either that or—"

Steve's radio squelched and he excused himself.

"Sheriff Burns?"

He recognized Deputy Edgerton's voice. The man sounded agitated.

"Yeah?"

"It's Detective Shade."

Steve's heart skipped a beat. He'd taken but two steps back from the group of men and upon hearing Veronica's name they'd stopped talking.

"Wh-what-what about her?"

"She's... she's gone."

Sheriff Burns nearly staggered. When he'd left the hospital no more than an hour ago, she'd been fine. Tired, in shock, maybe, but physically fine.

"What?" he gasped.

"Yeah, she took off. She went to go see the guy from the fire? The internal affairs guy? Then she just ran. The IA guy said she got a call but didn't know what it was about."

Blood flooded the sheriff's system, causing his extremities to tingle.

She's... she's gone.

He cursed under his breath and did his best to collect himself.

"Any idea where she went?"

"No, I'm sorry, but I didn't know what to do."

"Sheriff Burns, over and out."

There was no need to explain anything; the captain, Peter, and Freddie had heard it all. Deep down, none of them were surprised that Veronica hadn't heeded their instructions to stay put.

She was too stubborn for that. And Steve didn't expect Deputy Edgerton to physically stop her from leaving—he probably would have gotten his ass kicked if he'd tried. But the man should have had enough common sense to at least follow the detective.

Steve cursed again and then his radio squelched a second time. He answered it immediately, expecting to hear Deputy Edgerton's voice and hoping that he would say that he'd made a mistake, that Veronica was sleeping peacefully in her hospital room.

He was wrong on both accounts—it wasn't even Deputy Edgerton.

"What?"

"Sheriff Burns, it's Deputy Carter."

Once more, eyes bored into him.

Deputy Carter... Deputy Carter...

It took Sheriff Burns a few seconds to put a face to the name.

"Go ahead."

"We've got a situation at Bear County Correctional that requires your attention."

"Situation? What kind of situation?" Steve asked quickly, preparing to tell the deputy to take care of it, that they had more important things to deal with right now.

Once again, Sheriff Steve Burns was wrong.

"It's Ken Cameron, sir. He's dead."

Chapter 37

FIVE, SIX. I CROSSED THE River Styx.

Veronica elected to take an Uber to Bear County Correctional. Her car was back at Dr. Jane Bernard's office and her first instinct was to get the driver to take her there to retrieve it. But while she'd snuck away from two deputies in the hospital, the sheriff and perhaps even Freddie, were likely to have returned to the site of the fire. Getting away from them would prove considerably more difficult.

There was no satisfaction in being vindicated, in having her initial suspicion that Ken Cameron was behind this coming true.

For one, it reinforced the idea that her synesthesia wasn't infallible. She'd sat across from Ken and when he'd admitted to calling *Marlowe* and she had been convinced that he was lying.

Second, considering that the ex-cop was locked up this entire time, it raised the question of who he was using to perform his dirty work on the outside.

"You want me to wait here?" the driver asked.

Veronica looked at the prison. It was well past visiting hours now, but she thought she could once again leverage her relationship with Steve to get inside.

What Veronica planned on doing once in Ken's presence was another question entirely.

"No, I'm good. Thanks."

Veronica exited the vehicle and hurried up to the gates. As expected, her badge got her through the front doors. Unfortunately, that's where her progress ended. The prison seemed to be on some sort of lockdown.

"What's going on?" Veronica asked the first deputy she saw. She was hoping that she'd encounter the same man as before, the one with the gray hair and wide eyes, but that wasn't the case.

The much younger deputy pursed his lips and indicated in no uncertain terms that visiting hours were over and that she was to leave now.

Veronica once again pulled out her badge.

"My name's Detective Shade with the Greenham PD."

The deputy was unimpressed.

"Bear County employees only past this point. After the lockdown, you can return and—"

"Veronica?" She turned in response to her name and saw Kristin Newberry starting her way. The gray-haired woman was wearing her coroner's jacket and looked exhausted. "I didn't expect to see you here."

Likewise.

Kristin Newberry only showed up when there was a body.

"Who died?"

Kristin shrugged.

"Not sure, just got here."

Breathing heavily, Veronica asked the same question to the deputy who had stopped her.

The man's upper lip curled.

"Like I said before, you can't be in here. Now, would you please leave the premises?"

"Was it Ken? Tell me it wasn't Ken Cameron."

"That's it, you're trespassing."

The deputy reached for her arm and Veronica recoiled.

"I wouldn't—" Kristin started, but she was interrupted.

"Deputy Hill, stand down. Do not touch her."

The deputy froze and Veronica turned to see Sheriff Steve Burns coming toward her.

"Sheriff, she's with Greenham PD and we're on lockdown so—"

"What were you going to do, Deputy? Arrest her? Throw her in jail?"

"She was trespassing, and I was trying—"

"Why don't you go on break."

Deputy Hill's eyes darted to Veronica.

"It's-it's lockdown. Everyone—"

"Go on break, now, Deputy Hill."

Great, that's all I need, Veronica thought as the deputy stormed off following an angry glare, *another enemy.*

"Detective Shade is my guest. She's welcome here," Steve said to anyone who would listen. He was all business now. "Kristin."

The coroner nodded at him.

"We have to stop meeting like this, Sheriff."

"I wish."

"Sheriff? If you'd follow me, I'll take you to the body."

Now, it was the deputy who had greeted Veronica the last time she'd been here—too late, of course.

Please don't recognize me.

Their eyes met.

"Detective Shade, nice to see you again. I have those phone records for you."

Shit.

Steve might not have been himself lately, but he wasn't so far gone that he didn't pick up on this. But before the sheriff could ask what she'd been doing here, and, perhaps, what she *was* doing here, the deputy continued.

"One body—happened in the showers. No cameras in there, as you know. I have a list of the inmates who were in there with him at the time—all D Block—and all of them have been sequestered, but so far no one's talking."

"Who's the victim?" Veronica asked softly, even though she already knew the answer.

She just had to hear it.

The sheriff and his deputy ignored her.

"We're reviewing security footage to map his movements before the incident, but so far nothing stands out."

"Any idea of motive, Deputy Carter?"

Five, six. I crossed the River Styx.

"Who's the victim?" Veronica asked again.

"He's a cop. I'*nt* that motivation enough?"

The four of them were walking down the hall—Steve, Veronica, Kristin, and Deputy Carter—when Veronica stopped suddenly and grabbed Steve's arm.

"Who's the fucking victim?"

The sheriff looked at her. He had sweat on his forehead and his pupils were dilated even though pretty much all of Bear County Correctional was bathed in bright artificial light.

"Ken Cameron," Sheriff Burns said at last. "Ken Cameron was bludgeoned to death in the shower."

Chapter 38

FREDDIE WATCHED SHERIFF BURNS RUSH off. He wanted to go with the man but couldn't. Bear County Correctional was Bear County business, regardless of the victim. And the tension between Captain Bottel and the sheriff was palpable.

"This is going to be a PR nightmare," Captain Bottel muttered to himself.

Freddie had a different thought entirely: Ken Cameron didn't deserve to die. Imprisoned, yes—he had put the life of an innocent young woman in danger—but killed?

Definitely not.

A deputy closed the rear doors to the cargo van loaded with Dr. Bernard's files. He looked around, searching for the sheriff, but when he didn't see him, he approached the next highest level of authority.

"That's the last of them. Where am I taking the evidence again?"

Before Captain Bottel could answer, Freddie spoke up.

"They're expecting them in Matheson."

"Ah, right—that's what I thought. Thanks."

As Freddie watched the van's taillights recede, he felt a knot form in his stomach, a result of guilt as much as hunger. His reasons for suggesting that the evidence goes to Matheson had little to do with averting the media's attention.

And everything to do with his son.

In truth, he didn't share the sheriff's nor Veronica's view that media involvement was a negative thing in this case. Quite the opposite, in fact.

Freddie looked over at Peter who was on the phone, probably trying to reach Veronica, while at the same time sucking on a cigarette as if it was the last on Earth.

If anybody would understand, it was Peter Shade.

Peter had adopted a traumatized child and had given up everything for her. He'd sacrificed a promising career and then, beating all odds, had become a police captain.

In the end, he'd given that up for Veronica, too.

Yeah, Freddie thought, *Peter would understand. He would do anything for his daughter. And I will do anything for my son.*

"Captain, I can head back to the office, review the security footage around the hardware store and this place. Might come up with something new, now that we have a make and model. Then I really need to get some sleep."

Captain Bottel never took his eyes off the office building and Freddie wondered what was going through his head. He knew very little of the man, other than the fact that he'd come from Washington to accept this post. Rumor had it that Pierre Bottel and Mayor Tom Dixon were close, that they'd both served in Afghanistan years ago.

To date, all of Freddie's interactions with Pierre had been cordial, and while he'd initially wanted to hate the man, he quickly realized that this wasn't going to be the case.

But seeing him deal with the current stressful situation, around Peter and the sheriff, made his opinions of the captain waver.

"What about Detective Shade?"

This was another worrisome quality. They'd been talking for a good ten minutes and this, during a lull, was the first time that Captain Bottel had even mentioned Veronica.

"She's with the sheriff," Peter said, speaking up for the first time.

The captain finally looked away from the building.

"She's a special consultant for Bear County on this case," Freddie reminded Bottel when it looked as if he was going to address Peter harshly.

"Right. Sleep might do us all a little good. I'll have people looking for the Mazda and Dr. Bernard around the clock. We'll debrief, with Sheriff Burns, in the morning."

He grunted an affirmative and then glanced at Peter.

"I know this is your daughter but—"

"I'm going to get some sleep, as well."

Peter flicked his cigarette to the ground and rubbed it out with his heel.

The hell you are, Freddie thought.

Like Veronica, Peter Shade was a stubborn bastard. And with his daughter being at the center of this case and Dr. Jane Bernard still out there somewhere?

He wouldn't sleep until the man was caught.

Captured, put behind bars, or dead.

A simple nod to both men, only one of which was reciprocated, and then Freddie retreated to his car.

He drove slowly away from the scene, but as soon as he could no longer see the flashing lights in the mirror, he accelerated.

Freddie also picked up his phone and dialed a number.

Rather predictably, there was no answer. Freddie tried again.

And again, and again.

Someone picked up on the fourth attempt.

"Yeah?" the man sounded as if he was drunk or half-asleep. Maybe both.

"Terry, I need to see you."

A groan.

"I can't."

Freddie squeezed the phone between his thick fingers.

"This isn't a request. It's an order—I need to see you. *Now.*" Freddie heard what sounded like the man with the limp and the terrible haircut rising from either a bed or a chair.

"It's just... after last time... I don't think I can help you anymore."

Freddie said nothing for a good ten seconds.

"H—h-hello?"

"Terry. I don't think you understand. Either you meet me outside your house, your piece of shit apartment, or I'm going to kick in your front door and drag you out for everyone to see. It's up to you."

Freddie pulled over, slamming on the brakes hard enough to make them squeal. Then he stared up at the fire escape, counting the number of windows until reaching eight. A light went on, the crooked blinds became momentarily more crooked, then a shadow appeared.

"You're not—you're not here, are you?"

"Two minutes, Terry. Two minutes and then I kick in your door and make a scene."

It took closer to five for Terry to make his way outside and five more to hobble down the fire escape. Freddie gave him a break on account of his limp.

The confidential informant was wearing a filthy white muscle shirt and a pair of dark gym shorts.

Freddie leaned over and opened the passenger door.

"Get in."

The man burped as he sat down, and even though he covered his mouth, the smell of booze on his breath was toxic.

"This is unexpected, I was—"

"You ever seen heroin packages marked with a snake on them? A snake eating an eyeball? Like an emblem of some sort?"

Terry dramatically screwed up his face.

"What?"

"It's like an outline of a snake eating an eyeball? The heroin comes from New York."

"Heroin?"

Freddie lost it. He reached over and grabbed the man by the shoulders and pulled him close.

"Yeah, heroin! Have you ever seen a bag of heroin with a fucking snake eating an eyeball on it? These questions only again harder, Terry!"

The man sobered a little.

"I ain't never seen nothin' like that. Serious."

Freddie let go. When he reached for the glovebox, Terry recoiled, but the detective had no intention of assaulting him again. He rifled through the contents, before yanking out an old McDonald's napkin. With a pen that every cop carried in their breast pocket, irrespective of uniform, he drew the image that Troy Allison had shown him as best he could. Admittedly, it wasn't great, but it had to be more illustrative than his verbal description.

"This." He shoved it into Terry's face. The man tried to take it, but Freddie wouldn't let him. "Have you ever seen this before?"

It was almost comical the way that Terry inspected the drawing, tilting his head this way and that.

"Naw, man, I'm real sorry, but I've never seen it."

"Heroin—new on the streets."

Terry tucked his stringy hair behind his ears.

"I don't know anything about heroin, Freddie."

"Detective Furlow," Freddie corrected.

"Okay, sorry, Detective Furlow, I've never done heroin before. Never even seen it. I fence jewelry, Fred—*ahh*, Detective Furlow. You know this."

Snarling, Freddie shoved the napkin into his pocket.

"Who does then? You must know someone who deals this shit?"

Terry started to shake his head.

"Nobody? Nobody?"

"S-s-sorry."

"Fuck!" Freddie slammed his meaty palms on the steering wheel.

"I'm real sorry, Freddie. I-I-I don't know anything about heroin. But-but-b-b-but you know about last time? When I helped you set up, like, that sting, you know? I haven't been paid and I need—"

A rabid stare stopped the man mid-sentence.

"Get out."

"Okay, okay."

Terry had his hands up and it took him too long to open the door.

"Get out! Get the fuck out!" Freddie shoved Terry just as he finished fiddling with the handle. The CI fell on the curb and Freddie gunned it, nearly running over the man's one good leg.

In his rearview mirror, he saw Terry slowly rise to his feet and then give him the finger.

Freddie didn't slow.

It was a long shot, of course. He *knew* it was a long shot. Terry only dealt in stolen jewelry, that was what he was arrested for before being turned CI, and that was what his rap sheet was full of: selling stolen goods.

Not drugs—never drugs.

But Detective Furlow's once large cadre of confidential informants had long since dwindled. Some had been arrested, some disappeared, some, rare, had turned their lives around.

None were of any use.

But there was one CI—not his, but his partner's—who had a history of drug use and abuse.

And the man was going to help.

Freddie wrenched the steering wheel so hard that it sounded like he was twisting an old leather belt.

Dylan Hall was going to help. Whether he wanted to or not, that tall piece of shit was going to help Freddie keep his son out of prison.

Chapter 39

"He called me."

The men were talking, outlining Ken Cameron's final movements before he was murdered in the shower.

"He called *me*."

When still no one paid her any attention, Veronica reached out and grabbed the back of Steve's arm. He jumped and pulled back, even though she'd barely pinched him.

"Ken Cameron called me. That's why I'm here. He called me from… here. From Bear County Correctional."

"He *what*?" Steve was beyond incredulous.

Veronica lowered her hand.

"I was in the hospital speaking to…" Veronica almost said *Cole*, but just conjuring the man's name reminded her of the kiss she'd given him on the forehead. In and of itself, nothing particularly scandalous. The real issue, however, was what she'd felt before *and* after kissing him. Veronica looked down when she continued, "I got a call from Bear County Correctional, and he—" Another hesitation, this one having nothing to do with emotional infidelity. Veronica raised her eyes now and stared at Steve. "—he said, *five, six, I've crossed the River Styx.*"

Veronica noticed that Steve's right hand was shaking, and he used his left to make it stop.

"What else—" the sheriff cleared his throat. "What else did he say?"

Veronica shrugged.

"Nothing. Just hung up, so I raced over here."

"Right." The sheriff corralled a serious-looking deputy. "I need you to get video footage from the telephone room and I want call logs from the last two hours."

"I can—" Deputy Carter began, but Steve silenced him.

"No, you're staying with us." Then, to the other deputy, the sheriff said, "I want that footage loaded up in the security room in five."

"Yes, sir."

"What's this River Styx stuff?" Deputy Carter asked. "Did he say anything like that when you visited him earlier?"

Veronica winced.

"What?" He glared at her. "You were here earlier?"

Veronica debated lying but quickly quashed the idea. She nodded.

"When? *Why?*"

Once again, Veronica grew self-conscious.

"I came here after the show. I thought... I thought it might be Ken Cameron who had called in."

"From prison?" Steve was too tired or too out of it to hide his contempt.

"I know, I know," Veronica said defensively. "I know it couldn't be him, but..."

The sheriff made a face and then shook his head in disgust, which made Veronica feel ashamed and dirty. His hand started to tremble again, too. It was as if Steve was a different person than even a few weeks ago.

What the hell is going on?

"And did he mention anything about the river?" Deputy Carter cut in, clearly sensing the tension between them.

"No, nothing. Ken had nothing to do with this."

Except, he did—he had to. He'd called Veronica, maybe not when she was on the show, but earlier tonight.

Five, six, I've crossed the River Styx.

"What does it mean?" Veronica hadn't meant to speak out loud.

"River Styx or the rhyme?" Deputy Carter asked with a shrug.

"Both?"

It dawned on Veronica that she hadn't thought about the rhyme much at all, only that it served as a sort of preemptive calling card.

Was it important? Did it matter? Or was it just the inane bastardization of a children's nursery rhyme by a psychopath?

"Well, I'm no scholar, but I think River Styx is from Greek mythology. Separates the world from Hell or something like that."

"And swimming in it makes you invulnerable," Steve said absently. There was an odd lilt to his voice.

"Right." Veronica recalled something of the myth of Achilles. "What about the rhyme?"

"All I know about that is that it's been around forever. Eighteen hundreds, maybe," Deputy Carter offered.

"Thanks. Now let's go see the body," Steve seemed anxious now.

If they ever had a moment to themselves, Veronica made a promise to ask him what the hell she'd done wrong.

If there had been any doubt that Ken Cameron's murder had been connected to Gina's death, Cole's attempted murder, and Jane's abduction, this was dashed the second they entered the showers.

There was one major shower room for all Bear County inmates, a twenty-two by twenty-two-foot square comprised almost entirely of small alternating gray and white tiles. Lining the outer wall, spaced at regular intervals about three feet apart, were plain silver shower heads, complete with two dials beneath them. In the center of the room, there was a large pillar, which also had shower heads on it, effectively maximizing the number of men who could shower at any given time. A rough calculation suggested that this number could be as high as twenty.

But today, right now, nobody was showering.

The tiles were still wet, and the shoe covers that coroner Kristin Newberry made them all wear were instantly sopping. Several taps dripped incessantly, oddly in rhythm, generating shrill backdrop music.

To enter the shower room, Veronica had to pass through a hallway just wide enough to walk single file. The entire left wall was a window looking into the shower room, clearly, the location where guards who wanted to stay dry and still keep their eyes on the inmates could post up.

Privacy was in short supply in Bear County Correctional.

And yet, someone still managed to get to Ken without being seen.

The ex-Greenham police officer's body lay on the other side of the pillar, mostly obscured from view. As per Kristin's instructions, they encircled the pillar from opposite sides, keeping a wide berth. Veronica thought this unnecessary; running water would have long since washed away any evidence.

Ken Cameron was lying face down, the tiles around his head pink with blood mixed with water. What made the scene particularly disturbing was that the man's face was nearly completely flat against the ground. From the side, there was no visible space between the gray and white tiles and his mouth or eyes, or any section of the face that was generally set back from the chin or brow.

Someone had smashed Ken's features effectively flat. But not before driving part of his head into one of the metal shower heads, if the chunks of hair and flesh still dangling from one of them was any indication.

And yet, none of this violence was a clear indication of a link to the other victims, with Gina or Cole or Jane.

It was the liquid soap that tipped Veronica off, making the phone call—*five, six*—redundant.

It was everywhere. It was splattered all over the walls, the floor, even the ceiling in some places. It was as if someone had taken a bottle of liquid soap—the kind that claimed to clean your hair, face, balls, and body—and sprayed it haphazardly throughout the shower.

Where it touched puddled water, it bloomed, going from thick strands of deep indigo to intricately patterned snowflakes that were closer to turquoise in color.

It wasn't quite the right shade, Veronica always saw more navy than turquoise, but the effect was close enough.

To her, it looked like sweat.

And what did you wash off in the shower? Sweat.

Veronica's synesthesia was already on high alert, painting the entire room in vibrant, yet mostly transparent, oranges, reds, and yellows. The addition of the blue was uncomfortable, but the effect wasn't nearly as disorienting as back at Gina's house.

First the paint, Veronica thought, *then the gas. Now, the sweat.*

She considered this for a moment—it wasn't quite right.

No, first the song. A different song, but a song, nonetheless. Then the paint, gas, and sweat.

"What's with all the soap?" Deputy Carter asked.

Steve knew, of course. He'd been there, he'd listened to the man on the phone during the interview. But the sheriff said nothing. When Deputy Carter answered his own question a second later, it became apparent that he wasn't a *Marlowe* fan.

"A distraction? Maybe an attempt to block the view from the window?" The Deputy indicated the thick glass separating the shower from the hall.

This wasn't likely, given that there was no soap on the actual window.

"I don't think so," Kristin Newberry said. "More likely it was to ensure chaos." She slid her wet shoe cover in a thick strand of soap. It glided effortlessly. "I bet after Mr. Cameron went down and everyone started to run, a lot of people slipped and fell."

"It happened around shift change, and there is no video in here, but I'll ask some of the deputies," Carter said.

Veronica was impressed. It sounded like a reasonable theory. One that made sense.

Her idea, of this all being by design to fuck with her senses seemed less sensible.

But it was the color, the pattern. Kristin was right, this was designed to cause chaos, but inmates falling on the evidence was just collateral damage.

It was designed to cause chaos in *her*, in Veronica Shade's mind.

And it worked.

The showers were humid, and Veronica felt sweat, real sweat, form on her forehead and beneath her arms. The waves of blue coming off her blended with the soap on the ground and walls, once again triggering a bizarre, watercolor-infused vertigo.

Steve, perhaps sensing a change in her posture or maybe he needed support as well, leaned up against her.

The coroner set her black toolbox on the ground next to the corpse. She opened it, slipped on a glove, then gently lifted Ken Cameron's head.

Veronica looked away.

The dichotomy from earlier in the day was too much to bear. In the interview room, Ken had been angry, then smiling and smug. In the shower... even the most base expression was impossible when your face was reduced to bloody porridge.

And Veronica was responsible.

She loathed Ken Cameron, but he didn't deserve this. Nobody—well, maybe Trent Alberts and Herb Thornton—deserved *this*.

"I-I-I can't... I can't..."

Veronica stumbled toward the door, but her feet were wet and the tiles slippery. She fell to one knee, causing a puddle of blue soap to spread even wider. Exact color or not, Veronica quickly lost the ability to distinguish between her synesthesia and reality. It was like being back at Gina Braden's house.

She closed her eyes and strong hands—Steve's hands—helped her to her feet. Within moments, the phantom visions behind her lids began to fade.

They always faded.

"I'm okay." Veronica opened her eyes. "It's the fire—I think I need some air."

"I'll take you outside," Steve offered.

"No," she said, straightening. "I'll be all right."

With every stride Veronica put between herself and the horrible scene in the shower, the more strength she gained. In the hall, she felt well enough to look back at Ken Cameron's face one last time.

I'm sorry.

It seemed ludicrous to apologize to the scumbag, but it also seemed somehow right.

I'm going to find whoever did this to you, and to Gina, and Cole, and Jane. And I promise—I promise *I will make them pay.*

Chapter 40

THE SNAP THAT THE CORONER'S gloves made as she pulled them off caused Sheriff Burns to jump.

"Nothing surprising," Kristin said, her gaze drifting through the window and into the shower room where CSU was bagging Ken Cameron's corpse. "Manner of death, blunt force trauma to the face and head. Cause of death, homicide."

Sheriff Burns nodded.

"Thank you, Kristin. Now go home and get some sleep."

The sexagenarian raised an eyebrow and adjusted her gray hair into a loose bun.

"Sleep? I don't think so. I have a deposition tomorrow at eight." She checked her watch. "Nine hours to go and I haven't even started yet."

Steve gave her an appreciative nod.

"Thanks."

Before leaving, Kristin turned to Veronica.

"You going to be okay? I'm not a doctor, I only play one on TV, but if you need—"

"I'll be fine. Thank you."

With some space between her and the body now, Veronica's frantic mind had calmed somewhat. But like following all storms, only after the winds die down can the real damage be assessed. Veronica became aware of something that just might be more disturbing than Ken Cameron's gruesome murder.

She didn't smell anything different. Even after her blatant lie to the coroner, amongst several others uttered inside the shower, Veronica detected no change in smell. The residual scent of gas and fire was still ever present in her nostrils, but that shouldn't have mattered; the smell of gas was inside her head and it should have intensified.

But it didn't.

Is this like Benny's song? Is my ability to detect lies gone now, too?

For several seconds after Kristin left, Veronica just stared into the shower. Even after Ken Cameron's body was completely wrapped and he was hoisted onto a gurney, she continued to stare.

The emotional toll of the day, combined with the psychopath messing with her synesthesia, was enough to thoroughly exhaust her. Sleep was the last thing on her mind, but Veronica knew that it would come eventually, whether she wanted it to or not.

"Sheriff, you want to look at that footage now? From before the shower and in the phone room?"

"Yeah, let's take a look." The crack in Sheriff Burns' voice was evidence that he also felt gripped by fatigue.

Deputy Carter led Veronica and the sheriff away from the showers and through several secured doors. Eventually, they found themselves in a small, dank room that contained a large desk upon which sat six computer monitors arranged in a rectangular pattern.

When they entered, a man in a swivel chair turned to greet them.

His dark hair was styled in a crew cut and a thick wad of tobacco caused his lower lip to jut unattractively. His deputy shirt was half open, revealing a white T-shirt beneath.

"Deputy—" when the man in the chair saw the sheriff, he reached for the Dunkin' Donuts cup to spit out his chaw while at the same time attempting to button his shirt.

"Don't worry about any of that," Steve said. "Show me the tapes."

The man spat out the chewing tobacco but left his shirt unbuttoned.

"Yeah, sure." He spun around and pulled up a series of videos. "First, the footage of the inmates on the way to the shower. I also have video and audio of Ken Cameron on the phone."

"The shower, first."

The man spat in his cup and pressed play.

Veronica recognized the hallway as the one with the window leading to the shower. She counted. She counted four men, all with their heads down, two black, one Hispanic, and one white, before seeing Ken Cameron. Like the others, his eyes were also at his feet, but whereas the other inmates strutted, his gait was choppy, irregular. At one point, he stopped, and a muscular light-skinned black man nudged him forward. Ken disappeared into the shower blind spot and six more men followed. Twelve in total.

A guard came last, stared through the window for maybe half a minute, then left the way he'd come.

"That's pretty much it."

"Are they normally like this?" Veronica asked.

The man looked up at her.

"This is Detective Shade, she's a special consultant on the case," Steve explained.

The man nodded.

"Yeah, pretty much. They all walk around like that, slouched shoulders, head down. They think it's cool, I guess, but they also do it so they don't look suspicious."

"They look pretty suspicious to me," Veronica remarked.

"That's the thing, they all do it all the time so that if one is being suspicious they don't stand out."

"What about that man that bumped Ken? Pushed him forward?"

"LeVon Trykes, assault and battery. Beat up a man who grabbed his son at the park."

Veronica asked the deputy to rewind the tape and pause it with the best image of LeVon they could get.

She didn't recognize him. His name didn't ring a bell, either.

If LeVon was the psycho on the phone, his connection to Veronica was unknown.

"What about when they came out?"

Kristin Newberry was right. It *was* chaos. The twelve—eleven now—men were no longer concerned with looking cool or suspicious, they were just running scared, shoving each other as they tried to get away from the shower. Two deputies struggled to get by them, moving against the flow of traffic. Veronica focused hard, trying to detect traces of blood or excess soap on their half-naked bodies, to identify a possible suspect.

She saw nothing useful.

With a frustrated sigh, Veronica blurted, "Why wasn't there a deputy watching them?"

The man at the desk raised an eyebrow toward Steve, who nodded.

"This is D-Block, ma'am."

"D-Block?"

"Yeah, most of the time these inmates behave themselves. Don't require 'round the clock supervision."

"Ha, well, not this time," Veronica said with more spice on her tongue than intended.

"We're not allowed cameras in the shower, even in the prison. That's the law," the deputy said defensively. "And we're short-staffed. Sometimes we leave the D-Block—"

"It doesn't matter," Sheriff Burns interrupted. "What matters is we find out who did this. Now show me the footage from the telephone room."

Chapter 41

"THEY LOOK LIKE THE SAME group of guys," Veronica remarked as soon as the footage from the telephone bay started to play.

"That's 'cuz they are. D-Block showers together, uses the phone together, eats together."

Veronica recalled what the deputy had said about LeVon Trykes.

"Are they all violent offenders?"

"Not all. At first, inmates are grouped according to the nature of their crimes, but that doesn't always tell the whole story. LeVon has one assault on his record and that one was... understandable, I guess? Not the same as a thug with a rap sheet longer than a list of his bastard children. We reshuffle inmates according to potential."

Implied here was that Ken Cameron was one of these nonviolent violent offenders. Low risk. Perhaps a candidate for actual rehabilitation.

Veronica pictured the man's flattened face.

Not anymore.

They all watched the video play out.

Ken Cameron was second in line this time, with LeVon in front of him and not behind. The big black man used the phone for so long that the deputy elected to run the video at two times speed. He paced as he spoke, moving from one side of the archaic-looking pay phone to the other. Sometimes his back was to the camera, sometimes he stared directly at it. For what it was worth, Veronica didn't see anything in LeVon's features that would suggest less than a half hour from now, he would be collapsing the front of Ken's face. Would a man with just one assault on his record be capable of such violence?

Perhaps.

LeVon eventually hung up the phone and walked right by Ken without saying a word. Unlike in the pre-shower footage, before going to the phone, Ken looked directly into the camera. He almost seemed to know that Veronica would watch him, even though that was impossible.

But did he know what was going to happen? That he only had about a half-hour to live?

Ken grabbed the phone, dialed a number, waited for the collect call to be accepted, and then spoke. This all took ten seconds, maybe twelve.

And then he walked out, his posture identical to that of the men walking to the shower.

No looking at the camera this time.

"This is the number he called."

Veronica's phone number appeared on one of the monitors but before she could say anything, the deputy was already playing the audio.

She mouthed the words at the same time as they came out of the speakers.

"Five, six, I've crossed the River Styx."

When Veronica realized that everyone had overheard her, she said, "He called me."

The deputy was skeptical.

"What?"

"It was me he called."

"You? Why would he call—" the man's jaw dropped as he finally realized who Veronica was. "Oh, shit. You're—"

"Doesn't matter," Steve said harshly. "We think that someone told Ken to make the call. We need to find out who that was because it was probably the same person who killed him."

A daunting task. They had no idea when one of the other inmates might have approached Ken and instructed him to make the call. It could have been after Veronica's visit, or it could have been a month earlier. It could have even happened in the shower any number of days before Ken's last. If that was the case, they'd never know.

Either way, it was a lot of tape to review.

"Can we compare the list of people in the phone room and those in the shower?"

"Sure," the deputy said. "But it's probably just going to be all the D-Block men."

"That's fine. Just confirm who was there and then forward me a list of their rap sheets."

There was a finality to Sheriff Burns' voice, suggesting that they were done here.

Veronica didn't want to leave—they had one more victim but were no closer to finding out who was behind this.

There had to be a clue here somewhere. With all these cameras... they had to have picked up *something*.

"I also want you to compile videos of all Ken's interactions with other inmates after Detective Shade's visit this morning. Send it to my phone."

The deputy, momentarily forgetting who he was speaking with, reached for a tin of chewing tobacco on the table as he prepared to get started.

"Oh, sorry."

"Just as soon as you can."

Steve left the room with Veronica and Deputy Carter.

"Sheriff, my shift was up two hours ago," Carter said. "If you need me to stick around, I can, no problem."

"No, that's alright. Just make sure that all D-Block men are separated and in isolation for the night. Maybe that will help loosen their tongues and get them to start talking. In the meantime, we all need to get some sleep."

Deputy Carter nodded.

"Detective, I've got that list of phone numbers that Ken Cameron dialed that you asked for."

Before Veronica could answer, Steve spoke up.

"Just leave them at the front and I'll grab them on the way out."

Deputy Carter left the two of them alone.

"I think sleep is a good idea," Steve said.

Veronica couldn't argue with that but did anyway when it became apparent that Steve meant for her and not the both of them.

"I can't sleep now. Not with Jane—"

"You're exhausted, Veronica."

"So are you."

"Yeah, I'll be home soon. Just need to finish up some paperwork."

Was he lying? Veronica couldn't tell.

"Please."

"Okay. Just a few hours. And you'll be home soon?"

"I will," Steve promised.

Veronica was going to pull her phone out and call an Uber to take her to her car, but the idea of seeing all those missed messages was overwhelming.

Steve put a hand on her shoulder in a strangely awkward gesture.

"Don't worry, I'll have a deputy drive you home."

Veronica knew that this meant she'd also have someone stationed outside her house, but while earlier she would have considered this patronizing, she was a Greenham Detective, after all, it was comforting now.

She might have told her father, Steve, and Freddie that the unsub was more interested in hurting the people around her but seeing Ken Cameron's face changed all that. Twisting Gina Braden's neck around was one thing, bashing a man's face into smithereens was another.

No, having someone camped outside her home wasn't such a bad thing.

***

"Detective Shade? We're here."

A hand grazed her shoulder and Veronica startled awake.

"Don't touch me."

The deputy pulled his hand back as if it had been scalded.

"I'm sorry, I just wanted to let you know we've arrived."

Veronica had slumped in the passenger seat of the deputy's car, and she shimmied herself into an upright position. She must have fallen asleep the second she'd sat down.

Through the window, she saw that they had indeed arrived at her home.

See? I promised Steve I'd go home and sleep. Now, I've done both... maybe not in that order, but still.

"By the way, your phone was ringing," the young deputy informed her.

"No surprise there." Veronica opened the door and got out. But before closing it, she leaned back into the car. "You're not going anywhere, are you?"

Color rose to the deputy's round cheeks.

"The sheriff, he, *uhh*, he said—"

"Don't worry about it. Thanks for the ride."

Veronica was so tired that it took her a few moments to remove the correct key for her front door. A few more to realize that it was already unlocked.

And she never left the door unlocked. Neither did Steve. No cop did.

Three, four, lock your door.

Her hand instinctively went to the gun on her hip. The gun which wasn't there.

What the hell?

Veronica patted both sides of her body and then beneath her arms for shoulder holsters that she didn't own.

Where the fuck is my gun?

She looked back at the deputy's car.

"Detective Shade? Is everything all right?"

"Is my gun in your car?" She knew she sounded like a boot but didn't care.

"Your... gun?"

"Yes, my gun," she barked. "Is my gun—" Veronica was already turning the door handle and she pushed her front door open without thinking. "—in your car?"

The tinkling of a tiny bell proceeded Lucy coming to greet her. That was a good sign. If someone had broken in and was waiting for her then Lucy would be in hiding.

This was reassuring, but not so much so that she was willing to just barge into her house unarmed. Veronica squatted and gestured toward Lucy, indicating for her to come outside.

"Detective? I don't see it. Detective?"

Veronica ignored the deputy.

"Come here, Lucy. Here, girl. Here—" Veronica stopped. The cat's black nose was covered in something dark red.

Blood.

Veronica leaned forward and pushed the door open wider.

"No!" she screamed when she saw the bright red stiletto lying on the wood. When she realized that it was still attached to a leg, Veronica sprinted into her house, gun or no gun. "Jane! *No!*"

PART THREE: A REAL HERO

Chapter 42

IF DYLAN HALL DECIDED TO run, that was it. The gig was up. There was no possible way Detective Freddie Furlow would be able to catch him.

But when he hollered, calling the man's name in the dark alley, Dylan didn't run.

He turned.

At six foot nine, Dylan was unmistakable, but he was also nearly unrecognizable. Since the last time Freddie had seen the career criminal turned confidential informant, he'd put on weight, gone from emaciated to lean. His cheeks were full, and they had color to them. Dylan's pupils were so perpetually dilated from using that Freddie couldn't remember his eye color. Today, they were a light hazel, clear and lucid.

His hair was thick, full, and dark.

Instead of sporting just a pair of underwear, the man wore ripped jeans and a white T-shirt, the crow tattoo on his forearm confirming his identity if his height wasn't enough.

But while Freddie had some difficulty recognizing Dylan Hall, the opposite couldn't have been said.

As soon as Dylan saw him, a sneer appeared on his face.

"You come back to thank me for saving your life? I accept cash or credit."

"Not exactly." Freddie paused and added, "but thank you. If you weren't there, I probably would've been beaten to death with a salad bowl."

Dylan laughed. The high-pitch cackle suited his crane-like appearance.

"You ever find out why Devon was carrying around a salad bowl?"

"No, and I don't care. I don't have much time, Dylan. I'm looking for somebody."

Dylan stopped smiling. They were standing roughly fifteen feet apart and when Freddie moved to close this distance by half, Dylan tensed.

"Don't run. Please, don't run. I just need your help."

"I'm not your CI—not anybody's CI, really, after I had to out myself to save your fat ass."

Freddie nodded, which sent a ripple through the soft skin beneath his chin that traveled all the way down to his belt buckle.

He licked his lips.

"I know, I know. I just need your help." Freddie pulled out his wallet and looked inside. He grabbed one twenty, reconsidered, then pulled out a second. "Please."

He held the money out to Dylan, but the man made no attempt to take it.

"Why don't you tell me who you're looking for, first?"

Six months ago, Dylan would have snatched that money up faster than Freddie could devour a large fry. Now, he was patient, calculated.

This wasn't looking good.

"The thing is, I don't really know what I'm looking for." Dylan made a face. "No, wait. Hear me out. I'm desperate. I'm looking for a man who's pushing new product on the street. Heroin. You might've seen it, it's got a—"

"I don't do that anymore," Dylan interrupted. "I'm clean, and I'm staying clean."

"I know, I know. I just need a name. Any name, really. The new product on the street, on the package it's got a snake—"

"Do you know how hard it is to start over after what I've been through?"

Freddie didn't know, and quite frankly, he didn't care. What he cared about was his son, Randall, and keeping him out of federal prison. But he knew he had to listen to Dylan's story if he wanted to get anything out of the man.

"I have no idea."

"Next to impossible, that's how hard. Almost everyone who passed through that hellhole of an orphanage, everyone I know, either ended up dead, on the streets, or in prison. And I mean *everyone*."

Freddie's mind turned to Renaissance Home. Located in Matheson, the orphanage was one of the smaller in the state. But it was big in reputation in all the wrong ways. An all-boys facility, run partly by the church and funded by the state, with minimal supervision by either, was a recipe for a disaster.

There was definitely some truth to Dylan's words. After all, Renaissance Home had twisted and demented Veronica's brother, Benny, in unimaginable ways.

"I'm sorry."

"Fuck your sorries, fatty." Maybe Dylan hadn't changed that much, after all. "I don't want your sympathy."

"What do you want then?" Freddie held the cash up again.

"To stay *out*. That's what I want. Matter of fact, I don't want your money. I'm trying to get right."

This wasn't going the way Freddie had hoped. He thought it would be an easy flip, and it should have been. If Dylan had still been using, the man would've taken the cash and sold out his own mother.

But his sobriety had come with baggage in the form of morals. And that was a problem. Freddie had promised Troy Allison someone higher up the food chain, but at this point, he'd settle for a low-level street dealer.

Someone.

Anyone.

"Look, I know—"

"What do you know? You know what the fuck I been through? Huh? You know what it was like in the home?"

"No, I don't. And I won't pretend I do. I'm just... I'm asking you for help."

Dylan crossed his arms.

"I'm sorry, I'm out of that life. I can't help you. I *won't*."

Freddie felt his anger mounting and tried his best not to let it take over. With men like Dylan Hall, if you pushed, they pushed back. Cop or no cop, cash or no cash, that's all they knew.

Survival. And you didn't survive as a lamb among wolves.

"You think that it's easy for me to be here? It's no secret that I don't like you, Dylan. I don't like what you did to Veronica, and I don't like the fact that you used to deal. But I'm still here, and I'm asking—*begging*—for your help. I'm looking for anybody involved with the new heroin on the street. It has an emblem on it... a snake eating an eyeball. Please."

For a moment, it looked like Dylan was going to break, that he would agree to help.

But then he shook his head.

"And I'm telling you that I'm out of that life, have been for a while. I don't know anybody in the game no more."

Freddie licked his lips again.

"Right, but you can find out? You can—"

"I'm out, and I'm not going back. Sorry, fat man. I can't help you."

And then Dylan turned and ran, leaving Detective Freddie Furlow standing in the dark alley by himself, wallet in one hand, cash in the other, and no one to give either to.

Chapter 43

Panic and guilt were incredible facilitators of recklessness, and Veronica was no longer concerned with her own safety.

She ran to the body lying in the front hallway of her house.

The woman was on her stomach, hands by her sides, legs straight and together. The swirls of hot colors that Veronica's synesthesia created obscured the scene, but not so badly that she didn't recognize the sticky puddle around the woman's head for what it was: blood.

Veronica dropped to her knees, her hands hovering above the body, not sure what to do.

"Jane?" she whispered. Then she repeated the name with more authority. "Jane!"

She continued to move her hands above the woman's head, not quite touching her as if there was some sort of force field preventing contact.

"Jane."

A reply came in the form of a meow.

Lucy nuzzled up to Veronica, and seeing the blood on the cat's nose for a second time broke the spell. She grabbed the woman by the shoulders and flipped her over.

"No." Veronica fell on her ass and scooted backward. "No!

Tears welled in her eyes, and Lucy tried harder to comfort her, but only succeeded in smearing blood on Veronica's shirt.

"Why is this happening? What did I do? What did I *do*?"

She wasn't a religious person, but desperation was a well-known stepping stone to faith. Her eyes went skyward, seeking answers.

When none came, Veronica closed her lids. The swirl of colors, the same ones from Gina Braden's house, from Jane's office, from her own home, impregnated the darkness. She waited for them to subside.

"Why?" she whispered. "*Why?*"

Veronica took a deep breath and opened her eyes. Now that her synesthesia had become muted, she got a better look at the scene.

That's when she noticed the gun.

No, not *the* gun—*her* gun.

The one that had put two bullet holes in the corpse's face, one in the forehead and one below the left eye.

Veronica recognized her service pistol immediately, the small nick on the handle, the inch-long scratch near the muzzle.

"Oh, shit! D-d-don't touch anything—oh, man!" Veronica didn't turn to look at the deputy who clumsily rushed into her home. "Sheriff, I-yeah, I need you. At... at... at Veronica's house."

Veronica caught only bits and pieces of the conversation that the man had with his superior, something about nearly being here, something about whether or not she was okay. She couldn't take her eyes off the two crimson bullet holes. The one in the victim's forehead was uncannily similar to Gloria Trammel's. Identical, in fact. But as Veronica stared at it, it started to change—it grew, expanded, took over all the victim's features, like a black hole surrounded by a bloody corona.

It continued to get bigger until it swallowed her entire head.

"Oh my God, what happened?" Hearing Steve's voice brought her back from the brink. His familiar arms lifted her up and pressed her against his chest.

"I-I-I—" That was it. That was all Veronica could muster—the most selfish letter in the alphabet.

"It's okay," Steve told her softly. "It's—"

He stopped and Veronica knew why. The sheriff had seen the blood on her shirt and her gun on the floor.

His arms were suddenly no longer comforting, they were taut. And then they released her entirely.

"Veronica? What the hell did you do?" Steve's face was pinched.

"What?" Veronica wasn't sure she'd heard correctly. Did he just accuse her of doing this? Impossible.

"Veronica?"

Impossible, but true.

"What the fuck, Steve? I didn't do this! How could you think that?"

Steve immediately tried to take his words back, but it was too late. She'd seen it in his face. He really thought she was capable of something like this. Veronica wasn't sure who this said more about, her or him.

"I didn't hear a shot or—"

"Outside, deputy. Now," Steve barked. The young man bowed his head and left them alone. "I didn't mean to suggest that—"

"No, you did," Veronica countered. "I know you did. But that..." she was about to say that that didn't bother her, but it would have been a lie. It bothered her. A lot. Her sheriff boyfriend thought she was capable of murder. What the actual *fuck?* "What bothers me, is that if you thought I did this, then someone else will, too. I—I came home, and she was just... there. I didn't even have my gun, Steve. I didn't have it after I left the hospital—couldn't find it."

"Yeah, she was asking me if—"

The deputy had returned.

"Get the fuck out!" Steve shouted. "*Now!*"

Jesus Christ, what is wrong with you?

Veronica had been living with Steve for more than six months and she had never seen him like this. So agitated, so wound up.

So different.

"Did you touch the body?" Steve asked, the hint of accusation still clinging to his tongue.

"Yeah, I turned her over. I wanted to see if she was still alive."

Veronica suddenly remembered something that the young deputy had said back in the car.

"Shit."

"What?"

Veronica fumbled to pull out her cell phone. She ignored all the text messages and missed calls and dialed her voicemail. Her finger was shaking badly as she typed in her four-digit pin.

A pleasant voice informed her that she had one new message.

Veronica didn't need to hear it to know who it was.

And what they were going to say.

Still, the woman's words sent a chill up her spine.

"Seven, eight," Marlowe whimpered. "I've sealed your fate."

Chapter 44

LESS THAN FOUR HOURS AFTER they'd convened outside Dr. Jane Bernard's office, they were all back together again. The only difference this time was that they were investigating an actual murder and not attempted murder.

Marlowe Lerman, the eponymous woman behind the TV talk show, lay dead in the front hallway of Veronica Shade's home, a bullet in the brain and a bullet in the cheek.

She'd been killed with Veronica's gun. Bear County coroner Kristin Newberry informed them that they would have to get a Medical Examiner from Portland to come in, probably Dr. Thorpe if she was available, to confirm this, but everything was consistent with her service pistol.

While no one outside of Sheriff Burns had come right out and accused her of anything, Veronica knew how it looked. And it would only get worse when the news got out that Marlowe was intending to do a follow-up special about synesthesia, and about her.

Veronica, pissed about being exposed on live TV, invites Marlowe over to air her grievances. Tells the woman *not* to do the special, that she'd already exposed her secrets, making things difficult at work and at home. The argument gets heated, fueled by the stressful events of the day. Marlowe doesn't help things by running her mouth, the only thing she's good at, and it degenerates into violence.

Veronica shoots her twice then, realizing what she's done, collapses. Sheriff Boyfriend arrives, banishes the first deputy on the scene, and starts to clean up the mess.

That was the narrative, clear as day.

It wouldn't hold up in court, much less any real level of scrutiny—the timeline didn't make sense, not to mention that Veronica hadn't fired a gun in weeks—but it was complicated and messy.

Just like the interview on *Marlowe* had been.

Then there was Gina Braden and the pen with Veronica's fingerprint on it that had mysteriously ended up on her corpse. Not to mention Ken Cameron, whom Veronica had put in prison, being killed hours after she'd visited him.

None of this seemed to Veronica like a real attempt at framing her, but instead, something to make her life, and her work, impossible.

"Your heart rate is through the roof, and you're dehydrated. I can hook you up with an IV and something to help you sleep."

For the second time that night, Veronica found herself in the back of an EMS truck. This time, Veronica wasn't lying on a gurney but sitting on the opening, legs dangling over the edge.

"I'm fine."

Veronica looked down at her hand. She still had a PICC line in from her time at the hospital.

The EMT sighed.

"With all due respect, Detective, you're not fine. Your heart rate is too high, and your electrolyte balance is off."

Veronica didn't hear the rest of what the man said. She was too busy focusing on Detective Furlow, Captain Bottel, and Sheriff Burns, trying to read their lips. None of the men were happy, that much was obvious, but Freddie looked the most upset. He kept trying to speak but was continually interrupted by his superiors.

They evidently came to a conclusion, because Captain Bottel nodded and the three of them started toward her.

"You're not going to accept any treatment, are you, Detective?"

"No. Thanks."

Veronica pushed herself off the back of the truck.

Blue hues were coming off all three men, but Steve was sweating the most.

"Detective Shade," Sheriff Burns said. He was locked into professional mode now, as he should be. "We've decided to remove you as a consultant on this case. Now—"

"*What?*" Veronica couldn't believe what she was hearing. She'd thought they were coming over with a plan, a course of action to find this bastard, not remove her from the case. "No way."

"I'm sorry, Detective." Captain Bottel took over. "We can't risk jeopardizing the case if—"

"What case? What *fucking* case? We don't have a case. All we have is bodies."

"Bodies that keep piling up around you."

Veronica glared at Steve.

"What are you saying? I didn't—"

"Please, let's just try and stay calm," Freddie interjected. "It's for the best, Veronica."

"For the best?"

Once again, Captain Bottel took center stage.

"Detective Shade, this is only temporary. Just until we—"

Veronica lost it.

"This is your fault!" she yelled, pointing at the captain. "You wanted me to go on that show. You wanted to boost Greenham's image. Not me. I didn't want anything to do with it."

Freddie moved his girth between her and the other men.

"Everyone just needs to calm down."

His bulk broke her line of sight of the captain. That and the realization that it should have been Steve stepping to her side and not her partner tempered her fury.

Still, Veronica needed to get a final word in.

"I never wanted to do the show. All I wanted was to do my job."

"And you'll get your chance, Detective Shade. Like I said, this is only temporary. I'm really sorry but I'm going to need your badge," Captain Bottel said.

"My badge?"

Veronica should have expected this, and deep down she knew it was coming. It was the only thing that the captain could do. If she stayed on the case, everything she touched would be poisoned. From a legal standpoint, as well as a PR one, having Veronica Shade on the case was a non-starter.

She was actually surprised that this hadn't happened sooner. That didn't make it sting any less, however.

And her dad… where was Peter?

"She doesn't have it," Freddie stated. "Whoever took her gun from the hospital, took her badge, too."

Veronica looked at her partner.

What's he doing?

She could feel the badge in her pocket.

Did he know? Was Freddie lying on purpose?

If it hadn't been for the damn fire, she would've known for certain.

"Yeah," Veronica confirmed hesitantly. "He took my gun and my badge. He killed Marlowe, and he has Jane."

They needed to remember that.

No matter how fucked-up things got, Dr. Bernard was still being held hostage.

And that was the strange thing: Gina and Marlowe had been murdered. Cole had been held hostage, but only for a short while before he'd nearly been killed, too.

So, where the hell was Jane?

All signs pointed to her being dead, but Veronica couldn't—wouldn't—believe that.

"Okay," Captain Bottel said. "I've arranged for the two of you to stay at a motel for the night."

At first, Veronica thought that the captain meant Steve and her. But then Freddie nodded.

"Wait, the two of us?" Veronica asked.

"Yes. Detective Furlow has volunteered to remain by your side until this is over."

Veronica pictured how angry Freddie had been moments ago.

Volunteered? I don't think so.

"Okay," Veronica relented. "Just find this bastard." She leveled her eyes at Steve. "Find this bastard and find Jane."

Chapter 45

GREENHAM PD DIDN'T SPLURGE. THE Phoenix was a twenty-four-room motel built in the sixties and never renovated. If Veronica was inclined to ask, which she wasn't, the reasoning behind Captain Bottel selecting this place was to not attract attention.

Truthfully, the only thing it attracted was cockroaches.

And the captain hadn't lied about Freddie being beside her at all times. The room had two beds, both singles, covered in thin comforters.

But the shower worked, and the water was hot. That was the first thing that Veronica did after checking in, under Mr. and Mrs. Yates. She took a scalding shower, grateful to scrub her skin clean of smoke and fire and sweat.

For thirty minutes, Veronica stood under the water, letting it cascade over her body, turning her skin pink.

She placed a forearm against the outdated tiles and closed her eyes. Veronica was so tired that she almost fell asleep, just like that, standing in the shower of a forty-dollar-a-night motel room.

But then she saw the bullet hole in Marlowe's head. That ever-widening wound. That black hole of emptiness.

Freddie was sound asleep by the time Veronica got out of the shower. The shitty single bed upon which he lay was so flimsy that it sagged beneath his weight.

And the man snored. Jesus, did he ever snore. Even in her exhausted state, Veronica doubted that she'd be able to sleep beside him with that rusty chainsaw starting up every half second.

Captain Bottel had been nice enough to let her get a change of clothes from her house, with one Bear County deputy and one Greenham cop watching her at all times, and Veronica slipped them on.

It felt good to be clean, but this was short-lived.

What she did next was dirty.

Freddie had put all of his gear, his wallet, badge, and car keys, on the table between the two beds.

She grabbed her partner's keys and scooped them up. They jangled noisily, but an air horn siren wouldn't have been able to wake Freddie. Veronica was backing toward the door when she spotted something else: Freddie's holster and gun. He'd probably put those on the table, too, but they'd slipped off and were now sitting on the floor against the wall.

Taking her partner's car was one thing. But his gun?

You never touched another cop's gun. *Ever.*

But hers had been stolen. Stolen and used to kill Marlowe.

Worse than touching another officer's weapon was needing one and not having it.

That was what Veronica told herself as she bent and removed Freddie's pistol from his holster. She slipped it into the back of her jeans, then teased her gray Oregon Ducks sweatshirt over top of it.

No, she didn't feel dirty. Veronica Shade felt downright filthy.

Freddie didn't deserve this. And it wasn't like running away from Deputy Edgerton at the hospital, either. Captain Bottel had given Freddie a direct order to stay by her side, equal measures to protect her as to make sure she didn't reinsert herself back into the investigation.

But what choice did she have?

Veronica couldn't just lie down and sleep while everyone she came in contact with today was murdered.

No chance.

Veronica left the motel room, closed the door behind her, and then got into Freddie's car. She was forced to toss a whole bunch of fast food refuse—bags, drink trays, empty fry containers—into the backseat just to make room. Freddie's heavy body had damaged the springs inside the seat, and Veronica sunk so low that she could barely see over the steering wheel. She fiddled with the controls, trying to raise it up, but it was no use—the seat was broken.

Freddie has to lose some weight. Yesterday.

Veronica started the car and put her arm over the passenger seat and looked out the back window. She'd just forced the angry gear shift into reverse when there was a knock at the window.

She nearly wet herself.

"Shit!"

Veronica moved her hand from the headrest to the gun in the back of her pants. But then she saw who it was and rolled down the window, instead.

"Grand theft auto has a minimum sixteen-month sentence in the state of Oregon," Freddie informed her.

Veronica glanced around, looking at the worn seats, the torn upholstery, the garbage that was pretty much everywhere inside the car.

"Nothing about this shitbox qualifies as grand. Most I'd get for stealing this thing is a slap on the wrist and a free coffee."

Freddie chuckled dryly.

"All right, unlock the door and let me in. If we're going to do this, we're going to do this together. Oh, and don't even think about it—I'm driving."

Chapter 46

SHERIFF BURNS HAD ALL OF the footage from Bear County Correctional sent to the computer in his office. After a quick stop at Daphne's for a hot cup of coffee, which had nearly turned into him accepting her offer of coming in for a bite to eat, he was back at it.

But focusing was difficult. He had so much on his plate—so much, so much, so much...

He'd been clenching his jaw so tightly that his temples hurt.

More Oxy—he needed more Oxy.

Fuck, he didn't need more Oxy. He needed to never use it in the first place.

But that fucking bear...

That was Steve's nightmare: the bear.

Every time he lay down and closed his eyes, Steve could hear the goddamn thing behind him. It started with just a growl, but it got progressively louder. Soon, it was a throaty sound, like a low-filled toilet flushing, wet and hollow.

He would run, of course, but he was never fast enough. Then the bear would be so close he could feel it sharing his air, making him claustrophobic.

But when Steve finally turned, it wasn't an animal chasing him, at least not the kind with fur and fangs.

It was his wife.

The worst part is that she had a hole in her head. A hole just like Gloria Trammel and Marlowe Lerman had.

I should've never gotten mixed up with Veronica. From the start, I knew it was a bad idea. And now someone is coming for her... someone is killing everyone around her.

Steve sighed and rubbed his eyes, trying to clear his vision so that he could get back to watching the videotapes again.

Focus on finding this guy.

One, two, I'm coming for you motherfucker.

There were twelve inmates in Cellblock D, all with crimes ranging from fraud, theft, to assault. No murders, no extreme violence. Nothing even close to bashing someone's face completely flat.

Ten of the men were in the showers when Ken had been murdered, eleven in the telephone room when he'd called Veronica.

But Steve couldn't find a single link between any of them and Veronica. *Nothing.* She hadn't arrested any of them, hadn't so much as spoken to them, so far as he could tell.

In fact, there didn't appear to be a link between these inmates and Ken Cameron, either, aside from sharing a cell block with the ex-cop. But there had to be one. All D Block inmates were behind bars when Gina and Marlowe were killed, and Cole and Jane were snatched.

It couldn't have been one of them. It had to be someone on the outside. But who?

Steve slapped his computer mouse across his desk in frustration.

They had three bodies now, and the only things they had in common were a white Mazda 3 and Veronica Shade.

Deputy McVeigh had given him the figures on the car: there were more than half a million Mazda 3s sold in the USA between 2004-2009, about a quarter of which were white. Narrowed to those with Oregon plates, they had a grand total of nearly thirty-thousand vehicles. And that was if the plates belonged to the car and weren't lifted from another.

But there was only one Veronica Shade.

Steve reached into his pocket for another pill. He came up empty.

That was… impossible, right?

Steve searched his other pocket, but they weren't there either.

Fuck.

Then it struck him: he'd changed his outfit back at Veronica's. His pills were in his other pants.

"Fuck."

Steve couldn't think. Couldn't function.

Couldn't sleep.

Couldn't help Veronica.

Couldn't do anything.

He looked down at his hand. It was shaking violently.

Less than a month.

Dr. Kinkaid had given him the 'script less than a month ago. That's how powerful the drug was, that's all it took.

Thirty days.

Steve was no idiot. He knew he was in trouble. But so was Dr. Bernard. So was Veronica.

When this was over, when they finally fucking caught this guy, he'd get help.

He had no choice.

But not now.

Steve rose out of his chair and stretched his back. There was an uncomfortable tightness to his skin where the scars from the bear attack had formed.

"Fuck this."

He left his office and took the stairway to the basement level. It was after midnight and the halls were quiet. Almost every deputy, including those working overtime, was canvassing the streets, searching for a suspicious white Mazda and Dr. Jane Bernard.

It was almost too easy.

Enter the evidence room, cut the video feed, and grab the box with the name Vinny Pasquale written on the side.

Vinny was a low-level drug dealer who had been convicted of three years for intent to distribute. He'd pleaded out, but Bear County still kept the evidence for six months before incinerating it.

No one would notice a few missing pills.

Steve took the box off the shelf and opened it.

"Damn it."

Last time he was in here—the time when he'd stupidly forgotten to wipe the video evidence only to find it mysteriously missing later—Steve had grabbed the last of the Oxy.

He rooted around the box, which was mostly paperwork and a few photographs, but there were no more pills. Steve's eyes drifted to the shelves next, to the hundreds of evidence boxes sitting on metal shelving. He tried to read the labels, but everything was blurry as if someone had smeared petroleum jelly all over the labels.

There was no time to find another case like Vinny's. A case that had what he needed and that nobody would notice if it went missing.

Steve looked back into Vinny's box one final time. There were no pills, but there were other drugs.

There was a baggie of yellowish powder.

Heroin.

Steve shook his head even as he picked up the evidence and buried it in his palm. Then he slid it into his pocket and replaced the box on the shelf just like it had been.

His breathing had become shallow, labored.

It was insane. Everything about this was absolutely crazy.

Heroin… c'mon. Junkies used heroin. Shit, Anthony Wilkes—*MEENIE*—had overdosed on heroin. It wasn't like smoking a joint, or even in the same ballpark of doing a weekend bump of coke.

This was *fucking* heroin.

But if it could help him think straight...

Steve left the evidence room and hurried up the stairs back to his office.

He wasn't about to do heroin.

He took painkillers because he was in pain. Painkillers that a doctor had prescribed. That was all. There was nothing wrong with that, either. There was nothing—

"Sheriff?"

Steve's back was to Deputy McVeigh, and for a brief moment, he thought about running. McVeigh had the footage of him robbing the evidence room, there was no doubt about that. The only copy.

He had been holding on to it, but now that Steve had stolen heroin—he'd gone too far. He was going to be arrested right here, right now by his own Chief Deputy.

Sweat broke out on his entire body.

"Sheriff?" Deputy McVeigh repeated.

He cleared his throat and turned.

"Marcus, I know—" Steve stopped when he saw not one man, but two. Deputy McVeigh and a big, bald black man who was holding his hat against his chest.

This was it. McVeigh had brought backup and the deputy was ashamed of having to arrest his boss.

"Please, all I ask is that you wait 'til tomorrow. Wait until we catch this guy. Then I'll go quietly."

McVeigh pulled a face.

"Go quietly?"

Steve blinked.

Could he have been wrong? Was this about something else?

The timing, though...

"What can I help you with?" He tried to project an air of authority but failed terribly.

"It can't wait until tomorrow. Deputy Milligan has something to say."

Steve was still in disbelief, but he wasn't so shell-shocked that he couldn't lead the two men into his office.

"Close the door behind you." His voice had almost returned to normal.

McVeigh did as he was asked, then nudged the deputy.

"Go on, Ronnie. Tell the sheriff what you told me."

The man, still unwilling to meet Sheriff Burns' eyes, played with the brim of his hat, massaged it, rolled it between his fingers.

"I stopped somebody in a white Mazda 3." Deputy Milligan's voice was impossibly small coming out of such a large man.

"Speak up."

"Sorry. Yesterday morning, before any of these crimes started, I stopped someone. I think—I think it might have been our guy."

Steve was completely alert now, withdrawal or not.

"Why do you think that?"

"He was—he was creepy and... weird."

The left half of Steve's mouth curled upward.

"You think it's our guy because he was creepy?" This sounded like a whole lot of bullshit, a waste of time.

"Yeah, but also because he had paint in the backseat. Like six buckets."

Steve immediately grabbed his mouse. Thankfully, it still worked.

"What's the plate number?"

"I don't... I don't remember."

"You don't remember?" Steve shook his head. "You have the report? What was the citation for?"

He navigated his pointer to the Bear County traffic citation database.

"'Speeding. But I—I didn't give him a ticket."

"What? Why not?" Steve was becoming increasingly frustrated with Ronnie Milligan's strange behavior.

"What the fuck is going on, McVeigh?"

"Warning—I gave him a warning," Deputy Milligan blurted.

No, he didn't. Steve knew the parlance among his deputies. Deputy Milligan *let him go* with a warning.

This man in the car, likely the man who was hunting and killing everyone who associated with Veronica, had offered Deputy Milligan a bribe.

And he'd taken it.

Shit.

"What was the tag number?"

"I-I-I don't know."

"What do you know, Deputy? Do you know anything that can help? Like what he looked like? His name? Anything? Or are you just wasting my time?"

"His name was Dante. I don't know the last name, but I remember his first name was Dante."

"Is that all? Was he white? Black? Tall? Fat?"

"White—he was white. Dark hair, but he was wearing a cap. Didn't see much else."

By now, Deputy Milligan's hat was nearly folded in half.

"You're relieved, deputy. Off duty until I say otherwise."

Ronnie Milligan's eyes went wide.

"I need the money, I—"

"I said go!" Steve shouted. "Now!" McVeigh started to go with the deputy, but Steve called him back. "Stay here."

There were thirty thousand white Mazda 3s in Oregon.

But only one was registered to someone with the first name Dante.

Neither Deputy McVeigh nor Sheriff Burns said anything as they stared at the man's photograph.

The man who was behind the twisted song: *one, two, I'm coming for you. Three, four, lock your door. Five, six, I've crossed the River Styx. Seven, eight I've sealed your fate.*

"Nine, ten," Steve whispered. "I'm coming for you, you piece of shit."

Chapter 47

"WHAT DO YOU EXPECT TO find, Veronica?" Detective Furlow asked.

Veronica didn't answer because she didn't know. All she knew was that there was a clue somewhere in the files. There had to be.

The filing cabinets and their contents were mainly unmarred by the fire, with only two of them exhibiting dark burn marks on their blue fronts. There were some dents, as well, but these were from when Veronica had pulled them off the wall.

And when they'd fallen, several locks had broken off. At least, that was the story that Veronica would tell if anyone felt so inclined to ask. The heavy-duty bolt cutters that she'd found in the Matheson evidence locker? Sheer coincidence.

But this was all moot. News of what case these were from hadn't reached Matheson yet. All these cops knew was that Greenham had an overflow problem and that they were going to be keeping some evidence safe for the time being. Veronica showed the two boots working the midnight shift her 'stolen' Greenham PD badge and that was enough to gain them access.

"I have no idea how they're organized, so you start with those over there, and I'll start with these."

If Freddie had any reservations about looking through Dr. Bernard's confidential notes, he didn't voice them. He didn't say much of anything, really. And her partner's jovial nature outside the roach motel had been short-lived.

There was something on his mind, something related to FBI Agent Jake Keller, and Veronica would ask about it.

Eventually.

Just not now.

As it turned out, in many ways, Dr. Jane Bernard's filing system was a lot like her: slightly archaic, and while not ugly, the system was far from beautiful. Patient names, last names, followed by given name initials, were written in block letters on the tabs of each creme-colored folder. Inside each of those were smaller folders with dates—session dates, most likely. These held Dr. Bernard's handwritten notes.

A digital system would have been far more efficient. The folders themselves were organized in alphabetical order and the first locker that Veronica opened contained surnames starting with P. She was looking for S, for Shade, but she quickly flipped through these just in case something triggered a memory or anything at all.

None did.

She expected the next cabinet to be filled with Qs and Rs but was met with Bs instead. Veronica scowled and took a step back.

"They mixed up the order."

"I got Ws here," Freddie remarked. "Sheesh, how many patients did she have?"

Did.

A simple slip-up or foreshadowing?

They needed to find Jane.

Veronica was convinced that Dr. Bernard was different, that the unsub was keeping her alive for a reason, that she was more important than Gina or Marlowe. Wishful thinking, to be sure.

But sometimes wishes were all you had to keep you going.

Despite the ominous use of the verb in the past tense, Freddie had posed an interesting question. For all her years visiting Dr. Bernard, Veronica had only ever seen a handful of patients coming and going. This was particularly odd, given that she had the propensity to show up at all hours.

In addition to being one of a handful of psychiatrists commissioned by the City of Greenham PD, Dr. Bernard specialized in childhood trauma and was often on call to help treat survivors of an increasing number of mass shootings in the State. If Veronica had to hazard a guess, there were upwards of a few thousand folders spread out over all the lockers.

Were there other patients who had spent as many years with Dr. Bernard as Veronica had?

"Found the Ss."

Veronica closed her locker and walked over to Freddie.

"There was an F file mixed in, but the rest of the folders in here are Ss."

Veronica nodded but even when Freddie took a step away from the locker, she hesitated.

Was it because she was nervous about what she'd find or what she *wouldn't* find?

Fuck it.

Veronica swallowed her discomfort and attacked the folders. She scrolled quickly through the names, Sabra, Scander, Seal, the miscategorized F file, Fiori, and finally, Shade.

Veronica's file was thicker than the other Ss, but about the same width as the F file, and in line with some of those she'd already flipped through.

Still, at almost nine inches thick, it was impressive, especially considering how little Jane used to write during their meetings—a word here, a sentence there.

But over the years, it added up.

"I think—I think I need to be alone," Veronica said, as she removed her file.

"I get it. But please, Veronica, don't run this time." Veronica looked over her shoulder at her partner. "Please?"

"Okay. Promise."

"I'll be close. Just going for a walk."

Veronica watched Freddie leave the evidence room. He still wasn't right, something was off. The old Freddie would have given her space if she requested it, but he wouldn't leave her alone. Not with a psycho out there targeting her and those around her.

But once again, Veronica had more pressing concerns and she pushed this aside, banking in her own folder, a mental one marked 'to be dealt with later'.

Veronica's hands were shaking worse than Steve's when she finally gathered enough courage to open the folder.

Veronica Shade, nee Lucy Davis, age 11.

Beneath her name, Dr. Bernard had listed her height and weight, hair, and eye color. She'd even paper-clipped a small photo from third or fourth grade to the upper right-hand corner of the first page.

Veronica stared at the photo. It felt as if she was looking into her past, a past filled with nightmares.

She shook her head and started to read.

It took five minutes for the tears to spill.

It took six for anger to overwhelm her.

Wait a second...

Veronica flipped back to the first page.

Veronica Shade, nee Lucy Davis, age 11.

Lucy Davis.

"She knew," Veronica whispered. "Jane knew all along."

***

It had come to this. Time was nearly up. Even if Troy Allison honored the forty-eight-hour hold before arresting Randall, of which there was no guarantee, Freddie had to do something tonight. Tomorrow, when it was light out, cops would be crawling everywhere. Searching for a white Mazda 3, but with their eyes peeled for anything suspicious. And at north of three hundred pounds, Freddie was anything but inconspicuous.

There would be no rookie cop manning the Matheson Evidence room, there would be signing in and out, and records and video and...

Tonight—it had to be tonight.

Veronica was so engrossed in her reading that she didn't see Freddie reenter the evidence room. And despite his size, she didn't notice him moving up and down the aisles, either.

For some reason, the person that came to mind was Peter—his old friend Peter Shade. He was probably the best cop that Oregon had ever known, definitely the best cop in Greenham PD history.

And he'd been summarily dismissed. Why? Because his daughter was determined to solve important crimes? Because of bureaucratic bullshit that didn't matter?

What mattered were people like Peter. What mattered were people like Dr. Jane Bernard. And what mattered were people like Freddie's son, like Randall Byers. They made mistakes, but they were good people.

It wasn't difficult for Freddie to find what he was looking for. DEA Agent Troy Allison had likely put it on display, like some sort of trophy or reminder or God knows what. The time for hesitation was over. Freddie knew what he had to do. Just like Veronica knew that she had to be here, that she had to look through the files, Freddie had an obligation, as well.

The only difference was that while he suspected Veronica would leave the Matheson Evidence room empty-handed, Detective Freddie Furlow most definitely was not.

Chapter 48

VERONICA WIPED THE TEARS FROM her face. She'd come here with the hopes of finding out who was behind the murders, to discover who hated her so much that they would kill nearly everyone she'd spoken to today.

She was no closer to this end. But her visit to the Matheson Evidence locker was far from a complete waste of time.

In fact, it was quite an enlightening experience.

And equal parts infuriating.

Veronica debated taking the folder with her but decided against it. She would come back though, that was for certain.

She met Freddie in the hallway. He looked as if he'd been sleeping while leaning up against the wall.

"Well? You find anything?"

Veronica shrugged.

"Yeah, but I don't know how it can help us." Veronica tapped her foot and chewed the inside of her cheek. "I don't know what to do now, Freddie."

She normally didn't think twice about looking vulnerable in front of her partner. But everyone seemed like a stranger today.

Even herself, especially after what she'd just read.

To her surprise, Freddie didn't make a big deal of it.

"What if…"

Veronica's eyes shot up and a wry smile formed on her lips.

"You with a what if? Alright, I'm game. What if what, Freddie?"

Despite the effectiveness of the man's joke cutting the mood, Freddie's face was the same as it had been with Agent Keller that morning.

Which is to say, grim.

"Well, what if whoever is behind this is from the streets."

Veronica's brow lowered.

"From the streets? Why would you think that?"

"Well, you have your intuition, and I have mine."

Freddie was usually an open book. Him being obtuse was rarer than him eating a vegetable that wasn't in the immediate proximity of a hamburger patty.

"But—wait, no." Veronica shook her head. "This is about that vendetta you have, right? You think it's Dylan Hall who's behind this?"

"I never said that." Freddie pushed off the wall with considerable effort and Veronica followed him past the guard—who gave them a nod—and outside.

"Yeah, but that's what you're thinking, right? That Dylan is somehow behind this? Freddie, he's clean. Has been for a while now."

"Once a junkie, always a junkie."

Veronica took Freddie's keys out of her pocket and her partner tried to grab them.

"No way, I'm driving."

Freddie gave her a disapproving look but didn't stop her from sliding into the worn driver's seat.

"Look, I'm not saying it's him. To be honest, it's probably not him. But we have every cop, deputy, PI, everyone even tangentially related to law enforcement out there looking for this guy. Maybe someone on the streets can help, tell us something the law can't."

Another surprise. Freddie wanting to ask Dylan Hall for help.

She was skeptical that it would bear fruit, but Freddie was right about one thing. Them driving around looking for a car was a waste of time.

"Okay. Why the hell not?"

Veronica knew where Dylan lived. He'd graduated from the alley to a tiny apartment right here in Matheson. In truth, it was pretty awful. The neighborhood was one step up from the ghetto and the apartment, with a front door that somehow had gaps on all sides, was what people not familiar with actual crack dens would refer to as a crack den.

But it was an improvement.

And Dylan Hall was clean.

Veronica knocked twice, and despite the late hour, the door was answered in moments. She hoped this was because the apartment was so small that it took no time to get to the door rather than the occupant expecting a delivery.

If Dylan's appearance was any indication, it was the former. He looked good. In stark contrast to the peeling paint on the walls and the broken parquet floors, Dylan looked new and fresh.

"Detective Shade?" Genuine confusion crossed the man's face. "What are you doing here?" Even his voice seemed fuller, less squeaky.

"I need your help." As she reached for her wallet, Dylan's eyes drifted over her shoulder.

"Naw, I told your fat partner already. I don't know nothin' about no heroin. I'm out, and I ain't going back."

"What?" Veronica, thinking that Dylan must still be half-asleep, pulled out forty bucks and held it out. He didn't take it. "I'm not looking for drugs, Dylan. I'm looking for a murderer."

"*Murderer?*"

"Can I take a piss?" Freddie suddenly asked. Veronica glared at her partner. "What? I have to go."

"Not in here you ain't," Dylan said. Then to Veronica, "I'm trying to get my shit together. I'm pretty much useless as a CI ever since I saved the fat man. I don't know nothin' about no heroin or no murder."

"I really gotta piss. Seriously, I'll just be a second."

"This ain't Central Park. Piss outside."

"I'm not an animal. Let me use the toilet."

Freddie was obviously trying to get inside the man's apartment. Why? Did he think that there was evidence in there? Or worse, did he think that's where Dylan was keeping Dr. Bernard?

Veronica suspected neither—she thought that this was still part of her partner's twisted vendetta against the ex-con.

There was no hint of violence here, the only yellow coming from Dylan were the sweat stains on his white T-shirt. And even those were old—they were no longer giving off blue hues.

"*Hmm.* No."

"Fuck, okay," Freddie said, finally relenting. "I'll be right back."

Veronica watched him waddle around the side of the apartment before turning her attention back to Dylan.

"Fuckin' weirdo," Dylan muttered.

"Look, I know it's hard. Take the money, Dylan."

Two times a charm.

"I'm sorry, Veronica, but I don't know nothin' about no murders. Closest thing I came across was that cop friend of yours, the one who tried to frame me."

It took Veronica a beat to realize that he was talking about Ken Cameron.

She swallowed dryly.

"I knew this was a long shot, but this guy—he's after me."

Dylan's dark eyes were lost in a squint.

"What?"

"Yeah, I didn't know where else to go, to be honest. But this guy, singing this fucking kid's song..." Veronica was rambling but couldn't help it. "He's coming after everyone I've spoken to today. *Everyone.*"

Veronica closed her eyes and ran a hand through her hair.

"Gee, thanks for stoppin' by."

First, Gina, then Cole, and Marlowe. Then Jane. How could she forget about interrupting the two of them together? Jane and her father, half-naked.

Did that mean her father was next?

Veronica couldn't remember the last time she'd spoken to her dad. Had it been at her house after discovering Marlowe's corpse? No, he wasn't there. At the hospital... maybe.

Feeling a knot form in her stomach—add it to the collection—Veronica got her phone out.

"What song?" Dylan asked before she could dial her father's number.

"What do you mean?"

"You said this guy who's after you sang a song? What kind of song?" There was a tightness to Dylan's voice that wasn't there before.

"Yeah... you haven't seen the news lately, have you?"

Dylan cast a glance back into his apartment. Veronica heard a muffled thump, probably the man's cat, but saw nothing.

"I ain't got no TV."

"Right. It's a nursery rhyme: one, two, I'm coming for you. Three, four, lock your door. Five, six, River Styx, something like that. You—you okay?"

Dylan had gone white as a sheet. Ironically, he looked more himself now. Like the junkie that Veronica was used to seeing.

"Where did you hear that?" he asked with a gasp.

"I told you—that's the song that this guy sings before he kills." Another knot. "You sure you're okay?"

Dylan, suddenly weak, leaned up against the warped door frame. Veronica reached out but he waved her off.

"Have you—have you heard the song before?"

Dylan's Adam's apple bulged several times.

"Five, six, I've crossed the River Styx."

Now it was Veronica's turn to go pale.

"Where? Where did you hear that from?"

Dylan steadied himself and color began to return to his face. Now the sweat came. Smokey blue tendrils from the crown of his head and the tops of his shoulders.

"At the orphanage. At Renaissance Home."

Freddie appeared, looking lighter and fresher than he had moments ago.

"What's up? What'd I miss?"

Veronica didn't take her eyes off Dylan.

"You're not going to believe it, but he's heard the song before. At the orphanage—the place where they sent Benny. We need to go there, and we need to take him with us. *Now.*"

Chapter 49

"No fucking way," Dylan said. "I'm not fucking going back there. Nope."

Veronica politely declined the man's offer to sit on his couch. It was clearly something that had been picked up on the side of the road or acquired via dumpster diving. The cushions were worn, there were more cigarette holes than she could count, and it smelled like a wet dog.

Veronica wouldn't have been surprised if it was full of both lice and ticks.

But while she elected to stand, Freddie's options were more limited. He leaned up against the wall but judging by the discomfort on his face, this wasn't cutting it. Standing for prolonged periods was difficult given his size.

"You remember when I asked you about Renaissance before? When you were locked up?" Freddie asked.

Dylan grunted.

"Yeah, when you pricks in Greenham tried to frame me for that shit with horse-girl. What about it?"

"You didn't say much then. I was hoping that you could tell us a little more about your time there, now? Like how it relates to that song?"

Sobriety had done little to diminish the man's deep-rooted anger.

"Why? So you can pin somethin' else on me, too?"

"Please, Dylan," Veronica urged. "Anything you can tell us might help find this guy."

Dylan cast a distasteful look in Freddie's direction but some of his rage subsided.

"Fuck it—all right. Renaissance… shit, where to begin. Well, all good stories start with a big boss, I guess. The man in charge's name was Father Cartier—made it sound all French and exotic, but he was from Detroit, I think. Who knows—they just ship those pricks around. Anyways, he was fucking fat." Dylan lifted a chin to Freddie, "Not as fat as you, but still fucking fat. Gray hair that looked like dryer lint, walked around like his shit don't fucking stink. Never came near me, though. If he did, I'd knock his teeth out. Once, when I was eleven or—"

"Tell us about the song," Freddie interrupted, trying to keep the man on track. Dylan pursed his lips. "We don't have much time."

A strange choice of words. Time for what? To save Jane?

Dylan was painting an unfortunately familiar profanity-laced picture, but Veronica was still having a hard time piecing it together with her own life.

Benny had gone to Renaissance. Was that the link? But Benny was dead. Really dead this time.

"Yeah, that song. Well, some of the younger kids sang it most every night. I was in and out of Renaissance—" he held up three fingers, "—adopted, you know? But I heard it a coupla times. One, two, I'm coming for you. Three, four, lock the door. Five, six, I crossed the River Styx. Seven, eight, I've sealed your fate."

Veronica sniffed but wasn't sure if she detected more gasoline in the air. The way that Dylan sang the song? There was a strong possibility that, despite his words, he was one of the younger kids.

Dylan wouldn't be the first person who turned to drugs to help cope with the traumatic abuse suffered as a child. Veronica just hoped that reliving these experiences didn't push Dylan back toward the needle.

"What does it mean? The song?" Freddie asked.

Dylan looked away now and Veronica couldn't help but notice an uncanny resemblance to her brother Benny. Not as a child, but as an adult.

When Benny had set himself on fire, he'd somehow managed to lock his eyes on hers even as his flesh bubbled and melted away.

Was it shame she'd seen in his looks? Maybe. Something closer to regret, perhaps.

"Like I said, Father Cartier was a piece of work. The kids sang that song as a reminder, kinda like, he's coming for you, don't forget to lock your door. But the thing is, he probably had the key—if fat Father Cartier wanted into your room, you couldn't stop him."

"What about the River Styx? What's that all about?" Freddie said.

Dylan shrugged. He was becoming increasingly agitated, alternating between rubbing his hands on the thighs of his jeans and scratching the back of his arms.

"Rumor had it, Father Cartier would take some of his favorites out to the Casnet River to swim."

"To swim?" Freddie blurted.

Veronica had seen parts of the Casnet River, but it was long and ran the entire western and southern edge of the Hilltona Forest. So far as she knew, there were no beaches. It was mostly rocks and rapids.

"You can't swim there," Freddie continued.

"I don't know what to tell you. That's the rumor. I don't know why they called the River Styx, either, but we did. Father Miller would stand on Donovan's Bridge and watch us boys try to cross to Hilltona."

The continual switching of tenses, from they to us to we, confirmed Veronica's first instinct: Dylan had been one of those boys.

Had Benny?

Did he used to go to bed singing that song, closing his eyes, and hoping that Father Cartier would pick someone else's room?

She wanted to push harder, to find out more, but Veronica had experience in spots like this. Push too hard, and someone was likely to break. Dylan Hall might be full of bravado, but it was just a front—his status as an ex-junkie made him more vulnerable than most.

Veronica now wished she'd taken a seat, bed bugs or not.

"Dylan, would you be willing to tell someone about this? Like make an official statement?"

Dylan cocked his head and rolled his upper lip.

"What you talkin' about?"

Freddie took over.

"What Detective Shade means, is that if you come in and give a statement, and some of the other boys corroborate what happened to you, then we—"

Dylan's eyes went dark, nearly black.

"I told you, fat man, it wasn't fuckin' me, all right? It happened to some of the other kids, the weak ones. That's who that rapist fuck Father Cartier picked on."

"Right, but—"

Veronica interrupted her partner. She suddenly felt like they were speaking to a child and tried to channel Dr. Bernard, how the psychiatrist had been with her when she'd been young.

"You don't have to admit to anything. You can just tell us at the station what you saw, experienced, or overheard happening. That's it. Say as much or as little as you want."

Dylan sucked his teeth.

"Yeah, we tried that—head shrink came in, blah, blah, blah, nothing ever happened. The kids—*they* just kept singing that song. Besides, what difference would that make?"

"What difference would that make?" Anger rose in Freddie's voice, which was uncharacteristic—that was her job. "Maybe to stop this predator? If he still works there—"

"He don't."

Veronica was inclined to try and calm her partner, but her mind was racing.

Could it be him? Could the priest be responsible for all this? Maybe Benny had done or said something that pissed him off? Threatened to go public with the abuse? Did Father Cartier think that Benny told her about it? But why this insane game? Why not just take her out?

"Well, wherever he works, then."

"Motherfucker's dead."

Silence.

"Yeah, dead of a heart attack, or so I heard. I don't give a fuck about him. You wanna know how many people went to his funeral?"

More silence.

"I don't know either because I wasn't there. But I bet you nobody went. Not a single fucking person. Not even those nun bitches who looked up to him like he was God."

"Okay, okay," Veronica said. "You don't have to make a statement. But I think you should come with us."

"I don't gotta go with you."

"No, you don't. But—"

"I'm *not* going with you."

Dylan was making fists with both hands.

Freddie moved away from the wall.

"It's probably better if we, *uhh*, if we go alone."

Better for whom?

Was on the tip of her tongue. Definitely not better for Dylan to be alone right now. But the man was right. They couldn't force him to do anything.

"C'mon let's go," Freddie encouraged.

Veronica reached into her wallet. She only had another forty bucks left but she didn't hesitate in handing that over, too.

She just hoped that the man would spend it on a new couch and not smack to stick in his arm.

"Thank you, Dylan. And… and I'm sorry."

Chapter 50

BASED ON THE RUMORS, VERONICA had expected Renaissance Home to be dark and somber.

Instead, she was surprised that the orphanage in Matheson was well-lit, and the expansive lawn out front neatly trimmed. Even at this late hour, the lights that shone on the gray facade cast it in a cheery glow.

Veronica parked on the street and walked up to the wrought iron gate, which, with the word 'Renaissance' worked into the metal, was perhaps the only foreboding thing about the place.

There was an intercom and a sign that said, *Visitors must check-in,* above it. Veronica pressed the button and waited. Eventually, a huffing Freddie arrived behind her around the same time that a voice emanated from the box.

"Hello?"

Veronica nudged Freddie and both of them held up their badges.

"Greenham PD. I know it's late, but we would like to speak to someone in charge. It's important."

They waited another thirty seconds and then the latch on the twelve-foot high gate disengaged.

Like the building in which she resided, the woman who introduced herself as Sister Margaret was cheery and bright. Her skin was like crumpled wax paper, but the eyes that stared out of the habit were vibrant.

"Detectives, I'm not sure how I can be of any help. Maybe if you come back in the morning?"

They stood in the doorway of the orphanage. Sister Margaret was a diminutive woman and Veronica could see past her and down a vast hallway. There appeared to be framed photographs lining the walls, but she couldn't make out any of the details. She tried to picture Father Cartier, just like Dylan had described him, big and fat, strolling up this hall, maybe smirking when the terrified sound of the kids singing that song reached his ears.

"Who's in charge here?" Freddie demanded.

Sister Margaret wasn't fazed by his temperament.

"I am. And I'm not really sure how I can help you?"

"And yet, you haven't even asked why we're here," Freddie remarked, his tone unchanged.

Veronica moved in front of her partner, hoping that the physical separation would cause him to calm down a little.

"We just want to talk. Can we please come inside?" she asked.

"It's about the River Styx, in case you were wondering."

The glint in the nun's eyes dulled but only momentarily.

"Of course, come on in."

Sister Margaret stepped aside and held her arm out. Veronica went first, and Freddie followed.

Behind them, the nun closed the large wooden door and the sound of the heavy latch engaging echoed up and down the hall.

The interior of Renaissance Home had to be doom and gloom, didn't it? If even part of what Dylan said happened here was true, then there had to be some degree of pathetic fallacy at play.

But once again, the storyteller in Veronica was disappointed.

The lights were dimmer inside, but this was understandable—it was nearly two in the morning. But it was a far cry from dark.

"We can go this way, to my office." Sister Margaret indicated to the left.

Veronica couldn't take her eyes off the long hallway straight ahead.

"Can we walk this way?"

"I'd rather go to my office. The boys' rooms are that way, and they're asleep."

Freddie saw something on her face.

"Let's go this way—we'll be quiet, promise."

Again, that dark shadow crossed over the nun's features.

"Sure, why not?" This was accompanied by a tight smile.

They moved slowly, mostly on account of Freddie struggling to keep up. And they were quiet—the loudest thing was the giant keyring on the nun's hip that jangled with every step.

Veronica was glad that they didn't rush. It afforded her enough time to look at the dozens of framed photographs on the wall.

She let Freddie handle the questions.

"We wanted to ask you a few questions about the River Styx. Judging by the look on your face earlier, I'm guessing you know what we're talking about."

Most of the photos were action shots of what Veronica presumed to be orphans. The older ones were faded and had become sepia in tone.

"Yes—yes, I know it. Years ago, the kids used to sing it as part of a song."

The nun's nonchalance was alarming, but Veronica was too focused on the photos to pay much attention.

There was a muted coloring to the entire hallway, she realized.

Orange and yellow. A tinge of red.

Something that had happened here, likely long ago, triggered her synesthesia.

"Let me guess, when Father Cartier was still around?"

"I think so, God rest his soul."

Freddie grunted.

"Officer—"

"Detective," Freddie corrected.

"Right, Detective. I'm very tired and we start early here at Renaissance. If you were to just ask me directly what you think I might be able to help you with, we can probably speed this up."

"Abuse," Freddie said flatly. "We're here because of claims of child abuse at Renaissance by Father Cartier. That's where the song came from, right? One, two, he's coming for you... Father Cartier was the one coming for them, right? Coming to break—"

"That's preposterous. Father Cartier was a great man. He helped those boys—he was the father they never had."

This, Veronica couldn't ignore.

She whipped around.

"What father would do that to them? What kind of father would rape these boys?" Veronica got right in the nun's face. She remembered what Dylan had said about the nuns here, about how they'd revered Father Cartier. "Let me guess, you never saw him do anything wrong, did you? Father Cartier was a saint?"

"Father Cartier was a man," Sister Margaret corrected, her tone placating. "But he was a great man. Kids just like to make up stories, and I don't know who—"

"Stories?" Veronica spat. "What kind of kid makes up stories about being *raped*? About being terrified to—"

"Detective Shade!" Freddie shouted. It was his code word for her, letting her know that she'd taken things too far. "Please, calm down."

Behind the nun, Veronica saw the doors to the orphans' chambers. They had large brass handles and beneath those, old-fashioned keyholes.

The colors that spilled out of those locks were intense.

That was where the violence had taken place.

Veronica was so angry now that she was hissing.

She couldn't stop thinking about Dylan and her brother. About all those boys on the wall behind her.

Veronica also thought about her own life. Renaissance Home was an all-boys' orphanage, but those that housed girls were no different.

She could have been dropped off, abandoned.

Nobody thought of orphanages as places of deep, resounding love. Orphans often came with heavy baggage and those in charge weren't always best equipped to deal with their special needs.

A man beats his wife into a coma and a judge sentences him to eight years behind bars. A freak car accident takes the lives of mom and dad. A crackhead mother abandons her newborn outside a fire hall.

Special. Difficult.

Bullying runs rampant in orphanages—hierarchies are developed and staunchly maintained.

But this level of violence? Of abuse? No, that shouldn't exist. Not with kids. Not with anyone.

"We don't want to take up too much more of your time, Sister Margaret," Freddie said. "I think if we had a list of past and present orphans, that might help us."

"That is going to be a bit of a problem."

There was something so strange about this nun. Veronica had just accused the man who used to be in charge of a horrible crime, deplorable, and she just shook it off as if it was nothing.

Was it because she'd heard this all before? Had there been an investigation and Father Cartier was cleared?

What the fuck was going on here?

"If this is about a warrant, I can assure you that—"

"No, I would give you the files if we still had them," the nun said raising her shoulders. "Unfortunately, not long after Father Cartier passed, we had a—"

Fire.

Veronica was almost certain that the nun was going to say fire.

She didn't.

"—flood. Our records were ruined. Some of them just completely turned to mush while others became so moldy that we had to get rid of them."

Convenient.

Freddie frowned giving him a guppy-like appearance.

"What about digital records?"

The nun shook her head.

"Unfortunately, funding is rather tight and the only records we had were by paper and pen."

That fucking smile again. It seemed to Veronica to be the pious woman's way of saying fuck you without saying a single word.

"Well, you must know some of their names though, right?"

"I know—"

"Like Father Cartier's favorites? Do you remember their names? The ones he took swimming?"

"I'm—"

Freddie tried to stop her, tried to physically move her back, which shouldn't have been a problem given their size and weight discrepancy. But it was.

Veronica was agile and fueled by fury.

"What about Benny Davis? Do you remember him? *Huh?*"

Veronica came this close to grabbing the nun by her habit and throttling her—that's how incensed she was.

Throttling a fucking nun. A nun who had let two cops into an orphanage at three in the morning because they needed help with a case.

What would her dad think about her now?

Veronica was on the verge of calming down, but things went south when the nun opened her mouth again.

"I thought you looked familiar. You're his sister, aren't you? Little Benny Davis—"

Veronica lost it.

She reared back and slapped the nun across the face. The sound was loud and like everything in the hallway, it echoed. The nun spun with the blow, causing the keys on her hip to jangle loudly, adding to the cacophony.

"Veronica!"

Realizing what she'd done, Veronica jumped back. Her shoulders banged uncomfortably against the wall behind her, and a photo crashed to the ground.

"You need to leave, now!" Freddie ordered. Veronica stepped forward and her partner, thinking that she was going to take a swing at the old nun again, put a hand on her chest.

Veronica hit the wall again, not as hard this time, but it caused more photos to fall.

One of them landed face up and Veronica stared at it.

It was a group of boys standing in two rows, like a classroom picture. At the bottom was a list of their names. Standing in the back row, in the center, with his arms wrapped around the two boys closest to him, was Father Cartier.

He looked exactly the way she thought he would.

"Maybe there is a list of names after all."

"Veronica, you need to go—Sister Margaret, I'm so sorry for this."

"I think you both should leave." No longer did the nun have a fuck you voice, but a wavering one.

Good.

"Just—gimme a sec. Freddie, please."

Veronica picked up the two other fallen photos and looked at them. They didn't have what she needed, what she wanted.

Veronica leaped to her feet and started scanning all the photos on the wall.

Where is it… where is it… there.

A polar plunge—that's what it felt like. Veronica couldn't breathe, her heart couldn't even beat. Every single cell in her body was flash-frozen.

Benny Davis.

Her brother.

In the faded picture, Benny was standing beside another boy. Neither were smiling. The scars on his head and neck were pink and raw—there was no date on this action shot, but it must have been taken less than a year after the fire.

Veronica still couldn't believe that all these years, Benny was right here. In Matheson. Less than a few hours away, no matter where in the state her dad took her.

"Fuck." Veronica wiped at her eyes, but they were dry.

One, two, I'm coming for you.

If anyone deserved that abuse, it was her, not Benny. She'd played the game. She'd won EENIE, MEANIE, MINEY, MO.

And she had chosen herself. There was no greater, selfish sin than that.

"Veronica, we should go now."

Veronica was inclined to agree but then she looked at the photo again.

"Wait—"

"No, we can't wait. Let's get—"

Veronica shook her partner's meaty hands off her.

"Wait! I... I know this boy—this kid!" She wasn't pointing at Benny now, but at the orphan beside Benny. Like her brother, he looked sickly, pale, but instead of a scarred scalp, he had shaggy dark hair. Veronica looked past Freddie at Sister Margaret, who was still crouched and holding her left cheek. "Who is this? Who is this?"

"Leave. Get out of here, now." A meek command.

"Tell me where—ah, fuck it."

Veronica quickly scanned the photos on the wall.

"Veronica?" Freddie said, softer now.

"Wait—wait, wait, wait."

She found it. The 'class photo'. Benny was there, and so was Dylan, who stood out because even at such a young age he was head and shoulders taller than the rest.

In the back was the boy with the midnight black hair.

Veronica took the photo off the wall and pointed at him.

"It's him—he was at the library when I took the book out," Veronica whispered. "He was also in the hospital—he was the doctor talking to Steve. And—and I think—Freddie, I think I've seen him at Dr. Bernard's office before." Now the tears came. Not a deluge, but just a misting. Veronica glanced at Freddie through foggy vision. "This is the man we're looking for." She looked at the legend beneath the photo and found the boy's name. "Dante Fiori—that's who's behind this."

"Get out!" the nun suddenly screamed.

Veronica tucked both photos, the one with Dante and her brother, and the group shot, under one arm.

"Gladly," she said with a sneer. "But I'll be back—I'm coming back for you."

Chapter 51

"Dante Fiori," Steve read out loud. "He owns a white 2007 Mazda. Last known address, 714 Willington Ave. in Matheson."

The photograph was old, taken during the man's arrest more than four years ago. Short dark hair, almost buzzed, pale features. Slight, with high cheek bones.

Steve didn't recognize him.

He leaned closer to his computer monitor, but Dante's appearance still triggered nothing.

"I've never seen him before," Deputy Marcus McVeigh remarked. Then he snapped his fingers. "But that name... hold on a sec."

Before Steve could stop him, McVeigh was already rushing out of his office.

Dante Fiori... Dante Fiori...

The name and face meant nothing to the sheriff. Unlike McVeigh, he hadn't seen or heard it before. Despite the day's revelations, Veronica's past was still very much a secret. Steve had no idea who her friends were let alone ex-boyfriends. He'd long since given up asking, too, concluding that Veronica didn't lead a normal life—she simply didn't have friends or a history of love.

Her synesthesia explained why—at least in part. The fact that her father forced her to move around as often as he did was also a contributing factor.

But still... Dante Fiori... *nothing*.

Steve thought that he'd feel something when the murderer who was stalking his girlfriend was finally revealed. But there was no *voila* moment for Steve, no instant recognition.

"Who the fuck are you and what do you have to do with Veronica?" he whispered.

Determined to find out more, to identify the link tying this all together, Steve performed a deeper search of the Oregon criminal database. Dante Fiori didn't have an extensive record, but he was in the system. The man's crimes ran the gamut from petty theft to robbery, with a couple of assault and batteries sprinkled in. Never spent any real time behind bars.

But it was the man's first crime, disorderly conduct, that drew Sheriff Burns' attention. It wasn't the crime itself that was of interest but what Dante had written in the "address" box of the arrest sheet.

Renaissance Home.

"What the hell?"

Renaissance Home was the same orphanage that Veronica's brother, Benny Davis, had been shipped off to.

This couldn't be a coincidence.

Steve was in the process of searching for a home page or other information pertaining to the orphanage when McVeigh returned. He quickly closed his browser and nodded toward the stack of papers in his chief deputy's hands.

"What do you got?"

"Check it out." McVeigh flipped through the pages before stopping and pointing at a line.

It was the same name—*Dante Fiori*—but Sheriff Burns wasn't sure what he was looking at.

"What is this? Where's this from?"

"It's a list of people who attended at least one of Gina Braden's CrossFit sessions over the past few months. Dante went three times. I knew I recognized his name from somewhere."

Steve read the name again.

"Where did you get this from?"

"From the gym."

Steve turned his chair and looked up at McVeigh, who was standing over him. He couldn't remember asking anyone to go to Gina's gym. In fact, he hadn't done much of any investigating into Gina's death.

Was it the drugs? Had they made him sloppy? Forgetful? Or was it because he was so emotionally charged? Because this case was personal, and it all revolved around Veronica?

"No, I mean, like, who got it?"

"Oh, Deputy Lancaster. I sent him out to the library and the gym after we discovered Gina's body this morning."

Another thought started to creep into Steve's brain.

Doubt.

Doubt that he was a half-decent sheriff, that he was good for Bear County.

Doubt that he could protect even those closest to him.

"Steve?"

Sheriff Burns cleared his throat, and he made a fist, trying to stop the trembling.

"Good work."

"Thanks," McVeigh said hesitantly. "I guess that's why Gina went into the store and bought the paint while this Dante guy waited in the car. Gina knew him, trusted him."

Once again, Steve fell silent.

"Do you want to head out to his house? Or should I—"

"Wait, do you remember the smoking woman in the robe?" Steve asked. His memory from this morning was foggy, but something wasn't sitting right with him.

"Yeah, Linda. What about her?"

"She said she saw Gina carrying the paint buckets inside. Why would she do that? Even if she bought the paint for Dante as a favor or something, why would she bring them into her own house? Storage? Seems odd, no?"

"I don't think that's what Linda said," McVeigh countered.

"What do you mean? The woman said she saw Gina bring the buckets inside. Thought she was doing a reno or something."

"No, I'm pretty sure she said she saw someone who looked like Gina, someone wearing Gina's hat, carrying the paint."

Steve rubbed at the pasties in the corners of his mouth with a finger.

"Right, you're right. And Deputy Milligan said that the guy in the car was wearing a hat. Goddamn it, it wasn't Gina carrying the paint. Gina was already dead."

"Probably."

"Fuck." Steve was embarrassed. Not because he'd forgotten a minute detail, but because he'd botched pretty much everything when it came to this case. His main objective had never been to find Dr. Bernard or to capture a killer. It was to get high. "Fuck."

"It's alright," McVeigh consoled. His voice seemed genuine, but there was a gleam in his eyes that Steve didn't care for. But there was nothing he could do about it. McVeigh had the videotape of him breaking into the evidence room. And now the chief deputy was just biding his time, waiting for the best opportunity to take his shot. "So, you want me to put the call in? Send a team to Dante's residence?"

"Yeah." Steve's throat was as dry as his lips now. "Six-man team, maintain a perimeter. Observe, do not engage. If there's any movement from inside, they are to wait until we arrive before they do anything at all."

"Got it."

As McVeigh leaned out of the room to relay the sheriff's directives, Steve went back to his computer.

His search for Renaissance Home didn't come up with much. Just a homepage, generic, reiterating what Steve already knew: that it was a state-funded, church-run, orphanage for boys.

An idea occurred to him then and he went back to the list of inmates from D-Block.

And there it was, staring him right in the face.

"Clyde Krause," he said out loud. McVeigh wrapped up his call and returned to his side. "Check it out: Clyde Krause attended Renaissance Home as did Dante Fiori. That's the link."

Steve addressed his computer again, calling up D-Block inmate Clyde Krause's visitor logs.

The man only had two: six months ago, a Sister Margaret Fortin, and three weeks ago, Dante Fiori.

If there was any residual doubt that Dante was their man, this shattered it.

"So, three weeks ago, Dante meets with Clyde and then yesterday, after Detective Shade unexpectedly visits Ken Cameron, the man is murdered," McVeigh said, musing out loud.

Even though Steve was convinced that Dante was behind the murders, there were still many holes in the case that needed to be filled.

Like motive, for one.

And there was a glaring problem, punctuated by another search that revealed that Clyde Krause hadn't used the phone in over a month. He had been in the shower when Ken was killed, but not in the phone room.

Today, technically yesterday now, Veronica had gone on *Marlowe*. Gina, who had already been kidnapped by this point, calls into the show, and the psychopath, Dante, taunts them with his song.

Everything followed a specific sequence after that: Veronica met with Cole, then Ken, then with Dr. Bernard.

How could Dante have orchestrated all of this for today? For this *exact* day? Three weeks ago, *Marlowe* hadn't reached out yet—the dollmaker wasn't even cold. But that's when Dante met Krause, which was the only time he could have told him to kill Ken and spread that blue liquid soap everywhere.

"Do we have footage of the meeting between Clyde and Dante?" McVeigh asked, clearly thinking the same thing that Steve was.

"We should."

As Sheriff Burns sifted through video footage from Bear County Correctional, Deputy McVeigh's radio squelched.

"No car in the driveway, Deputy. No movement from inside, either. Lights are all off. How do you want us to proceed? Over."

McVeigh cursed.

"Sit tight. Maintain perimeter. Update me if you see any movement. Over, out." Then to Steve, he said, "He's not coming back to his house. He wouldn't be that stupid."

Sheriff Burns grunted an affirmative.

"Here, this is the meeting," he said, then pressed play.

Once again, any expectation of a great revelation was quickly dashed.

Clyde Krause was a big man with a shaved head and a scar behind his left ear. He was led into the room by a deputy and seated at a round metal table.

A few seconds later, another man walked in, this one more slight, with shaggy black hair. Dante was a little thicker than in his arrest photo, but not by much. And even though his back was to the camera, something about his gait struck Steve as familiar.

Dante took a seat across from Clyde, and they exchanged a few words. Then Dante took out a small photograph and showed it to the man, which Clyde stared at for a good twenty or thirty seconds before nodding. The picture returned to his pocket and that was it.

"What's that picture? Ken Cameron?" McVeigh asked.

"No, Clyde and Ken are both in D-Block. All Dante would have to do is say Ken's name, not show him a picture."

"Then who?"

Steve pressed play again. Right before exiting the room, Dante looked up at the camera and the sheriff paused the video.

He looked almost like a different man compared to his mugshot.

And Steve recognized him immediately.

"*Ffffuck.*" The word came out as a moan.

"What?"

Almost everything fell into place then and Steve knew who was in the picture that Dante had shown Clyde.

"I know this man. He—he was the doctor at the hospital after the fire. He was standing outside Veronica's room."

Chapter 52

"I don't… I don't really understand why we're going back there, back to Matheson," Freddie said hesitantly. "We should call Captain Bottel, let him know what we've found."

"And say what? That even though I'm off the case and that you were supposed to babysit me, we kept on digging? That we, I dunno, kinda illegally read confidential files and then interrogated a CI?"

"Well—"

"The captain's going to know soon enough, anyways. That nun is gonna call the cops, report that I slapped her."

Out of the corner of her eye, Veronica saw Freddie wince and suddenly felt bad about dragging her partner through the mud with her. He was a grown man, he made his own decisions. When she'd taken his car keys, he could've stopped her.

Except he couldn't, because he was bound by loyalty.

"I lost it, I know," Veronica said with a heavy sigh. "I'm sorry. But this case… it's about me and it's about Benny. I can't stop."

Freddie nodded ever so slightly.

He understood, of course.

"But why are we going back to the evidence locker?" The man's voice cracked, and Veronica couldn't help but think that this wasn't entirely due to lack of sleep.

"Because, before, when I was looking through the Ss for my name, there was one file that was misplaced. That's not a mistake that Dr. Bernard would ever make." Veronica glanced at the photo of her brother and the other boy that she'd removed from the broken picture frame and had placed on the dash. "I didn't read the last name. All I know is that it started with an F."

"And you're sure you've seen this guy at Dr. Bernard's office before?"

In her mind, Veronica pictured the last time she'd barged into Jane's office unannounced. Dante had been there alright. She remembered him with his head down, his hair in front of his face as he left.

"Yeah, I'm sure."

Freddie snatched the pictures and looked at them both, one in each hand, as Veronica continued to drive toward the Matheson Police Station.

"And you think this Dante Fiori guy put his file next to yours on purpose?"

"I'm sure of it."

Freddie raised one thick shoulder.

"But how would Dante know that you would get access to the files? I mean, they were in Dr. Bernard's office. It's not like she would have just let you look at them."

"Yeah, but he set the room on fire," Veronica reminded him.

"Right, okay, so you had access to them, but how would he know you would actually read them?"

It took Veronica only a single beat to come up with the answer.

"Because he read *my* file, that's how—he knew how I would react once Jane went missing." Veronica shuddered. "That's how Dante knew about me, about my synesthesia, about everything."

This is what she'd thought from the very beginning, but now she was absolutely certain of it. Instead of feeling vindicated, Veronica only felt violated.

"*Riiiight.*"

Freddie was still looking at the pictures and his lack of confidence in Veronica's reply annoyed her.

"I'm telling you, it's the truth."

His eyes darted to hers, and there was an unexpected coldness to them.

"Is this your superpower telling you or...?"

Not only was this the completely wrong time to make a joke, but Veronica didn't think it was one. Not with that icy stare.

"What?" she balked. "What are you talking about?"

Freddie backed down.

"Nothin'. I just don't think it's a good idea to go back there."

"Fine. I'll drop you off wherever you want to go."

"It's my car," Freddie reminded her.

"I'll get mine then."

"No, I'm sorry—I'm just tired." He rubbed his eyes for effect but Veronica, whose nasal passages seemed to have cleared somewhat since visiting Renaissance, detected a strong whiff of gas.

He wasn't *just* tired. There was something else going on.

"I can drop you off, you can grab my car, or we can switch. Up to you. You don't have to come with me."

"It's fine." There was a finality to her partner's voice that convinced her to drop the subject.

The past twenty-four to thirty-six hours had been draining for all of them, not just her—Veronica forced herself to remember that. Yet, everyone in her life, from her father, to Steve, to Freddie, seemed different even before everything had gone down.

She couldn't hold the fact that her father was sleeping with Jane against him—he was a grown man and she was a grown woman. But he'd been short with her in a way he hadn't been in years. A subtle, yet noticeable difference.

Then there was Steve... there was something serious going on with her boyfriend. He was on edge, seemingly on the verge of snapping at every little thing. It could be the stress, sure, but the sheriff had nearly resorted to violence on several occasions. Not only was that not like him, but it scared Veronica. She thought she knew what kind of man he was. She thought she loved him.

Maybe there was a darker side to Steve. Maybe she didn't really know him at all. Veronica had tried to look into his past and had come up blank. Asking Steve directly was a non-starter. At the time, Veronica thought that fair, given her own shrouded history, but now that her life story had been aired like dirty laundry, maybe it was time for him to come clean, too. And if Steve refused?

The unexpected image of Cole Batherson lying on his hospital bed came to mind.

"Why did Cole get my dad fired?" Veronica asked, wanting to change the subject of her thoughts. "And don't even try to tell me it was because he missed the meeting with the mayor. I'm not that stupid."

For a while, this was exactly what she'd believed, however.

"Freddie?"

The man averted his gaze.

"No, don't do that. Tell me."

"Maybe—" he looked at her. "Maybe Cole isn't such a bad guy."

"And maybe Gordon Trammel was an angel. What are you talking about?"

"It's just—it's not my place to say."

Veronica threw up her arms.

"What the fuck is with everyone and their secrets?"

Oh, shit.

It was one of the stupidest things she could've said for a myriad of reasons. And Veronica regretted opening her mouth.

"Okay, you want to really know what happened?" Freddie said, his eyes boring into her now. She'd never seen him this incensed before, especially not at her.

And there it was again, people not being who they seemed. Freddie continued unprompted.

"Cole didn't get your dad fired, Veronica. *You* did."

"What?" Veronica gasped. "What are you talking about?"

"You got him fired, Veronica."

"That makes no sense. What did I do?"

Freddie sighed and his tone softened a little.

"Cole was being pressured by everybody. The department, the mayor… even the fucking union wanted a scapegoat for the Ken Cameron disaster. Nobody could believe that a man like that could exist in the police department for as long as he did without somebody knowing about it."

"And they thought *I* knew?"

"No. But you weren't exactly present. You left, remember? You were warned to stay on task, to do everything by the book."

"But—but we were looking for people who stole watches, Freddie. There was a killer out there, remember?"

"I remember you not checking in. I remember you nearly getting me killed. I remember not knowing where you were half the time."

Veronica cringed.

"I thought you said that Cole was a good guy? How could he be a good guy if he tried to get me fired?"

"You don't get it." Freddie shook his head. "He didn't."

"I don't understand."

"Cole went to your dad, showed him his report. It was... sparkling. No mention of you, of anyone. No mention of misconduct, all rainbows, and unicorns. A bunch of horseshit, but still."

"Then why did my dad get fired?"

"Because Peter was smart, and Peter had been in the game for a long time in many different departments. He knew if Cole submitted that report, if he didn't come up with a scapegoat, they'd fire him."

"But—"

"Not done yet. And after Cole was fired, they'd send someone to replace him. And that person might not be so nice. They'd question everybody, and let's just say that you're not the most popular in the department."

Veronica finally understood.

"If someone else from IA came in, I'd be cut loose."

"Pretty much."

"He—my dad told Cole to change the report," Veronica said. "To implicate himself, to make it look like it was his fault that he never spotted Ken Cameron's tendencies earlier."

Freddie nodded.

"Yeah. He knew he'd get a full ride and the mayor was more than happy to accept the report, no questions asked. Mayor Dixon agreed to say nothing disparaging about your father, just mention that they were cleaning house, reorganizing the department. Corporate buzzwords. It was a win-win for everyone."

"Except for my dad."

Freddie shrugged and the loose skin beneath his chin jiggled.

"He's moved around a lot, I think he kinda liked the idea of staying put."

And that lasted for how long? Three months? If that? Then he started screwing my psychiatrist.

"Anyways, I'd think about that before you were so harsh on Cole."

Veronica pictured Cole's handsome face, marred with soot.

Maybe… maybe he's not such a bad guy after all.

Back to that again, bad guys, people not being who she thought they were.

Freddie fit that mold to a *T*. Like Steve, he was short-tempered, irritable. Fine, understandable enough—everyone had their bad days. But he'd always been someone she could count on. Someone she could trust.

Veronica wasn't so sure if that was the case anymore.

Unlike with Steve and her father, she thought she could pinpoint the moment when Freddie had changed. It had been that morning—Freddie's oddly intense meeting with FBI Agent Keller.

"Is everything all right with you?" Veronica asked in a voice she hoped would express her genuine concern.

"Like I said, just tired."

Again, a lie.

Veronica clenched her teeth. It was clear that her partner didn't want to talk about it, but from her own experience, she knew that sometimes the best medicine was the most difficult to swallow.

"Freddie… I saw you this morning with Agent Keller."

"You spying on me now?" Freddie snapped.

Veronica was taken aback by the man's vitriol.

"No, I just saw you. You looked like you—"

"I'm just tired."

Frustrated by this repeated lie, Veronica doubled down.

"You're lying, Freddie. You can't lie to me. I want to help, but—"

"You know what? Take me to your—no, just drop me off here."

"Freddie, c'mon. I'm just trying to—"

"Drop me off!" Freddie's booming voice filled the car and Veronica shrunk into the oversized seat.

She'd never heard the man yell before. It was impressive. And terrifying.

Veronica was reminded of the way that Steve had acted when he'd stormed *Marlowe's* stage.

"Okay," Veronica said reluctantly. "Fine."

She pulled over to the side of the road. They were perhaps ten minutes from Matheson PD and Veronica was tempted to ask if Freddie was sure, to apologize, to suggest that they just keep going, but the man's jaw was set, and so was his mind. To top off the bizarreness of the situation, Veronica was actually driving his car.

But no matter how pissed off her partner was, she wouldn't give it up. She needed to get back to Dr. Bernard's files, she needed to read what Jane had written about Dante Fiori. The man had been inside her head, and now it was time for her to enter his.

"Here, at least take my keys. My car is at Dr. Bernard's—"

Freddie snatched the keys and got out of the car, slamming the door behind him for good measure. An old hamburger wrapper dislodged from the door pocket and landed on the seat.

"—office."

Freddie had his back to her and was already walking away.

Veronica wanted to call out to him, explain to him that she was only trying to help. But best-case scenario, she wasted her breath and Freddie ignored her. Worst case, they would get into a deep discussion that would slow her down.

Veronica put the car in drive and continued on her route to Matheson PD, a single thought on her mind.

What the fuck is going on with everyone today?

Chapter 53

STEVE KNEW HE WAS IN trouble. The shaking had spread from his hand to his arm, and now, every few seconds his shoulder started to twitch.

A cold sweat had broken out on his forehead, but he felt like he was burning. All symptoms of the flu, but Steve wasn't sick.

He had no choice but to send Deputy McVeigh to Dante Fiori's house—anywhere but by his side. He also commissioned his chief deputy with the task of asking one of their most dependable judges for a warrant to enter their suspect's home.

All tasks for a sheriff, which made McVeigh, even though he tried to hide his emotions, incredibly happy. If things kept going this way, maybe he wouldn't have to threaten Steve with the evidence locker footage. Maybe his addiction would drive him out of office without any of the deputy's influence.

On the way to the hospital, he called Dahlia. There was still more he needed to confirm about his theory.

The woman didn't answer until the fifth ring.

"H-hello?" She sounded half-asleep.

"Dahlia, it's Sheriff Burns."

"Oh." Steve heard her sit up. "What can I do for you, Sheriff?"

"Marlowe—" he caught himself. He'd nearly said that Marlowe was dead. Dahlia didn't know that—couldn't know that. Steve scolded himself and then quickly changed his approach. "I know that Marlowe is protective about her information, and I respect that. But there's something I need to know. This is... I can't impress on you how important it is."

It's so important that it could mean catching your boss' killer or letting him get away.

"I already gave you the recording, and if Marlowe finds out about—"

"Marlowe won't find out." Steve snapped. If he thought that telling Dahlia that her boss was dead would do anything other than cause the woman to break down, he would've broken the news over the phone in a second. "I need to know how the interview with Veronica was set up."

Fuck, it felt wrong, speaking as if Marlowe was still alive, deceiving this well-meaning woman. It felt like he was taking advantage of Dahlia's abuse.

Steve's shoulder twitched so violently that his entire body shook.

"What... what do you mean?"

"Who called who? Did you reach out to Greenham PD, or did someone call you?"

There was a short pause.

"Marlowe was looking for stories about powerful women for a week-long theme. We called Greenham PD."

Steve scrunched his nose.

"You sure?"

"Yeah, it was—no, wait a second, I'm sorry I'm sleepy. Someone called me, told me about her, said to reach out to Greenham. I looked into her story and that's when—"

"You're sure that someone called you first?" Steve interrupted.

"Yeah. Yeah, I'm sure."

That's what I thought.

"Thanks."

Dahlia coughed dryly.

"What's this—what's this about, Sheriff?"

"Nothing—go back to sleep." Now Steve initiated a pause. "And I'm sorry. I really am."

"For—for what?"

Steve hung up just as he pulled into the hospital parking lot.

It came as no surprise that no one recognized either a photo of Dante Fiori, his mugshot, or the still he'd printed from the man's recent visit to Bear County Correctional. Administration claimed that not only was Dante Fiori not a doctor on staff, but he'd never been a patient, either.

He debated asking to see the video footage from earlier in the day but, in the end, decided that that would just be a waste of time. If this ever went to trial, it might prove useful: Dante had posed as a doctor to gain access to Veronica's room for one reason.

To steal her gun, which he later used to murder Marlowe Lerman.

But that didn't matter now.

After instructing security to be on the lookout for someone who fit Dante's description, and to archive all video footage from the last week, Steve left the hospital less than half an hour after he'd arrived.

Next stop: Renaissance Home.

The link between Dante and Veronica was clearly related to her brother and they intersected at the orphanage. That was the best that his addled mind could marshal.

He was parked outside the large wrought-iron gates, preparing to get out of his car, when his radio crackled.

The sound was so startling that he actually cried out.

"Sheriff Burns?"

Holy fuck.

It took Steve seven breaths—he counted them—to calm down enough to answer.

"Yeah?"

Yeah—that's all he could say.

Pathetic.

"Breached Dante Fiori's residence at 3:56 am." Of course, Deputy McVeigh sounded official, sounded as if he'd gotten a good night's sleep.

"And?"

"He's not here. Dr. Bernard neither."

No surprises there, at least. It would have been fitting if Jane had been inside Dante's, if McVeigh had rescued the psychiatrist. It would signal the end of his tenure as Bear County Sheriff, but at least then he'd be able to move on.

Steve's thoughts mimicked his uncontrollable movements: disjointed, fragmented. Inappropriate.

"Anything else?"

"Uhh, yeah, I'm not really sure—"

"Just fucking tell me, Marcus. Stop with this bullshit posturing and tell me what you found."

"Right, sorry, sir. Well, we found something in the basement. A shrine, so to speak."

Steve squeezed his eyes tight and shook his head.

He knew what the shrine was all about before his deputy so much as hinted at it.

"We have pictures of Veronica, lots of pictures. Most are recent. Surrounding these are photos of the victims. Gina, Cole, Dr. Bernard. There's one of Marlowe, too—Veronica is in the shot. It looks like it might have been taken from the set."

Steve shut his eyes. He thought he could picture Dante as one of the cameramen, but this might just be projection. He was high at the time, after all.

"Anything else?"

"Yeah, uhh, there's a picture of you here, too. You and Peter Shade."

Steve was alarmed but not surprised.

"Any photos of her brother? Of Benny Davis?"

He heard McVeigh rifling through what sounded like a thick stack of photographs.

Jesus, how many pictures did this psycho take?

"To be honest, I'm not sure what Veronica's brother looks like. Is he—"

"Just send them to me. Snap a pic and send me a copy of everything you see there."

McVeigh groaned.

"That'll take at least—"

"Yeah, well, just do it."

You're not the sheriff yet, boy.

Steve switched off his radio and got out of the car. He had little experience with orphanages, and the only interactions he'd had with churches were at his wife's insistence. But he didn't think that nuns were supposed to be so hostile.

"No, ma'am, I'm not from the City of Greenham. I'm the Bear County sheriff and the last time I checked, Matheson is located in Bear County. Now, I just want to—"

Steve stopped speaking when the gate unlocked. Moving quickly, he made his way to the front door.

An elderly nun dressed in a black habit stood with her arms crossed over her narrow chest.

"I'm glad you're here—I was just about to call somebody."

Steve was suddenly on high alert.

Was Dante here?

The nun's lack of urgency suggested not, but she also probably knew Dante from his time in the orphanage.

"Really?"

"Yes." The nun wrinkled her lips. "That woman slapped me." She pointed at her left cheek, which looked a little red. "Right here."

Again, unexpected.

"What woman? Who?"

What the fuck is going on?

"Some policewoman. I don't remember her name, but she had this man with her, a huge man."

Steve winced.

Freddie and Veronica were supposed to be at the hotel. He didn't really believe that they would stay there, but why would they come here?

And why the hell would Veronica slap a nun for Christ's sake?

"I'll look into it," he said, knowing that he would do nothing of the sort. "What did they want?"

The woman had sharp eyes and she leveled them at Steve. It appeared to the sheriff as if she was being selective with her words.

"They wanted access to records, wanted a list of previous orphans at Renaissance Home."

"And did you give it to them?" Steve looked past the woman and into a wide hallway. The walls were bare, but there were multiple squares that were darker than the surrounding area along its length. He also noted a few small pieces of glass on the floor.

To him, it looked like someone had recently removed a series of photographs.

"No, I didn't. I told them that they were destroyed in a flood."

The nun moved a little, and while she was too small to block Steve's entire view of the hall, she just happened to place her head directly in the path of the missing photos.

"The reason why I came here, ma'am—"

"Sister."

"Sorry, Sister. The reason why I came here is because I wanted to ask you about a former… student." He almost said patient.

The nun squinted and Steve had the sneaking suspicion that she already knew who he was going to ask about.

What wasn't clear was if this was a result of Veronica and Freddie inquiring about Dante or if she just assumed it was him from past experience.

"Dante Fiori? Do you know him?"

"Dante… no, I don't think so. Was he recent?"

"Long time ago. You sure?"

"I'm sorry, Sheriff, my memory isn't as good as it used to be."

This seemed like a lie. The woman might be old and creased, but she was still sharp.

"What about Benny Davis?"

A slight twitch, nearly imperceptible. If Steve hadn't currently been dealing with a bout of uncontrollable spasms of his own, he might not have noticed.

"No, sorry."

Sheriff Burns stared at the nun, giving her a moment to reconsider. She didn't, and he knew that this, like everything else, was a dead end.

"One more thing, Sister." Sister came out with a little extra zeal and the nun picked up on this. Her arms tightened. "You doing some renos in there?"

"…renos?"

"Yeah? It looks like some pictures are missing from your wall."

"Oh, that. Well, that police lady, she took two of them. Stole them."

"Right, but it looks like there's a lot more than two photographs missing."

The nun didn't even turn around.

"I'm very tired, Sheriff."

"Hmm. Me, too." He tipped his hat. "Thank you for your time."

He was already making his way back to his car when she hollered, "I want that woman arrested!"

Not going to happen.

Once behind the wheel, Steve took out his cell phone. McVeigh had already sent him dozens of photographs from Dante's house—of course he had. He scrolled through the images with the speed of a serial polygamist on a dating app, feeling a chill when he passed images of Gina and Marlowe.

Not even his own photo, taken yesterday while he'd been in his car with Veronica outside the *Marlowe* set, made him stop scrolling.

It was an older image that finally stayed his hand. It was faded, almost completely devoid of color. He wasn't sure how he knew, but Sheriff Burns was certain that it had been one of the pictures on the wall of Renaissance Home. Probably one that Veronica had taken.

It showed Benny Davis and Dante Fiori, bare-chested, arms around each other. In the background, Steve could see a fast-flowing river. It should have been a happy photo. It would have been, if they'd been smiling.

Only they weren't, and there was deep pain in both young boys' eyes.

Steve exhaled all the air from his lungs.

He knew what he had to do.

People weren't going to like it—people being primarily Veronica Shade.

But he had to involve the press. He had to get Dante Fiori's face in front of the camera, and a description of his car out to the media. Somebody had to know where he was hiding.

Somebody had to know where he was keeping Dr. Jane Bernard.

Sheriff Burns just hoped that they led him to a person and not a corpse.

Chapter 54

VERONICA HAD BEEN RIGHT. IT was Dante Fiori's file that had been pressed up against hers. And this was no accident. He'd put it there, knowing she'd find it.

What was a surprise was that it was nearly as thick as her own.

The first entry was from nearly fifteen years ago when Dante was eleven. It followed a familiar pattern, one that started out as reserved and untrusting, to the boy gradually opening up over several years.

About fifteen pages in, corresponding to roughly an equal number of sessions, Dante made the first mention of a friend. As far as Veronica could tell, there was no mention of this friend's name anywhere in the heavy folder.

But she knew exactly who this other boy was.

It was the boy from the photo she'd stolen from the orphanage.

Dante Fiori's friend was Benny Davis.

It would take hours to read all of Dr. Bernard's notes, and Veronica didn't have the time nor the stomach for it.

She wasn't sure if Dr. Bernard had deliberately been obtuse when it came to writing about Dante's abuse or if that was just how the man had recounted the horrific events that transpired at the hands of Father Cartier.

It didn't matter—a victim of abuse herself, Veronica was an expert at reading between the lines.

And the more she read, real or implied, only served to anger her further.

Skimming the pages felt wrong, like skipping chapters in a biography, but it was necessary. Over time, Dante's sessions became more structured, less manic.

Then, about four months ago, Veronica detected a change, a reversion.

Eleven-year-old Dante was back. And he was still fucking pissed. Only, not so much at Father Cartier anymore.

At someone else. Like his friend, this person went unnamed. Also like his friend, Veronica knew who it was.

And so she should.

Because it was her.

The problem was that Dante's frame of mind degenerated so quickly and violently that it was impossible for Veronica to understand the impetus behind it. Then, a month ago, things became borderline incoherent. And these were Dr. Bernard's writings, her interpretations. In person, Veronica assumed Dante was downright psychotic.

"What the fuck happened four months ago?"

Veronica took a break to rub her eyes.

It was too much. Even what she'd been through as a child didn't compare to Dante's upbringing.

Dante and Benny and probably Dylan, too.

The sun would rise soon, and that would mark nearly an entire day that Dr. Jane Bernard had been missing. While this was clearly no normal case, Veronica couldn't ignore the facts. If a victim wasn't recovered after the first twenty-four hours of a kidnapping, the odds of them ever being returned alive dropped precipitously.

The only thing working in their favor was that Dante had a history with Dr. Bernard.

Veronica shook her head.

Was this really a positive?

Maybe not.

If what Dylan said was true, and Veronica had no reason not to believe him, then Father Cartier was working at Renaissance Home up until the day he keeled over from a heart attack.

Why hadn't Jane done anything to make the abuse stop?

Veronica quickly scrolled back through the notes.

It didn't appear as if Dante opened up about the abuse until he was older, and it wasn't clear if he was still at Renaissance at that time. Even if Dante had left by then, there were other boys. Other boys being abused in the orphanage.

Molested.

Raped.

Veronica was running out of time, and so was Jane. And while these tales of abuse were eye-opening, they weren't anything new. Dylan had already told her and Freddie about Father Cartier.

You wanna know how many people went to his funeral? I don't know either because I wasn't there. But I bet you nobody went. Not a single fucking person. Not even those nun bitches who looked up to him like he was God.

What Veronica needed was a way to find Dante. And she remained convinced that that information was there. Buried in these notes.

But where?

Veronica flipped to the very last page. Dante's final session with Dr. Bernard had been roughly three weeks ago.

And, by all accounts, it had been brief.

Dr. Bernard had written a single word: *Report.*

Veronica frowned.

Report what? Report the crimes committed against Dante? Or report Dante?

Did Jane know that he was close to snapping?

If anyone had known, it would be her. But she couldn't have predicted this. Couldn't have predicted that she was destined to become one of Dante's victims.

Frustrated, Veronica flipped the final page over.

There was more here. Only, it wasn't in Dr. Bernard's hand. It was Dante's writing.

Crooked, all capital letters.

Four simple, familiar lines.

ONE, TWO, I'M COMING FOR YOU.
THREE, FOUR, LOCK YOUR DOOR.
FIVE, SIX, I CROSSED THE RIVER STYX.
SEVEN, EIGHT, I'VE SEALED YOUR FATE.

The final line in the last 'E' dragged all the way to the bottom of the page.

Veronica read the nursery rhyme three times, and after the third, an idea came to her.

She was inside Dante's head now, the way he had been in hers.

And she knew exactly how to get the man to come out of hiding. It would put her directly in the psychopath's crosshairs but that was only fitting.

Because that was what she deserved.

This was Veronica's fault.

And so long as no one else associated with her got hurt, she was okay with facing the consequences.

However terminal they may be.

Chapter 55

FREDDIE FELT TERRIBLE ABOUT WHAT had happened, at lashing out at Veronica the way he had.

But he had no choice. He couldn't go back to the Matheson Evidence room. It was too risky. And he couldn't tell Veronica about his meeting with Agent Keller, either, because this would only prompt more questions.

For all her faults, Veronica was a smart and capable cop. She would dig until she uncovered the answers she was looking for.

But some secrets were best left buried. Even though Veronica wasn't at fault for the disaster that was the *Marlowe* TV show, she was partially to blame for her history becoming public knowledge.

Going on live TV was a risk, a risk she'd known and willingly took.

It wasn't a risk Freddie was inclined to accept.

An Uber dropped him off at Dr. Bernard's office, but it took longer than he'd hoped to grab Veronica's car. The entire building was still a crime scene, and while her vehicle wasn't part of this, it was still close enough that he couldn't just jump in and drive off without others noticing. If a beat cop recognized him, and, quite frankly, he was difficult to be mistaken, they were likely to report his presence—his presence *without* Detective Shade accompanying him—to Captain Bottel.

He'd be called in, regardless of the hour.

And the clock was ticking.

Freddie waited in the darkness until there was a shift break, and then he made what to him qualified as a mad dash to Veronica's car. In reality, it was more of an aggravated shuffle than anything else.

He really did not like to run.

But it worked. Nobody noticed him getting in the detective's car and nobody noticed him driving away.

DEA Agent Troy Allison was standing outside the dilapidated headquarters smoking a cigarette when Freddie pulled up.

The bald man saw him park and get out, but nothing about him changed. When Freddie was within ten feet of Troy, the man leaned inside the door to the building and snapped his fingers twice. Then he went back to smoking.

Two seconds later, the door swung open, and Randall Byers came out. He was trembling and his eyes reflected the headlights of Veronica's car like two lighthouse beacons.

"Wh-what's happening?"

Randall saw Freddie and ran to his father, trying his best to embrace him. The thin boy could barely get his arms halfway around his waist, but Freddie swallowed him whole. Randy reeked of sweat and old cigarettes.

After a beat, he looked at DEA Agent Allison. The man had lit another cigarette and was staring at the glowing ember as if it were the most interesting thing in the world.

"Thank you," Freddie said, giving his son another squeeze. "Thank you so much. This —"

The man exhaled an impressively tight stream of smoke.

"I know what you did."

Freddie felt a lump form in his throat. He opened his mouth, but no words came out.

That was okay because Agent Allison wasn't done yet.

Still staring at his smoke, the man said, "I know what you did, Detective Furlow. And I know who you are. Never again. Do you understand me? *Never again.*"

This was a threat. Not a thinly veiled cryptic message, but a threat and a promise all wrapped into one.

Freddie was ashamed of what he'd done. But it had been necessary. Peter Shade had done things that others would balk at to save his daughter, things that had negatively impacted others, and he had done the same.

Freddie nodded, and then he hugged Randall more tightly. His son entertained this for another twenty seconds before backing away.

"Come on, I'll take you home," Freddie said, leading the way back to Veronica's car. He opened the passenger door before realizing that Randall was still standing in the middle of the parking lot.

"Come on, let's go."

Freddie cast a worried glance in Troy's direction, thinking the agent might change his mind.

"I'll just take a cab." Randy pulled out his cell phone.

"Don't be silly, I'll drive you. Your mother's probably worried sick."

Bringing up the boy's mother, his ex-wife, was a grave mistake.

"I bet they are." Randy's voice had hardened, and he no longer looked frightened. Instead, he looked angry. "But you can't go back there. Not after what you did."

Freddie sighed.

It had been so long, and so much had changed since that day.

"What I did?"

"Yeah, what you—"

Freddie sneered. He was sick and tired of being everybody's whipping boy.

"What I did is save you from going to prison."

"I'm not—"

Freddie pointed at his son.

"What I did was risk everything to keep you out of jail. That's what I *fucking* did."

Freddie didn't think he'd ever sworn at his son. Before, or after that day.

Randall looked frightened again.

"Now, get in the car."

He didn't move.

"Randy, get in the—"

"What did you think was going to happen?" Randall asked. Frightened or not, Freddie had forgotten that this wasn't the same boy he knew. This wasn't his son—it was someone completely different. "That you'd just come and save me and then everything would be okay? That it would be like nothing happened? Is that what you thought?"

Freddie's chest suddenly tightened.

"G-get in the c-car."

Randall shook his head.

"It doesn't work like that, Dad. That's just not the way things work. Not with me, not with Kevin, and especially not with mom."

Freddie wanted to say, *I know that*, but he was suddenly short of breath. And his arm… his left arm felt numb.

"Dad?"

Freddie's vision became cloudy. He blinked, but that failed to clear the motes that floated in front of his eyes.

"Dad?"

He dropped to his knees. It felt as if his heart was being crushed by a vice. A vice that had been placed in a scorching oven.

Detective Freddie Furlow managed a weak croak and then fell on his face, and everything went black.

"Dad! *Dad!*"

Chapter 56

As expected, Marlowe's handler Dahlia was first to arrive. It was early—4:45 am—and Veronica had just parked in the studio lot three minutes before Dahlia pulled up in her electric car.

Veronica watched the diminutive woman with her large glasses for a moment, feeling a pang of guilt. She'd witnessed Marlowe treating the girl like shit, and as disgraceful as this behavior was, being a handler on a show this big was huge. In some respects, Hollywood was still old school. You had to eat shit to get your breaks.

This was a steppingstone to something greater.

But that stone was about to crumble.

Veronica got out of Freddie's car. Her legs were like bricks and she had a throbbing headache.

"Dahlia!" She waved an arm over her head. "Dahlia!"

The woman had a binder across her forearms with a cup and a metal straw balancing on top. Startled to hear her voice, the cup wobbled and nearly fell.

Probably because her mind was so fatigued, Veronica was reminded of a story she'd heard, ironically taking place somewhere in Hollywood. A woman was in her home chatting on her cell phone, sipping from a similar style of straw. She wasn't paying attention and tripped on the corner of a coffee table. When she fell, the straw penetrated first her eye and then her brain.

She died instantly, still holding the phone in her hand.

Wouldn't that be something, Veronica thought. *Wouldn't that just be the kicker—me, responsible for another death.*

"Hi," Dahlia said hesitantly.

Veronica took the woman's drink.

"Let me help you with that."

"Thanks. What-what are you doing here? Are you going to be on the show?"

The show... shit.

Veronica had forgotten about the follow-up show, the one exploiting her and her condition.

Dahlia stared at her expectantly. Her glasses had slipped down her nose but with her hands full, she was unable to push them back up.

"No, I won't be on the show. There-there won't be a show, Dahlia."

Tilting her head back to see through her glasses, and with the lenses magnifying her pretty eyes, Dahlia looked like a child.

A child whom Marlowe had chastised and disciplined as she saw fit.

"What do you mean? Does this have something to do with the sheriff's call?"

Veronica raised an eyebrow. She knew that it was better to break the news quickly, tear the Band-Aid off as fast as possible, but this was a development she hadn't expected.

"Wait—the sheriff called you? Sheriff Burns?"

Steve had also called Veronica, several times, in fact, but she'd turned off her cell phone. He'd only try to convince her to stay put, that they would take care of things.

"Yes. He was asking about how your episode was set up. I told him that someone from your department reached out first."

That couldn't be right.

"No, you guys called us."

Dahlia shook her head and her glasses slid down a little more.

"That's what the sheriff thought, too, but you guys called us, asked if we were interested. You guys were very specific about the date, in fact. I know, because I took the call."

Veronica racked her brain. That didn't make sense. Greenham's PR department said that the show reached out to them. And specific dates? What was that all about?

"Detective Shade, I'm very sorry and I don't want to be rude, but I have a lot of work to do before today's episode."

Veronica regained her focus, deciding to worry about who called whom later.

"There won't be an episode," Veronica said. "I'm so sorry to have to tell you this, Dahlia, but…"

The waterworks started before she finished the sentence.

"No, it can't be…" Dahlia whined.

Veronica, unsure of how to act and haunted by memories of telling Kathleen Astor that her daughter was dead, just did what came naturally. She wrapped her arms around the woman. The binders fell from Dahlia's arms and coffee splashed on the back of her shirt, but neither of them cared.

"How-how did she die?" Dahlia asked between sobs.

Rip the Band-Aid off, fast.

"She was murdered."

"Murdered?"

Veronica let the woman go and took a step back. Dahlia was a mess, and she was doubtful the woman could see much with all the tears that streaked the lenses of her glasses.

"I'm really sorry. I am. And I know you want answers. I just can't give them to you now."

"I don't understand."

"I know. But, Dahlia, I need your help. I need your help bringing Marlowe's killer to justice. Can you do that? Can you help me?"

Chapter 57

"CITIZENS OF BEAR COUNTY, I'M here before you today because we need your help."

Sheriff Steve Burns stared out over the crowd. It was much smaller than the one he'd previously stood before when they'd found the girls dressed up as dolls in the woods. He'd invited all media outlets, and he really did need them to help find Dante and Jane. But Steve didn't want a circus and had fallen short of telling them that there was a violent psychopath on the loose. A man who had already killed three people, including a celebrity, and had taken another hostage.

His hand was shaking so badly that the piece of paper he held flapped like a kite. Steve placed it on the podium and smoothed the page absently.

"We are currently looking for this individual." The sheriff indicated Deputy McVeigh who held up the photograph that they'd taken of Dante Fiori from when he visited Clyde Krause. "His name is Dante Fiori. He is twenty-seven years old, five foot ten and a half inches tall, and weighs approximately one hundred and sixty-five pounds. He is pale and has shaggy black hair, but he may have changed his appearance. He drives a white Mazda, year 2007, with Oregon plates." The sheriff looked down at the paper on the lectern and read off the tag number. "He is to be considered armed and dangerous. If anybody has seen or sees Dante Fiori, please call either Greenham PD or Bear County Sheriff's Department immediately. Both numbers should be on your screen now. I repeat, you are not to approach Mr. Fiori. You are not to speak to him. If you see him or have seen him over the last few days, call one of these phone numbers."

This got the press' attention.

"Does this man have anything to do with the fire in Greenham?" one reporter shouted.

"At this time, we are only describing Mr. Fiori as a person of interest. But he is considered armed and dangerous. I repeat, do not approach him."

"Sheriff is—"

The follow-up question was cut short, as several of the reporters were suddenly talking amongst themselves. One of them was holding up his cell phone and showing it around.

Steve covered the microphone and leaned over to McVeigh.

"What's going on? How the hell did they find out about Marlowe?"

McVeigh shrugged and said something to a deputy behind them, who nodded and entered the building.

"Sheriff, is Marlowe Lerman really dead?"

The question came as a shock to the sheriff.

"What?" Steve's hand was still covering the microphone. He removed it. "We're just—we just need Bear County's help finding Dante Fiori."

How the fuck did they find out about Marlowe?

"Is she really dead?"

"I..." Steve didn't know what to say.

"Is it true that Dante Fiori has something to do with Marlowe's death?"

The questions came fast and furious now.

"Does this have anything to do with what Detective Veronica Shade said on *Marlowe* this morning?"

"This morning?" Steve hadn't meant to speak—the words just fell out of his mouth.

"Yeah, Veronica Shade was on the show this morning," the same reporter continued. "She said... she said Marlowe was dead. Can you comment on this, Sheriff Burns?"

Steve grabbed the mic in his palm and leaned toward his deputy.

"What the fuck is going on, Marcus?"

The man gave him a dumb look and Steve thought that perhaps he was behind this. That this was one of his tactics to embarrass the sheriff.

"Wrap this shit up," Steve ordered.

With reporters continuing to shout questions at him, he turned and entered the building. Then he grabbed the very first deputy he saw.

"What are they talking about? Was Detective Shade on *Marlowe* this morning?"

"Wh-what?"

Steve pushed the man away and then shouted to everyone within earshot.

"What is this shit about Detective Shade on Marlowe this morning?"

The deputy who McVeigh had spoken to moments ago, appeared with a phone in hand.

"Yeah, Sheriff, she was on the show—just an hour ago. Here."

Steve grabbed the phone, his eyes first noting the time in the upper right-hand corner. It wasn't even seven yet.

Then he saw her: Veronica Shade.

It was just her in the frame. Below her was the show's name in neon pink script, as well as Veronica's in bold text.

Her hair was a mess, and her eyes were red. She looked beyond exhausted.

Steve pressed play.

"Many of you will recognize me from this show just two days ago. For those of you who don't, my name is Detective Veronica Shade with the City of Greenham Police Department.

I have some terrible news to share with you, and this is the way I think she would have liked her fans to hear about it: on Live TV." Veronica lowered her eyes for a second, before looking directly into the camera again. "Marlowe Lerman was murdered yesterday night, and the man who killed her is named Dante Fiori."

What the hell is she doing? Veronica, what the fuck are you doing?

Steve wanted to avoid a circus and Veronica wanted to avoid the media.

This was the opposite of both.

Veronica leaned forward before continuing, her eyes narrowing to mere slits.

"Now, I'm speaking to you Dante because I know you're watching me. You've been watching me for weeks." She paused. "You're a coward. A *bleep* coward. You hurt everybody around me because you were too scared to confront me yourself. You're scared. And you're also a liar. You said you crossed the River Styx, right? Five, six, I've crossed the River Styx? Isn't that the way your *beep* song goes? Huh? But you never crossed it. Neither did your friend. And that's your fault. I'll give you one more chance to try, though, just like Father Cartier did all those years ago. One final chance."

The video cut to black.

What. The. Fuck.

The River Styx?

Five, six, I crossed the River Styx?

What the hell was Veronica talking about? What does this have to do with the song?

"Sheriff? You good?"

The phone was bouncing in his hand, and he thrust it back to the deputy. Then Steve took out his own phone and dialed Veronica's number.

Just like the previous ten times, it went straight to voicemail.

"Veronica? Where the fuck are you, Veronica? Call me back. *Call me back!*"

He tried Freddie next, but that too went to the answering machine. He didn't bother leaving a message.

"Fuck!" Steve reared back and launched his phone across the room. It struck the wall just above a seated deputy's head and exploded. Glass and plastic rained down on him. "*Fuck!* Where is the River Styx? Can someone please fucking tell me where the fuck is the River Styx?"

Chapter 58

Her plan was to get there first. Being unfamiliar with Donovan's bridge that crossed the narrowest point of the Casnet River, she wanted to get a lay of the land, to plan escape routes, should they be needed.

But he was already there. Veronica spotted Dante's car, the same white Mazda she'd seen back outside Gina's house what seemed like a decade ago. The backseat was littered with empty paint cans—dozens of them.

Either Dante had gone straight there mere minutes after her special episode of Marlowe aired or he was here the whole time.

Veronica put it at fifty-fifty.

She saw the blue paint next. Like surrounding Ken Cameron's body in the Bear County Correctional shower, the paint was everywhere. It was on the grass, the trees, rocks. Everywhere.

The paint cans were just tossed to the side.

Sweat.

Veronica heard the Casnet before she saw it. Loud, angry waters. The blue paint made it up to the entrance of the wooden bridge before things changed.

First, the smell.

Gas.

The odor was strong. Veronica didn't see any red containers, but they were there just as they'd been in the broom closet with Cole Batherson.

Donovan's bridge was maybe twenty feet long and eight feet wide.

The blue paint violently transitioned into red, then orange and yellow. Some of the water had splashed onto the bridge from the river below, making the paint runny and causing it to swirl in places.

Being outside dispelled some of the illusion, but it still made Veronica conscious of her footing.

She walked onto the bridge—one step, two.

That's when she saw him.

It was the man from the hospital, the man at Dr. Bernard's office, and it was also the man from the library. Veronica wasn't one hundred percent certain, but she thought he might have been a cameraman during the filming of *Marlowe*.

She didn't notice Dante at first because he'd stripped nude and had covered himself in the fiery paint. It was all over him, covering his legs, stomach, even his face. The man had used it to pull his shaggy dark hair back from his forehead.

The only thing that wasn't covered in paint were Dante's eyes.

They were black, just like in the photograph that she'd taken from Renaissance and was now tucked into the back pocket of her jeans.

Dante was standing in front of the wooden railing. He was holding what looked like a rope in both hands. It dangled between his legs, and then through them as it disappeared behind him.

He saw her then.

And when he did, he grinned a horrible grin.

"You like what I've done for you?" the man said. His voice was high and tight, probably because he was forced to shout to be heard over the river.

Still, there were enough similarities for Veronica to recognize it from the show.

One, two, I'm coming for you.

Veronica understood. Dante had done all of this, all of this preparation to mimic her synesthesia in order to eliminate any advantage she might have over him.

Water splashed, soaking Dante's back and he laughed.

The gas smell all around the bridge would make it impossible to know if he was lying. The blue paint? A surrogate for his sweat.

The warm colors masked impeding violence, but this, Veronica thought, was redundant.

Because Dante wasn't just capable of violence, he *was* violence. She saw it in those black as night eyes of his.

She'd read about it in Dr. Bernard's notes.

Dante Fiori was completely, and utterly insane.

Veronica reached behind her, not for the faded photo, but for Freddie's gun. She drew it out the back of her jeans and aimed the muzzle at Dante's forehead.

She had never been the best shot, but her accuracy wasn't terrible. If Veronica was forced to fire and didn't hit him with the first bullet, one of the next two would strike its mark. Besides, he was naked. She could see that he didn't have any weapons on him, other than that rope. Although, she couldn't fathom how he intended to use it.

"Ah, ah, ah," Dante mocked. "You won't need that now. Soon, yes, but not now."

Veronica didn't lower the gun.

"Why don't you step forward so I can hear you better."

"I can hear you just fine. And I think you can hear me, too." Dante's voice rose a few octaves. "*One, two, I'm coming for you. Three, four, lock your door. Five, six—*"

"Shut up!" Veronica took two steps toward Dante. "Shut the *fuck* up!"

Dante's face dropped.

"Lower the gun."

Veronica ignored him.

"Tell me where Jane is. Tell me what you did with her?"

Dante smiled again.

"What I did with her? What I did with *her*? How about what she did with me?"

Veronica wasn't following.

"Oh, poor girl. You think because you read the file I left you that you know all about me? Hmm?"

This was a distraction, nothing more.

"Do you know what Dr. Bernard did when I told her about what happened to me? To us?"

"I have no idea. I just—"

"Well, why don't you ask her for yourself?"

Dante suddenly moved to his left. He didn't take a step so much as he glided across the paint-slickened bridge.

Veronica froze.

Dr. Jane Bernard was standing on the other side of the railing, her feet on a wooden buttress no more than six inches wide. Her hands were tied in front of her, wrapped in duct tape first and then with the other end of the rope that Dante was holding. Her ankles were taped as well, and a piece covered her mouth. This was stained by a single tear of blood coming from one of her nostrils.

The psychiatrist's blouse was torn, and her hair was a rat's nest. Like Dante, her entire body was covered in paint. But unlike the psychopath, her paint was blue, not red and orange.

But the only thing Veronica cared about was her eyes. They were open, and she was alive.

God damn it, the woman was alive.

"Welcome to my inferno, Veronica," Dante said. "Or would you prefer if I called you Lucy?"

Chapter 59

"Why are you doing this?" Veronica tried her best not to whine, but exhaustion had stripped her of what little control she had left of her voice, her body. "What did I do to you?"

Dante laughed.

"What did *you* do to *me*? You ask all the wrong questions, Lucy. You really do." He flapped the rope, splashing some paint into the air. And then Dante turned and looked down at the Casnet. "You know why we called this the River Styx?"

Veronica didn't want to talk about the river, she wanted to talk about why Dante had killed Gina, Ken, and Marlowe. But the man was unhinged, his thoughts roiling like the water below, barely coherent. Having read his file, Veronica thought she was prepared for this.

She wasn't.

"Greeks believed that the River Styx separated the Earth from the Underworld. Now, Benny and me don't know much about Greek mythology, but it was in one of the books we read. A kid's book, a mix of legends with a make-believe hero who saves the day." Dante sighed and Veronica moved forward a little more, trying to figure out how to get to the man before he could let Jane go and send her falling backwards into the river. "Father Cartier would make us—his special orphans—strip naked and jump in the freezing water. Then he would tell us to swim across. He would stand here," Dante indicated the spot in which he presently stood, "and watch us, with a grin on his fat fucking face. He made us a promise: if we swam all the way across, if we got to the other side, he would leave us alone."

Veronica looked beyond Dante and even Jane. The Casnet River was full of sharp rocks that broke the surface and while the water wasn't quite moving fast enough to be considered rapids, she couldn't imagine two, or more, skinny pre-teen boys trying to swim across.

"Benny and I would try our best. Dylan, too, but mostly me and Benny. See, in the myth, if you crossed the River Styx, you'd end up in the Underworld—Hell, I guess. But in our lives? Everything was reversed. Hell was Earth—Renaissance was hell. And anything was better than Renaissance. I mean *anything*. We wanted to be in the Underworld. Begged for it, tried our hardest to swim across. But you wanna know what happened?"

Veronica couldn't help but imagine her brother, with his burnt scalp and neck, trying to cross the river. Bobbing up and down like that yo-yo he loved to play with, sputtering, coughing. On the verge of drowning but still desperately trying to make it to the other side.

"You never made it," Veronica whispered.

"Maybe you are smart, after all. No, Lucy, we never made it. We almost did once, though. Benny was nearly across, three-quarters of the way. Maybe more. But then a wave came and buried me. I tried to tell Benny to keep going, to make it to the Underworld, but I don't know if he misunderstood or..." Dante shook his head and his paint-soaked hair fell in front of his face. "He came back for me. Grabbed me and dragged me back to shore. And the whole time—the whole *fucking* time, Father Cartier was laughing. Laughing and waiting. *Hell* was waiting for us, Lucy."

As Dante paused to reflect on the horrors he'd experienced as a child, Veronica looked to Jane. Her eyes were bulging and wet, but Veronica didn't know whether this was from the river or from tears. She knew better than to indulge a madman, but Dante was the only one who had answers to her questions.

"You said it isn't about me... is it about her?" Veronica indicated Dr. Bernard who shouted into the tape that covered her mouth. "Are you pissed at her because you told her what happened at the orphanage, and she did nothing? Are you pissed because she never stopped Father Cartier from abusing you boys?"

Dante laughed again. The sound made Veronica's fillings rattle.

"Dr. Bernard is weak; she couldn't stop anything. She tried, though, I'll give her that. She tried. But that cunt of a nun—she shut everything down."

Veronica knew he was speaking of Sister Margaret.

"You know, we had locks on our doors—three, four, lock your door." A tittering laugh. "And every single night we locked them. But then we'd hear *her*. She'd walk down the hall, those fucking keys jangling with every step."

Veronica was transported back to a few hours ago. She was looking at the colors swirling out of the massive keyholes on the boys' doors. And Sister Margaret was walking... slowly... cling... clang... cling... clang.

"That bitch would unlock the doors. Sometimes, we were sound asleep and wouldn't even notice. But even if we did, we knew better than to lock them again. And if she unlocked your door, you knew *he* was coming."

"Then why? You did this—" Veronica stopped herself from saying, *to me*. "—to everyone around me. *Why?*" Her words bordered on begging now.

"Because, Lucy," Dante turned his head skyward as he shouted her birth name. "Because the esteemed Dr. Jane Bernard made me think I could change. That I didn't have to be the killer *he* made me. That I could be good, or if not good, then at least not *bad*."

"I don't... I don't understand."

Dante threw his head back again. As he did, his hands came up and yanked the rope. Dr. Bernard was pulled forward and her stomach banged off one of the bridge stanchions. When she rebounded, her weight, similar to Dante's, pulled the psychopath backward. He dug his heels in at the last moment and Jane's momentum stopped, her body hovering over the rocky river roughly twenty feet below.

"Of course, you don't. Of *courrrrrrse*, you don't." Dante rolled his eyes dramatically. "Benny said you were the stupid one, the mean one. I killed him. I *fucking* killed him."

Veronica wasn't following. Clearly, he couldn't mean Benny.

"What? Who? Who did you kill?"

Ken Cameron?

Wrong again.

"Father Cartier, *Luuuuucy*. That's who! I killed him. About four years ago, I snuck into Renaissance, and I found the fat fuck naked in his bed. I was high on something... I don't even remember what. Something Dylan gave me. Anyways, I think that Father Cartier had just come back from paying a visit to one of his special orphans. He was sweating, dripping with it. *Disgusting.* I only wanted to beat him up a little, you know? But then when I started hitting him, he woke up and looked at me and I swear—I *swear* to you, Lucy—he smiled. That *fucker* smiled. And I just couldn't stop. I put a pillow over his face and yelled at him. Yelled at him to stop smiling. And when I pulled it back, he finally had." Dante paused to lick his lips. Then he tugged on the rope and Jane teetered. "I told her. And she... she helped cover it up."

Veronica couldn't tell if Dante was lying—the gas smell that the man had poured on the bridge was still too strong—but

Jane's expression, at the very least suggested that it was possible.

Dylan had told her that Father Cartier had died of a heart attack. Could he have been wrong? Could Dante be telling the truth?

Veronica hadn't read anything in Jane's notes about this, but if it were true, it wasn't as if she'd broadcast it to the world or leave handwritten evidence.

"That nun raised hell, but Dr. Bernard here told her that if she opened her mouth, if she said that Father Cartier died of anything other than a heart attack, she'd find every single boy who had ever stayed there and she would get them to tell the world what he did."

Except there was no list of boys. Because there was a convenient flood that ruined the paperwork.

"I don't care that you killed him, if he did what you said he did, Father Cartier deserved to die."

Veronica was partly humoring the man, not wanting to make him even more irrational for fear that he would drop Jane into the Casnet. At this height, she put the chances of survival at sixty-forty against. But tied up and unable to brace her fall or swim?

Less than five percent.

But Dante's words made her think of her own decisions. Like putting a bullet in Gloria Trammel's head.

During the mandatory psych sessions that followed, they'd called it 'the shooting'. Only, that was downplaying it, turning it into a euphemism. It wasn't just a shooting, it was a killing.

Veronica Shade had shot and killed Gloria Trammel.

The dollmaker was dangerous, there was no doubt about that. She'd killed and would kill again. Worse, she'd made her own daughter an accomplice.

But deep down, Veronica knew she could have taken Gloria out with a bullet in the shoulder, maybe one in the stomach.

Most worrisome, was that, at the time, that hadn't even crossed her mind.

She'd shot to kill.

"I knew you would say that."

"Why, because you read my file?" Veronica replied, throwing the man's words back in his face. "Is that why? You don't know me, Dante. You don't know me at all."

"Oh, oh, oh, oh, that's not why. I read your file, yes, I did, but that's not how I know you."

Veronica should have seen this coming, too. She should have prepared herself for what came next.

She recalled Dr. Bernard's notes and how Dante regressed about four months ago—that was when he started to go off the rails. That was also around the time that Benny—Holland—had died. They had hidden that well, Veronica and her father, but if Dante was watching her…

And then, about four weeks ago, Veronica had killed Gloria Trammel. And not only had there been no attempt to cover that up, but Greenham PD had actively flaunted it, and paraded Veronica around like some hero.

"To be honest, I didn't even know who you were. Benny talked about his sister all the time, of course, about Lucy, but I didn't know it was *you*." Dante's eyes suddenly bored into hers. "He told me about the game, about how you killed your family. How you tried to kill him."

Veronica shook her head and almost smiled. This was bordering on insane, now.

"That's not—"

Dante tugged the rope and Jane shouted into the tape.

"Don't you lie to me!" Dante sniffed the air dramatically. "I smell gaaaaaas! I can tell you're lying! You killed them! You killed your family... *eenie, meenie, miney, mo, catch a tiger by the toe...* you killed your mom and dad and tried to kill Benny, too."

"Bullshit."

"Don't lie—"

"Bullshit," Veronica shouted. "Trent and Herb killed my parents. I was just a kid. I had no choice."

She was acutely aware that this conversation was eerily similar to the one she'd had with her brother before he'd set himself alight and wasn't surprised. After all, both Benny and Dante had been through similar trauma.

And both were borderline insane.

"That's not what he said, your brother. He said you were mean. He said you were mean *before.*"

Don't indulge, don't even listen.

"What are you talking about?"

"He said you abused him and your parents."

"What? That's a lie."

Veronica's eyes darted to Jane, but the terrified woman now refused to look at her.

Dante chuckled.

"You wouldn't know a lie if it slapped you across your pretty face. Benny said you cut your father's finger off. Said you grabbed a knife while he was chopping onions and you sliced his finger right off."

It was absurd... but something about it also rang true. Sort of. Dante's words triggered a memory in Veronica, a memory of her dad pretending to cut off his own finger and then faking blood with ketchup.

That was what happened.

She didn't really cut his finger off. That was ridiculous.

"And then there was the time you put bleach in your mother's ice cream. Remember that? She ate some, then vomited. Your brother had to get her water."

"That's… that's not what happened. My dad gave the ice cream to me… and… and it had peppers in it, not bleach. Jesus."

Fucking gas. If only she could sniff out this lie.

It was a lie, of course, it was also the incoherent ramblings of a madman. What Dante said wasn't true.

Of course, it wasn't true.

It couldn't be true.

"I didn't know your new name—I just knew you as Lucy. Mean, nasty Lucy. But then I saw you. I saw you that day when you barged into my session with Dr. Bernard. I saw your eyes. Gold-flecked, just like Benny's. I knew it was you. So, I started to follow you. You were doing good, real good. And I started to think to myself, if you, Lucy Davis, a killer, a murderer of her *own* parents, could restart your life, maybe I could, too. Maybe I didn't always have to be a killer. Maybe I could move on. I even started to forgive you for what you did to Benny and your folks, started to believe that same bullshit that Jane told you, that you were just a kid, that you had no choice."

It suddenly dawned on Veronica that she was wrong, that this whole paint and gas charade wasn't to eliminate any advantage that her synesthesia might give her. Or, that it wasn't *just* to even the playing field. It was because Dante was jealous, he wanted something special, too. Veronica had been abused, endured horrible things that no child should ever experience, and she'd gained what people, Freddie, Dante, maybe even Steve, referred to as a superpower. It was strange to think of this as a reward, but she was convinced that this was what Dante thought of it.

And what did he get?

Nothing. Just continued rape. There was no superpower, no relief, no reprieve. For Dante Fiori, he experienced all nine levels of hell at the same time.

"What was it that Benny liked to say? *No matter how old, the will to survive is something you get at birth?*"

Close, but not quite.

The will to survive is ingrained at birth, Lucy. Young or not, you had a choice. And you chose yourself.

"Don't talk about him," Veronica warned through clenched teeth. The gun in her hand wavered. "Don't you fucking talk about my brother."

"Why? Because you know what I'm saying is true? Lucy, Lucy, Lucy… you were doing so well. But then Gloria Trammel came along. You know what they say, once a killer always a killer. You shot her in the head. You *murdered* her because you couldn't help yourself."

Veronica shut her eyes, but Bev Trammel materialized out of the darkness. She was gesturing for the little girl to come closer all the while she was reaching for her gun. Veronica had put the innocent girl in harm's way to save herself. And then she'd killed Gloria.

"I had to." Veronica's voice was weak. "I had no choice."

"That's what I'm saying, Lucy! That's what I'm *saying!* We don't have a choice—once a killer, always a killer. One, two, I'm coming for you. Three, four, lock your—"

Veronica strode forward, leading with the gun.

"Shut the fuck up! Just shut the fuck up!"

Dante wanted her to kill him, that much was clear now. He wanted her to prove that nothing they did mattered.

In a twisted way, Veronica killing Dante would justify his own slayings, his own twisted belief that he had no control over what he'd done. Dante had killed because he had to, that he was either born this way or Father Cartier had turned him into a beast from which there was no coming back.

"—door. Five, six, I crossed the River—"

"I'm fucking warning you! Shut the fuck up!" Veronica's finger tensed on the trigger.

"—Styx. Seven, eight, I've sealed your fate."

Veronica closed one eye and took aim.

"Don't do it, V. Please don't do it."

The voice startled Veronica and she glanced over her shoulder.

"Dad? What—what the hell are you doing here?"

Chapter 60

"PLEASE, VERONICA," PETER SHADE SAID, his palms out in front of him. "Put the gun down."

Veronica's mind was a mess now, and the paint, the fucking paint that Dante had splashed everywhere, only added to the confusion.

He was going to kill Jane, he was going to let go of the rope and she was going to fall to her death.

Wasn't he?

"Wh-wh-what are you doing here?"

"Just put down the gun."

Veronica whipped her head around to look at Dante.

"Veronica—"

"That's not her name. Her name is Lucy," Dante said in his tittering voice.

"Don't listen to him. Everything that happened today is a lie. He tried to set you up—the fingerprint on the pen in Gina's pocket, the gun he stole from the hospital used to kill Marlowe, none of it will hold up. It's just a trick, smoke and mirrors. He did this, not you."

"I don't—I don't understand... what are you doing here, Dad?" Veronica felt tears coming on. "Why are you here?"

There was only one answer to this.

It was because he knew about the River Styx—he'd seen her plea on *Marlowe* and knew where Veronica wanted to meet. Dr. Bernard must have told him about Dante and Benny and everything else that happened at Renaissance House.

He'd lied—her father had lied, and Veronica had never been able to detect it. Peter said he didn't know what happened to Benny after he'd become an orphan.

But he knew all right.

Worse, was that Peter and Jane had conspired against her. In the notes that Dr. Bernard had taken during their sessions—private, confidential sessions—there were things written in the margins about her life that she didn't even remember.

Like the fire. Like Trent and Herb.

Like her birth name for Christ's sake. Veronica hadn't even known that.

How long had Peter and Jane been seeing each other? How long had they been plotting against her?

And how could things have been different if Jane had told her about her past? All those years, pretending not to know the origins of her synesthesia.

What about her childhood? Was she a bad seed, like Dante said? Had she done those things to her mother and father?

They seemed unfathomable. But up until a month ago, so had shooting someone in the head.

Dante's voice unexpectedly entered her mind.

Once a killer, always a killer.

And now his voice entered her ears.

"We can't change, Lucy!" Water splashed against Dante's back. "Once a killer, always a killer!"

"Don't listen to him," Peter urged. He moved toward her. "He's insane. You're better than this, *V*. You are."

"He hated you. Benny *hated* you. He told me that—"

Veronica grabbed her temples. The gun was cold against her skin.

"Stop, I can't—please, stop. *Please.*"

But Dante was a madman, and he didn't know how to stop. That was part of his pathology.

"He told me—"

"Shut the fuck up!" Peter yelled, but Dante just spoke over top of him.

"He—your brother, Benny—he told me that if they'd picked him, he wouldn't have hesitated."

"Veronica, don't listen. Please," Peter begged.

She pointed the gun at Dante again.

"He would have told them to kill you first. Lucy, the abusive sister. The one nobody in the family liked. Why do you think that Trent chose you, huh? You think it was really because of the game—because of *eenie, meenie*?" He lowered his voice until it was barely audible. "I'll let you in on a little secret, Lucy. They know who's gonna win as soon as they start. And they picked you for a reason."

Colors swirled everywhere.

"They picked you because they knew you would kill them."

Images flashed inside Veronica's addled mind, dichotomous images. A scene of her dad pretending to cut his finger, then him actually screaming, the ketchup becoming blood. Veronica spitting out spicy ice-cream, her mom vomiting up bleach.

"I don't—I don't know what's real anymore."

Tears soaked her cheeks.

"I thought I could stop… you know?" Dante continued his ramblings. "Dr. Bernard told me I could." He imitated Jane's voice. "*You can be someone different every day you wake up. The choice is yours.* Yeah, right—that's fucking bullshit. Every day in Renaissance Home we woke up in Hell, and every day he would rape us. I could pretend I was the mythical hero, could pretend that I could stop him. But no amount of pretending would prevent Sister Margaret from walking down the hall and unlocking our doors and Father Cartier grunting and groaning as he flipped our naked bodies over. Then I realized something: I didn't need to pretend. I could kill him. And I did. Once a killer, always a killer. *Once a killer, always a killer.* I couldn't stop. I killed Gina—I actually liked her, you know, but I had to kill her. I said your name, by the way, when I was twisting her head around. I said *Lucy Davis did this*. And then when I got Clyde to kill Ken, I made him say the same thing. And Marlowe, her too. *You* did this."

Every time Dante mentioned a name, their likeness flashed in Veronica's brain. Gina Braden, covered in paint, her neck broken. All the woman had done was let Veronica sign out a book—it wasn't even for her.

Then Ken Cameron, with his face completely flattened and smashed to a pulp.

And Marlowe, who was a bitch, no doubt, but who didn't deserve to be shot and murdered in the front hall of Veronica's home.

"You don't have to do this, V." Peter pleaded. "You don't."

"But you do, Lucy," Dante countered. "That's what I'm telling you! You have to. It's who you are, it's who *we* are. Benny—"

"Don't talk about him, please."

Benny Davis—Holland Toler—soaking everything in gas, including himself. Benny, telling her that she already chose who got to live once and how she wouldn't get that chance again. And how he'd decided that no one was going to leave this time.

He'd been smiling when he set his shirt alight. That was the worst part.

Benny had been *fucking* smiling. Like he knew.

Like he knew what Veronica was.

"Benny knew what you were!"

"Why did you kill those people?" Veronica begged. "Why?"

"I had to. Just like you have to kill me."

Veronica wasn't even sure if Dante had spoken these words or if she'd read his lips.

Or if she'd just made them up entirely.

The same goes for what happened next.

Dante smiled and for the first time since beginning his diatribe, the smile reached his black eyes.

Two things followed next. With Dante's focus locked on Veronica, Peter inched closer to him. That, and Dante flicked his wrist. Not like before, not to make Jane teeter, but Veronica thought that he was about to throw the rope over the side of the bridge.

And if he did that, Jane would die.

"Once a killer, always a killer," Dante whispered, raising his arm even higher.

Veronica's vision exploded in violent red splotches as she pulled the trigger.

"No!" Peter shouted as she fired off a second round, then a third. "*No!*"

Chapter 61

SHE WASN'T A GOOD SHOT, but she wasn't a bad one, either.

The first bullet hit Dante in the side, or at least Veronica thought it did—it was hard to tell because of all the swirling colors and paint. The second missed. The third struck him in the neck.

Dante stumbled backward, the rope dropping from his hands. He hit the handrail and then, just before pitching over, their eyes met one final time.

And, like Benny, Dante smiled.

Then he was gone.

No longer holding the rope, Dr. Bernard was left standing on the buttress that was too small for her feet. She managed to stay upright for a few seconds before slipping.

Ex-police captain Peter Shade wasn't much smaller than Freddie, but unlike Veronica's partner, he could fucking run.

The man was in a full sprint before Veronica fired her third shot. He launched his body across the bridge, grabbing the end of the rope that Dante had just dropped with both hands. It was slick with paint, and it slipped between his fingers, but he adjusted his grip and held tight.

"Help me! V, grab the rope!" Peter screamed from his stomach.

Veronica dropped Freddie's gun and then fell to her knees.

She held her head in her hands and sobbed.

"V!"

Once a killer, always a killer. Once a killer, always a killer. Once a killer, always a killer.

Peter grunted and heaved.

"V, I need your help! *Now!*"

The desperation in her father's voice drove her to her feet. She was like a zombie when she grabbed the rope, an automaton when she pulled. Together they managed to hoist Dr. Jane Bernard to the railing and then, with Veronica holding the rope tight and anchoring her feet on the only piece of wood she could find that wasn't slick with paint, Peter helped her to safety.

Peter tore the tape from Jane's mouth and then kissed her before wrapping the terrified woman in a tight embrace.

Jane was saying something, apologizing Veronica thought, although she couldn't make out the exact words over the sound of the raging water.

It was strange how everything Dante had said was crystal clear, whereas Jane was barely audible.

Veronica dropped the rope and stumbled to the edge of the bridge.

"V? What are you doing? *V?*"

Peter thought she was going to jump.

He was wrong. Veronica was a killer, not suicidal.

But she needed to see.

Veronica put both hands on the railing and peered over the side.

At first, there were only jutting rocks and foaming water.

But then she spotted him.

Dante Fiori must have struck a rock on the way down—his leg was bent at an odd angle, and his hips seemed out of true. But for some reason, the river hadn't swept the man away. Instead, he'd been forced to the other side, toward Hilltona Forest. As Veronica squinted through tears and mist from the river, she saw that his left hand was stuck in some shrubbery, which kept him from being pulled downstream.

He made it, Veronica thought, more tears filling her eyes. *Dante finally made it across the River Styx.*

A shot rang out and Veronica flinched.

She turned, expecting... she wasn't sure what to expect, but it definitely wasn't her father with her gun—no, Freddie's gun—pointed up to the sky.

He fired again.

"I did this, V," Peter said, the inner corners of his eyebrows high on his forehead. "Me. Not you—you didn't shoot him. You did not shoot him. *I* did."

"Yes." Jane nodded enthusiastically. "Peter shot Dante."

"V, I did this, okay?" Peter reiterated.

"You lied to me," Veronica said.

Peter didn't deny this claim.

"I'm sorry, but you need to tell me you understand. I did this. I shot Dante, you grabbed the rope, okay?"

Veronica attempted to wipe the tears from her eyes but only managed to smear paint all over her face.

"You lied to me," she repeated.

"Veronica, this is important, okay?"

She glared at Dr. Bernard.

"You lied to me, too."

"We only did what we—"

Veronica started backing away.

"That stuff that Dante said... that stuff about my parents, about the knife and the bleach... was that true?"

Peter looked ashamed.

"No, of course not."

Veronica was nearer to the water now, and the air was less polluted with the scent of gasoline.

Until her father spoke, that is.

"You're still lying to me," Veronica whispered.

"Please, V," Peter protested. "I shot Dante. That's what happened. It's important we get our stories straight."

Get our stories straight...

"You fucking lied to me, and I'm done with both of you."

Veronica turned. Both Peter and Jane yelled at her to come back, but she walked off Donovan's bridge without so much as a glance over her shoulder.

Chapter 62

"**WHAT THE FUCK HAPPENED?**" **SHERIFF** Steve Burns demanded. "And where is Veronica?"

Peter Shade was comforting Dr. Bernard, holding her to his chest. The former was covered in blue paint, the latter in red and orange acrylic.

"Peter?"

The man let go of Jane and stepped forward. Then he pulled a cigarette out and lit it.

"She's fine."

"Yeah, I know she's fine," Steve snapped. "Where is she?"

Peter took a drag.

"I don't know. But… she's okay."

The man didn't sound so sure, and Steve threw his hands up.

"What the fuck happened here, Pete?"

On the way to Donovan's bridge, he'd listened to the call that ex-Greenham PD captain Peter Shade put into the dispatch. Several times, in fact.

And it didn't make sense.

Peter sucked on his cigarette before answering.

"I shot Dante and he fell over the side. Then Veronica and I saved Jane. It's not that complicated. He was going to throw the rope over. He threatened to do it and then when he flinched, I took the shot."

Steve had heard this before. It made even less sense now.

"You shot Dante with Detective Freddie Furlow's gun?"

"Yes."

How did you get his gun? And how come when you are crack shot, it took you five bullets, three of which missed, by the way, to hit a man standing no more than fifteen feet from you?

Steve continued across the bridge, not slowing. Behind him, he heard Kristen Newberry and the tech, CSU Paulie, following.

"Captain Bottel will be here in a few minutes," Steve hissed under his breath. He stopped just short of grabbing Peter's paint-covered shirt. "Get your fucking stories straight."

"Oh, shit, he's down there," CSU Paulie exclaimed. He and Kristin were looking over the side of the bridge.

"I have to go down there?" Kristin groused.

"Do you understand?" Steve asked Peter and Jane. "Get your shit together."

"It's no big deal," CSU Paulie continued. "Besides it gives me a chance to finally tell you why that show that you like, How to Catch a Predator, went off the air."

The words were background fodder to what Steve hoped was the most intense stare of his life. This situation was beyond fucked up. He had no idea where Freddie, the man responsible for looking after and staying with Veronica, was. Or how he'd lost his gun... which had been used to kill a man armed with a rope.

A goddamn *rope*.

None of it made sense.

"Well, you won't believe it, but they honed in on this DA in Texas?"

"Yeah, I remember that," Kristin said.

"This DA was sending naughty images to a young kid, underage of course, but get this, when the show tried to confront him in his house? The man put a gun in his mouth and blew his head off. Fucking—"

Steve couldn't handle it anymore. He turned to Paulie.

"For fuck's sake, would you just get down there and process the body?"

Paulie looked unfazed by the sheriff's words. He simply shrugged and continued down the slope.

Bear County Coroner Kristin Newberry was another story. She looked at Steve with a tired expression.

"You overheard what happened here, right, Kristin?"

The woman stared at him blankly.

Steve moved away from Peter and Jane and approached the coroner.

By nature, he wasn't a violent man. But a horrifying thought passed through his mind just then. If Kristin made waves, how far would he go to keep what really happened here a secret? To keep Veronica safe?

"I heard, Sheriff, and I understand."

Steve nodded.

"Good." Then he turned to his deputies who were busy trying to cordon off Donovan's Bridge. "I don't want the press anywhere near here. Got it? Not a single fucking camera anywhere near this place!"

The sound of a car approaching made Steve whip around. He was about to shout again, to ask how the hell the media found out about this so quickly, before noticing that it wasn't a news van. It was a Greenham PD vehicle. The car came to a stop near the end of the bridge and Captain Bottel got out of the passenger seat.

"Captain," Steve said. "We've—"

Chief Deputy Marcus McVeigh opened the driver's door.

What the hell?

Both men looked serious as they made their way in his direction, trying their best not to step in too much paint—a near-impossible task.

This is it, Steve thought. *McVeigh showed the evidence room footage to Bottel and they're both coming to arrest me now.*

But when neither man pulled out their cuffs, Steve began to relax just a little. A tiny amount. His nerves were frayed worse than a pair of jeans cut with blunt shears.

The captain surveyed the scene before offering Peter Shade a disapproving look. It was clear by his lack of surprise, that Captain Bottel had already been briefed on what had happened here.

And if they weren't here to arrest him, why was McVeigh in the captain's car? Why was he *driving* the captain's car?

"Where is Detective Shade?" Captain Bottel asked.

Unsure of the man's motivations, of whether he was interested in her well-being or looking to chastise or arrest her, Steve took his time in answering.

"She's fine," he said at last. "She's okay. She went to get checked out, but she's going to be okay."

The captain nodded.

"Good. About her partner, about Detective—"

"I'm sorry, I don't know where he is."

The captain couldn't be surprised that Freddie had done a shit job of keeping tabs on Veronica.

It was an impossible task from the outset. Anyone who had spent just five minutes with Veronica would know that.

"No, I'm sorry, you misunderstood. Her partner, Detective Furlow, is in the hospital. He isn't doing so well. Had a massive heart attack this morning."

"Jesus," Steve gaped. "Is he—"

Captain Bottel shook his head.

"We don't know, yet. Doctors are hopeful, but for now, it's touch and go."

Chapter 63

VERONICA HAD MADE A PROMISE, and no matter how tired she was, no matter how confused, upset, angry, or disgusted with herself, she was determined to keep it.

The first thing that struck her as odd was that Renaissance Home looked much more intimidating during the day. This was, Veronica knew, almost certainly because she was more familiar with its history now and had nothing to do with the building itself.

The second was that the wrought iron gate was open.

This would have been the time to pull her gun, but Veronica didn't have hers or even Freddie's now.

She strode up the stone walk to the front door. She raised her fist to knock on it, but then changed her mind and tried the handle instead.

It was unlocked and Veronica pushed the door open. It made a horrible creaking sound—some things didn't change, night or day.

Some things did, though.

Sister Margaret didn't come to meet her, and the hallway... the pictures, they were gone. Their outlines were still there—dark squares surrounded by sun-bleached paint—but the frames and images were gone.

The doors to all of the boys' rooms were closed, which was also unusual.

I'm very tired and we start early here at Renaissance.

That's what the nun had said.

Then why aren't the boys up yet? And where is Sister Margaret?

Veronica, recalling that the woman had said her office was to the left, headed in that direction. At the end of a much smaller hallway than the one across from the boys' rooms, was an office. There was a wooden cross hanging from the door and two nameplates on the wall.

Just reading both of them made her sick to her stomach: Father James Cartier and Sister Margaret Fortin.

"Sister?"

There were no windows, and the door was ajar.

"Sister?" Veronica repeated as she placed a hand below the cross and slowly pushed the door open.

Death.

That was the first thought that went through Veronica's mind when she peered into the office. This was unsurprising, given the scene before Veronica and the way her synesthesia inundated her vision with familiar warm hues.

Once a killer, always a killer.

Only she hadn't killed Sister Margaret Fortin.

The old nun had done that to herself.

There were strips of paper everywhere: on the desk, on the floor, stacks of ribbons lying on top of empty folders. Apparently, the Renaissance Home paper shredder had been working overtime.

Veronica didn't need to read them, to piece them together, to know what they were.

They were the orphanage records—they hadn't been destroyed in a flood. Margaret had shredded them all, because she knew that when Veronica returned, as she'd promised, she would come for them. Just like Jane had threatened, Veronica would hunt down every single one of the orphans and ask them to come forward, to talk about what the nun and her beloved priest had done.

Most would refuse, some were dead, but a small portion would agree.

And after Sister Margaret had finished destroying the records, she'd hung herself. The diminutive nun had looped a rope around a beam in the ceiling, then around her neck.

This narrative added up, and it made sense.

There was but a single piece of paper that hadn't been shredded. It lay on the corner of the desk and Veronica picked it up.

Even the suicide note matched the scene.

Veronica detected a flash of movement near the door. She glanced up from the paper.

It was a boy. He looked ten but was probably closer to thirteen. When their eyes met, he darted. This happened so quickly that Veronica wasn't sure if it was real or imagined.

It could have been Benny, or Dante, or Dylan, or any number of the hundreds of kids who had been abused in Renaissance.

Veronica let him go and read the suicide note out loud.

"He was a good man."

That was the note—that was all it said.

How wrong could a person possibly be?

A good man? From what she'd heard, Veronica was beginning to doubt whether or not Father Cartier was a man at all. More like some sort of demon, maybe even *Dis* in Dante's Inferno.

This got Veronica thinking about the good men in her life, or at least the ones she thought were good men.

Steve... Freddie... her father...

What did she know about good men?

Veronica thought that Cole was a bastard, and he turned out to be the best of them all. The only person who stayed true to themselves all the way to the end.

And her dad, Peter Shade? Why had he been so adamant that he take the blame for the shooting? A noble gesture to make up for decades of deceit? Or had there been another reason? Was it because despite the rampant crime and drug use in Bear County, there had been only two police-related shootings resulting in a fatality over the past eighteen months... and both had been committed by Detective Veronica Shade?

Another thought occurred to her then. Something darker.

Or did Peter Shade know something about her? Something *else* about Veronica that he'd been keeping a secret? Did he believe what Dante had said about her being a bad seed even as a child?

Veronica scowled.

She would never know because she would never speak to her father or Jane again.

Veronica shook her head, trying to clear her mind. This was mostly ineffective but sufficient enough to keep her plodding forward. To this end, she pulled two items out of her pockets: her cell phone and the photo of Dante and Benny.

She stared at the latter while dialing Bear County coroner Kristin Newberry's number on the former.

"Hello?"

"Hi, Kristin. It's Detective Shade."

"Oh," there was a commotion in the background. From the sounds, Veronica surmised that the coroner was still out at Donovan's bridge. "Captain Bottel's been asking about you."

"Yeah, I know."

"What can I help you with?"

"Well, I had a question about an old case. Really old, before I was a detective."

Before I'd even heard of Renaissance Home.

"Okay... do you have a case number or..."

"Father James Cartier." Veronica paused and Kristin said nothing. "Do you know him?"

"What's this about, Detective? I'm very busy here."

A distinct change in tone, an indication that the coroner knew exactly what this was about.

"I'm wondering how he died."

"Heart attack," Kristin answered immediately.

Veronica waited. In the background, she heard Steve shouting something incoherent.

"Detective, I would be very careful about asking too many questions. Especially if they involve deaths under mysterious circumstances."

She's looking at Dante Fiori's corpse now, Veronica knew.

"You're probably right. But—but I just have one more question for you, then I won't ask anything about Father Cartier ever again."

Silence.

"When did he die?"

"When?"

"Yeah, the date."

"Four years ago. Around this time. I don't remember the exact date."

Around this time…

No, not around this time, Veronica thought. *It was two days ago, the day that I went on* Marlowe. *Four years to the day—exactly four years to the day.*

"Oh, and when you're done there, I have another body for you."

"You're kidding? Murder?"

Veronica looked around the office, at Sister Margaret, the shredded papers, the desk—she took everything in.

The narrative added up and it made sense. Except for one thing…

Veronica walked around and grabbed the chair from beneath the desk. She carried it over to Sister Margaret's body and placed it beneath the nun. After cocking her head, she kicked it over.

"Naw," Veronica said, her eyes drawn to the photo of Benny and Dante. "Not a murder—suicide. No mystery to this one."

Chapter 64

"THE FINGERPRINT ON THE REAR taillight of Dante's Mazda checks out—it belongs to Deputy Milligan. He put it there when he'd pulled over Dante," McVeigh ignored the sheriff.

"At least he did that right." Steve pursed his lips. "Cut Ronnie loose."

Both Sheriff Burns and Deputy McVeigh were staring through the one-way glass at D-Block inmate Clyde Krause as they spoke.

"You sure?" McVeigh asked. "He's got a family and—"

"Let him loose." Steve nodded to himself. "Yeah, he's done. You ready?"

Before the deputy could answer, he pulled the door open and walked inside the interview room. Without a word to the inmate, Steve slapped the folder he'd been holding down on the table.

"Clyde Krause," he began. "You're serving six years for assault and battery. Before that, eighteen months for unlawful possession. Not that much time, all told." Steve paused for effect. "But capital murder? Look, I know the government put a stay on executions in the State of Oregon, but there are always exceptions. Like Trent Alberts. I can't say for sure, but maybe they'll make another exception for a cop killer. Unless, of course, you start talkin'."

"Ex-cop," the light-skinned black man with a shaved head corrected.

"Right, well, at least we're on the same page and you know why you're here. Let me tell you what I think happened and if I stray too far from the truth, you can correct me, yeah?" Just a glare from Clyde. "Good enough. So, here goes: about three weeks ago, you get a visitor named Dante Fiori. He doesn't say much, but he does show you a picture. That much we know for sure—we have it on camera. The rest—well, feel free to jump in at any point moving forward. This photograph features a pretty young detective. And Dante says to you, she's going to come in here, and she's going to pay a visit to your D-Block cellmate Ken Cameron. He doesn't know exactly when but thinks—*hopes*—it'll be around the fifteenth. Anyway, Dante tells you that after the detective visits, you have a job to do: you're to kill Ken Cameron. I don't think he tells you how—that doesn't matter—but what does matter, is that you're going to get some blue soap—it's gotta be blue—from the commissary and after the deed is done, you're to splash it all around." Still no reaction from Clyde. "But before all that, you're going to bribe Ken, or threaten him, but I think bribe. You're to tell him to make a phone call to that young detective's number. And Dante gives you a very specific line from a nursery rhyme that Ken is supposed to say. This about right so far?"

Clyde leaned back and crossed his arms over his chest.

"I'm going to take that as a yes. I mean, maybe it's not perfect, but it's close enough, right? But the thing," Steve brings the thumb and forefinger of his right hand together like a chef indicating he likes the sauce, "The thing I don't understand, the thing I can't wrap my head around, is why you would do this for Dante Fiori? Capital murder is a far stretch from assault and battery. Now, I know that you guys went to Renaissance Home together and I know some of what you went through."

Clyde snickered.

"You know nothing."

"Right, I won't pretend to know everything that went on there. But I know that it was bad."

Clyde sucked his teeth.

"In trying to figure this out, I made a list of reasons why one might be inclined to kill for someone else." Steve pulled a sheet of paper out of the folder and started to read. "One, romantic love. You love Dante and would do anything to earn his heart. Naw, I don't think so. Two, blackmail. That doesn't sound right, either. You have no family, no girlfriend. Nothing of real value outside these walls. Three, money. But... Dante doesn't have money. So, you can see my conundrum, Clyde. I just don't understand your motivation."

Steve could tell that Clyde wanted to elucidate him—like most criminals, part of the fun was bragging about their crimes—but he wasn't so idiotic as to incriminate himself for murder. That was okay because they'd planned for this, too.

"Hypothetically," Deputy McVeigh spoke up. "Can you hypothetically think of another reason why someone would kill for another?"

"Hypothetically?" Clyde asked in his baritone voice. "The fuck does that mean?"

"That means," Steve explained, "you aren't copping to this particular murder. You're just helping me understand, given your experience in a place like this, one possible reason that someone would kill for someone else—not you specifically, and not Ken Cameron. You aren't admitting to anything." The sheriff pointed up to the camera that was recording the interview. "And that's all on tape, on the record."

Clyde smiled.

"Just a guess, right? Cuz I didn't kill nobody."

Steve shrugged.

"Sure, a guess."

"Well, you missed a few, Sheriff."

"Like?"

"Like gang initiation, huh?"

Steve cocked his head.

"*Riiiight*, missed that one. Go on."

He knew neither man had any sort of gang affiliation.

"Well, how 'bout, returnin' the favor? If Dante—I mean, if *someone* killed for you, you might kill for them, right? I scratch your back, you scratch mine? That kinda shit?"

Aha.

Everything suddenly became clear. Clyde knew it, too, because he was smirking.

The D-Block inmate owed Dante because the man had killed for him. Tit for tat.

And there was only one person who Dante could have murdered to have that amount of sway with someone like Clyde Krause.

Father James Cartier.

"Hypothetically," Steve said dryly then indicated for his deputy to follow him out of the room. "Thank you, Clyde. This has been very... illuminating."

When they were once again staring through the one-way glass at the prisoner, Deputy McVeigh asked, "You want to charge him now?"

Not do you want to charge him, but do you want to charge him *now*.

"No. We're not going to charge him, *now*. We're not going to charge him at all."

McVeigh gawked in disbelief.

"What do you mean? He killed Ken—it had to be him. Dante told him to kill—"

"I know."

"If you know, then we should charge him. At least get the DA's opinion on this. I know that you didn't like Ken, Sheriff—I didn't either—but still. He's a murderer."

Steve took his hat off and scratched his forehead.

"We have eleven suspects in that shower and none of them are going to say a word. You guys let them stew overnight and pressed them already. None will talk. We have no cameras, no clear motive—at least not one that a jury is going to understand—and no evidence. So, our choice is to charge all eleven D-Block inmates with murder or none of them." Steve put his hat back on. "No, not *our* choice," he corrected himself. "*My* choice. And *my* choice is to charge none of them."

With that, Steve turned away from the glass.

"Sheriff? Sheriff? Where are you going?"

Steve didn't like the annoyance he heard in his Chief Deputy's voice, but he didn't stop.

"I have an appointment. You take care of Krause."

***

"Yes, yes—I have pain, doctor. It's in my back. Every time I move…" Steve stretched his right arm forward and winced.

"It looks like it's healed well," Dr. Kinkaid remarked. Steve felt the man's gloved hands on his bare skin and inhaled sharply. "The scarring might fade over time, especially if—"

"I don't care about the scarring." Steve softened his tone. "I just—it's the pain. I need it."

Dr. Kinkaid lowered the sheriff's shirt and walked in front of him. The man's eyes were on a clipboard and as Steve watched, he checked something off.

"And I… and I need a refill on my prescription." Steve's lips were tacky, and he licked them. This offered no relief. His hand was also shaking but making a fist didn't correct the problem this time.

Only opioids could do that.

Dr. Kinkaid didn't look up from his clipboard.

"How's work going lately, Sheriff?"

"What?"

Now Dr. Kinkaid raised his eyes.

"I asked how work was going? Has it been particularly stressful lately?"

Well, doc, if you must know, I've had three murders, including a prominent TV personality and an ex-cop, two attempted murders, including an esteemed psychiatrist, in Bear County this past week alone. Not to mention a psychopath whose death was… suspicious at best. I'm also nearly certain that someone, an ambitious deputy after my job, to be more specific, has video evidence of me stealing drugs from an evidence locker.

"I mean, not any more stressful than usual."

Check or X, Steve couldn't tell which the doctor marked on his damn clipboard.

"Personal life? How are things going with your personal life?"

Oh, we're going there, are we? Okay… I can't sleep. Haven't had a full night's sleep in more than a month. I have this recurring nightmare of the bear coming after me, but when I turn around, it's my wife. Only, she's dead. And this has put a damper on my sex life. Speaking of which… I just recently accused my girlfriend of murder—well, not directly, but close enough. Then when she tried to reach out, to help me? I pushed her away—pushed her away until she was gone.

"Not the best," Steve admitted. "But it's been worse." Also true.

An X this time—definitely an X.

"So? You think—"

"Steve, I'm not going to be renewing your prescription today," Dr. Kinkaid said flatly.

"What? Why not? I'm in—"

"Not today, or any day, for that matter. Opioids are serious drugs and while we try to prescribe them with every safety measure in mind, the potential for addiction, both physical and psychological, is always there. I'm going to be honest with you, Sheriff Burns—I think that you may need some help, some counseling at the very least."

"Counseling?" Steve slid off the examination bed. "I don't need counseling. I need a refill."

Dr. Kinkaid shook his head.

"No, you don't. Your physical wounds have healed, Steve."

"Now, it's Steve? A few seconds ago, it's Sheriff Burns, but now, you're trying to be all sweet, and it's Steve?"

"Please—"

"No, don't fuckin' 'please' me. And don't play your mind games with me, either. You don't know me."

"I may not know you personally, Sheriff, but please—"

Steve slapped the clipboard right out of the doctor's hands. As it clattered loudly on the hard tile floor, he pointed a finger in the man's face.

"I said, don't 'please' me."

Dr. Kinkaid looked frightened, but that wasn't what made Steve walk away. It was the fact that his finger was bouncing up and down like he was experiencing a minor electric shock.

Steve lowered his hand and backed out of the room.

"Sorry," he grumbled under his breath. "I'm sorry, doc."

What the fuck is wrong with me?

Chapter 65

VERONICA'S PLACE WAS A MESS—it was disgusting. CSU had done a decent job of cleaning up, but there was still fingerprint dust all over her main foyer. That stuff clung to everything.

All the blood was gone, except for in one spot.

Nobody had thought to wipe Marlowe's blood from Lucy's nose. Veronica grabbed a wet towel and cleaned the cat's snout.

Then she fed the animal, who must have been starving.

Upstairs wasn't much better, even though CSU hadn't done any work on the second floor.

After the fire at Dr. Bernard's office, both she and Steve had just dropped their clothes in the center of the room before hopping in the shower. It made the entire second floor stink of soot and ash.

Crinkling her nose, Veronica balled up her shirt, pants, and underwear, and threw them in the laundry. She grabbed Steve's shirt next, tossing it—*swish*—from across the room. She was about to do the same with Steve's pants when she felt something heavy in his pocket.

She reached in and pulled out a Ziploc bag.

What the hell?

There were nearly two dozen small white pills in the bag. Veronica knew what they were, of course, but it took a little longer for her to figure out what the sheriff was doing with them in his pocket.

She weighed the bag in her hand, trying to rationalize a different reason for their presence.

There was none, of course.

Steve had been prescribed meds following the bear attack, but that was going on a month ago.

And these weren't prescription.

They did, however, explain a lot.

Grinding her teeth, Veronica took the pills and threw them in the toilet. Being completely sealed and with some air in the bag, they floated on top of the water. She watched them for a moment, almost hypnotized by how they bobbed just a little on the surface.

When Veronica heard the front door open below her, she flushed them.

"Veronica? Veronica!"

Steve hurried up the stairs and rushed into the bedroom. He went straight for her, wrapping his arms around her in a heavy embrace. Then he kissed her forehead.

"I'm so glad you're okay."

Veronica said nothing. All she could think about were those pills.

"You are okay... right?" Steve asked, pulling back.

"Exhausted."

"Shit, me, too."

Veronica watched Steve's eyes dart about the room. He spotted his pants, which she had left on the floor, and he let her go to pick them up.

He felt each of his pockets and with every empty squeeze, Veronica saw more blue waves of sweat coming off him.

That's what he'd really come here for. Not to see if she was doing okay, but for his damn drugs.

"I flushed them, Steve," Veronica said softly.

"You *what?*" his voice was tight.

"I flushed the pills."

Steve was incredulous.

"You didn't. You *fucking* didn't."

Veronica nodded and took a step back.

"I did. You're not acting like yourself, Steve. You're sweating and short-tempered and, quite frankly, you scare me. You... you need help."

Steve rose to his full height and Veronica saw that his hands were balled into fists.

"*I* need help? *I* do?"

"Steve, please. I don't want to fight. I just need to sleep."

"Don't fucking please me. Those were *my* pills." He ground his teeth. "*Mine*. You had no right."

He stepped forward aggressively.

"Who are you?" Veronica whispered. She was starting to get scared, to second guess her decision to tell Steve what she'd done. "I don't even know you anymore."

"Well, I know you!" Steve bellowed. "*I know you!*"

Veronica's adrenals squeezed out their very last reservoir of adrenaline.

"You know me, huh? Really? You know me because of what Dante said on that stupid show? You don't know me, Steve."

A wicked grin appeared on the sheriff's face. Even though his uniform made him look older, Veronica had thought that Steve always looked handsome.

Until now.

Now, he looked ugly.

Hideous, even.

"No, I know who you are because Benny told me about you."

Veronica, who had been leaning forward slightly, now swayed in the opposite direction.

"What?"

"Yeah, your brother, he told me about you. Benny told me all about you... all about *eenie, meenie, miney, mo*."

Each word drove the icepick deeper into Veronica's heart. The pain on her face was so palpable that even Steve, lost in a withdrawal haze, thought he'd taken it too far.

"Shit, I don't—I'm sorry. I didn't mean it. I just—I need those pills, Veronica."

Veronica, shaking worse than Steve now, raised a finger and jabbed it at Steve's face.

"Get out," she said, and Steve started to backpedal. *"Get the fuck out and don't ever come back!"*

And just like that Steve was gone, leaving the front door wide open behind him.

Epilogue

CITY OF GREENHAM PD DETECTIVE Freddie Furlow heard a beep and opened his eyes.

He had no idea where he was, but that became evident in seconds. Freddie was lying in a hospital bed covered in a sheet and surrounded by medical equipment. There was someone in the room with him.

"Randy?"

A woman ducked out from behind an EKG machine.

"Did you say something?" the nurse asked.

Freddie licked his lips.

"My son? Did he visit?"

The pretty nurse angled her head downward.

"Not that I'm aware of, Mr. Furlow."

"What about my wife?"

"Ahhh." The nurse glanced at her clipboard. "Well, I don't see her as an emergency contact…"

Freddie closed his eyes and tried to take a deep breath, but his chest hurt, and he started to cough halfway through.

When it passed, he opened his eyes.

"What about my partner? What about Veronica Shade? Has she come in?"

The nurse offered him a placating expression.

"I'm sorry, Mr. Furlow, but no one has been in to visit you—not yet. If there's someone you'd like me to call, however…"

Freddie closed his eyes again, trying, and failing, to will away the tears that formed behind his lids.

***

Dylan Hall bounced his legs up and down as he lay on the cold hard bench and stared at the bald DEA Agent as the man chain-smoked cigarettes. Jail was much, much worse when you were sober, he realized.

"Mr. Hall, you're no rookie here. You know the deal. You tell me where you got the dope from, who sold you the heroin with the snake eating an eyeball on it, and I give you a slap on the wrist and let you go."

"I don't know anything about a snake eating a fucking eyeball, alright?"

The DEA Agent, who was leaning against the wall, not even looking in Dylan's direction, exhaled a noxious cloud of smoke.

"Sure, and I'm going to live 'til I'm ninety. Just tell me where you got it from, Dylan. Your games won't work with me."

Dylan jumped to his feet and ran to the cell bars. He gripped one in each hand, wrenching it tightly in his palm.

"I didn't get it from anywhere! I was framed! I was *fucking* framed. I'm clean, god damn it! I'm out! *I'm out!*"

Agent Allison smiled.

"Sure, you are, Dylan. Sure, you are."

***

Bear County Sheriff Steve Burns sat in his car parked outside the place he still owned, the place that was technically his home but that he hadn't been able to even go inside since Maggie Cernak had committed suicide in his barn.

"What the fuck are you doing?" he asked himself.

He wasn't expecting an answer and was surprised when it came.

Without even thinking about it, Steve had reached into his pocket, and he'd pulled out the small baggie. He lowered his eyes away from his pathetic reflection in the rearview mirror and glanced at his palm.

The plastic bag was slick with sweat, but the powder, the yellow powder inside, was dry.

And that was the answer. It had to be.

***

Bear County Chief Deputy Marcus McVeigh stared at the computer monitor as he clicked play for what was the twelfth time.

He still couldn't believe it.

After he'd seen Sheriff Steve Burns enter the evidence room on consecutive days, he'd been curious, especially considering how odd his boss and mentor had been behaving as of late.

When that failed to elucidate Sheriff Burns' motive, on the second day, he checked the footage.

McVeigh's first thought was that it was a mistake, that there was a rational, legal reason why Sheriff Burns had removed the drugs from Vinny Pasquale's evidence box.

He wasn't stealing them—no way. It couldn't be.

But no amount of mental gymnastics could explain what he saw.

McVeigh kept the video to himself, trying to wrap his mind around what was happening to Bear County. It had never been and was never going to be a utopia, but things had steadily gone downhill since the sheriff's arrival.

All things told, Marcus might have buried that tape—might have even deleted it.

Until today. Until the irrational way that Sheriff Burns had decided to deal with Clyde Krause, a cop murderer.

Now, he wasn't so sure what to do with the video.

Deputy Marcus McVeigh clicked the mouse and watched the video again, hoping that the thirteenth time would offer him insight into what to do next, that it would prove lucky.

***

Oregon State Trooper Phil Crouch typed the name into the missing persons' database and pressed enter.

He knew what the result would be—the same as it had been for the past two years.

Julia Burns, still missing.

Phil looked at the report in his right hand, then back at the computer monitor.

It couldn't be.

It couldn't be that Julia's fingerprint had shown up on a plastic explosive that failed to detonate.

The report had to be wrong.

In his mind, he pictured the scene he'd come across, the scene with then State Trooper Steve Burns standing in his kitchen, blood on his hands, a puddle at his feet.

The report had to be wrong because Julia Burns was dead.

And Steve had killed her.

***

Dr. Jane Bernard hadn't said much since being kidnapped by Dante Fiori. And while Peter Shade had some experience dealing with the grief of others, his ability to comfort her exceeded his skill set.

Peter tried not to wake her as he reached with his free arm and grabbed his laptop from the night table. Jane continued to breathe heavily as he opened it, and she didn't wake when he teased his arm from behind her head and started to type.

He should have done this years ago—Peter felt like an idiot keeping these records for as long as he had.

Why? Why after I purged them from the police database did I make a copy for myself?

It made no sense.

None.

Fucking none.

"What are you doing?" Jane asked sleepily.

Peter deleted the last known record of Veronica's—no, not Veronica's, but Lucy Davis' childhood.

The police reports. The ones from before the accident.

They were gone, now—gone forever.

"Nothing." He leaned over and kissed Jane.

Once a liar, always a liar.

Peter closed his laptop and replaced it on the nightside table. "Nothing at all."

***

"Detective Shade?"

Veronica was surprised to find Cole Batherson standing. She thought that when she popped in to find out how he was doing, he'd still be in the hospital bed.

The second surprise was that Cole looked good—he looked clean and healthy. The color had returned to his face.

The absolute polar opposite of Steve.

"Veronica, what's wrong?" His face became a mask of concern. "Are you okay?"

Veronica was about to fall back on her tried and true strategy of denial, to say that everything was fine. That she was okay.

But she wasn't.

She hadn't been okay for a long time.

And for some reason, Veronica didn't want to lie to Cole.

Instead, she shook her head and lowered her chin to her chest.

Cole reacted instantly, wrapping his arms around her and sitting them both down on the side of his bed. Then he just held her there.

He didn't say anything, didn't rock her like a baby, didn't do anything. Cole just held her until all of her tears had dried up.

Only then did Veronica pull away, and immediately felt embarrassed. Heat rose in her face, and her ears started to burn.

She was a detective—she wasn't supposed to be this soft, this weak.

"I'm sorry about what happened to you," Veronica said, wiping her face with her sleeve.

"You don't need to be sorry, Veronica. It wasn't your fault."

Veronica looked at him, stared into his soft eyes. It dawned on her how wrong she'd been about this man. How absolutely wrong she had been.

Veronica might have synesthesia, but it was no superpower.

It might tell her if someone was lying, it might tell her if someone was sweating, or if they were about to explode into a violent rage.

But it didn't tell you who they were, what they stood for.

And it was far from infallible.

Cole continued to stare at her until Veronica got uncomfortable. Her eyes drifted to the side of a stack of papers on the end of the bed.

"What are those?" she asked, trying to clear the air of the awkward tension.

"It's my—" Veronica picked up the stack of papers and Cole made no move to stop her. "It's my article for the New York Times. I had a lot of time to think while I was lying in this bed. I was planning on showing it to you before I sent it in, get your opinion. If you want, I'll tear it up. Tell them I didn't want to write it."

Veronica's first inclination was to tear it up, to tell Cole that she had no interest in being the feature of an article now or ever.

But she was also interested in what Cole wrote about her. She shouldn't be, but she was.

After I read it, Veronica told herself. *After I read it, I'll destroy it.*

It was well written, not Pulitzer worthy but good, and it was everything that she'd hoped the *Marlowe* interview was going to be.

Veronica wasn't sure where Cole had found his sources, but they must have been good because he'd used them to paint a fairly accurate representation of her life, of her early childhood, of the break-in, the fire, and her adoption.

It was heart-wrenching but tasteful. Accurate.

When Cole wrote about her synesthesia, he resisted the urge to glorify it and talk about it like it was a superpower. He was succinct and honest.

Gloria Trammel and Dante Fiori were mentioned, of course, they had to be. But Cole focused on Veronica and didn't pepper the text with gory details of their terrible crimes as others might have.

The paper shook mildly in Veronica's trembling hands as she neared the end of the article.

Lucy Davis had been through a terrible ordeal, an unfathomable tragedy. It shaped who she was, shaped the very fabric of her mind. And although Lucy changed her name to Veronica Shade, she never let what happened change who she was. Others had. Her brother had, as had Dante Fiori.

But not Veronica.

She took the things that hurt her and used them not to incite violence, even though violence is unavoidable given her past and her profession, but to help others.

And in a world where superheroes are depicted on the big screen as having bulging muscles or the ability to shrink or grow at will, the unassuming City of Greenham might just have a real hero in their midst. Not one who can read minds, but one who has a unique and misunderstood condition, one who goes by the name of Detective Veronica Shade.

"I'll take out anything or everything if you want. I'll even throw it in the trash. I just thought—"

"It's beautiful," Veronica said. The words surprised even her, but when she looked into Cole's eyes again, she didn't take them back. "I think you should send it. Get them to print it."

"Really? Because—"

Veronica cut Cole's words off with a kiss. She pressed her lips strongly against his, and at first, Cole resisted or was too surprised to reciprocate.

But then he leaned into her, placing a hand behind her neck as he slid his tongue into her mouth.

Veronica wanted nothing more than to just live in this moment forever. To revel in the kindness and compassion that was Cole Batherson.

But that was impossible.

Because even though what Cole had written was beautiful, it was also a lie.

A complete and utter lie.

Veronica Shade was no hero. And like Dante Fiori and Benny Davis, and to a lesser degree Gloria Trammel, she was a harbinger of violence.

Once a killer, always a killer.

Isn't that what Dante had said?

The only difference was when Veronica Shade killed, she did it with the badge in her pocket. And now, every time she closed her eyes, she heard the sound of murder ringing in her ears.

END

Author's Note

WHEN I FIRST STARTED WRITING Veronica Shade, Steve Burns, Bear County, *et al*, I never thought things would get this manic, this fast.

As my longtime fans are aware, when I write, I don't so much lead my characters as they lead me. With Veronica, I knew that things were going to get wild in Bear County—c'mon, they just had to—but I didn't know the time scale. Well, *#thrillogans*, it's only book three and the poop his hit the proverbial fan.

What I had (*kinda, sorta*) intentionally planned was to illustrate the many of the parallels between the cases (such as the watch heist and the dollmaker in The Scent of Murder) and the characters (think Freddie and Steve). I wanted to show that even though these cases and these characters involve similar situations and decisions, their motivations are very different. And, let's face it, despite living in a sound byte world with clips taken out-of-context than not, motives *should* matter. The real question remains, however, what are Veronica's motives?

I wish I could tell you, but, alas, this is Veronica's story, and she deserves the right to lead you along this insane adventure with her. It's not my place to say.

You keep reading, I'll keep writing.

Best,
Pat
Montreal, 2023

Made in the USA
Middletown, DE
19 September 2024

61102962R00217